ONCE IN A BLOOD MOON

DOROTHEA HUBBLE BONNEAU

Together we rise
Dorothea Hubble Bonneau

ACORN PUBLISHING

FROM THE TINY ACORN ...
GROWS THE MIGHTY OAK

FBI Anti-Piracy Warning: The unauthorized reproduction or distribution of a copyrighted work is illegal. Criminal copyright infringement, including infringement without monetary gain, is investigated by the FBI and is punishable by up to five years in federal prison and a fine of $250,000.

Advertencia Antipirateria del FBI: La reproducción o distribución no autorizada de una obra protegida por derechos de autor es ilegal. La infracción criminal de los derechos de autor, incluyendo la infracción sin lucro monetario, es investigada por el FBI y es castigable con pena de hasta cinco años en prisión federal y una multa de $250,000.

Once in a Blood Moon

First Edition
Copyright © 2020 Dorothea Hubble Bonneau
All rights reserved. No part of this book may be used or reproduced in any manner whatsoever, including Internet usage, without written permission from the author.

This story is a work of fiction. References to real people, events, establishments, organizations, or locales are intended only to provide a sense of authenticity and are used fictitiously. All other characters, and all incidents and dialogue are drawn from the author's imagination and are not to be construed as real.

Book cover by Damonza.

Book interior design and formatting by Debra Cranfield Kennedy.

www.acornpublishingllc.com

ISBN—Hardcover 978-1-947392-86-1
ISBN—Paperback 978-1-947392-85-4
Library of Congress Control Number: 2020907701

Written in honor of the author's late son,

Dr. Gregory James Fisk,

whose life and character empowered this novel.

ONCE
IN A
BLOOD
MOON

INTRODUCTION

Research for *Once in a Blood Moon* launched me on a fifteen-year journey that revealed many surprises. Early readers of the manuscript told me that coming upon such revelations took them out of the story as they pondered the feasibility of certain events. So, I'm providing some little-known facts that have been woven into the plot of this historical fiction novel.

Documentation and additional references are located in the *Source Material* section located at the end of this book.

In 1526, Magistrate Lucas Vasquez de Ayllon of Spain was given a commission by Charles V to establish a colony in what we now know as South Carolina. He set off from Hispaniola in mid-July of 1526. His three ships arrived in the "new world" on August 9 with five hundred men, women and children, which included African slaves and friars from the Order of Preachers.

Magistrate de Ayllon agreed to follow the dictates of the Law of Burgos, which forbade mistreatment of indigenous people and encouraged their conversion to Catholicism. Many settlers became ill and perished. Magistrate de Ayllon contracted an illness and died in October; dissension arose. When the new leaders were cruel to the slaves and the natives, the indigenous Cofitachiqui joined forces with the slaves and helped to force their Spanish captors to sail back to Hispaniola.

Free of captivity, the African slaves remained and made the South Carolina region their home, eighty-some years before the English settled in Jamestown.

Many African slaves from the Gambia region shared their extensive knowledge of rice cultivation with planters eager to make a profit. Their expertise brought prosperity to South Carolina and helped to secure a financial foundation for the new nation.

Diola (French spelling)/Jola (English spelling), excellent agriculturists, had developed two hundred varieties of rice seeds by the time they arrived in the new world. They maintained a unique social structure that valued equality which was demonstrated in gender roles and in the rotation of leadership hierarchy.

In 1800, the few free people of color who owned slaves did so to prevent oppression of family members. A minority exploited slaves for commercial purposes.

Divorce in South Carolina remained illegal until 1949.

In South Carolina, no law prohibited interracial marriage until the time of the Civil War.

Thank you for sharing this journey.
Dorothea Hubble Bonneau, Author

PART ONE

CHAPTER ONE

Heaven Hill Plantation, 1807

The air in the ballroom on the top floor of Heaven Hill Plantation is thick with July humidity and stale with afternoon heat. Alexandra half-hopes she'll pass out. Then, this humiliating minuet lesson will be over.

She had been skeptical when Mother asked her to assemble the house-help. Brimming with rare enthusiasm, Mother announced, "First, I want to thank all of you for your prayers. Not one person stopped me to check my papers when I traveled by schooner from Georgetown all the way to Charleston on my quest to find a suitable instructor."

Being able to pass for white has advantages, Alexandra thought.

Mother fanned herself, then continued. "I saved the best news for last. Madame Arnaud, the famous dance mistress, has agreed to personally prepare Heaven Hill's very own debutante for her coming-out ball." Everyone in the room had applauded, except Alexandra. The thought of dancing to please Mother's social climbing friends terrified her.

When the servants had been dismissed, Mother drew Alexandra close and said, "Tomorrow you begin preparation for the most wonderful event of your life. Madame Arnaud will arrive in time for breakfast."

Wonderful? If this lesson is any indication, the coming-out ball will be the worst occasion of Alexandra's life. Her shoes are too small, and her feet ache; Mother's standing on the viewing platform making a mental list of her mistakes; and her corset, a device invented by a sadist who didn't think women should breathe, is torturing her. Her fear of making a fool of herself at her debutante ball is the only thing that keeps her from running out the door.

"Take your position," instructs Madame Arnaud.

Alexandra curtseys before the dance assistant, who might have been handsome fifty pounds and thirty years ago. He bows. The viola trio plays Bach's Minuet #2 for the fifth time. Alexandra has taken three steps when Madame Arnaud shrieks, "No! No! No!"

The musicians lower their bows and avert their eyes. Madame stalks toward Alexandra gripping her *teacher's helper*, an elongated conductor's baton she uses to train students "who require a little extra incentive."

Alexandra's muslin dress, cut in the empire fashion of the day, has no padding to dampen Madame's stinging blows. Nevertheless, as the instructor raises her baton, Alexandra stands erect, lifts her chin and refuses to flinch when the teacher's helper strikes the back of her calf.

"From the beginning." Madame's voice, almost as deep as Papa's, doesn't match her petite frame and tiny pig-eyes.

Alexandra pulls her sweat-saturated gloves up to her elbows and takes her position opposite the sallow-cheeked assistant. *"Let my dancing please Madame this time,"* she prays.

Madame raises her baton. The musicians fit their violas to their chins, lift their bows and play a prelude to the minuet.

Alexandra freezes. She can't remember a single step.

Madame Arnaud shakes with anger. "Rise on your toes, then dip. Like so."

Odd, Alexandra muses. She loves the minuet music of Bach and Handel and Corelli, but the dance steps fly out of her head the instant the music starts. A place in her mind, hidden even from herself, rebels at the idea of dancing in front of an audience for the sole purpose of luring a husband.

She doesn't dare tell Mother, but the truth is she longs to become a famous violinist, maybe even a composer, not a show-piece wife able to entertain guests with her music on rainy winter nights. But she can't defy tradition without incurring a disastrous consequence, and she can't abide the thought of making a fool of herself on the ballroom floor. So, she smiles at Madame Arnaud, indicating she's ready to try again.

"One more chance." The menace in Madame's voice shatters the scant confidence she has mustered.

Madame nods. The musicians play. Alexandra rises and dips. She thinks she might succeed. Then she sees Mother casting her famous evil eye toward her, and she turns to the left instead of the right.

"Stop!" Madame Arnaud flings her baton. Alexandra ducks, just in time and stomps toward the door.

"I'm not through with you," says the dance mistress.

"Respect your teacher," warns Mother.

Alexandra turns to find Madame Arnaud standing so close that the witch's breath, a mixture of cloves and sour stomach, nearly makes her gag.

The dance mistress pontificates. "Of course, you realize, because of your—condition, it is essential that you master these steps before your coming-out ball,"

What condition? Alexandra wonders. But she doesn't dare ask.

Madame turns toward Mother. "As I've told you, the minuet has fallen out of fashion in some circles. Perhaps she could manage something... simpler."

Mother stiffens. "Bach's Minuet will open my daughter's coming-out ball."

"If Alexandra shows no improvement at our next lesson, I will be unable to continue with her instruction. I refuse to have my reputation ruined."

Madame Arnaud scoops up her teacher's helper and leaves

the room without kissing Mother on both cheeks in their French custom. The musicians fix their eyes on the exit and follow her out the door.

When she and Mother are alone, Alexandra braces herself. Mother's voice drops to a dangerous register. "You spend too much time playing your violin. If I were to sell it, you could dedicate more time to your dance preparation."

Nausea washes over Alexandra. Playing her violin gives her life meaning. Alexandra stares at the floor and presses her lips tight to stop bitter words from spilling out.

"No prospective husband wants a wife who will make a fool of him on the dance floor."

Alexandra bites her tongue.

"But, as playing the violin is your one talent that might attract a refined gentleman's interest, I've decided against selling it, for now."

"I'll practice dancing four hours a day," Alexandra promises. Even to herself, she sounds like an over-eager child, not a sixteen-year-old on the threshold of being presented to the world.

"Don't make promises you won't keep. I'm going downstairs. Put on something fresh before you come to supper."

"I'm not hungry."

"Suit yourself."

Mother glides out of the room.

Alexandra storms into her chambers and brushes past Lulu, who's dusting the full-length mirror. She throws open the door of her wardrobe, a carved mahogany masterpiece built into the west wall, and stares at her debutante dress.

That green gown dares her. *Defy your mother. Try me on. Practice the minuet you're so clumsy at. I'll make you look good.*

Alexandra turns to Lulu. "Help me on with my party dress."

Lulu doesn't move. "Your mother said you weren't to wear it until your coming-out presentation."

Alexandra pulls her sweat-soaked muslin dress off over her

head, drops it to the floor and stands in her camisole, arms up, waiting.

"Now," says Alexandra, "before Sampson comes in to light the small chandelier."

Alexandra follows Lulu's fearful gaze to the French doors that open from her room onto Heaven Hill's wraparound balcony, a feature that makes Mother's plantation house one of the finest Greek Revival mansions on the Santee River.

Alexandra strides over and pulls the damask drape closed, too hasty to notice that a corner has caught on the latch. "No one can spy now. Satisfied?"

"What if your little brother comes in?" Lulu asks.

"Jimi's down at the village with Papa."

Lulu crosses her arms and plants her feet.

"Worried about Mother? You know she goes straight to her chambers after supper."

"Sometimes she pays you a visit."

Alexandra raises an eyebrow. "Once in a blood moon. Lulu, we have to do this before Sampson comes in."

Lulu's lip quivers. Alexandra feels her servant's fear ripple through her own body. She softens her voice, but she doesn't change her mind. "You want me to be the laughingstock at my own coming-out party?"

"Of course not." Lulu's sincerity carries Alexandra back to their childhood, when they were still allowed to play together. The tears welling in Lulu's eyes as the dutiful serving maid helps her put on the green chiffon sting her conscience.

But she forgets Lulu's feelings the moment she twirls in front of the new standing-mirror Mother claims would be at home in the parlors of Versailles. The drape of the high-waisted gown shows off new curves. Just last year her hips had no shape. Perhaps wearing this dress really will make her look good when she curtseys and swirls at her debutante ball. The perfect shade of green accentuates her jade eyes and harmonizes with the deep mahogany of her skin. Maybe her audience won't think she's a child masquerading as a seventeen-year-old when she dances with the Brown Fellowship Society gentlemen she has yet to meet.

Alexandra stiffens when she looks at Lulu. "I can't practice dancing with you while you're wearing that bulky house-help outfit." She whips the blue silk ball gown out of her wardrobe, the one that will never fit her right on top, and presses it into Lulu's hands. "Put this on."

Lulu brushes her fingers over the river pearls sewn along the bodice. "We're grown, Miss Alexandra. Your mother says I can't wear your clothes anymore."

Alexandra never dreamed this day would come. When they turned five, she and Lulu, born just two days apart, had locked pinkies and promised to be best friends forever. As they grew older, they climbed trees, sailed boats made of leaves and pine twigs, and danced to the sounds of drums and ekonting down in the African-style village where Papa now lives.

Then, on Alexandra's tenth birthday, Mother flounced into her room and announced, "Alexandra Louise, the time has come for you to treat Lulu like the slave she was born to be."

Alexandra felt like she'd been kicked in the stomach by one of Mother's vicious billy goats. In her mind, she told Mother, *Lulu's my friend. I don't want a personal servant.* But the threat of punishment, for both of them, coerced her to say out loud, "Of course, Mother."

That night, when they were alone, Alexandra drew Lulu close and whispered, "I'll never lord it over you like Mother and her friends do with their help."

But now that her coming-of-age celebration is only five months away, her promise to be kind has turned into a lie. She is eager to play her violin for her guests. But the terror of impressing Mother's uppity friends when she dances the minuet, with men she's never even met, makes her tongue lash out as if it has a mind of its own.

"Put it on. Hurry." Alexandra sounds so much like Mother, she scares herself.

Lulu slips her arms out of her sleeves, lets her starched calico fall around her ankles and crosses her arms to hide her ample breasts. Alexandra turns away. She'd forgotten slaves don't wear undergarments. Lulu sighs as she pulls the blue silk over her head.

"You look gorgeous," Alexandra says. She sits on the stool in front of her vanity mirror and commands, "Do something quick with my hair."

"Yes, Ma'am."

Alexandra's lips curl into an involuntary smile. This is the first time Lulu has called her ma'am. A twinge of guilt chases off her rush of power.

As her servant's magic fingers recreate a hairstyle copied from Mother's *Dancing Master's* book, she reviews Lulu's reflection. If she had Mother's taste for beauty, she'd be jealous of that honey-colored skin. Lulu's almost light enough to pass for white, like Mother. She'd be envious of Lulu's bosom, blooming above the neckline of the low-cut dress—without the aid of a corset. And there's no doubt; if permitted to dance at a ball attended by influential free-people-of-color, Lulu's grace and looks would fan the desire of potential suitors and kindle the envy of every debutante in the room.

Even so, Alexandra prefers her own skin tone, dark as rich earth, like Papa's and Aunt Mamou's, a reminder of her African heritage. She's proud of her strong, slender body. And even though attracting a gentleman caller is a mild curiosity, she's most interested in spell-binding her coming-out audience when she plays her violin.

If only she didn't have to dance the minuet in front of all those people.

Once Lulu manages to coax Alexandra's hair into a topknot fastened by an emerald-studded comb, she nods and takes her position in front of the mirror. Smiling behind a fan that matches her dress, Alexandra hums Bach's minuet. The dress works its magic as she and Lulu spin and dip, giggling when they make the last turn.

"Thank you, Lulu," Alexandra whispers. Then she executes a perfect curtsey and looks to her servant for praise.

Lulu's eyes are riveted on the French doors.

"What?" asks Alexandra.

"Someone was watching."

"Don't be silly."

Alexandra turns and sees that an edge of the drape and the embroidered silk over-curtain have caught on the latch, leaving an opening large enough for someone to see inside. It's a good thing it's dim in the interior of the room. Day is yielding to night. The large chandelier hasn't been lit, and half the candles in the smaller one have burnt themselves out.

"Whoever it was probably couldn't have seen much," Alexandra says. But she doesn't sound convincing, even to herself.

One of the hall doors that opens onto the balcony slams. Maybe Jimi's come home early from visiting Papa. Alexandra can bribe her little brother with a chocolate and make him promise not to tell what he saw. But the footsteps are too heavy to be Jimi's.

Alexandra helps Lulu pull the house-help dress over the blue silk and plunks herself down on her vanity stool.

Just as Lulu starts working lavender oil into Alexandra's hair, Mother bursts into the room carrying a lantern bright enough to turn night to day.

"Good evening, Miss Josephine," Lulu says, dropping a curtsey and staring at the floor.

Mother sets the lamp on the bureau and paralyzes Alexandra with a hateful glare. "You were told not to wear that dress until your debut."

"I had to put it on so I could decide how Lulu should fix my hair to best show off the dress," lies Alexandra, proud that she's looking Mother in the eye and keeping her voice steady.

Mother lifts the hem of Lulu's calico, revealing the silk dress. She turns to Alexandra, her voice rich with venom. "You know Lulu's not to wear your clothes anymore." Mother narrows her eyes. "Do you have any idea what people would say if they knew you'd taught your girl a ballroom dance?"

"I'm sorry, Mother."

"You will be." Mother bobs her head toward Lulu. "Go down to the kitchen and tell Old Mary to fill a jar with water and fix a basket of shrimp and rice cakes."

"Right away, Miss Josephine."

Cold sweat drenches Alexandra. "I'll make it up to you," Alexandra whispers as Lulu rushes to the door.

Lulu dips a curtsey and hurries out.

Mother's shrill laugh turns into a coughing fit. When she's caught her breath, she turns to Alexandra. "Make what up to her? She's your slave, or have you forgotten again?"

"Then why can't I do with her as I will?" Mother's eyes narrow. Alexandra wishes she could call her words back.

"She's yours to train, but she's on my property ledger until five months from now when you turn seventeen, providing you prove you're worthy of being called a woman at your debutante celebration."

"What are you going to do to Lulu?"

Mother plucks the servant's bell from its holder by the door and rings three times. Sampson's signal! Alexandra wills herself not to show the fear that courses through her like acid. A loud knock rattles her resolve.

"Come in," Mother chimes in the tone she reserves for her favorite help.

Sampson, who's nearly seven feet tall, strides into the room dressed in his midnight-blue waistcoat. His posture is ramrod straight like Mother's. Unlike Mother, he could never pass for white. Although he's light-skinned, his black hair, cut short, with sideburns that reach nearly to his chin, is curly and coarse like that of most Africans.

"Sampson, Lulu's waiting in the kitchen. Lock her in the hog loft with some water and shrimp cakes," orders Mother.

"No!" Alexandra cries out.

Sampson hesitates.

Mother glares at him. "You have cotton in your ears?"

"On my way, Miss Josephine."

"Oh, and Sampson, in the morning, install the bars on Alexandra's balcony door. She's to be confined until I'm satisfied she's learned to comport herself with the dignity that will bring honor to Heaven Hill."

"Soon as the rooster crows, Miss Josephine." Samuel spins on his heel and hurries out.

"Mother, please don't. Those meat-eating hogs terrify Lulu. It's too dangerous."

"You ever see a pig climb the ladder to that loft?"

"Punish me instead. I made her put on the dress."

Mother gazes into the mid-distance. "Your juvenile actions have convinced me to invite Ichabod Collins to stop by the house."

"The speculator?" Alexandra struggles to catch her breath.

"You've shown me it would be best if I got rid of Lulu and bought you an experienced attendant."

"You can't sell Lulu!"

"I'm your mother. You're telling me what to do?"

Alexandra shakes her head.

"Of course, I wouldn't want to sell her until January, when the price of number-one girls will triple. You do remember why the price will triple, don't you?"

Alexandra nods. Mother has told her a hundred times. The price will soar when it becomes illegal to bring in slaves from Africa, starting on January first.

Mother taps the sharpened nail of her pointer finger on the

marble-top table, no doubt calculating how much Lulu might bring in a private sale.

"If I sell Lulu for a good enough price, I'll have enough money to purchase a skilled attendant who can teach you the things you need to know in order to lure a worthy suitor."

"I don't want to lure a suitor!"

Mother's shrill laugh sparks Alexandra's fury.

"You can't sell my friend!"

Mother slaps Alexandra. Words fly out of Alexandra's mind. Mother has never struck her. She wills herself not to cry. At first, she thinks she sees regret soften Mother's face, but she knows she's wrong when Mother says, "You better hope spending time in the hog barn will teach that girl the humility that will make her appealing to her new master, or she'll have the devil to pay.

"You're confined to your rooms for the duration of Lulu's time with the hogs. Miranda will bring your meals and empty your chamber pot." Mother starts to leave; then she turns back. "One day, you'll thank me."

As soon as Mother's out the door, Alexandra slumps to the floor. This is all her fault.

Lulu's shriek brings her to her feet. She throws open her French doors and steps onto the balcony. Moonlight sifts through the branches of the giant oak as Alexandra watches Sampson force Lulu up the outside ladder that leads to the loft over the hog barn.

She has to do something to ease Lulu's fear. But what? The song of a whippoorwill charming the night provides her answer. Even as babies, she and Lulu adored music.

Ignoring the punishment sure to follow, Alexandra stands on her desk chair and lifts her violin down from the top of the shelf of her drop-lid secretary. She steps out onto the balcony, relieved to see that Samuel left the loft shutter open when he removed the ladder. Steadying her violin under her chin, she raises her bow, and plays Lulu's favorite piece, Chevalier de St.

George's "Opus V." As she plays, the music ripples with light and hope. Alexandra is so transported, she doesn't pay any mind when Sampson opens her chamber door.

"Come here," he says in his God-voice.

Alexandra stops playing and turns to face the giant.

"It will be easier if you don't resist," he says, extending his arms. "I'll return it after I put up the bars in the morning."

She hugs her violin, as if protecting a child, and steps back into her room. Sampson closes the French door. Then he pries the instrument from Alexandra's trembling hands, picks up the case, and leaves.

Alexandra flings herself onto her canopy bed and rolls onto her back.

"Didima," she whispers, "if you're watching over me like you promised, I have a favor to ask. Lulu won't last a year if she's sent down South to pick cotton. Give me a sign if it will help for me to sneak down to the village and ask Papa to stop Mother from selling my friend."

Even though Alexandra's going on seventeen, the possibility of seeing Grandmother Didima's ghost terrifies her. She coaxes herself to sit cross-legged in the middle of her goose-down mattress and keeps her eyes open for a sign. Moonlight streams through the window panes of her French doors and paints her ceiling with monsters, but she keeps her eyes open.

When she hears the clock down in the foyer strike midnight, and no apparition has appeared, Alexandra is both disappointed and relieved. Then, as she reaches up to close the canopy curtain, the scent of gardenias perfumes the air.

Even a child knows the souls of the departed announce themselves with the fragrance they loved most while on Earth. The only gardenias at Heaven are all the way down in Papa's village garden. Didima wore a gardenia in her hair every day when they were in season. Her grandmother's spirit has given her a sign.

Alexandra has learned the hard way that there are consequences when a person doesn't obey a message from the other side. She'll have to go see Papa tonight, before Sampson has a chance to put the bars up. Lucky thing Mother never guessed she'd have the nerve to sneak out in the dark.

"Thank you for the sign, Didima," she says. "Now, please, help me be brave."

CHAPTER TWO

When Alexandra dangles her feet over the edge of her bed, an Ahoelra, one of those discontented African ghosts with mischief on its mind, slips into her head.

"*You don't have the courage to do this thing,*" the Ahoelra whispers.

"I do have the courage," she whispers back. The flame in her lantern flickers and dies. Sampson never did light the chandeliers. Darkness engulfs her. Alexandra shudders. The Ahoelra shakes with laughter.

Taking a deep breath, she touches her toes to the floor. She finds it warm and damp under her bare feet, like a living thing that has caught a fever.

"*You're going out alone, in the dark?*" asks the Ahoelra.

"Go away," Alexandra says as she slides her feet along the floor, testing for squeaky boards. When she makes it to the other side of the room without crashing into anything, she pulls open the French doors. Moist air swirls around her like silk, jasmine-scented with a touch of swamp rot. She peers into the moonlit night and smiles. Mother's lawns are shrouded in a caul of fog. With luck, she'll make it to Papa's village and back without Mother ever knowing she left the big house.

Pulling her black cloak over her dress, more for camouflage than warmth, she slips into her riding boots and steps out onto the balcony. Taking hold of the dew-slick railing, she feels her way to the back landing, grateful when she sees the porch lantern is still lit.

She hesitates. Do evil spirits really prowl through Mother's statue garden at night like some of the house-help claim? Fear ripples through her. She doesn't have time to go the long way. She pulls the lantern off the stand and follows its orb of light. Alabaster saints watch her with their marble eyes. A shadow glides in front of the Virgin and slips behind St. Joseph.

"*Go back*," warns the Ahoelra.

"It was a trick of the light," Alexandra says so loud that her own voice startles her.

Gathering her cloak, she races up the hill toward the man-made ridge that separates Mother's bastion of "refined" Carolina society from Papa's African world. When she reaches the edge of the pine forest, she stops. Will Papa help her save Lulu? Or will he be angry and say Mother's free to do what she wants with the house-help?

An animal cries out. Panther's prey? She wishes she'd brought a torch instead of this lantern with its feeble light.

"I can't do this," she whispers.

The Ahoelra purrs as she turns back toward the big house.

She's taken three steps when a vision of Lulu's lifeless body being carried from a row of cotton flashes into her mind. She turns toward the woods, steps into the dark maw of giant trees, and picks her way over the damp carpet of rotting leaves that covers the path. When she comes to the towering oak that marks the entrance to the sacred forest, she lifts her arms and looks toward the sky.

"Emitai, Creator of All Things, protect me," she prays to Papa's God.

She walks deeper into the forest. Wind whispering through longleaf pines grows to a roar. Something brushes the top of her head. She screams. Ducks down. Conceals the lantern behind her—as if that will help. She holds her breath and stays still.

When nothing more happens, she looks up and sees the culprit, a strand of moss dangling from a low branch.

The Ahoelra cackles, *"Lucky this time. Go back before it's too late."* But its voice sounds childish here in Papa's forest.

Turning onto the main path, she passes the stack of stones that mark the way to the ceremonial grounds. Scents of moss and burnt wood hang in the air, conjuring memories of magical nights when sacred shrine fires sent up sparks that intermingled with fireflies. She hears the echo of drums and the thrum of ekonting strings.

When they were little, and she and Lulu were still allowed to visit the village, they raised their hands as soon as the drumming started. They wiggled their hips and danced like birds set free from a cage.

As soon as the path opens on to the pasture, Alexandra tucks away her memories. If she doesn't focus, those new patrollers, so determined to enforce the slave curfew, could mistake her for a runaway and take her to jail—or worse.

The fog has dissipated, and the full moon bathes Papa's stables in silver light. Fragrances of hay and herbal liniment quicken Alexandra's anticipation. The village lies on the other side of the man-made hill that was built long ago to divert floodwaters. As she passes the corral, Cabai, her favorite horse, comes to the railing and nickers a greeting.

Alexandra strokes his nose. "I'd like to spend some time with you, but I have to go."

Her heart drops when she reaches the top of the rise. Warning fires that surround mud-and-thatch homes built around the village commons have been lit. There's no way she'll be able to steal into Papa's house unnoticed with those fire-tenders standing guard. They all know the terms of her parents' agreement. When it became impossible for them to live together under one roof, Papa and Mother divided Heaven Hill into two portions. Mother reigns over the big house with her retinue of slaves. Papa lives with free-people-of-color in the Diola-styled village modeled after the homeland his ancestors inhabited along the bank of the Gambia River.

From the day Alexandra turned fifteen, she has been forbidden to enter Papa's grounds until the time she's promised to a suitor approved of by Mother—unless there's an emergency.

Alexandra sends up a prayer, "Emitai, Creator of All Things, make Papa understand that Lulu will die if she's sent to pick cotton down in Georgia. And please, forgive me for treating her like my servant. She's my friend."

Alexandra's about to start down the path that leads to Papa's house and brave bargaining with the sentries when the hairs on the back of her neck stand on end. Someone's following her. She ducks into the bushes and crouches. She can hear the stalker coming up behind her.

Someone grabs her arm and pulls her to her feet. Alexandra turns and finds herself standing face to face with Oeyi, the village priest. The old man looks like a dream-spirit, dressed in his long red caftan and matching conical hat. This is the first time she's seen him up close. He's even taller than Papa. His complexion, even darker. The priest's obsidian eyes seem to glow in his unlined face. How can he be more than ninety years old?

"Come." Oeyi's voice ripples through her like the vibration of a deep-throated bell.

Didima once told her that Oeyi is so powerful, he can make himself appear in two places at once. Mother says he's the devil's shape-shifter, a worker of black magic.

"I have to see Papa," Alexandra says, struggling to keep her voice even. "My friend's life depends on it."

As Oeyi peers into her eyes, a wave of dizziness disorients her. "I know why you've come," he says.

She doesn't resist when the old man lifts the lantern from her hand, raises his staff, inset with crystals and festooned with feathers, and gestures for her to follow him down a barely perceptible trail.

Sounds of the night are silenced. As they move farther through waist high swamp grass, clouds of mosquitos assault them. Oeyi stops when they come to a vine-covered mound. He lifts the curtain of ivy aside. Alexandra follows him through a crevice into a man-made cave.

"Wait here," Oeyi says, handing her the lantern.

"Are you going to bring my father?"

Oeyi leaves without answering.

The acrid smell of animal droppings stings her nostrils; her stomach roils. When a high-pitched whine emanates from a narrow opening. She shivers. *Ghosts? Angry spirits? Wild animals?* She picks up her lantern, ready to run back to the big house. But when she reaches the cave exit, she realizes she'll never be able to find the way. So, she paces around the unlit fire pit. In the flickering lantern light, she sees that the walls are shimmering. Old Marcello, Heaven's blacksmith, whose Cofitachiqui ancestors intermarried with Papa's African relatives, has told her about the pearl-studded walls in the ancient temples of his people. She's about to move closer to get a better look when a chirping sound sends a chill up her spine. She ducks as a colony of bats swoops past her and out through the opening to feast on mosquitos.

Why had Oeyi brought her here instead of taking her to Papa's village? Just when she fears the old priest has abandoned her, she hears someone coming. "Let it be Papa," she prays.

But the footfalls are quick, not heavy and deliberate like Papa's. Alexandra flattens herself against the wall and tucks her lantern behind her. She hears heavy breathing and sees torchlight flicker near the cave entrance. Has a patroller discovered this mound? The Ahoelra *hisses.* Is she about to be captured and sold into slavery?

Her eyes are riveted on the entrance when Aunt Mamou

strides through the opening waving a pine torch in front of her and flashing her famous smile.

"Mamou!"

"Ali!" Mamou sings as she sets the torch in a sconce in the cave wall.

When Alexandra falls into her aunt's embrace, she feels like she's eight years old again. Then she stiffens. "Where's Papa?"

Mamou draws back. "Your father's not in the village."

"But I have to talk to him."

"He's in Georgetown seeing to a problem with a rice shipment. He'll be back tomorrow evening. It wouldn't be a good idea to tell him you've come here in the middle of the night. Sit with me, Alexandra."

Mamou gestures toward tree-stump stools that surround the fire pit. If her aunt intends to have one of her long talks, Alexandra will never get home on time.

"You'll be back before sunrise," Mamou assures her.

Has Mamou read her thoughts? Terrified by what her aunt will find inside her mind, Alexandra yearns to leave. But that vision of Lulu's lifeless body pops back into her head. She forces herself to sit still and allows Mamou to place her warm, fleshy palms on either side of her face.

Mamou's eyes roll up until only the whites show; her lips move, but she makes no sound. *Talking to her spirits*, Alexandra thinks. Mother calls it speaking with the devil's minions.

Mamou's eyes fly open. Her laugh startles Alexandra. Her aunt leans close and whispers, "I don't converse with friends of any devil."

Shaken by the accuracy of her aunt's clairvoyance, Alexandra nods. Mamou's quick smile prompts her to relax.

"I was studying your situation. There is a way you can save Lulu from the auctioneer's block. But you must do what I tell you, and you may not like it."

"How did you know I came about Lulu?"

"Seeing what's true is my gift—and yours too. When the time comes, you'll be able to summon visions at will. But, in the beginning, images will come to you in flashes."

Like the image of Lulu's lifeless body?

Alexandra has seen what she calls mind-pictures for as long as she can remember; often their predictions do come true; sometimes they serve as a warning.

"Breaking with society's rules terrifies your mother," Mamou says.

"Mother never breaks the rules."

"But you do. In your mother's mind, the way you act and what you say provides evidence of how effectively she's conveying knowledge of manners and propriety. She's right to be concerned. One misstep on your part will cast both of you from the world of privilege enjoyed by the few wealthy women-of-color who live in the low country."

Mamou closes her eyes and takes a deep breath. Alexandra can see her eyeballs moving under her closed lids, as though she's observing something from a hidden world.

"Uh, huh. I understand," says Mamou to an entity Alexandra can't see. Mamou opens her eyes and takes hold of Alexandra's hands.

"Apologize to your mother for treating Lulu like a friend instead of a servant."

"Lie to Mother?"

"Let me finish. Tell your mother you now understand your role. Agree to treat Lulu like she treats her help. Convince her you are the best person to train Lulu to become a valuable asset for Heaven Hill."

"But . . ."

"Say you understand. You don't have to tell her you believe she's right."

"I can't."

"Can't or won't? It's not worth shading the truth if it will save your friend?"

Alexandra stands, ready to leave even if she can't find her way.

"Running away from how things are won't solve your problem."

Alexandra sits back down.

"For now, Lulu belongs to you in name alone, but if your ability to teach her pleases your mother, she will legally belong to you on your seventeenth birthday."

Suddenly Alexandra understands. "And then I can free her!"

"It would be wise to wait a little while, but when she belongs to you, you can explain your earlier actions to Lulu."

Alexandra throws her arms around Mamou's neck. "Thank you!"

"Remember, you have to convince your mother you're ready to assume your role as young mistress of Heaven Hill. You must make her believe you have the skills to train Lulu to be an obedient slave."

"I'll try," Alexandra says.

"Trying isn't good enough. Do it. Listen carefully, Ali. Our African ways frighten this new establishment. But these interlopers know they need wealthy free-people-of-color to help them keep the peace between slaves and white slave owners.

"Your father, my brave brother, hopes you can master the social skills of the new order and that all the doors of Carolina society will open to you. He wants you to remember your African ways, but he also wants you to continue to study and to compose your music and to deepen your talent with your violin."

Lately, Alexandra has felt like she might break in half if she tries to live in two worlds at once.

"You don't have to live in two worlds. Live in one at a time. Part of growing up is being able to move from one situation to the next without losing touch with who you are. Think of it as changing into clothes that are appropriate for the situation. You wouldn't wear a dance dress to ride your horse, or a riding outfit to go to church. Remember, even though you change your clothes, it is you who rides the horse and you who goes to church."

Mamou lays her hand on Alexandra's cheek. "If anyone can build a bridge between the two worlds, you can."

"If I adopt all of Mother's ways, I might lose touch with my African roots."

"Tuck your love for your Diola heritage in a safe place in your heart. If you earn the respect of your mother's world, one day you may be in a position to share the legacy of your father's people with those who have ears to hear, colored and white alike."

"Papa isn't upset about me being presented at a coming-out ball?"

"He hopes you will be a great success."

"Honestly?"

"Honestly."

Relief washes over Alexandra. Every time she's gotten excited about the prospect of playing her violin in the Christmas concert, or wearing the jewels and beautiful dresses purchased for the round of parties that will announce she's an eligible young woman, a part of her has felt like she was betraying her African ancestors. Now, with her father's blessing, she can pour her heart into her upcoming concert audition and enjoy her celebration. If she succeeds, perhaps she really can be part of connecting both worlds.

"One warning," says Mamou, "Lulu is a terrible actress. So, until she clearly belongs to you, you must never tell her that you're ordering her around to keep your mother from selling her."

"That's going to be so hard."

"Every morning when you wake up, imagine Lulu's delight when you give her those freedom papers."

Oeyi slips into the cave. "It's time."

Mamou kisses Alexandra's cheek. "This visit will be our

secret. Neither of your parents would be pleased if they knew you had come to the village in the middle of the night."

Mamou takes off the cowrie necklace that has been passed to the women in her family down through the generations and slips it over Alexandra's head.

"Mamou, I can't take your amulet."

"You are the light of my soul. I was going to give it to you when you turned seventeen. It's an early present."

"But . . ."

"Let it remind you of your ancestors' strength."

CHAPTER THREE

By the time Alexandra and Oeyi reach the ridge that divides Heaven Hill into two worlds, the rising sun has turned the horizon from black to grey. Sampson will be coming soon to put the bars on her doors. She must hurry. She turns to thank Oeyi, but he's nowhere to be seen.

Gathering courage, she races through Mother's statues, hiding behind saints as she goes. When she gets to St. Michael, there's no more cover. She sprints to the back entrance and runs up the stairs to the balcony. She looks around. No one seems to be watching. Just as she's replacing the lantern, a rooster crows. She tenses, hunches down and creeps along the west side of the balcony toward her room. When she steps through her French doors, she sees Lulu stuffing pillows under the quilt on her bed.

"I thought you were locked in the hog barn," says Alexandra.

Lulu wheels around, her face grey with fear. "Where were you?" she asks as Alexandra slips off her muddy boots and hides them behind the drape.

"You'll pay if you tell a single soul I sneaked out."

"Would I be trying to make it look like you're in this bed if I was planning to tell on you? I was afraid you'd been kidnapped, then I saw your cloak and boots were gone. Where did you go?"

"That's for me to know."

Lulu flings the comforter on the floor and removes the pillows. "Why did Mother let you out so soon?" asks Alexandra.

"The hogs were testy. Your mother told me she was afraid I would fall in the pen and be damaged."

And then you wouldn't bring Mother a good price, Alexandra thinks. She wants to hug Lulu, to tell her she's glad the hogs didn't get her. Alexandra's stomach ties in knots as she follows Mamou's instructions and works her face into a scowl. "Stop standing there like a lump on a log. Go down and get my breakfast!"

When tears well in Lulu's eyes, Alexandra's stomach turns into a hot ball of acid. How will she keep up this charade?

On her way out the door, Lulu picks up a note from the dresser and stuffs it in her apron pocket. Alexandra snatches it and reads the message written with Lulu's artistic flourish: *je te remercie d'avoir soulage ma peur avec ta musique. Tu es une bonne amie.*

Bracing herself against the wall, Alexandra lies. "I was playing that music for me, not you. And why did you write 'bonne amie'? I'm your mistress, not your friend. Stop using French and forget the reading and writing I taught you!"

Lulu frowns. "Forget how to read and write? What's happened to you? Where have you been?"

"I've had a revelation, that's all. It's time we grow up and assume our proper roles. I'm hungry. Go down to the kitchen and get me a croissant and some cheese."

Before Lulu has time to undo the latch, someone pounds on the door. Lulu's eyes dart to Alexandra's muddy hem. She races to the bed and pulls up the quilt. Alexandra dives under the covers and whispers. "Don't give me away. Please."

Lulu rolls her eyes and races to unbar the door. Miranda, queen of household help, barges in clutching an envelope. Alexandra closes her eyes and takes slow, even breaths, praying that Miranda won't guess she's only pretending to sleep.

"You're slow as a snail," Miranda scolds.

"I'll be quicker next time, Miss Miranda."

Alexandra hears the trepidation in Lulu's voice.

"Why was this door locked from the inside?" asks Miranda.

Alexandra holds her breath. Is Lulu about to give away her secret?

"Once, Jimi wandered in when ..."

"Never mind. Wake Miss Alexandra and get her ready for her violin audition."

"Her audition's today?"

Alexandra peeks through her eyelashes.

"This," Miranda says, waving a letter like a flag, "was delayed on account of the storm that washed out the road to Pinnacle Plantation. At least that's what the boy who just brought it told me. Alexandra's audition is later this morning."

This morning? Alexandra presses her face into her pillow to stifle her gasp.

"If you ask me, the 'delay' was deliberate," Miranda mutters as she rifles through the dresses in Alexandra's wardrobe.

Alexandra's mind spins. Why would Tante Isabelle want to ruin her audition? From the time she was a little girl, her aunt has comforted her whenever she observed Mother giving her a tongue lashing.

Alexandra sees Miranda lay out her corset and audition dress, a pale, yellow silk trimmed with French lace, a favorite ornamentation of Mother's dressmaker.

"Have Miss Alexandra dressed, coifed and downstairs in one hour. I have to attend to her mother before she starts throwing things."

The second Miranda's out the door, Alexandra springs out of bed.

"I'm not ready to audition for Monsieur Martin."

"When he hears your piece, your violin teacher will beg you to play the first solo in that concert. I guarantee it. Up with your arms," Lulu says, careful not to let the muddy hem touch Alexandra's skin as she pulls the dress over her head.

How can she be so bossy when Lulu's being so nice to her?

Lulu's eyebrows shoot up. "Is that your Aunt Mamou's cowrie?"

Alexandra covers the necklace with her hands.

"You went all the way to your father's village alone? At night?"

"You'll be sorry if you tell."

"Why would I do that?"

Had her rude behavior made no impression on Lulu?

"Your Tante Isabelle might love you, but she'd have a hard time if she saw that amulet peeking up over the neckline of that low-cut dress."

"I need Mamou's magic with me."

"I could put it in your violin case."

Alexandra nods.

Lulu tucks the magical shell into a secret compartment under the lining of the resin compartment.

"Sit on your stool so I can get you ready." Lulu dips a hand-towel into the lukewarm water in the basin she'd brought up earlier, wrings the cloth nearly dry, and dabs dirt and pine sap off of Alexandra's face, hair and ankles.

Her friend's tender touch almost makes Alexandra lose control and blurt out that she must be stern so she can save Lulu from being sold. It aches to be so cruel. But she has to be convincing, or Lulu's sure to over-play being a slave and arouse Mother's suspicion.

"Hurry up. I need to practice."

Lulu pulls the corset tight enough to give Alexandra a hint of cleavage.

"I can't breathe."

"You want to look like a boy?"

CHAPTER FOUR

*A*lexandra trembles as she walks down the mahogany staircase and steps out onto the circular drive of Heaven Hill's elegant plantation house. Mother's new carriage awaits. No wonder she has the jitters. This is the most important day of her life. If Monsieur Martin gives her top billing in the Christmas Concert, she could become the most famous violinist in the low country. Well, that's an exaggeration. But if she dazzles her audience with her musical talent like Lulu promises, maybe her critics will overlook the mistakes she's sure to make when she dances the minuet in front of her ball guests.

Sampson descends from his perch in the driver's seat, adjusts his white and gold waistcoat and glides to Alexandra's side. Never looking her in the eye, he extends his hand. Resting her fingertips in his gloved palm, she steps up into Mother's new Clarence, an exquisite vehicle, recently purchased to impress South Carolina's elite young free men-of-color—and their parents.

As she's about to take her seat, Mother pierces her with a disapproving look. Her voice sounds flat and dangerous. "Didn't you learn a single thing in your deportment lessons? Smooth your dress under you before you sit, and cross your ankles like a proper lady."

When Alexandra's finally permitted to settle opposite Mother, she dares to ask the question that's been burning inside her since she left Mamou. "Mother, I can prove I have the ability to train Lulu to be an obedient slave if you will . . ."

"I need to rest." Mother closes her eyes and leans her head against the high back of the red leather seat.

Alexandra gazes out the window as they pass by the long-leaf pines that line the cobblestone drive leading to the main road. An armadillo waddling toward cover in the woods draws her attention. Watching the world roll by takes her mind off the coming audition.

Mother brings the back of her hand to her forehead, like the heroine of a tragic novel, and says, "How do you expect me to sleep with all that light pouring in?"

As soon as Alexandra pulls down the leather shade, the inside of the carriage turns into a coffin, but she doesn't dare complain.

Are other young women afraid they can never please their mothers?, she wonders.

Without opening her eyes, Mother says, "Remember, you are not to initiate a conversation with anyone but Cousin Callie, and you are to respond to Monsieur Martin in a respectful tone. Being too familiar with one's instructors is a sign of poor breeding."

A tendril of tepid air, ripe with the musky scents of swamp and forest, slips under the curtain and carries Alexandra to a time when Papa still came with them on their visits. She'd delighted in pretending she was a princess traveling from her castle at Heaven Hill to Cousin Callie's palace at Pinnacle Plantation.

Back then, the swamp that separates Heaven from Pinnacle was filled with fairies and elves and magical spirits. They waved to her from the highest branches of the cypress trees, trees she was convinced had the watchful eyes and earnest hearts of friendly giants.

She was eleven when her parents decided they could no

longer live under the same roof. The day Papa moved down to the village on the south end of the plantation grounds, she begged to live with him.

"You will be trained in the feminine arts. You will marry well and become the mistress of a grand plantation," Mother told her.

When Papa remained silent, all the fairies died, and the trees turned into ogres.

Alexandra withdrew into her private world where she played her violin and dreamed of becoming as famous as Phillis Wheatley, a slave brought from West Africa when she was eight, maybe even from the same village Papa's people came from. Phillis' owners taught her to read and write when they recognized her gift with words. When she was a young woman, she was invited to England where she recited her poems for the Queen. Following the publication of her book, Phillis was given her freedom.

As the carriage approaches Pinnacle, Alexandra's fingers find her seat and tap out the rhythm of the *Corelli* she's prepared with the hope of impressing Monsieur Martin. She would have preferred to play Chevalier de Saint-Georges, referred to by some as the Black Mozart, but Mother wouldn't hear of it.

She's almost reached the crescendo when Sampson turns the horses up Pinnacle's main drive. She lifts the shade a fraction of an inch. Outside slaves sing, stooping and standing and turning, like slow motion dancers as they work through rows of late-July rice. Then the carriage winds up the man-made hill toward the concert pavilion, built when the idea of Greek revival first impressed itself on the southern imagination. Mid-morning light bathes its marble columns in shades of ivory and gold, igniting Alexandra's desire to please Monsieur Martin.

When Sampson brings the carriage to a stop before the pavilion's gleaming steps, Alexandra leans forward to wake Mother. She stops when she sees a thread of bloody mucus trailing from Mother's lips, threatening to spot her lace shawl.

Is Mother ill?

Alexandra dabs Mother's mouth with a handkerchief. Then she takes a deep breath and whispers, "We're here."

Mother's eyes fly open. She glances around fearfully, still tangled in a dark dream. Then she sits up straight, presses her lips to a thin line, and adjusts her hat. "Comport yourself like a young lady, Alexandra. And remember, you and Callie have the same grandmother and the same claim to Paradis."

Mother doesn't add that Paradis, the family plantation that was usurped by the English when they invaded Martinique so long ago, will never be given back, despite the island's return to the French. Nor does she remark that Alexandra and Callie are really just half-cousins: Callie, whose complexion is as white as cream, hasn't got one drop of African blood. If Alexandra hadn't inherited jade eyes from Mother's side, she would be indistinguishable from her father's distant Diola relatives who still live in villages along the Gambia River.

Sampson reins the horses to a stop, hops down from the driver's seat and opens the carriage door. Alexandra is about to jump down when Sampson steps forward and extends his hand, reminding her that she is no longer a child.

"My violin and practice music, please," she says with what she hopes is the right mix of kindness and authority.

Mother rewards her with a rare nod of approval.

Sampson reaches into the carriage and retrieves the violin. Then he unlatches the back compartment, lifts out the satchel that contains Alexandra's practice music, and hands it to her.

"Thank you, Sampson," she says, attempting the inflected tone Mother uses with the house help.

With the hint of a smile, Mother says, "We mustn't keep my sister waiting, Sampson."

By the time the carriage resumes the drive to Pinnacle's big house, Alexandra has reached the top step of the pavilion. For good luck, she kisses the hand of the marble Athena who guards the entrance, then she opens the glass door and steps inside. The

French furnishings are sparse, but elegant. Mother's taste runs to rose and burgundy; Tante Isabelle's palette includes blues and creams, rich with vermillion accents.

Alexandra's mind fills with images of the Christmas concert when the stylish parlor will spill over with patrons clamoring to be noticed by their peers. Then she sees Callie stretched out on the blue velvet divan like an aloof lioness; her unpinned hair cascades to her waist like burnished gold; her mouth twists down in a pout.

Why has her cousin picked this day to be in one of her fire and ice moods?

"Good morning," Alexandra says, affecting a cheerfulness she doesn't feel.

Callie doesn't stir.

Dread washes over Alexandra. Has she arrived too late? Sampson had taken that detour around the part of the road that was still washed out. Had Monsieur come and left, too annoyed to wait? And why isn't Hera here to take her shawl?

Alexandra takes a deep breath to steady herself. "Callie, what a lovely gown," she says.

Callie turns her head a fraction of an inch and takes in her own reflection in one of the floor-to-ceiling windows.

Alexandra chokes down the flood of angry words threatening to spoil her chance to audition and steps out onto the balcony, clutching her violin case. After scanning the rose garden to make certain no one's watching, she slips Aunt Mamou's cowrie amulet out of its concealed compartment and holds it to her heart.

"Afraid Monsieur will discover he was mistaken about your talent?" chortles the Ahoelra.

"Stay away," Alexandra says aloud. She looks around to make certain no one was listening, then she rushes the amulet back to its hiding place.

Aromas of a rice and crayfish boil wafting up from the quarters put a worry in her mind. She didn't have time to eat breakfast before they left Heaven Hill, and she's exhausted from being awake all night. What if she doesn't have the strength to play well for Monsieur? Assuming he hasn't come and gone.

Movement at the far end of the vegetable garden catches her eye.

He's here!

She backs behind a column so she can watch him without being seen. Then she realizes her mistake. It isn't Monsieur coming up the path. Alexandra's fingernails bite into her palms when she sees a scantily clothed slave struggling to free herself from the jeweled collar at the end of the leash the new overseer holds tight with both hands. A thin stream of blood trickles down the slave's neck from where the collar has cut into her tawny skin. The beauty's eyes are sky-blue. Alexandra guesses she must have come from Sierra Leone, where Europeans have mixed their blood with Africans for centuries.

The slave cries out. Alexandra wants to scream at the overseer to let the poor woman go, but Mother made her promise not to say one word about the rules ordained by Callie's new step-father and his cronies.

Alexandra is still fuming when she hears footfalls and follows the overseer's gaze to a thicket of birch trees. She sees Monsieur stride onto the path to the pavilion, dapper in his black cut-away and beaver top-hat. A blush colors his normally pale face when his eyes alight on the slave's leash, pulled up so tight the poor woman is gasping for breath.

Monsieur will help her, Alexandra thinks as she eases herself to the side of the column so she can hear, but, hopefully, not be seen.

"Morning, Maestro," croons the overseer in a deep resonance that overmatches his short, muscular stature. "Or is it afternoon?"

Monsieur clears his throat.

Why doesn't Monsieur tell the overseer to unfasten the slave's collar? What is he waiting for?

"Mr. Ball said to inform you he expects his step-daughter to play the first solo in that musical affair y'all are planning. I tell you in confidence, he'll cancel the whole she-bang if you don't give Callie first billing. And, that would be a shame after all y'all's preparation."

Cancel the concert? Alexandra leans against the column to keep her balance.

"I received Mr. Ball's communication," says Monsieur.

There's a strain in his voice. Monsieur must be working himself up to tell the overseer that Alexandra will play the first solo.

"Of course, Callie will play first, provided both young ladies are up to their usual standard," says Monsieur.

Alexandra feels like the floor under her feet has fallen away. Monsieur lied to her. At their last rehearsal, he had taken her aside and all but promised she would play the first solo.

"Good day, Maestro," says the overseer as he yanks the leash.

Monsieur says nothing as the poor woman runs to keep the collar from biting into her neck.

Hera, Tante Isabelle's head-of-house, sails around the corner, strides to Monsieur and pierces him with her famous evil-eye. After waving him into the parlor, she spins on her heel, marches up the steps to Alexandra and whispers, "Don't you go blaming your tutor for panderin'. If he hadn't agreed, your aunt's new husband would have canceled the whole concert. You come on in and let your talent shine."

Hera grabs Alexandra by the elbow and steers her into the pavilion where Monsieur's already setting up the audition scores. Alexandra lays her violin case on a table and slides her practice sheets out of her satchel. Monsieur, who's standing so close she can smell the peppermint on his breath, doesn't so much as glance her way as he adjusts her stand to the proper height. He surprises her when he leans close and whispers, "You should have played first, Mademoiselle. Je suis désolé. But remember, the last solo, your solo, is the one the audience will remember—if you do well with your audition."

Alexandra moves toward him, as though drawn by a magnet. Hera inserts herself between them and turns to Monsieur.

"Miss Callie been waitin' on you since the sun peeped over 'All Hallows Hill.'"

Monsieur rushes over to set up Callie's score.

Hera scowls in Callie's direction. "It's time to practice, Missy."

Callie doesn't move.

"You hear what I said?" Hera steeples her fingers and waits. "Don't you dare embarrass your mama and your new daddy by making a fool of yourself because you haven't prepared."

Callie tilts up her chin. "I've changed my mind. I'm going to ask Mother to cancel the Christmas concert. Alexandra can play at her own plantation. The upper ballroom at Heaven will suffice for a solo recital. Or, maybe she'd rather go down to her daddy's African village and play for the heathens."

All Alexandra hears is the Christmas concert might be canceled. She can't let that happen. It wouldn't be the same to play at Heaven. Pinnacle's Pavilion, famous for its acoustics, is easy for audiences to reach by both river and road. Alexandra rushes to Callie and kneels by her side. "We've been preparing for this day since we were seven years old!"

Callie examines her newly manicured nails. "We're young women now, with the prerogative to change our minds."

"You have to play, Callie!"

Callie's laugh pummels the air. "Why? You'll be the star. Last time we practiced, Monsieur Martin hinted he'd give you the first solo, as long as your audition was up to your usual standard. I have a mind to throw my violin in the river and let the poor thing drown. In fact, I . . ."

"Ladies," Monsieur interrupts, "allow me to present the final schedule. Miss Callie, you will open the recital, provided you prove you are ready in your final audition."

Callie snatches the billing from Monsieur's hand. After

reading it over twice, she smiles and presses it into Alexandra's palm.

Alexandra can barely breathe. Monsieur has not only given Callie the first solo in the concert, but also the second and third.

"You'll play the final solo, Mademoiselle Alexandra." Alexandra lifts her eyes to Monsieur's. "The finale," he says, holding her in his steady gaze. "But before either of you plays in the concert, you must each perform well in your final audition."

As Monsieur adjusts Alexandra's music, his hand brushes hers. She's startled, then embarrassed, then pleased. She glances at Callie, relieved to see her cousin's attention has turned to Hera.

"Bring the violins," orders Callie, the color returned to her cheeks and the coolness to her voice.

Hera continues to pluck dead flowers from the daylilies arranged at the marble feet of Euterpe, muse of music and delight.

"You have lead in your legs? Bring the violins! Now!" demands Callie with a look that sends fire through Alexandra.

Hera snaps a dead bud off of a lily stalk, ambles over to the brass and glass music cabinet and tries every key on the ring that's looped through her belt. The last one, easily identifiable because it's brass and all the others are copper, unlocks the cabinet.

"Mademoiselle Alexandra, if your piece is satisfactory, you may take your concert violin home and use it to practice from now until the recital," Monsieur says as he lays Alexandra's velvet-lined case open.

Alexandra thrills at the prospect of practicing with the exquisite Grand Gerard Grand-mère brought her from the famous music shop on Rue Montmartre in Paris.

"What about my violin?" whines Callie.

"Guests first," says Hera, without meeting Callie's hateful gaze.

Alexandra positions the violin under her chin, closes her eyes and draws the bow across the strings. Petty thoughts about who will have the first solo vanish as her improvisation carries her to a vision of her Diola ancestors standing on the banks of the Gambia River, smiling and waving to her. As she continues to play, a three-string ekonting appears in the form of a shimmering spirit. It bows to her, then, with a flourish, it presents its cousin, the violin, which steps forward, shining from within like a new star in a cerulean sky.

Alexandra transitions from greeting her African relatives into a sensuous interlude. The music transports her into a world of color and shifting forms. She's so absorbed, she scarcely hears Hera address her cousin.

"Miss Callie, your violin's still waiting."

"Shut your ugly mouth!" Callie screams.

Alexandra stops playing and cradles her violin. She stares as Callie's features morph into the same reptilian scowl that earned Tante Isabelle's sister-in-law the nickname, 'The Witch with a Thousand Faces.'

Callie motions for Hera to approach. Hera shuffles toward her, head held high. Callie slaps the proud slave's face. "Get out!" Callie whispers.

I'll never slap Lulu, Alexandra thinks.

"There's a few things I have to do in here," Hera says, ignoring the blow.

Callie smiles her crocodile smile. "As you know, Mama gave me five slaves to do with as I please when I turned seventeen," Callie narrows her eyes. "Your grandson, Zeus, is a Number One Boy, if ever I saw one. The money I could make from his sale would be more than enough to buy that frisky thoroughbred I have my eye on—and you do know how I love to ride.

"A horse trader is going to pay a visit to Pinnacle this Saturday. I might just ask him what price Zeus would bring in the Charleston market."

Hold your tongue, Alexandra warns herself.

She thinks her cousin has won the match of wills until she sees fire smoldering in the old slave's eyes, and she recalls the rumor that Madame Calderon, Mistress of Bliss Plantation, up on the Pee Dee River, was poisoned by her discontented head-of-house less than a year ago.

Callie turns to Alexandra, lips pursed, nose in the air. "Colored folks have to know their place." When Callie places her hand on Alexandra's arm, she jerks away.

"Oh, my Lord, I didn't mean y'all," Callie says. "According to Mama, your daddy could walk into a court of law any day of the week and ask to be counted white on account of his old money, just like that boy from Berkeley County did. Folks say that man's skin is black as coal, like yours and your daddy's. I'm sure both of y'all could follow his example."

Alexandra clamps her teeth tight so angry words won't give her cousin an excuse to exclude her from the concert.

Callie continues, "It's common coloreds I was talking about. They might twang on a banjo, but they are incapable of playin' Mozart or Bach on a violin."

Alexandra plants her feet so she won't fall over from the dizziness that's come over her.

Callie never acted like this before her mother married Mr. Ball. Just when Alexandra's about to lash Callie with some cruel words of her own, Monsieur Martin says, "Let me fix that, Mademoiselle."

"Fix what?" demands Callie.

Alexandra wonders the same thing.

"Your cousin's scores are out of order," replies Monsieur, turning his back so Callie can't see what he's doing.

Alexandra's eyebrows shoot up when she sees Monsieur tuck an envelope into the pocket of her violin case before adjusting her scores. He presses a finger to his lips. "Pour tes yeux, seulement," he whispers, without looking at her.

For her eyes only? Alexandra breathes in his peppermint-scented breath. "Merci," she whispers.

"What're y'all whisperin' about over there?" Callie asks.

"I told your cousin it is impossible to play if a score is not perfectly placed. Shall I fix yours as well?" asks Monsieur Martin.

"My score is just fine," retorts Callie.

"Ladies, prepare to play," Monsieur says, throwing a smile in Callie's direction.

Alexandra's relieved that his eyes don't linger on her cousin.

The young women raise their bows, bosoms riding high in their Greek Goddess gowns.

Chapter Five

Callie's audition earns high praise from Monsieur. Now, it's Alexandra's turn. Her violin sings, laughs, weeps, scolds, laughs again, then falls silent. She drops her bow hand to her side and wills herself not to make a display of her exhilaration. Neither Callie nor Monsieur Martin moves.

When Alexandra dares raise her head, Monsieur is staring at the polished floor. Her piece disappointed him; she's certain of it. He's struggling to tell her that she has failed the audition.

When she's given up hope, Monsieur claps his diminutive hands like a delighted child. "Bravo!" He lifts his hazel eyes to hers. Tears stream down his cheeks. A shock of triumph thrills through her. Monsieur holds her in his unabashed gaze. Fire uncoils from her private place. Is he casting a spell?

Alexandra catches a glimpse of Callie's mouth twisted into a perverse smile. "I feel a headache comin' on." Callie lifts the back of her hand to her forehead.

Alexandra roots her feet to the floor and watches as Callie swoons. Monsieur catches her. What else can he do? He lowers her to the settee, kneels by her side and touches his hand to her cheek. He speaks gently, his voice full of concern. "You don't seem to have a fever."

Callie's eyelids flutter. Alexandra's stomach lurches.

When her cousin's fingertips graze Monsieur's lips, he jumps to his feet as if bitten by a snake. Alexandra covers her smile with her hand. There's a tremor in Monsieur's voice when he says, "Mademoiselle Alexandra, come see to your cousin while I fetch her mother."

"Mais oui, Monsieur," Alexandra says as casually as she can manage.

Why couldn't Callie allow her a few minutes to bask in Monsieur's praise?

"I want you to stay with me, Monsieur Martin," says Callie, reaching for his hand. "I feel so safe in your company. Let my cousin fetch Mama."

Monsieur whisks his hand out of Callie's grasp.

"Watch over her," Monsieur tells Alexandra.

Monsieur's almost to the door when Callie says, "Wait. I'm improving."

Wonder of wonders.

Monsieur rushes over to Alexandra's music stand. She's so focused watching Monsieur, she doesn't notice her cousin sneaking up behind her.

Callie clasps Alexandra's shoulders with cat-claw hands, presses her lips to Alexandra's ear and murmurs, "Your solo at the end was a jewel."

Callie's compliment washes away Alexandra's anger. From the time they were little, Alexandra has looked up to her older cousin. Callie whispers, "Making love with a man could never be as good as that, no matter what Jillian says. Don't you agree?"

Jillian, Callie's sinful new step-sister, has used a combination of perfect manners and feminine wiles to create a corridor of adult trust that has provided her the freedom to 'taste life's forbidden delights' without adults guessing what she's up to.

"That's uncouth!" blurts Alexandra, trying to wrest herself from her cousin's grasp.

Callie digs her fingernails into the soft flesh on the underside of Alexandra's arm and maneuvers around until they're face to face. She slides her hand up to the back of Alexandra's neck and presses so close Alexandra catches the scent of jasmine blossoms pressed between her cousin's breasts.

"But I guess we'll never know about intimacies with a man until we are much older. Will we?" whispers Callie. She releases Alexandra with a shove that sends her stumbling into a music stand. The music scores scatter. Mortified, Alexandra drops to the floor and starts scooping up the fragile pages.

"Je suis désolée, Monsieur."

"Allow me." Monsieur extends his hand to help Alexandra to her feet.

Callie giggles, casts a glance to Monsieur and says, "Isn't Alexandra the clumsiest person you've ever seen?"

Alexandra wishes she could disappear.

"No harm done," Monsieur says. But Alexandra can see the concern on his face as he scrutinizes his prize pages. After he's made a show of putting the music back in order, he announces. "Ladies, I am happy to say that you are both ready to play in the Pinnacle Parlor's Christmas Concert."

Callie takes hold of Alexandra's hands. Alexandra stiffens.

"Don't be a spoil sport."

Mother's always telling Alexandra she takes Callie's careless comments too seriously. Maybe developing a thick skin is a requirement of growing up. Alexandra grabs hold of her cousin's hands and leans back. They whirl around the room like they have since they were four years old. After three turns around the parlor, Alexandra's anger fades. When they're out of breath, the young ladies slouch onto the white brocade loveseat, fan themselves with their hands, and close their eyes to stop the room from spinning.

When her dizziness subsides, Alexandra senses her dress has pulled down too far. She opens her eyes, horrified to see that one of her breasts has popped out of the scooped neckline. She lowers her lids and peeks through her eyelashes as she inches the dress up. When she dares to glance at Monsieur, he's concentrating hard on rolling his scores into scrolls and tying them with blue ribbons. He hasn't seen her fiasco. She hopes. She watches him slide his rolled parchments into his oiled shoulder case. Her breath catches when he lifts her violin and kisses the underside of its smooth brown neck. Alexandra looks at her cousin, relieved to see Callie's eyes are still closed.

Suddenly, Callie jumps up, fully recovered.

"Monsieur," Callie says, batting her eyes, "I don't believe I'm quite prepared. Could you find the time to offer me a private lesson?"

"I'll speak to your mother about scheduling a session," Monsieur says.

Before Callie has a chance to respond, Monsieur turns toward Alexandra. "Mademoiselle Alexandra . . ."

"Oui, Monsieur?" She wishes she hadn't sounded so eager. The last thing she wants is for Callie to guess that she has an affection for Monsieur which extends beyond the normal feelings a violin student should have for her teacher.

Let him propose a private for me too, she prays.

"May I count on you to practice three hours every day, until we meet for our final rehearsal?"

Alexandra's heart drops. "With pleasure, Monsieur Martin," she says, trying hard to conceal her disappointment.

When Monsieur reaches the door, he turns back to face them. "My heart still soars on the wings of your magnificent strings."

As he nods in their direction, Alexandra convinces herself that he sees only her.

He takes off his hat, rakes his fingers through his hair and punctuates his praise with a bow. A shiny black lock falls over his flushed cheeks. As the door closes behind him, Alexandra notices a page of music has slipped under the settee. She picks it up and races out to the porch.

"Monsieur!" she calls, holding the page up for him to see. He runs up the stairs two at a time to fetch it.

It's common for a French gentleman to lift a lady's hand a hair's breadth from his lips and kiss the air above it, but Monsieur holds Alexandra's eyes in his gaze, touches his lips to her hand, and sends so strong a fire through her that she nearly forgets where she is. He steadies her with a firm grip, never taking his eyes from hers.

A guttural laugh shatters the spell. Alexandra looks down and sees the overseer leering at them from behind the rose arbor.

Monsieur withdraws his hand, which is suddenly cold and clammy.

Paralyzed by a dark feeling she can't name, Alexandra watches Monsieur rush down the lane without looking back.

She shouldn't have allowed him to touch his lips to her flesh. A lady would have withdrawn her hand and scolded Monsieur for taking liberties. But the way he had looked into her eyes sent a shock through her that rooted her feet to the floor.

"Why's he in such a hurry?" Callie stands in the doorway with a smirk on her face. Had her cousin seen Monsieur kiss her hand?

"He was so odd today," continues Callie. "Reminded me of a woodpecker, or maybe a penguin the way he strutted about in his starched white shirt and black tails. What d'ya think, penguin or woodpecker?"

"I thought he looked like an elegant young man," retorts Alexandra, relieved. If her cousin had witnessed the impropriety, she would have mentioned it.

"Young? He's twenty-five years old!" Callie peers into Alexandra's eyes. "You weren't too disappointed when he gave me the first solo—and the next—and the next—were you?"

Alexandra shakes her head, refusing to be baited.

"Never mind, we have more important things to think about."

Without taking a breath, Callie throws down the gauntlet. "Race you," she says as she sprints across the groomed lawn to the back stairs of the big house.

CHAPTER SIX

By the time Alexandra catches up, Callie is ringing the call-bell attached to the windowsill.

"Let's go on down to the hardpan on the riverbank and dance," Callie says, her mood turned from venom to honey.

Callie rings the bell again with a distinctive rhythm meant to call a specific slave. A little girl, whose skin gleams like polished teak, dashes up from the garden clasping a bouquet of pink peonies. Her gauzy shift floats up behind her like dandelion fluff.

The girl drops a low curtsey at Callie's feet.

Callie takes hold of Alexandra's hand. It's all Alexandra can do to keep from laughing as she watches the child stare at their entwined fingers: ebony and alabaster.

"Stop gawking," barks Callie. "Go put those flowers in the little silver vase my daddy brought from Charleston. Then bring me the blue quilt from the bottom shelf of my chifforobe. The one with lilies-of-the-valley embroidered on the hem."

The little girl's eyes remain glued on the cousins' hands.

"You have cotton in your ears?" Callie asks.

The wide-eyed girl jerks to attention, bows awkwardly, and races into the house, holding tight to the flowers.

Callie twirls the back of her hair around her little finger. Her eyes dart from Alexandra, then back to the floor.

"What's wrong?" Alexandra asks.

"Nothing."

"Tell me, Callie."

Callie sinks onto the porch swing and pats the seat next to her. As soon as Alexandra settles beside her cousin, Callie clears her throat and drops her voice to a whisper.

"I want you to know how bad I feel about having to limit our concert audience to a handful of abolitionists and Quakers. My real father's relatives remain forever loyal to y'all Degambia's, so they'll be there. But Mr. Ball struggles with the fact that you and I are blood-relations."

"I didn't know the audience would be limited," blurts Alexandra.

"Like I've said a trillion times, whenever Daddy's daddy came to visit, he told us the story about how your grandpa saved Pinnacle after that 1760's hurricane washed away all of our seedlings. My daddy's daddy bragged that your grandpa gave him so much of his fast-growing rice seed that he brought in a bumper crop the next spring.

"And then there was the time our daddies were fighting side by side with the Swamp Fox, and your papa pulled my daddy out of a pool of quicksand."

Alexandra watches Callie squirm, all the wiliness bled out of her face, "Mama says, and I agree, it's ignorant to lump your family together with common slaves just because y'all's skin, yours and your daddy's, that is, is black as night."

Alexandra can feel beads of sweat forming on her forehead. She keeps her gaze steady, hoping Callie won't notice.

"To quote Mama," Callie tilts up her chin. "'Post-revolution interlopers don't realize that the Degambia family was the very first in this area to plant rice, the crop that brought wealth to the Carolinas, and hence to this nation.'"

Alexandra's laugh is too shrill.

"You laughing at me?" Callie asks.

"You sound exactly like your mother."

"I'll take that as a compliment." Callie leans close and whispers, "I think the newcomers are ashamed of their common heritage. They simply can't bear the thought that some of their dark-skinned neighbors are more skilled, and more accomplished and prosperous than they'll ever hope to be." Callie clasps both of Alexandra's hands. "Tell me, how could someone who's barely more intelligent than a monkey play Mozart?"

"When did you get the new girl?" Alexander asks, hoping to turn the conversation to a new topic.

"Day after Mama ordered the orchestra for my big party. Haven't named her yet. Any ideas?"

"She didn't come with a name?"

"We always give our slaves a new identity to match their new place."

"How old is she?"

"Six or seven, I guess." Callie pauses. "Sleeps on a nice little rug by my bed, holding tight to her fan in case I get hot and need some breeze."

Callie's voice fades. "Sometimes I wake up and hear her callin' for her mama. When Mr. Ball asks if she's giving me any problems, I don't tell him about how she cries in the night." Callie sighs. "Mr. Ball can be so overbearing. Mother says I must respect him, because he's taken it upon himself to adopt me and offer me his name. If only Daddy hadn't died." Her voice drops. "I want to stay a Panier, but I've learned not to voice my opinion on that matter."

Alexandra's startled by the fear she sees flit across Callie's face.

"No matter what anyone says, no man will ever replace my real daddy." Callie looks around to make sure no one's listening. "It chills me to the bone when Mr. Ball trains the pick-a-ninnies with his horse quirt."

"Have you told your Mother?"

"I tried. She told me I must respect my new father's ways.

When I said he wasn't my real father, she started crying, so I let the matter drop. Can you keep a secret?" Callie asks.

"You know I can."

"Mr. Ball says your daddy spoils your slaves rotten by letting them plant private gardens and giving them Sundays free to use for their own purposes."

"I told you, all the people who live in the village are free, like Papa. Their ancestors joined the Cofitachiqui Indians and chased their Spanish captors back to the Sugar Islands in 1526. And my father's people . . ."

"Skip the history lesson. According to today's law, if they don't have papers to prove they're free, they're slaves."

Does Papa have papers? Alexandra wonders.

"Truth to tell, y'all've bragged on your daddy's African ways so long, you've convinced me that your daddy and his kin are real smart. He knows contented darkies work harder. That's why your rice yields are the best in the low country, which brings me to my secret."

Callie checks to make certain no one's listening. "I've decided to follow your daddy's example. Of course, I'll never recreate an African village. But I can offer some rewards."

As if on cue, Callie's girl returns with the quilt. Callie works her face into a frown. "Try to be a little quicker next time," she says as she raises one eyebrow and rains scorn down on the fearful child.

"Yes, Miss Callie."

"Did you put the flowers in the silver vase?"

"Yes, Miss Callie."

Callie takes a ginger candy from her pocket and drops it in the little girl's hand.

"Thank you, Miss Callie!" The little girl trips over her own feet in her attempt to execute a presentable curtsey.

"Tell Mama and Aunt Josephine that Alexandra and I have gone to play hide and seek in the maze garden. Stand in the doorway like I taught you and wait for a lull in the conversation."

"Yes, Ma'am."

"Hurry on, now!" commands Callie.

The little girl rushes into the house saying, "Hide-and-seek in the maze garden," over and over to herself.

"She might have just shuffled along if I hadn't given her that candy. Your daddy's influence. See what I mean?"

Even without Callie's experimental kindness, Alexandra can see that the little girl has a generous nature that would please Papa's side of the family. But it's her potential value on the property ledger that would impress Mother.

Callie pops up out of the porch swing, reaches behind the flower pot and produces her mother's copy of *The Dancing Masters*. The complete book of contemporary dances includes instructions about how to execute the minuet, along with renderings of a daring new dance: the waltz.

"I borrowed it from Mama's shelf in the library."

"Does she know you have it?"

"I'll put it back before she misses it. Come on, let's go practice!"

Alexandra and Callie have sneaked down to the river and danced barefoot on the hard-pan since they were seven years old. The adventure has always been heightened by the black satin river that rises and falls with ocean tides. But Callie has changed. Alexandra feels afraid to go down to the river alone with her cousin.

"I don't think I have enough energy left to dance today," lies Alexandra.

"You don't know how to waltz yet. You do want to make a favorable impression at your first real ball, don't you?"

Mother has invited Monsieur Martin to attend the coming-out. Alexandra tricks her mind into believing that Monsieur had drawn away from the overseer's glare to protect her virtue—not his reputation. And if he'd stood up for that poor slave, Mr. Ball might have prohibited him from returning to Pinnacle. Her feelings distort reason. Alexandra longs to impress Monsieur. She imagines dancing with him before bedazzled spectators. She panics. He's an accomplished dancer. What if the orchestra does play a waltz? She'll make a fool of herself.

"I guess I could go down and dance for a little while," Alexandra says, rising from the porch swing.

Before the young women reach the bottom of the stairs, they see a stranger wearing the sheriff's badge galloping toward them from the back road. Three of his deputies ride hard on his heels.

Callie leans close to Alexandra. "Let's duck behind the snowball bush before they see us," she says. She sets the quilt on the porch swing and hides the *Dancing Masters* behind the geranium planter.

But the men are coming too fast. The girls are only half way down the stairs when the men rein their lathered horses to a stop.

The new sheriff, who wears a top hat too small for his head, points at Alexandra.

"Girl! Git me some water."

Alexandra edges toward Callie and reaches to take her hand. Callie moves away. Cold sweat drenches Alexandra.

"You deaf? Git me some water. Now!" The stocky man's eyes graze over Alexandra's body. He clucks his tongue and turns to Callie, "You're too old to be dressing your slaves in your own clothes like they was dolls. I recommend you burn that fine dress to avoid being tainted by the sins of Hamm."

"These are my clothes!" says Alexandra.

The sheriff and his deputies laugh.

"Tell him, Callie! These clothes are mine."

"You let your girl speak to you in that tone?" The sheriff asks.

"I'm not her girl!"

Alexandra plants her feet. Callie backs toward the door.

"Callie! Tell him."

Callie edges into the house and eases the door shut.

Alexandra faces the sheriff. "My daddy will want a word with you," Alexandra says, her fire rising.

When she sees a vein on the sheriff's neck pump the venom that makes men crazy, the hairs on the back of her neck stand on end. She sighs with relief when Tante Isabelle glides out the back door like a cool breeze. Mother follows, arms akimbo, lips pressed tight.

"Where's Sheriff Adams?" asks Tante Isabelle in her blue-velvet voice.

"Heart attack. He'll recover more than likely, but he won't be back to work for a long time, if ever. Traveling judge deputized me. I'm following up on a slave who escaped from the Georgetown jail. You seen a big, black buck with a crooked nose and a little finger missing on his left hand?"

"I haven't made the acquaintance of such a man," says Tante Isabelle. "How are Mary and Margaret getting along?"

"Who?" asks the sheriff.

"Sheriff Adam's wife and daughter."

"Don't know 'em."

"Y'all are new to the Georgetown area, aren't you?"

"Yes, Ma'am."

"Surely, you've heard of Heaven Hill, the oldest plantation on the Santee," continues Tante Isabelle.

"Yes, Ma'am," says the sheriff.

Alexandra can tell he's lying from the way he shifts in his saddle and looks to his men to provide him with the correct answer.

"Well then, I am pleased to present the mistress of that famous plantation, Miss Josephine Degambia." Mother curls her lips into her Mona Lisa smile and nods.

The sheriff tips his hat.

"And her daughter, my niece, Alexandra Degambia," Tante Isabelle continues.

The sheriff's eyes bulge as Alexandra forces herself to curtsey.

"Carolina Gold, the most sought-after rice in the world, is shipped all over the world from Heaven Hill, but I'm sure you knew that, Sheriff. Where'd y'all say you're from?" Tante Isabelle doesn't wait for his answer. "Now, if all y'all are still thirsty, you and your men are welcome to use the well in back of the blacksmith's shop. The water's fresh and sweet, sure to cool you down on a hot day like this. When you're done, be so kind as to show yourselves to the main road."

The sheriff turns his horse and kicks it to a canter. When he and his deputies are specks on the horizon, Callie slips onto the porch from the back door followed by Alexandra's mother. "Shall we stroll in the maze garden?" Callie asks Alexandra.

"I don't feel up to walking with you," Alexandra snaps as she pushes back her tears and draws a ragged breath.

"Don't you young ladies allow that rude man to dampen your plans," says Tante Isabelle. "He'll be dismissed as soon as I have a talk with the mayor. Aunt Josephine and I are addressing the invitations to your Christmas concert. Come in the house and have congratulatory lime-and-lemon."

"Already had some," says Callie. "We'd prefer to soothe our nerves in the garden."

Alexandra starts to protest, then thinks better of it. Callie's still liable to see to it that the concert is canceled if she's riled.

"A walk through the garden will do you good. Just stay away from the roses in those dresses, and don't go down to the river. Understand?" Tante Isabelle waits for a response. "Did you hear me, Callie? I said not to go to the river."

"Yes Ma'am, I heard you," Callie says, offering her best Sunday-School smile.

CHAPTER SEVEN

C allie skips down the path that leads toward Tante Isabelle's garden maze—and the river. Alexandra lags behind. She fantasizes punching her cousin in her perfect upturned nose. But that would ruin her chance to play in the concert. She carefully summons her words. "Why didn't you tell that new sheriff I'm your cousin?"

Callie digs holes in the gravel with the toe of her boot. "I went in to get Mama. You could have come inside instead of provoking that man."

"And let him think I was your slave?" Alexandra glares at Callie. "The color of my skin never used to bother you."

"It doesn't bother me now. I held your hand in front of my new slave, didn't I?"

"She's a little girl."

Callie's voice deepens. "The sheriff could hurt us."

A horrible thought pops into Alexandra's mind. "Callie, has Mr. Ball hurt you?"

Callie stiffens and becomes unreadable. "Of course not," she says, too loud. "I really do need to go down to the river and dance so I can clear my head. You can come or stay."

"The river? You promised your mother . . ."

"I told her I understood what she said, I never told her I agreed not to go farther than the garden maze."

"Jillian teach you how to shade the truth?" asks Alexandra.

"You never told a white lie to your mother?"

Touché.

"You want to practice dancing like you said?" asks Callie. "Or would you rather make a fool of yourself when everyone's judging your ability to dance at your coming-out?"

Callie turns to go. Alexandra imagines tripping over her feet at her ball and giving Mother's high-toned friends a reason to smirk behind their fans.

"I'm coming," Alexandra says, but her insides scream, *this is a mistake.*

When Callie turns down the ancient Indian trail that weaves through Pinnacle's overgrown forest, Alexandra tenses. Last time she and Callie came this way, a coral snake dropped off the low-hanging branch of a bush right in front of her. She froze and the snake slithered away. But it seemed like an omen and Alexandra vowed she'd never participate in one of Callie's deceptions again. But here she is, less than two months later, sneaking down to the river.

Alexandra stuffs her skirt into her pantalettes, climbs up on the lowest branch of the Granddaddy Oak and scoots next to where Callie sits dangling her bare feet.

She's about to slip off her stockings and tuck them in her shoes when Callie says, "There's something you should know."

"What?" Alexandra asks, horrified Callie's going to confess she's also in love with Monsieur.

"Jillian knows about our place on the river."

Alexandra heaves a sigh of relief.

"What on earth did you think I was going to say?" Callie continues without waiting for a response. "That sneak Jillian followed me down here one morning when I was comin' to dance. I had no idea she was behind me. Anyway, we made a pact and sealed it by exchanging jeweled hair baubles. She said she wouldn't tell that I went to the river to dance if I agreed not to tell she brought her beaux down to our sand bar." Callie raises her eyebrows.

"We signal to each other when we're coming to the river by turning the geranium pot on the back porch around, so the white flowers face the lawns and the red flowers face the house."

"Race you," Alexandra says before Callie has a chance to ask what secret she's hiding.

They tuck their shoes into the crook of a branch, jump down, tie their skirts up around their waists and splash through the swampy grass.

"I won," Alexandra announces when she reaches the cool, hard sand. She turns to face Callie, who's ogling the river.

"Old Joe!" whispers Callie.

Two years ago, Old Joe, a twelve-foot alligator, gobbled up a little girl who'd waded into the river when her mother was washing clothes.

"Stay way back from the water," Callie cries out.

Alexandra follows her cousin's line of sight and sees something brown moving toward them in the current. A page of music floats atop the slow-moving black water, and sinks.

"Get out!" Callie yells.

"It's Monsieur's music bag," Alexandra shouts as she wades in, fishes out the leather music bag and drags it on to shore. The scores fall out in a rush of water. Alexandra sinks to her knees and tries to separate the fragile pages so she can lay them in the sun. She stops when they start to rip.

"Maybe they'll come apart when they dry," Callie says.

What if Monsieur tried to cross the river when the tide was rising. What if he fell in? Maybe he can't swim! Or what if someone pushed him?" Alexandra's fear expands as the image of the overseer leering when Monsieur kissed her hand flashes in her mind.

There's a rustling in the brush. Jillian and Mr. Ball burst through the trees on twin Arabians. They rein their horses to a quick stop and throw up a shower of sand.

"You promised not to tell!" shouts Callie.

Jillian flashes a wicked smile.

"Something's happened to Monsieur Martin," says Alexandra. "We have to help him."

"Do we, now?" Mr. Ball asks through clenched teeth.

Fear floods through Alexandra when she sees spider webs of blood in the huge man's eyes. But Jillian's face, devoid of recognizable human emotion, frightens her more.

Mr. Ball trots over to Callie. "Git on up!" he bellows, as he thrusts his hand out to pull her behind him. Callie steps back.

"Mr. Ball, didn't you hear what Alexandra said? We found Monsieur Martin's music floating down the river. Something awful must've happened to him."

Mr. Ball bends down, grabs Callie under the armpits, and heaves her up. "Throw your leg over the horse's neck."

Callie maneuvers herself so she's sitting astride in front of the pommel. Mr. Ball pulls her so close that her back is jammed against his front.

"Wait till I tell Mother you bruised my arms again," says Callie.

Alexandra's hands ball into fists.

Mr. Ball turns to Alexandra. "Git up behind Jillian."

Jillian screws her face into a scowl. "I don't want a darkie ridin' on my horse."

"I ask your permission?" bellows Mr. Ball.

Alexandra starts to run up the path that leads to the bridge where Monsieur might have fallen in the river. Mr. Ball steers his horse to block her.

"Git up behind Jillian. Now!" Mr. Ball raises his horse quirt.

"Don't hit Ali!" yells Callie.

Mr. Ball presses the stubble of his beard into Callie's neck. "Say please, and call me Daddy," he says, the quirt still raised. "And put a little sugar on that tone."

Alexandra's stomach roils when Callie turns around, smiles and bats her eyes.

"Don't hit her, please, Daddy."

"Give the girl a hand up, Jilli." Mr. Ball's growl is so treacherous, neither Alexandra nor Jillian dare protest. Jillian extends her hand. As soon as Alexandra is balanced on the rump of the horse, Jillian wipes her palm on the horse's mane.

"Don't touch me," Jillian hisses. "Hold on to the back of the saddle."

The horses gain as much speed as they can manage on the narrow, vine-bordered path.

Alexandra struggles to hold on as Jillian kicks her horse to a canter.

"Slow down," Callie says when they approach the magnolia tree. "We have to get our shoes."

Mr. Ball leans forward in his saddle and digs his thumb into the flesh of Callie's forearm. "Don't be telling me when to stop and when to go. Got that, Sweetheart?"

"But..."

He slips his arm around her neck.

"Go ahead," Callie says, her eyes cat-steady. "While you're at it, leave a mark that Mother can see."

Mr. Ball releases her, rolls a wad of tobacco from one cheek to the other and spits. He grips his saddle horn so hard, his knuckles turn white. Then he spurs his horse to a trot.

As soon as the path widens, Jillian and Mr. Ball urge their horses to a gallop. When they come to the end of the sun-dappled forest, they burst forth with demon-energy and race across Pinnacle's manicured lawn, throwing up chunks of lush green grass.

Alexandra sees Mother and Tante Isabelle standing still as statues on the upstairs balcony. Even from this distance, she can feel the steady heat of Mother's anger. Mother disappears into the house and re-emerges on the front porch. Jillian reins her horse up so fast that Alexandra tumbles on to the cobblestone drive. Good thing she has cat-instincts; she rolls as she falls and avoids serious injury.

Mother runs down the portico stairs, yanks Alexandra to her feet, and wipes the dirt off her face. "Where are your shoes?"

"Mother, Monsieur Martin—"

Before Alexandra can finish her sentence, Sampson brings up the carriage. "Madame," he says, dutifully offering his hand to help Mother to step inside. Alexandra pivots and races toward the river, trying to ignore the sharp pebbles cutting into the soles of her bare feet.

"Get back here!" Mother screams.

Hera, who's racing to meet Alexandra, tries to thrust the violin case into her arms, but Alexandra runs right by the well-meaning slave.

"I have to find Monsieur," Alexandra tells her.

Hera grabs Alexandra's arm and spins her around. She leans close. "Too late for that."

"What do you mean?"

"What's done is done. Night's just around the corner. Y'all won't be safe out on the road after dark." Hera presses the violin case into Alexandra's arms. Sampson grabs her around the waist and carries her toward the carriage. She tries to kick free, but he holds her fast in his tree-trunk arms, hoists her into the red leather seat facing Mother and locks the carriage door from the outside.

Alexandra follows Hera's gaze up to where Callie's looking down from her window. Her cousin starts to wave, then someone comes up behind her and pulls her out of sight.

Alexandra takes hold of Mother's hands. "You don't understand. We found Monsieur Martin's . . ."

Seized by a coughing fit, Mother jerks out of Alexandra's grasp and dabs at her mouth. Fear and anger run riot inside Alexandra when she sees spots of blood on Mother's handkerchief and a spray of red on the bodice of her dress.

When she recovers her breath, Mother says, "Your concern should be with the journal those men found in your tutor's pocket. Tell me the truth, Alexandra, did you agree to meet that scoundrel in secret?"

"What are you talking about?"

"You heard what I said."

"Have I agreed to meet Monsieur Martin in secret? Of course not! What happened to him, Mother?"

"Nothing you need to know." Mother takes a sip from her medicine flask, pulls down her window shade, and closes her eyes.

"Please, tell me what happened to Monsieur," Alexandra begs.

Mother's eyes fly open.

"Please, Mother, tell me..."

"You are not to mention that abominable man's name, ever again. Sit still and be quiet. I'm going to rest my eyes. I only hope I can find a competent deportment tutor capable of curbing your willful ways."

Alexandra's fingernails bite her palms.

When they pass by the Pinnacle's welcome fountain, Alexandra opens the drape just enough to see out. A breeze ruffles the surface of the pool where four marble horses rear up to greet visitors. Water sprites sparkling on the surface of the fountain pool conjure a vision of Monsieur Martin struggling against a maelstrom of black river water.

Alexandra's whole body shivers as vivid images flash in front of her eyes one after another: men whose faces she can't make out push Monsieur down into the water; the butt of the sheriff's gun glints in the sunlight; Monsieur seeks purchase on the riverbank with one hand; with the other, he clings tight to the leather pouch that holds the music scrolls. The blunt end of a horse quirt crashes down on his head. He lets go of his precious music scrolls as blood streams down his forehead. Alexandra hears the phantom men laugh.

Her visions fade as suddenly as they had appeared. Alexandra tries to bring the mind-pictures back, to see if Monsieur survived.

No luck.

She recalls Mamou's words: "In time, you'll be able to call up visions at will, but, in the beginning, they'll come to you and leave again, unbidden."

Just show me if Monsieur's alive, she prays.

No voice whispers in her ear. No image flashes in her mind. Then she remembers that Aunt Mamou's amulet is still in the secret compartment of her violin case. She'll put it around her neck as soon as she has some privacy. Maybe it will help her conjure a vision of Monsieur Martin's fate.

A pair of wild geese flying just above the tree line captures her attention. "Storm's coming," she says aloud, "or maybe it's already here."

"Be still." Mother's voice sounds flat and dangerous.

Someday, I'll stand up to Mother, Alexandra promises herself.

The stale warm air and hypnotic rhythm of the wooden wheels scramble her thoughts as she drifts into a dreamless sleep.

CHAPTER EIGHT

When the carriage finally rumbles over the cobblestones that lead up the drive to Heaven's big house, Alexandra awakens, relieved to see Mother's still asleep. It's night, and no light can seep in, so she opens her drape. Darkness amplifies the sound of raindrops plinking on the carriage roof. A flash of lightning illuminates the austere features of Mother's face.

Has she ever been happy?

Thunder rattles the sky. Still, Mother doesn't stir. A furious wind begins to blow as Sampson guides the horses into the covered carriage house. He opens Alexandra's door and holds it with two hands. "Go on in. I'll stay with your mother until she wakes up."

Foul swamp air gags Alexandra as she clutches her Grand Gerard case and starts up the stairs that lead into the big house.

"Alexandra!" Mother screeches.

Alexandra's stomach knots. She turns.

Orange light streams from carriage house lanterns, framing Mother's face. Her hand shakes as she points at Alexandra. "If you had even an ounce of social grace, you might have said, 'Forgive me, Sheriff. I am a guest in this house. My girl remained at home. If she had accompanied me, I would have told her to fetch water for you and your men. Allow me to see if I can find someone to bring you refreshment.' If you'd said that, you could have walked into your aunt's house with your head held high."

Mother glares. "Instead, you forced my poor sister to come to your rescue and risk her reputation."

I risked Tante Isabelle's reputation? How? Papa would be proud I stood my ground, Alexandra thinks.

Mother continues, "I have a headache coming on. I'll advise you of your punishment in the morning," She turns to Sampson. "Tell Lulu to go down and sleep in the kitchen quarters so Alexandra can reflect on her behavior in solitude. In the morning, install those bars on her French doors. Make sure to do it this time."

Before Alexandra can protest, Grand-mère, a ruddy-faced, elfin woman with a crown of white hair, rushes out the door onto the carriage house landing.

"Grand-mère!"

"I thought I heard your voice, Ali."

When Grand-mère stands on tiptoe and hugs her, it's all Alexandra can do to hold back her tears.

Mother pushes past Alexandra and pecks the aging woman on both cheeks, a perfunctory gesture devoid of affection.

"I thought you were coming next week, Maman," Mother says.

"My letter must have been delayed because of that round of storms." There is no apology in Grand-mère's voice.

Mother addresses Sampson. "Don't stand there like a stick in the mud. Take Alexandra to her rooms."

Mother turns to Grand-mère. "I'll speak to you at breakfast, Maman."

Sampson clamps his huge hand around Alexandra's arm and steers her toward the door.

Just before they step inside the house, Alexandra hears Grand-mère tell Mother, "What I have to say can't wait."

Lulu is setting out bedclothes when Sampson ushers Alexandra into her room. His voice takes on a sweet tone when he addresses Lulu. "Miss Josephine says you're to go on down and sleep in the kitchen quarters so Miss Alexandra can spend some time in reflection."

Is Sampson's obvious affection for Lulu fatherly, or something else?

Lulu hurries past Alexandra without looking in her direction. Sampson follows. He shuts the door and turns the lock from the outside.

A noisy exchange floats up through the bedroom grille. Alexandra slides her listening horn out from under her mattress, presses it to the fireplace grate, and listens. Everyone thinks the horn is a toy, but when there's no fire blazing in the East sitting room, it enables Alexandra to make out what's being said.

"I saw your face fall when the doctor placed that sweet child in your arms."

Grand-mère's voice.

"You'd hoped Alexandra would be able to pass for white like you."

Morbid fascination keeps Alexandra glued to the listening horn. She gasps when Grand-mère tells Mother, "I suspect you've been influenced by that new preacher's nonsense about the darker the skin, the greater Hamm's contamination."

"It would just be easier if Alexandra were lighter, especially in these times," replies Mother.

Alexandra feels dizzy.

"Here's the truth, Josephine. I haven't one drop of African blood, nor have I done a single thing that makes me stand out from other human beings. In Martinique, your quadroon father was loved by Whites and Coloreds alike for his multitude of wise and compassionate acts. I wish you had been older when he passed so you could remember him.

"Then, there's my second husband, Isabelle's father, who was white to the core. I learned, too late, that he married me for my money and for the estate I inherited when your Grande-Tante Yvette passed. A thimble full of alcohol turned that man into a brute. Within five years of our marriage, he'd gambled away half of my fortune. He never did one thing to endear himself to our community. Although, to his credit, he accepted you as if you were his own, but only because he thought you were white. I didn't disabuse him of his misconception. He died before your mother came of age to marry.

"Your husband Ajamat is tall and handsome, noble and wealthy, and as black as a moonless night, a condition to which you did not object when you had no dowry. Why you divided this plantation and forced your husband to move out of this fine house is beyond me."

"He chose to leave."

"It's no wonder with the way you carried on about his African ways. He loves his people and his heritage. But when he married you, he agreed to build you this elegant home and to live here with you on your terms, as long as he was free to spend some time in his village. That man adored you. I think he still does. Heaven only knows why. At least you live on the same property and put up a front of living as man and wife in the view of the outside world."

"If your lecture is finished, I'd like to go to bed," says Mother.

Grand-mère, the only person in the world who can get away with ignoring Mother, continues, "Your daughter is a beautiful, talented human being. Both Ajamat and Alexandra are proof that the color of one's skin counts for nothing in God's eyes, and anyone who says it does has an ear turned toward the devil."

"I have to go up and lie down," Mother says.

"I'm not finished."

"My head's splitting."

There's urgency in Grand-mère's voice as she continues. "That new sheriff stopped by. There's something off about the man. He said to tell Ajamat he saw water trickling through the north levee that borders the road to town. Sampson was about to go down to the village and tell him when Jimi, who'd been listening at my side, begged to go instead. I gave him permission to ride his new horse to the village after he told me you let him go alone all the time."

"You had no right, Maman! Jimi rode down there once, with Sampson following far enough behind to make him think he was alone. Did you stop to think there was a storm coming on?"

"Offering a boy responsibility he can handle is what builds his confidence. Besides, it wasn't raining then."

"This is my house, Maman. You will not tell my children what they may and may not do. Do you even know if he arrived safely?"

"I'm certain he did. He's a competent young man."

"He's a little boy."

"Time to let him grow up, Josephine."

Alexandra hears someone pound on the door downstairs.

"I'll get the door," says Miranda.

Has Miranda been in the same room with Mother? Or was she eavesdropping in the hall? Alexandra hears the door open.

As it's uncouth to make a public display of family discord, Mother and Grand-mère fall silent.

Miranda greets the visitor, but Alexandra can't make out what's being said. Then she hears Miranda pad back into the sitting room.

"Forgive me for intruding on your conversation, Miss Josephine. But Alphonse from over at Pinnacle says he has an urgent message for you."

"The driver?" asks Mother.

"Mr. Ball demoted him to stable boy. He said he had to speak to you in private."

Alexandra hears Mother and Grand-mère leave the sitting room, so she climbs under her silk coverlet, stretches out on her on her bed and stares at the top of the canopy cover.

"I don't care if Mother doesn't love me."

"Don't you?" asks the Ahoelra inside her mind.

Alexandra's surprised by the odd sense of relief brought on by Mother's honest revelation. She hadn't denied a single word about disliking Alexandra because of her dark skin. Alexandra had always believed she couldn't please Mother because she was defective in some horrible way. Now she knows it's only the color of her skin that puts Mother at jagged angles with her.

Ironic, her little brother Jimi, who can nearly pass for white, will be the one to move to the village when he turns fifteen—even though he prefers Mother's world. Alexandra, who favors the Diola way, is supposed to be sanded and chiseled into Mother's conception of a 'polished woman.'

A bolt of lightning illuminates the room. Alexandra counts the seconds. One thousand one, one thousand two. Thunder roars across the sky. She goes to her window. Mesmerized by runnels of water that chase each other down the glass panes, Alexandra's thoughts carry her to Monsieur Martin, who might be lying out in this rain, beaten and bruised.

She senses he's still alive. *Don't let Monsieur Martin die,* she prays. Then she remembers the note Monsieur slipped into her violin case. Hands trembling, she opens the case and takes out his letter. She pulls down the writing surface of her secretary and slices the envelope open with her ivory letter opener. She's about to take out the note when she hears someone fumbling to unlock her door. She tucks the envelope under her ink blotter and slides the violin case under her bed. Then she tiptoes to her bed and dives under the covers. She turns away from the door and squeezes her eyes shut. The lock clicks open. Whoever it is comes in the room, approaches the bed and leans close.

"Always sleep in your clothes?"

Alexandra throws off the blankets, falls into Grand-mère's arms and sobs. Grand-mère holds her and rocks her until her tears are spent.

"All cried out?"

"Oui, Grand-mère."

Grand-mère sits on the bed and takes Alexandra's hands in her own. *"Je t'adore, ma petite."*

"I love you, too, Grand-mère."

"Alphonse came all this way to tell me that Callie and Isabelle are—having a little challenge with Mr. Ball. My intention was to help you prepare for your concert and your coming-out party, but I'm going to have to leave for Pinnacle tonight."

Alexandra squeezes Grand-mère's hand. "Don't go. It might be dangerous. Callie's step-father..."

"No need to worry about me. When my late husband died, I still had title to that acreage Mr. Ball has his eye on. If he crosses me, that land will never be his, and he knows it."

Grand-mère's gaze rests on the toy horn. "Listening at the grate?"

Alexandra hesitates, then nods.

"Grand-mère, does Mother like me at all?"

"She's concerned for her future, and yours. Many of those wealthy families from the Brown Fellowship Society have adopted the absurd idea that marrying a woman with light skin is better than creating a union with a quality woman of beautiful ebony hue. You're a prize, Alexandra. Anyone who can't see that is a fool."

"I don't want to marry a man from the Brown Fellowship. I don't want to marry anyone." Alexandra summons her courage and asks the question that's been on her mind for a long time. "If the shade of a person's skin is so important to Mother, why did she marry Papa?"

"You've never heard the whole story, have you?"

Alexandra shakes her head.

"It's time you did."

Grand-mère sits on the bed next to Alexandra.

"I can't explain without telling you about Paradis."

"Your sugar plantation on Martinique?"

Grand-mère nods. "When the English drove the French from

Martinique, Paradis was a prize they craved. One devastating day, your grandfather was out in the sugar fields. Our neighbor, Renaud, drove up in his carriage and said the English were coming and our lives were in danger, and we had to leave with him immediately. I told him we had to wait for your grandfather. He convinced me that your mother, who was only six months old, could be hurt, maybe killed, if we waited. So, I scooped her into my arms and fled, praying that Charles would make his way to us. When we arrived at the port, Renaud introduced me to a man who was helping French people escape to Charles Towne, as it was known then. I paid him with the diamond and emerald necklace your grandfather gave me when we married.

"Three months after we arrived at my Tante Yvette's home in Charles Towne, I learned my dear Charles had been killed." Grand-mère pauses, closes her eyes and draws a breath to steady her emotions. "I was white; my aunt and uncle were white; neighbors and friends assumed your mother, a lovely baby with ivory skin like mine, was white. They'd never met my late husband. Only my aunt knew your grandfather was mixed. Tante Yvette convinced me we must perpetuate the fiction that your mother was white. I acquiesced against my better judgment. After all, your aunt and uncle had taken us into their home.

"Your mother grew up believing she was white. Two years after we arrived, I married. My second marriage produced another daughter. Tante Isabelle was born when your mother was three-years-old. Even though your mother and Tante Isabelle were separated by three years, they enjoyed each other's company.

"When your mother was seventeen, a dashing young planter who had stolen her heart, inherited a lovely plantation on the Ashley River. He asked her to marry him. It almost drove her to commit suicide when I told her that her grandfather was mixed; color had become a distinction that prevented most people from marrying someone of mixed race because they felt it lowered their status.

"Your mother knew she couldn't marry the young man she loved. It was well-known that he and his family abhorred the idea of a white person marrying a person with so much as one drop of African blood. If she didn't tell him about her background, and they had a dark-skinned baby, her very life and that of the child would be in danger. It nearly broke that young man's heart when your mother lied and told him she didn't wish to marry him.

"It was her love of horses that gave her the will to live. She used to ride astride, galloping down the beach like the horse goddess Epona, her auburn hair flying up behind her like angel wings.

"Isabelle married when she was only sixteen. After two miscarriages, your cousin Callie was born. I feared your mother would become a spinster. Then, just after she turned twenty-one, a miracle occurred. Your father arrived in Charleston, the city had been renamed by then. He came to sell two of his famous Arabian horses.

"Your daddy's money persuaded your mother that she could still become the mistress of a prosperous plantation. I don't know how she managed it, but she let your father know she was mixed and that she was available. He fell head-over-heels in love. Not wishing to draw attention and create a scandal in Charleston, where everyone knew your mother's family, they kept their relationship a secret. Your father's home was way up on the Santee, so your mother and father only saw each other on occasion before they married.

"Your mother has always had a talent for business. Your father told her how he lived simply in his African-styled village, even though he possessed great wealth. She agreed to marry him—if he would build her a Greek Revival plantation house and would guarantee that she'd have the right to run it in her own way. A little more than two years later, he informed her that the last of the furnishings she requested had been moved into this very house.

"They took a schooner to Georgetown where they were married in a private ceremony. A washed-out road blocked by fallen trees prevented them from proceeding directly to Heaven Hill. So, one of your father's French business associates offered them his country home to stay in. They spent their wedding night in a secluded cottage. The road was cleared in three days.

"Your mother was impressed by the barouche carriage with its gold scrolling and four matched Arabians, one of her many wedding gifts your father had given her. He adored her. She hoped she might come to love him, in time. When the road was passable, he told her he had saved the best surprise for last.

"He had sent word ahead, and before they proceeded up the drive to the big house, which she had only seen in drawings, they stopped at his beloved village for a welcoming celebration. The villagers, he reminded her, were all free-people-of-color, and should be treated as her equal.

"When your mother saw your father's people dancing and heard them playing their ekontings and drums, she was horrified. She told your father she would not live on the same plantation with heathens and devil-worshippers.

"It was too late for an annulment. Your father proposed a compromise. His genuine love for your mother had not been diminished by her outburst. He agreed to build a barrier between her big house and the village. She would have full charge of the house and its grounds, and she would never have to see the villagers again. He would split his time, living part of the week in your mother's domain and spending the balance of his time in the village, his base for overseeing the rice and indigo fields.

"He had promised she could rule the house, so, though it grieved him, he turned a blind eye when she purchased slaves. You were born less than one year after your mother took possession of this house. Two years later, your Aunt Isabelle and Uncle Charles moved to the property adjoining Heaven with Callie, who was a year older than you. The two of you became playmates.

Tante Isabelle and your uncle had owned a starter plantation on the Ashley that had been subject to perpetual flooding, so they were delighted when a friend of your father's sold them Pinnacle Plantation, which was just on the other side of the swamp from Heaven.

"Your families took turns visiting one another on a monthly basis. You and your Cousin Callie, who shared a love of adventure, became fast friends. Six years after you came along, Jimi was born. Even though they had you and a beautiful son, your parents had grown apart. It became too challenging for them to live under the same roof. When you were eleven and Jimi was five, they agreed to remain married, according to South Carolina law, and to divide the plantation into your mother's world and your father's village.

"They also agreed that when you turned fifteen, you would live exclusively in the big house so you could concentrate on your coming-out ball and hone the skills that would enable you to run a plantation house one day. Once you were promised, you could visit the village. You loved both worlds and, until you turned fifteen, you traveled freely between them.

"Jimi was to move to the village when he turned twelve."

Alexandra sighs. "Sometimes I wish I were a boy."

"I know what your preferences are, Alexandra. I agree it is ironic. You favor your father, while Jimi is more comfortable in your mother's world. But life is what it is. To survive and to thrive requires stretching and adapting while holding fast to one's soul."

Grand-mère pats Alexandra's hand. "Your mother does love your music, Ali, and that's a big part of who you are. In her way, she wants the best for you."

The day's events have made quicksand of the ground Alexandra has always believed was firm and dependable. Words don't begin to express the confusion she's feeling. But she is certain of one thing, Mr. Ball is dangerous and she's afraid of what he might do to the people she loves.

"You have to be careful at Pinnacle Grand-mère."

Grand-mère pulls her shawl close and adjusts her hat. "Like I told you, when I dangle the possibility of selling that parcel Mr. Ball wants, I believe I can talk that man into treating Tante Isabelle and Cousin Callie like royalty."

Alexandra kisses Grand-mère on both cheeks. "Tell Callie I love her."

Grand-mère is almost to the door when she turns back. "If things don't work out for you here, when you come of age to make your own decisions, consider living near me. There's a small, affluent community of free-people-of-color in Charleston who are starting a school. They'd welcome your fertile mind and your musical gift, and I could set you up in a little house I own on Chalmers Street."

Alexandra's heart sinks at the thought of leaving Heaven. Even with its faults, it's all she has ever known.

Grand-mère reads the expression on her face. "Why am I talking nonsense? This is your home." Tears glisten on Grand-mère's cheeks as she leaves the room.

Alexandra feels empty as she walks over to the French door, steps out onto the balcony and watches Grand-mère's carriage drive down the cobblestone lane and out of sight.

The storm has passed, and the moon is winking on and off through racing clouds. Thunder rumbles in the distance. The stench of fish and something dead rises up from the swamp. Alexandra goes back into her room, closes the door and draws the drapes. Then she takes Monsieur's note out from under the ink blotter. Her breath catches as she reads the first page, penned in scarlet ink:

*A Writing from Jean-Jacques Rousseau's Novel, Julie
hand-lettered for Mademoiselle Alexandra Diola Degambia
by her admirer, Jean Marie Martin*

Monsieur Martin is her admirer? At first, she's ecstatic; feelings she has for him are mutual. Then she remembers his music floating on the surface of the river. She dares to pose the question she's been evading—is Monsieur alive? Has he been ripped from her life forever? Maybe reading his letter will help. She discovers Rousseau has written *Julie* in the form of letters. The first, addressed *"To Julie,"* is written in dark blue ink.

*Excerpts from **Julie***
by
Jean-Jacques Rousseau

"You know that I entered your house only at the invitation of your worthy Mother. Knowing that I had cultivated some agreeable talents, she believed that they would not be without usefulness, in a locale wanting in masters, toward the education of a daughter she adores...

"I hope I shall never so forget myself as to say to you things that are not suitable for you to hear, and fail in the respect I owe even more to your morals than to your station and your charms..."

The next line is circled in gold ink.

"I have no desire for a happiness that will diminish yours..."

Suddenly, Alexandra understands the heartache Mother must have felt when she told the man she loved she could no longer see him. As she reads on, she's delighted to learn that when Julie confides she cares for her suitor, he responds with fresh ardor,

"Oh how shall I withstand the torrent of delights that floods my heart?"

The second page contains Monsieur Martin's personal sentiments:

Dearest Mademoiselle Degambia,

Monsieur Rousseau enjoins us to be true to our feelings. In his passage to Julie, he mirrors my greatest hope, but Julie is not the object of my affection. Your music has opened the door to my soul. If there is the scantest chance that I might meet with you in private, at a place of your choosing, please return the enclosed ribbon to me at our final concert rehearsal, with the excuse that it must have fallen into your open violin case as I was tying up my scrolls.

Although I long to speak to you unsupervised, I assure you that my intentions are above reproach. I will understand if you decline my invitation.

I remain your devoted servant,
Jean Marie Martin

A postscript, written more hastily reads:

"I have confidence that, as you play your violin, you will transport your audiences, as you have transported me."

The blue ribbon, tucked into the bottom of the envelope, smells like roses. Alexandra can't stop her tears when she thinks about Monsieur Martin's sacred scrolls floating down the river. A vision springs into her mind: Monsieur lies in the mud on the river bank, unable to move because he's tied to a tree root. His eyes are open, and he is breathing. The vision seems so real that she reaches out to touch Monsieur's outstretched hand. When the vision disappears, she knows he is still alive, but his life is in peril.

She stuffs her pillows under her blankets to make it look like she's sleeping in her bed and steps out onto her balcony, determined to go to the village again, at night, and beg Papa to help Monsieur. He must have returned from Georgetown by now. She's thankful it has stopped raining.

By the time Papa's stables come into view, feathery clouds drift across the moon like ghosts. Good. The wind must have changed direction and sent the storm racing off in another direction. Alexandra hears the horses snort and paw the ground. *Why are they so agitated?*

She stands still and listens. Shivers spread down her shoulders when she hears laughing and sees men coming down the wagon trail carrying torches.

Monsieur Martin could die, she tells herself. *Don't run back home.*

She turns the wick in her lantern all the way down and lowers herself into the damp, knee-high grass. An army of chiggers feasts on her ankles. The men are coming closer. They're talking loud and fast, covering their fear with idle chatter. If only they were close enough for her to hear what they're saying.

Cabai's high-pitched whinny pierces her. Alexandra hunches down and creeps toward the corral fence.

The men stop talking. She can hear their booted feet slogging through the mud toward the corral. She sets her lantern on the ground. Fear turns her legs to water as she struggles to climb up on the railing to get a better view. She can see four people carrying pine torches. They're headed straight toward the corral.

Patrollers? She trembles. *They didn't see her lantern light from so far away. Did they?*

As the men edge around to the back of the corral, she eases

herself to the ground. They've come close enough for her to make out their words.

"Ain't right for a darkie to own all this land," says a boy-man whose voice is just turning.

"Or for that white music teacher to make eyes at the African girl, no matter how rich her father is."

She recognizes that man's voice. It's Mr. Ball's overseer.

"You see, Steven, that's why we come to teach them a lesson. Mixing white blood with black is an abomination in the eyes of the Lord."

That must be the boy's father.

She peers through the slats in the corral fence; torchlight frames four pairs of boots.

"Seems a shame to burn up all these fine horses," the boy-man says.

They're going to set fire to the corral?

"We talked on this, Son. Everyone for a hundred miles around knows who these horses belong to. So, we can't steal 'em. Throw your torch in that trough of dry hay, over there under the overhang, and prove you're a man."

That trough, attached to the corral fence, is saturated with pine sap. Even if the hay's damp, it'll go up in flames.

Alexandra needs to unlatch the gate. She wedges her foot between the bottom boards of the fence and hoists herself up high enough to lift the bar off the outside hook.

She climbs up and is about to reach over to release the inside bar when the boy-man asks, "Y'all hear that?"

Quiet as a cat, she lowers herself back to the ground and crouches.

One of the men asks, "You still believe those baby stories about African ghosts, Steven?"

The men giggle. But she can hear doubt in their high-pitched voices.

Alexandra sends up a prayer: *Help me save the horses.*

A cloud slips over the moon and throws a net of darkness over the land. Did her prayer work that fast? Is Oeyi working his magic?

The men's nervous laughter provides enough cover for Alexandra to slide under the bottom board of the fence without being heard, but the angle of the wood rails makes it impossible for her to climb up and get to the lock from the inside. She closes her eyes and calls out with her mind, the way Aunt Mamou taught her: *"Cabai!"* The stallion trots over to her. She grabs his mane, swings herself onto his back, leans down over his neck and urges him toward the inner latch on the gate.

"Heave your torch, Son."

The boy hesitates, then he says, "Cain't do it, Pa."

"Cain't, or won't?"

"These horses don't deserve to die."

"Give me that, you yellow-belly!"

A strong arm heaves the torch. The hay smolders; the wood flames up.

Alexandra tries to lift the lock-bar, but it doesn't give.

A barn owl screeches as it passes overhead. Its white wings beat the air. A drum sounds in the distance.

"Let's go before we have a bunch of crazy heathens chasing us!"

As the men start back up the path. Alexandra hears the snap of the trap Papa set to catch that panther that had carried off a colt last spring. A scream shatters the silence.

"Help me, Pa," pleads the boy-man, but the men must be too far down the road to hear him, or maybe they thought the boy had tripped and they wanted to teach him a lesson.

Sparks fly up in the trough. Alexandra slides off of Cabai's back and whips off her cloak. Smoke threatens her as she beats out the fire and stomps out the last of the burning embers. The horses swish their tails and paw the ground.

Alexandra hears the boy whisper, "Lord, I don't want to die."

Part of her believes that he deserves to bleed-out. But he's so young. And he did want to save the horses. Besides, if his father comes back to help him, he won't be able to open the trap and the boy will lose his foot—if he doesn't lose his life first.

Papa had shown her the sequence of levers to push and pull in order to release the trap if a horse—or a person, accidentally tripped the lever.

"I don't want to die," the boy is struggling to hold on to his torch.

Alexandra squeezes under the fence and goes to him. "Lie still," she whispers.

"Don't kill me," he begs.

The boy's eyes roll back. She's surprised to see he doesn't look much older than Jimi, even though his voice is starting to change.

"I'm not going to hurt you. Take a deep breath and hold the torch still."

She works the boy's belt off and tightens it into a tourniquet above the place where the trap has clamped onto his ankle. Then she pushes and pulls the levers, and the lock springs open. The boy yelps. She rips off part of her dress and wraps it tight around the wound, then she helps him to his feet. He's able to hold his weight. No broken bones. The boy looks into her eyes and seems to want to say something, but he turns and hobbles down the path without a thank you, holding tight to his torch.

Alexandra needs to go tell Papa what happened. When she climbs the fence, she sees torchlight bobbing toward her from the hill that leads to the village. Had the boy's father doubled back around? She steps down from the railing and presses herself flat against the corral fence. The gate opens and closes. The moon has come out from behind that cloud. Torchlight illuminates a flash of red.

Oeyi? she inquires.

The village priest moves toward her and looks into her eyes.

He traces her cheek with the palm of his hand.

Transfixed by his gaze, Alexandra is filled with the sensation that she's made of particles of light. A sound like rushing water soothes her. When her ordinary senses return, she sees Cabai nuzzling Oeyi. Some of the other horses are still stomping the ground, their ears pinned back. Raising his hands above his head, Oeyi chants the song Aunt Mamou used to sing to her when she had nightmares. The agitated horses grow calm and gather around the old man.

Alexandra tenses when she sees Papa striding toward the corral, brandishing a pine torch. His eyes blaze with barely contained rage. For the first time in her life, she understands why he's called 'The Panther,' that powerful animal able to conceal the fire in its soul behind an opaque gaze.

Papa grabs Alexandra's wrist. She plants her feet and looks into his eyes. "What are you doing here?" he asks.

"I found my teacher's music floating down the river. Monsieur would never abandon his music. I think someone tried to kill him. He may be injured. Please, Papa, send your trackers to find him."

Papa's grip loosens, but she's unable to read his face. Oeyi draws Papa aside and speaks to him.

"Saved the horses?" she hears Papa say.

Oeyi hands Papa what's left of her fire-eaten cloak. "Risked her life," she hears Oeyi say as the old man glances in her direction. Papa fingers the holes in her cloak. He turns toward her. "Walk with me, Analai," he says, his deep voice full of tears.

Papa used her Diola name, the way he had when she was a little girl.

She follows him to the man-made cave where she had spoken with Mamou. When Papa fits his torch into a sconce, pearls in the woven wall-mats glitter.

Alexandra pulls off her boots and sets them next to Papa's sandals. When she sits beside him on one of the tree stumps that surround the fire pit, her memory travels back to the time she was a child and she knew she had a place in Papa's heart.

It seems as though Papa's peering into her soul. "You and Jimi are free because your grandmother's white and your mother is free."

Why is he telling her something she already knows?

"Copies of the papers that prove your status are in Grand-mère's wall-safe in Charleston—if anything should happen to me . . ."

A chill passes through Alexandra. How could something happen to the Papa?

". . . the big house will pass to your mother to live in until she dies. Heaven's lands will be divided between you and Jimi. If my lawyer can prove I have the right to own property, you will become the heiress of Heaven Hill, and Jimi will become the heir."

"Nothing will happen to you, Papa."

"These new people are hungry for power. They'll demand proof that the villagers and I are free, but because our ancestors drove their Spanish captors back to the Sugar Islands way back in 1526, we have no papers. If I can be declared white in a court of law, like that planter in Berkeley County was, I can maintain my claim to Heaven Hill, and I can list Heaven's villagers on my slave ledger, as is required by law. I'll let a little time pass, then I'll take them to Boston and set them free."

Alexandra trembles when she realizes how sheltered she's been at Heaven Hill. Until recently, she'd thought only a handful of uneducated people judged a person by the color of one's skin.

"Come," says Papa. Using his torch to light the way, he motions for Alexandra to follow him deeper into the cave. He stops when they come to part of the wall that's a shade lighter than the earthen walls around it.

"Watch," he says as he pulls on the twisted stem of what looks like a vine.

Alexandra hears sprocket wheels whir. A section of wall springs opens to reveal an iron safe Alexandra estimates is two feet square. When she looks more closely, she sees the 'vine' consists of twisted strands of metal. Papa takes a key attached to a cord around his neck and opens the lock. Inside there are six leather pouches, each the size of a grown man's head. Papa hands one to her. It's so heavy, she almost drops it. She unties its drawstring and looks inside.

"Gold?" she asks.

"If authorities seize Heaven, go to Marcello's blacksmith shop, then come here for the gold. Marcello will help you and Jimi escape to your Grand-mère's, where you can retrieve the papers that prove you're free. If your grandmother isn't there, make your way to Judge Calvin's on Chalmers Street; he has duplicate documents.

"You'll have enough money to live comfortably. You may want to go North, or maybe to France. Or, you could become part of the free-coloreds who have created a community in Charleston."

Oeyi whistles a warning.

"Don't tell anyone about this gold," Papa says as he enfolds the key in Alexandra's hand. "Keep this key in your fireplace safe. You're strong and intelligent, Analai. I am proud of the young woman you've become."

Alexandra throws her arms around Papa. He strokes her hair, then he places his hands on her shoulders and looks into her eyes.

"From now on, wearing your feelings for all to see will be a luxury you can't afford. One more thing," Papa says. "Don't tell anyone about the corral fire. Those men won't brag about their failed attempt, and we don't need to draw attention to Heaven Hill."

She doesn't want to leave him, but she has to get home before the sun comes up and Mother discovers she's not in her room.

"I understand, Papa. I came here to tell you about my music tutor . . ."

"My trackers found your teacher bound up in a net staked to a tree root on the bank of the irrigation canal. In another hour the tide would have come in and drowned him. In a month, animals who live in the swamp would have picked his bones clean."

"He's alive!"

"He'd only been there a few hours. Aunt Mamou's nursing him back to health. When he's strong enough, trackers will help him get back to France."

Tears of relief stream down Alexandra's cheeks. She throws her arms around Papa again. "I love you, Papa!"

"Honor your teacher by making your music. Your love for him opened your heart, but now you must let him go. Aunt Mamou looked into the fire and saw there is another man to whom your true love belongs."

"I'm just glad he's safe," says Alexandra. But her tears betray her.

Papa draws back and peers into her eyes. "It's best to let the authorities think your teacher is dead. I'll have the trackers bring Jimi back to the big house in the morning. It's hard to believe he slept through all this commotion." He sighs. "I could say you shouldn't have come, but if you hadn't been so brave, we would have lost the horses. All is as it is meant to be."

Alexandra's heart swells with contentment as Papa takes her hand and leads her out to where Oeyi waits next to Cabai.

The priest whispers something to Papa. Papa nods. When he turns to Alexandra, he's smiling.

"Oeyi and I agree that you should make an euwuum pact with Cabai before you go back to the big house."

Excitement surges through Alexandra at the thought of the magnificent horse becoming her spirit animal.

Papa unsheathes his hunting knife and hands it to her.

Alexandra looks into the horse's liquid black eyes. She keeps her gaze steady as she cuts a thin line across her palm. Cabai shivers when she makes a shallow puncture in his flank and presses her palm to the horse's wound to mingle their blood. Then, she throws her arms around Cabai's neck, buries her face in his mane, and whispers, "We'll always be together in our spirit bodies."

Cabai presses his forehead to Alexandra's. Then Papa cups Alexandra's face in his huge hands.

"Be brave. Be strong. Show no one your tears. Honor your ancestors."

Papa holds Alexandra in his gaze. "Remember, if something happens to me, keep your brother safe."

Alexandra nods.

Papa turns and walks up the path to his village without looking back.

CHAPTER NINE

It's still dark outside when Alexandra slips back in through her window. "Lulu?" she whispers. Then she remembers Lulu was sent to sleep in the kitchen. Good. The fire in the fireplace provides enough light for her to make her way to her hearth and open the safe concealed by fireplace bricks. She places the key inside.

Her dress reeks of smoke, so she takes it off and hangs it deep inside her wardrobe. Then she shoves her wet boots under her bed. After sponging off, she changes into a dry nightdress and climbs under her bed covers. As soon as her head is on the pillow, she falls asleep and dreams she's flying through the sky on Cabai's back.

She can barely open her eyes the next morning when Sampson pounds in the bars on the outside of her French doors, making a prison of her room. She falls back asleep, despite the noise. The next thing she's aware of is Miranda setting a dinner tray on her side table.

Alexandra feels disoriented. "What time is it?" she asks.

"You slept all day, and now it's night."

Alexandra collects her thoughts. "Is Jimi back home?"

"It started pouring this morning. The rain's turned the road to slop. Jimi probably won't be coming back from the village until the weather clears. Your mother is furious."

Rain drops plink on the bars.

Miranda sets down the supper tray and checks Alexandra's chamber pot, which is still empty. "Eat, then try to get back to sleep, or you'll have your days and nights turned upside down," Miranda says, then she leaves the room.

Alexandra feels ill after eating just three spoonsful of chicken soup. Whenever she closes her eyes, she sees visions of traps springing shut, and fires igniting and horses rolling back their eyes in panic. When the clock downstairs strikes three, she starts to drift off. Then she hears something inside her wardrobe scratching at the underside of the trap door that's connected to the escape passage that leads from her room out to the well.

From the day Papa told her about that trap door, she's been terrified something evil would come into her room through that secret passage. Whatever's making so much noise is too big to be a rat, or even a raccoon. She eases herself to the floor, squeezes under her bed, wraps herself in the spare sheet she keeps stuffed in her pillowcase and presses herself against the wall. If anyone looks under her bed, he'll see a tangled sheet and think the help must have done a careless job. When she's sure every part of her body's covered, she lies still and listens.

Whoever wants to get in is trying to open the lock on the passage side of the trap door. Sweat runs down the back of her neck. Then the sound changes: Thump, thump. Thump, thump, thump.

Jimi's signal!

She slithers out from under the bed, crouches near her wardrobe and waits to make sure her ears aren't playing tricks on her.

Thump, thump. Thump, thump, thump. "Help me!" Her little brother's voice is muffled by thick oak flooring. She shoves her shoes out of the way, moves the Oriental rug and pulls up on the latch. The spring-hinge gives way. Gears grind. The trap door unlocks. She pulls up on the leather strap.

Jimi stands on the top rung of the ladder holding a lighted

pine torch. She grabs it, runs to her basin, and puts out the flame. She turns toward Jimi. "You could have burned down the house!"

He starts to cry.

She notices her little brother's hands and feet are smeared with mud. She sees his forehead is streaked with dried blood.

"What happened?"

He climbs out of the wardrobe, trying his best not to soil the expensive dresses hanging on the rack above him. His mouth moves, but no sound comes out.

Fear seizes Alexandra. "Jimi, tell me what happened."

He wheezes; he can't catch his breath. When she kneels and holds him close, his body feels like it's made of damp wood. His hollow eyes stare into a void. She helps him to remove his muddy boots.

"Tell me," she urges.

"Papa . . ." he starts to speak, then he sinks to the floor, trembling.

She strokes his back until he calms down.

"What about Papa?" she whispers.

"Papa's gone," he says in a voice so quiet she can barely hear him.

"Where did he go?" she asks, wondering if Papa set off in that storm to see his lawyer.

A shudder ripples through Jimi's shoulders.

"Let's get you into dry clothes."

Jimi doesn't resist when she strips him down to his drawers. Holding his limp hand, she guides him to the rocking chair in front of the fireplace. He sits and stares into the fire while she hangs the iron pot on the hearth hook and fills it with water from her bedside pitcher. When the water's warm, she dips in a towel and wrings it dry. With a soft touch, she dabs away mud and dried blood. After she pats Jimi dry, she hands him an out-grown blouse and the split riding-skirt she'd worn when she was about his size.

Jimi frowns.

"Sorry. It's the best I can do right now," she says.

When he's dressed, she kneels beside him. "Please. Tell me what happened."

When his words finally start, there's no stopping him.

"Just before the storm came in, I was helping Papa muck out the corral. I started to ask him why the hay was burnt when the sheriff and his men rode up and said, 'Thought you might like to know the levee in your east field's leaking.'

"'There aren't leaks in any of my levees,' Papa said. 'But thank you for your trouble.' Then the sheriff said, 'Saw it with my own eyes. Tide's coming in. Follow me if you don't want salt to ruin your fields.' Papa and I mounted our horses and followed the sheriff and his men."

Tears spill out of Jimi's eyes.

Alexandra rests her hand on his quivering shoulder. "Go on."

"I tried to stay close behind Papa, then something spooked Zeus. He stopped in the middle of the road, and no matter how hard I kicked his sides, he wouldn't budge. So, I got off and tried to lead him. Finally, I let go of the reins, and he turned and took off like his tail was on fire. I went a ways up the road to find Papa. Ground fog was rolling up from the swamp. I couldn't see anyone, but I could hear men yelling."

Jimi takes a breath and balls his hands into white-knuckled fists.

"I followed the sound of their voices. I could see the sheriff and his men up the road. They were closing in around Papa. I stepped off the road, hunched down and sneaked through the grass. I could hear water trickling through a break in the levee. The fog cleared, and it started to rain. The sheriff and his men leaned forward when Papa knelt down to taste the water. 'Salt,' Papa said. Then he stood, glared at them. 'You did this.' The men moved in on Papa and punched him, over and over. I picked up a stick and started running to help him. When I got there, blood was running down Papa's face.

"Papa saw me. 'Run, Jimi!' he yelled. But I didn't listen. I hit them as hard as I could. One of them clubbed me in the head with the butt of his gun. They laughed when I stumbled back. 'Tie the kid to a tree,' the sheriff said. 'We'll break him like a colt and sell him down South.'"

Panic rises in Alexandra. "Papa got away. Right?"

Jimi continues to speak as if he's in a trance. "The sheriff looked me in the eye. 'This is what happens when darkies don't know their place,' he said. Two of the men held Papa, another man punched him in the stomach. The sheriff untied a shovel from his saddle . . ." Jimi freezes, his eyes glazed. He dry heaves.

"Jimi, tell me."

"The sheriff brought the shovel down—on Papa's head. I saw the light go out of his eyes, like it did when my dog Sadie died."

Alexandra hears Papa's voice inside her head. *Be brave.* She swallows her sobs.

Jimi continues in a low voice that seems to belong to someone else, someone older. "It started to rain harder. The tide was coming in, and the canal was running high." Jimi buries his head against Alexandra's shoulder and whispers, "They threw Papa in the water."

Maybe Papa woke up and swam to safety, Alexandra tells herself. But she knows the truth.

She grips her little brother's hands. "Jimi—how did you get away?"

"A man with an eye patch turned toward me. 'Go get the kid. He saw what happened,' he said.

"The rope they tied me with was wet enough to stretch. I slipped my hands out of the knot and ran through the grass toward the bend in the river. They ran after me, but I had a head start. I squatted, slipped down the bank and grabbed a tree root, like I used to do when you and I played tag and hiding games. I smashed myself against the bank of the river and held tight.

"My hat came off and got stuck on a branch that was floating down the river. I heard shots. Bullets splashed in the water. 'Got him,' said one of the men. I guess they thought that branch was me and the hat was on my head. I heard the sheriff say, 'Here's our story . . .'"

Jimi's voice breaks. He takes a deep breath and continues. "'. . . the kid fell in the water; the father jumped in to save him just as a wall of water came roaring down from upcountry. We tried to rescue them, but they both drowned.'"

Alexandra and Jimi sit side by side, staring into the fire. Paralyzed by sorrow.

A rooster crowing in the dawn snaps Alexandra out of her grief. She promised Papa she would protect Jimi. Jimi saw the sheriff kill Papa. The sheriff will want to get rid of any witnesses. She kneels beside Jimi, places her hands on his shoulders and looks into his eyes. "The sheriff wants you dead. No one can know you're alive, not even Mother. Understand?" Jimi nods.

They hear someone coming down the hall toward her rooms. "Hide!" Jimi slithers under Alexandra's bed.

Act like nothing happened, Alexandra tells herself as she drops Jimi's muddy clothes into the secret passage and lowers the trap door. She pulls the rug into place and arranges the shoes, but she can't take the time to lock the latch.

Alexandra dives under her covers just as the lock turns on the outside of her door. Miranda marches into the room and bangs the door shut.

"You woke me up," Alexandra snaps. "Where's Lulu?"

Miranda purses her lips and throws open the drape. Early morning light filters through Sampson's bars and paints stripes on the wall.

"Rise and shine. Your father's eating breakfast at the house. You need to look presentable when you come down."

Alexandra sits up. "Papa's here?"

"Not yet. Probably got delayed by all that mud in the road."

Alexandra's hope dies.

"Do your business. I'll be back with a basin of clean water. You'll have to dress yourself since Lulu isn't here, and I have to tend to your mother."

"Where is Lulu?"

Miranda exits without answering. The lock on the outside of the door clicks back into place.

Thank the heavens Miranda was in a hurry. She didn't notice the muddy water in the basin.

"Come out," she tells Jimi.

A dull sheen has replaced the light that used to dance in her brother's eyes. She feels like crying, but she remembers her promise to take care of her brother. Mother's number one rule pops into her head: *A refined lady remains composed in the face of sorrow and fear, even when it seems like her whole world is falling apart. A lady knows how to create order out of chaos.*

Alexandra draws in slow, even breaths, looks Jimi straight in the eye and says, "You're so brave. Papa would be proud of you." Then she kisses him on both cheeks, like Grand-mère would have done if she'd been there.

"I'm not brave. I didn't save Papa."

A noise rattles the trap door and makes her jump. She grabs Jimi's hand. They run and hide behind the drape. She hears her shoes slide as the wardrobe door opens. Someone comes toward them. Alexandra squeezes Jimi's hand.

"Come out," whispers Oeyi.

Alexandra and Jimi emerge from behind the drape, still holding hands.

"Jimi's not safe here," says Oeyi.

Alexandra nods.

"Did Papa survive?" she asks, hoping Jimi had been confused.

Oeyi shakes his head. "Be brave, Analai." *Papa's words.* "We have to go," Oeyi says as he puts his arm around Jimi and guides him toward the trap door. Before they climb into the passage,

Oeyi holds Alexandra's attention with his hypnotic gaze. "When the sheriff delivers the news of your father's death, make him believe you're hearing it for the first time. Your brother's safe, as long as those people think he's passed over." He adds, "Your father would be proud of you, Analai."

Alexandra fights back tears.

"Come, Djimidene," says Oeyi.

Alexandra kisses her little brother on the forehead. *"Je t'adore."*

Jimi hugs her back. "I love you, too."

"Hurry!" Oeyi turns to Alexandra. "Get rid of any sign that Jimi was here."

When they're gone, Alexandra scrubs the mud off of her wardrobe floor, then she throws the muddy water, Jimi's torch and the soiled towels down into the passage. She adjusts the rug and latches the trap door.

"Let this be the right order," she whispers. If Miranda sees one shoe out of place, she might guess someone came up through that escape passage.

CHAPTER TEN

The room is in order, and Alexandra is dressed and ready by the time Miranda returns. "Let me put up your hair." Miranda arranges Alexandra's hair into a simple knot. "Lulu got called down to the Quarters to help Tete bring her baby into the world. Old Willa thinks Lulu has the makings of a midwife. If she's right, it might save Lulu from the auction block. Willa doesn't have long for this world, and every plantation needs someone who can deliver a baby."

Alexandra tenses. Mother's already told Miranda about selling Lulu.

"Put your shoes on and come on down." Miranda leaves the room.

Alexandra steps into her shoes, collects her nerves and walks down the hall where Mother's Christian saints pass judgment on mortals from gold-gilt frames. She takes a breath, opens the carved oak door, and steps into the dining room.

Mother sits alone at one end of a polished mahogany table, large enough to accommodate forty people. Her plate is heaped with crab cakes, cheese, pastries and fresh plum jam, none of which appears to have been touched.

"Good morning, Mother," Alexandra says, trying not to let her mounting panic slip into her voice.

"You took your sweet time. My breakfast is ruined on account of you."

"I thought you were waiting for Papa and Jimi."

Mother ignores her comment. "A boy brought word that the sheriff will be stopping by this morning."

The room swims. Alexandra feels like she might faint.

Mother's gaze drifts to the door. "Your father better be here by the time that sheriff comes." She nods at Tildy. The indentured Irish girl, waiting in the corner, pulls out Alexandra's chair.

"My crab cakes are cold," Mother says, casting blame to Tildy this time.

"I'll bring you another breakfast, Missus." Tildy scoops Mother's plate onto a tray and goes out to the kitchen house, separated a fair distance from the big house as a precaution against fire.

Mother glares at Alexandra. "Cat got your tongue?"

Before Alexandra can summon something to say, Lulu rushes into the room.

"Miss Josephine, I can't thank you enough for letting me help my cousin bring in the babies. Tete had twin girls!" Lulu's face shines.

"Is that blood on your apron?" Mother asks.

"Forgive me, Miss Josephine. I'll go change." Lulu dances out the door, inebriated by the miracle of two successful births.

Less than a minute later, Miranda ushers the sheriff into the dining room. His shoes trail dirt.

Alexandra grips the arms of the chair to keep herself from grabbing the cheese knife and stabbing Papa's murderer.

"I asked him to wait in the sitting room," apologizes Miranda.

The sheriff slouches and squints, one thumb looped around his belt, the other fondling the butt of the pistol that protrudes from his tooled leather holster. He doesn't remove his hat when he speaks in his toneless voice. "Sorry to be the bearer of bad news."

Alexandra can see Mother straining to make a pleasant mask of her face.

"Your husband and your little boy was scooping mud to shore up the break in the levy when a big wave of water come down and knocked the little fella into the irrigation channel. Your husband jumped in to help him. He couldn't reach the little fellow. Another wave come and swept them to their deaths."

Mother starts coughing so hard she can't catch her breath. Alexandra kneels by her side and offers her a sip of water. Mother finally settles. She waves Alexandra away and stands, resting her hands on the table for support. "How did you say it happened?"

The sheriff's eyes shift. "Someone 'round here should have learned to build a proper levee."

A more violent coughing fit seizes Mother. Alexandra watches her dab her mouth and fold streaks of blood to the inside of her napkin.

"Like to drown myself trying to help 'em," says the sheriff.

Alexandra clamps her teeth down to keep from screaming that the sheriff's a liar.

Color drains from Mother's face, but she regains her composure as the sheriff's tongue flicks out and runs along his upper lip. Mother stands straight as a flagpole, not a trace of sadness registering in her granite features.

Alexandra senses her Mother's poise wearing on the sheriff's nerves.

"My deputies found the bodies tangled in the roots of a toppled cypress."

Dread seizes Alexandra. "Jimi's dead? And Papa, too?"

"Found your father's body tangled in a fallen tree. The little fella's hat was washed up to shore. The water caught his little body and swept him out to sea."

The sheriff stares hard at Alexandra. Had she given away her knowledge that Jimi is alive?

"Poor Papa and Jimi," Alexandra cries, releasing a flood of damned-up tears.

"That was a mighty current, I tell you. Swept that little guy out to sea like he was a twig." The sheriff's voice cracks. "God rest their souls. No pain compares to that of losing a child."

Alexandra wants to yank out the sheriff's lying tongue. Anger turns her grief into wracking sobs.

"Alexandra! Take hold of yourself!" commands Mother.

"Papa and Jimi are dead, and all you say is not to cry!" Alexandra screams, sniffing up the last of her tears. That should convince the sheriff she doesn't know Jimi's alive.

"Terrible sorry for your losses, Ma'am."

Mother glares at Alexandra, then she turns toward the sheriff.

"Thank you for coming to tell us," says Mother in a flat voice. "I know it's not easy to be the bearer of bad news. I'll have my carriage driver gather some men to retrieve my husband's body and take it down to his village for a proper funeral." Mother pauses. "Would you like some warm tea with milk, and a biscuit, before you go out into this untimely cold?"

Guilt hoods the sheriff's eyes. He takes off his hat. His eyes roam. "Nice house," he says. Then he adds, "Ma'am, there's something else I want you to know. That music teacher won't be tryin' to take advantage of your daughter no more."

Alexandra grips her butter knife. *Hold your temper,* she tells herself.

"I was told that despicable man had been 'taken care of,'" says Mother. "Forgive me for not seeing you to the door." Mother turns to Miranda. "Show the sheriff out."

Before he has left the room, Mother adds, loud enough for the sheriff to hear, "And tell Tildy to come wipe away all this mud he tracked in."

The sheriff follows Miranda out, hat in hand.

Alexandra stands and starts to leave the dining room, but her knees give way. She sinks to the floor, unable to hold back a new round of tears.

Mother scowls. "Save your histrionics for the privacy of your room."

Tildy waltzes through the door, carrying a new breakfast on a silver serving tray. Lulu follows in a spotless uniform. Both stand motionless. Waiting.

"We won't be eating, after all," says Mother. She turns to Lulu. "Do you know where Miss Alexandra's black linen dress is?"

"The grieving dress? Yes, Miss Josephine."

"Put it on Alexandra, then come to my room, and I'll give you the mantilla she's to wear out of respect for the departed."

"What's happened?" blurts Lulu.

"The Lord has called Master Ajamat and Jimi home."

"They're dead?" blurts Lulu. Mother nods.

It takes Lulu a full minute to gather her wits and respond. "I'll see to the dress, Miss Josephine."

Mother's face is a mask of calm, but Alexandra notices that her hands are trembling.

CHAPTER ELEVEN

$\mathcal{A}$ lexandra stays by Mother's side as she makes arrangements for the funerals. The process begins with a war of words between the Catholic priest and Oeyi. After three days, they agree. Papa's body will be taken to the village ceremonial square where traditional Diola rites will be performed. Jimi's child-size coffin, which contains only his hat, will travel to the village grounds and remain there until after the African ceremony has been performed. Then his little coffin will be carried to *Mary Queen of Sorrows Cemetery* in the oak grove behind the big house.

When the arrangements are complete, Mother tells Alexandra, "I won't attend your father's funeral."

"But, Mother . . ."

"I'm not a hypocrite, Alexandra. I will arrange for Sampson to take you in the carriage. When the ceremony is over, he will drive you to *Queen of Sorrows* for Jimi's Mass."

"I'll walk to Papa's funeral," says Alexandra.

Alexandra's grateful that Lulu attends to her needs on the day of the funerals.

"Miss Josephine says I have to polish the silver today. You be all right going alone?" Lulu asks.

"I'll be fine."

When she passes by the stables on her way to the ceremonial grounds, Alexandra sees Cabai hanging his head over the meadow fence, as though he's expecting her. "You know Papa's crossed-over, don't you?" She presses her forehead to his and strokes his mane.

"I have to go now."

Cabai bobs his head and whinnies.

Lost in thought, Alexandra trudges up the trail that leads to the village square. A thin stream of smoke curls toward the cloudless sky. Burning cedar perfumes the air. When she reaches the top of the hill, she's glad to see that fresh pine boughs have been laid across the top of a man-made arbor that surrounds the oval field of close-clipped grass. When she enters the grounds, women wearing pagnes of woven flax, dyed in multiple shades of indigo, reach out to touch her, offering their sympathy.

Aunt Mamou, who looks more like Papa than Alexandra ever realized, approaches. She leans close and whispers so only Alexandra can hear. "Jimi's with Oeyi." Alexandra nods, glad Mamou knows Jimi's alive. Mamou takes her hand and leads her toward Papa's viewing platform. The sight of her father steals Alexandra's breath. His upright body has been tied into a high-backed wooden chair attached to the poles of a pine-bough litter. There's no sign of the bloating or bruises she expected to see. The medicine workers must have used powerful herbs and mud poultices to draw fluid from his body.

Papa is dressed in a pagne woven from sacred cloth dyed black, representing spiritual energy, and red, symbolizing both life and death. His eyelids have been sewn open, and even though a dull sheen covers his eyes, he seems to possess awareness. She senses his longing to tell his story. Mamou withdraws to give Alexandra a moment to be alone.

I love you. I miss you, Papa, she tells him inside her mind. *I know what happened to you. Jimi's with Oeyi. I'll keep him safe, like I promised.*

She senses Papa wants to raise his hand and bestow his blessing. She longs to turn back time, to when he was alive.

Mamou approaches, lays a gentle hand on Alexandra's elbow,

and steers her to their appointed seats on a raised platform at the west end of the ceremonial grounds. They sit side by side, watching, as four young men carry Papa's chair to the center of the grounds and set him between the trunks of four straight young pines that have been stripped of their branches and pounded into the ground. A swath of black cloth is stretched across the tops of the tree-trunks to provide shade for Papa and for the open coffin in which Jimi's hat has been laid.

Three groups of villagers gather around Papa. The men take their places in the outer circle, dressed in pagnes dyed in earthen hues. The women, whose heads have been freshly shaved out of respect for Papa, stand in the second ring. They wear copper bracelets to ward off angry spirits drawn to funerals by misery. The children, in the circle closest to Papa, wear black pagnes. They all circle Papa to the beat of a drum. Then the ekonting musician plays a single note, and the people form lines on either side of Papa and turn toward the eastern entrance of the arbor.

The oldest women of the village enter and stand in two rows, as sentinels, while the oldest men dance through the opening, chanting the sacred song they've been singing all night long. Endowed with other-worldly grace, the men perform the Nyakul, the funeral dance, to the rhythm of drums and the mystical melodies of ekonting strings.

Kahoeka, benevolent ancestors like Didima, who have chosen to watch over their descendants when they pass from this world, materialize as vapors before Alexandra's eyes. Alexandra has never seen the spirits so clearly. Ghosts who relish creating discord also hover above the people's heads, shadows seeking the food of human weakness. She understands for the first time that the *Ahoelra*, who invades her mind, comes only when she's angry and fearful. She wills herself to remain strong and alert.

Mamou stands and nods. Six of Papa's age-mates enter through the eastern entrance. On their shoulders, they carry a dugout canoe supported on horizontal poles festooned with cow skulls. The drum beat intensifies as they move toward Papa. They lower the canoe and place Papa, still in his chair, inside. After they have secured the chair, they face the entrance.

The Questioner, the oldest woman in the village, enters. She has been rubbed with ash; she wears a grey pagne. Amethyst and copper beads are imbedded in wing-shaped scars on her face. The revered elder steps forward to interrogate Papa's corpse. Alexandra knows that if the canoe dips from front to back, it means the answer to the woman's question is, "yes." If it dips from side to side, the answer is, "no."

The drumming stops. The ekonting sounds a single note. Papa's age-mates raise the canoe to their shoulders and walk in a circle. They stop in front of the old woman. She lifts her hands to the sky.

"Ajamat, is it true, as the new sheriff claims, that you died when you tried to save your son, Djimidene, from drowning in the flood?" Her voice seems to be traveling from another world.

The crowd holds its breath and waits. The canoe dips from side to side: "No."

The women throw up their arms. They weave through the line of children then dance toward the canoe as they sing the women's funeral song. Then they move backward to their original positions and wait.

Once again, the men carrying the canoe in a circle around the old woman and stop in front of her. She poses her second question.

"Ajamat, did you take your life because you were tired of living?"

Once again, the canoe tips from side to side: "No."

"Ahhhhhh," the villagers sigh in the single voice of one who has learned the answer to a secret.

When the old woman steps forward the third time, she says, "Ajamat, show us who has taken your life."

The drum beats as the women raise their hands over their

heads and move toward the canoe. They open their hands toward the sky, begging Emitai to reveal who has done this terrible thing.

The front of the canoe rotates, then stops and points toward the back road.

Rumbling sound shakes the ground. Alexandra sees riders galloping toward the village. The sheriff and his men burst into the ceremonial grounds and rein their horses to a stop.

"Move aside!" the sheriff orders.

The people stand and face the sheriff and his men. They crowd close together to protect Papa, forming a shield with their bodies. The sheriff urges his horse forward. Papa sits erect in his funeral chair, watching.

The people glare at the sheriff. The drumming starts up again. The melody of the ekonting shifts from sadness to anger.

"Is this the man who killed you?" asks the old woman.

The canoe dips forward and back, forward and back, to the quickened cadence of the drums. The people accuse the sheriff with narrowed eyes.

"Stop!" shouts the sheriff, trying to conceal the terror in his eyes. The women in the circle continue to chant while the old men dance the *Nyakul*, their bodies trailing ribbons of light as they turn to the left and to the right.

Alexandra's attention is drawn to the top of an ancient cypress where a panther, Ajamat's ewuum, crouches in a fork of the branches, its yellow eyes glowing.

The sheriff's horse throws back its head and paws the ground. No one but Alexandra and the horse seem to see the panther. She watches as the big cat moves down the tree. The sheriff's horse rears; the sheriff falls, but his boot catches in the stirrup. He gyrates, trying to dislodge his foot.

When the panther leaps to the ground, the horse turns and gallops back down the road, dragging the sheriff through the dust. The sheriff's men race to catch the horse's reins. Alexandra watches as the panther's image fades.

The drum falls silent as Ajamat's age-mates set the canoe on the ground. All eyes turn as one toward the empty road. Voices trill with heartache. Women tear at their clothes and cry out. Finally, Mamou nods. The villagers become still and part as Sampson and four of Mother's housemen pick up Jimi's coffin and carry it on their shoulders toward *Mary Queen of our Sorrows*.

Alexandra lingers. When she stands before Papa's chair and bows, she thinks she sees a tear glistening on his cheek. Then she hears his voice, softer than a whisper, "Be strong. Take care of your brother. You have work to do."

She nods, then she turns toward the road.

As she follows Jimi's coffin, she wishes she could wail and spend her grief like the village women, but tears will make her weak and dull her mind.

Has she built a wall around her grief so that she can honor Papa's wish for her to be strong in order to protect Jimi? Or, has her heart turned to stone, like Mother's? Deep in thought, she follows the procession to *Mary Queen of Sorrows*.

Alexandra steps through the chapel door, instantly soothed by light streaming through 'Mary's Window.' Papa had the exquisite stained glass installed two years before he moved down to his village. Now, the saint's compassionate eyes reach into Alexandra's soul and ease the pain in her heart.

Mother sits alone in the front pew, her eyes fixed on the child-sized coffin that rests on a wooden stand near the sanctuary railing. Not daring to disturb Mother's serenity, Alexandra sits in back.

Miranda watches from the doorway; slaves aren't allowed inside the chapel. From an elevated podium, a white-haired priest intones a blessing over Jimi's hat. After the Mass, he assures Mother that when the hat is buried, Jimi's soul will be taken up to heaven.

Alexandra aches to tell Mother that Jimi is alive. But she

knows Mother would insist that her little brother be returned to the big house, and that would put his life in danger.

After the service, Alexandra follows Mother and Miranda to the rose garden behind the big house. A fit of coughing wracks Mother's frail body. She sinks onto a wrought-iron bench, all the luster gone from her eyes. When Mother lowers her handkerchief, Alexandra sees it's soaked with blood. She sits beside Mother. When she starts to put her hand on her shoulder, Mother jerks away and turns her back as if Alexandra carries a disease.

Miranda approaches and beckons Mother to follow her. As Mother stands and follows her favored servant toward the big house, the hem of her long, black dress skims the ground. still damp from last night's rain. Her black lace mantilla conceals her pale face. She has become a shade, nearly passed from this world.

Alexandra trails behind them. She can't bear to be alone right now.

CHAPTER TWELVE

lexandra finds Mother and Miranda in the front sitting room, facing one another in matching parlor chairs. She should be the one sitting opposite Mother, not the house help. Alexandra moves behind Mother, grateful, that she hasn't been asked to leave.

"This might tell you why your sister didn't come to pay her respects," Miranda says as she hands Mother an opened envelope.

Without looking in her direction, Mother hands the letter to Alexandra. "Read it out loud."

A wave of pride washes over Alexandra when Mother gives her this important task.

Dear Josephine,

Mr. Ball has clarified the error of my perceptions. I will no longer visit you at Heaven Hill, nor will I be able to extend an invitation for you to return to Pinnacle.

Mr. Ball has made clear to me that it is against God's will for the white and colored races to indulge in social interaction. Accordingly, I must rescind my invitation for you to join us on Thanksgiving Day. It is obvious that due to the absence of Monsieur Martin, there will be no Christmas concert.

Please do not send correspondence, as your letters will be destroyed upon receipt.

Sincerely, Isabelle Ball

P.S. Please burn this letter as soon as you have read it, for your sake and for mine.

Alexandra thinks back to that horrid day on the sand bar when Mr. Ball terrorized her and Callie, and Tante Isabelle came to her defense. Were these really her aunt's thoughts, or had Mr. Ball threatened his wife? Even though the betrayal pains Alexandra, her heart aches for Mother, who has always considered Isabelle not only as a sister, but as her best friend.

"Miss Josephine, I don't believe your sister knows what happened to Master Degambia and Jimi. Mr. Ball must have intercepted your letters," consoles Miranda.

"She's my half-sister," Mother says as she stands and walks up the stairs without looking back. Alexandra goes outside, wondering if Grand-mère knows about Papa's death.

Until now, Alexandra thought Heaven's big house was an elegant testament of the love Papa once felt for Mother. Now late afternoon sun paints the huge edifice in oranges and reds that make it look like a dying, garish creature. Exhausted, Alexandra goes inside, drags herself up to her room and falls across her bed.

She's sleeping soundly the next morning, dreaming that she and Cabai are flying around a crescent moon, when Lulu shakes her awake.

"Go away. I'm having a good dream."

She squeezes her eyes shut, trying to block out the morning light. If Lulu leaves her alone right now, maybe she can slip back into her dream and block out Papa's death and Jimi's absence and Mother's illness.

"You have to get up," says Lulu.

"I want to sleep."

Lulu stands her ground. "The assessor and the sheriff are on the way here. Miss Josephine says they're trying to steal Heaven."

Alexandra leaps out of bed. "Help me on with my black dress."

Alexandra's jaw drops when she walks into the front sitting room. The best furniture and all the hand-painted vases from France have been removed. Miranda and Mother are stuffing the bronze crucifix into a cedar chest, already crammed with precious possessions.

"Alexandra, put Mary in the passage," Mother orders.

Alexandra frowns.

Mother wheels around. "Not Mary the cook, stupid girl. Mary-the-Mother-of-God! It will fuel that Protestant usurper's vengeance if he realizes we're Catholic in addition to being colored."

Stupid girl? When Papa was alive, Alexandra hadn't minded Mother's casual barbs as much. Now Mother's hateful words feel like knives.

Lulu, who's been posted as a look-out, calls down from the landing on the stairs.

"They've turned down the lane, Miss Josephine!"

Alexandra wrangles Mary-Mother-of-God inside the bookcase panel that conceals a hidden nook. Rage seizes her when she glances through the window and sees the sheriff riding his horse alongside the assessor's gleaming black carriage. She suppresses her feelings, falls into line next to Miranda and Lulu and awaits Mother's instructions.

"Lulu, tell Sampson to see to the sheriff's horse. Then ask Old Mary to set up a tray with blueberry scones and pomegranate juice."

Lulu rushes out of the room.

"Miranda, answer the door. Show those pretenders you are

awed and delighted that they have come to pay their respects."

Miranda bristles.

"Do as I say, Miranda. For Heaven's sake."

Mother turns to Alexandra. "I've set out that piece of lace you've been making for your trousseau. While you sit and work it, you are to be my second pair of eyes and ears. No matter what transpires, you are to keep your thoughts to yourself. Is that clear?"

Alexandra has no wish to contribute to Mother's stress. "Of course, Mother." She sits and takes the pillow and box of pins onto her lap, glad Grand-mère chose to pass on the art of lace-making the nuns in Martinique had taught her.

Mother draws a deep breath and rushes up the stairs. When she gets to the landing, she turns. "I'll come down when the time is right." Her lips curl into a sinister smile.

Alexandra jumps when the assessor raps on the door so loud she suspects he used the brass handle of his cane. Her hands freeze above the lace-making pillow as she watches Miranda take a deep breath and open the door.

"My, my! To what do we owe this great honor, Mr. Sheriff and Mr. Assessor? Do come in. Miss Josephine be spillin' over wid happiness when she see y'all've come to call."

Alexandra gawks. Mother requires all the slaves who work in the big house to speak the King's English.

Alexandra struggles to hide her smile when she sees 'Mr. Sheriff's' face is still bruised from being dragged by his horse. Wariness has replaced his arrogance.

The assessor reminds Alexandra of a bespectacled egret as he sweeps past Miranda, careful not to let any part of his body come into contact with hers. He struts around the sitting room as if he owns Heaven. The sheriff, not so agile, limps inside and leans on his cane.

"May I take y'all's hats, Gentlemens?" asks Miranda, casting her eyes to the floor.

"No need." The assessor whips his top hat from his balding head and holds it close, as if he's afraid Miranda might be planning to steal it. His beady eyes dart about the room.

"Please make yourselves to home while I goes upstairs and tells Miss Josephine she have a pair o' distinguished guests."

Alexandra glances up from her lace. She sees the sheriff grimace as he props himself against the wall, then she watches the assessor glide about the room appraising how much gold each picture frame and figurine might put in his pocket. When he stops behind Alexandra, the hairs on the back of her neck stand on end. Is he calculating how much she might bring on the auction block?

The assessor's heavy breathing and the smell of his clove-scented breath make her feel like vomiting. She bites her tongue to keep from remarking that it's obvious these 'guests' are commoners; they have no manners. Willing her hands to stop trembling, she pulls a thread into a knot, achieving a steady rhythm as the assessor makes his way to the grand piano and bangs the lowest note. Alexandra pricks her finger. A drop of blood blossoms on the lace. She'll have to start the whole piece over. He pounds the key again.

She wants to scream that the piano was tuned just last week, but she bites her tongue as she fantasizes jamming a pin into the assessor's eyes. She might even do it, if the sheriff's stubby fingers weren't curled around the butt of his pistol. She takes a deep breath as she recalls Papa's instructions to protect Jimi. She can't afford to antagonize these powerful men.

Mother finally floats down the stairs, green eyes flashing, auburn hair streaming over the high collar of a black dress that accentuates her svelte figure. She carries her ledger and a large envelope.

"My, my, I hear your position has become permanent, Sheriff. So good of you to take time to call on us. I know how busy important men like y'all must be."

Mother sets her papers down on a side table and offers her hand. The sheriff ignores her gesture.

Mother responds with a clap that startles the assessor's monocle out of his eye. On cue, Lulu rushes into the room, balancing a silver tray set with flutes filled with pomegranate juice and a plate set with scones.

"Do sit down, Sheriff," says Mother in a voice that could melt frost. "But first, if you would be so kind, introduce me to your associate."

"I'm the County Assessor," the assessor says dryly.

"Your name?"

"We are here on business."

"Y'all are from up North, I presume," says Mother.

Silence follows. Finally, the sheriff says, "I'm from North Carolina. He's from New York. But he's lived in Charleston for more than two years."

The assessor shoots the sheriff a hateful look.

"Two whole years, my, my. Lulu, offer your tray to these— gentlemen," says Mother, affecting the Southern accent she deplores.

Lulu carries the tray over to the sheriff; he selects the largest scone.

"No time for refreshments," the assessor snaps.

But the sheriff has already taken a bite. He stuffs the rest of the scone in his mouth and gulps down some juice. When the assessor catches his eye, the sheriff sets the half-empty glass back on the tray. From the expression on his face, Alexandra guesses the assessor thinks Mother's trying to poison them. Poison the assessor and the sheriff in their own house in the middle of the day? He clearly thinks they're fools.

Alexandra fixates on the mole on the assessor's long, narrow nose. If he were a woman, people would say he has the mark of a witch.

Mother sits on a parlor chair and crosses her delicate ankles.

"Cook's pomegranate juice is a marvelous drink," Mother motions Lulu over and takes a goblet. She sips her drink slowly, then she smiles and says, "But, if you prefer, Sheriff, we do have tea as well, or brandy, perhaps?"

"Brandy?" blurts the sheriff.

The assessor glares.

"Not now," says the sheriff.

The assessor sits opposite Mother on a straight-backed chair. "I'll come to the point. We hope you'll be able to keep your plantation. Regrettably..." he pauses to polish his monocle. "... it's beyond our power to stay the course of the law."

The assessor's upper lip curls up, revealing a row of perfect white teeth.

"Before you continue," Mother says, "you might want to avail yourself of these legal documents that arrived from the courthouse in Georgetown two days ago."

Mother hands a parcel of papers to the assessor.

"As y'all can see from the date, my husband was declared white before his unfortunate demise, and the village workers were added to his property ledger under the heading, slaves."

Alexandra perks up. Papa's lawyer won the case. It must have galled him to make slaves of his friends, but it was the only way to ensure they wouldn't be sold to cruel masters. He intended to manumit them as soon as possible. *Now what will happen?*, she wonders.

"According to my husband's will, Heaven Hill is to be conveyed to my husband's blood-tie heirs, with the provision that I remain in charge of this house until the end of my days. The moveable property, including the house help, belong to me, free and clear. As my young son has also passed over, the land will be conveyed to Alexandra, my husband's daughter, when she turns seventeen."

A shock passes through Alexandra. She knows nothing about planting and harvesting.

The assessor hands Mother his stack of papers. "It pains me to inform you that your late husband, who had not been declared white before his last ship left port, was unable to obtain insurance. He ventured with your plantation's capital when he sent last year's entire crop of Carolina Gold to a vendor in Bordeaux."

"He sells his rice on the London market," says Mother. As she peruses the documents, all trace of her accent vanishes.

The assessor continues in his know-it-all voice. "It must have seemed a good opportunity to trade with France, though I can't fathom why, since Napoleon has reinstated slavery in the sugar-growing colonies, a practice to which Mr. Degambia appeared to be opposed."

The assessor hands Mother a letter stamped with an official seal. She reads it aloud. "I regret to inform you that your husband's ship, 'The Kainoe,' was apprehended by a British man-of-war. The ship and its cargo have become the property of the Crown."

"This letter's over three months old," snaps Mother.

Alexandra steams. These men had orchestrated Heaven's take-over from the day Papa's ship was seized.

The assessor clears his throat. "Had your husband shored up his levees properly, next year's rice profits might have covered much of the loss. My agriculturist took a look at your fields, Missus Degambia. You won't be able to plant for at least a year, until all the salt has leached out of the soil."

Alexandra jumps to her feet, spilling her bobbins across the floor. "My father's levees were built well enough to withstand a hurricane. You're a..." Mother's coughing fit stops Alexandra mid-sentence; she sees blood splattered across the lace on Mother's sleeve. The assessor sees it too.

Alexandra sits. *Control yourself for Jimi's sake*, she warns herself.

"Please excuse my daughter. I am working to correct her impetuous nature."

The assessor continues, "Another matter, Madame, we have located the registration of your house slaves, but your husband's transfer of his workers to his property ledger has no date and signature. As there's no legal documentation, those ninety field workers will become the property of the State, as will this plantation. The law clearly states, and I quote, "All Negroes and Indians who do not have the papers to prove they are free are to be considered slaves." Your husband's debts fall to you— and to his heir, heiress in this case. If you fail to pay your debts within the month, the entire property will be seized, moveable property included."

Alexandra jumps up.

"Murderer!" The sheriff's eyes widen with fear. He suspects she has proof that he killed Papa. She thinks fast. "You'll kill us if you steal Heaven!" She can see from the expression on his face that he's still worried she can prove he killed Papa.

Mother grabs Alexandra's arm. "Sit down and work your lace." She digs her fingernails into the soft flesh of Alexandra's underarm. Mother turns to the assessor and declares, "My attorney will be in touch with you."

"I feel generous today," says the assessor. "Allow me to draw up a conveyance that permits you an additional year to pay what you owe, with interest, of course. Perhaps you will be able to bring in a sizeable crop of indigo by then. But, if you personally vacate the premises, the plantation will be taken over by the authorities."

Mother purses her lips and nods her head. "Very well."

Alexandra grinds her teeth. The assessor is gambling that Mother will die before that year's up. If that should happen before Alexandra's seventeenth birthday, there will be no legal recourse.

Alexandra remembers Papa's gold. She's about to tell the assessor they have the funds to pay Heaven's debts now, then she realizes the sheriff would only find a way to steal that, too. She'll tell Mother about it as soon as the assessor is gone.

The assessor draws up the contract and offers Mother a pen for her signature. She picks up her own pen and dips it in the inkwell on her desk. "I'll contact you after my attorney has reviewed the terms of this arrangement."

The assessor slides his remaining files back into his case.

"Forgive my daughter's lack of manners, gentlemen. Grief has robbed her of her civility." Mother keeps her voice light as she adds, "Did I mention that in addition to our lawyer, our dear friend, Judge James Calvin from Charleston will assist us in these matters? Surely, you've heard of him. Everybody of note in the low country respects Judge Calvin's reputation."

"Our attorney will be in contact with you as well," the assessor says as he snaps his case shut.

"Miranda, please ask Sampson to bring the assessor's carriage and the sheriff's horse to the front drive."

Mother smiles and turns to the sheriff, "Perhaps y'all'll have time for refreshments after this little matter is settled."

"Miranda," Mother says, "would you be so kind as to escort these men to the door?"

As soon as interlopers are out of earshot, Alexandra says, "Mother, I know how we can save . . ."

Mother cuts her off. "The assessor and the sheriff are powerful men. They can help us, or they can hurt us. You have given them a reason for the latter."

"Mother, please, listen . . ."

"Not one more word. When will you learn it's necessary to court people with power and make them believe that you have something they can use?"

"That's not what Papa taught me."

"And look where it got him. I have no intention of dying, or of vacating these premises within the year. I have every confidence that Judge Calvin will confirm that the listing of villagers on your father's ledger was completed in a timely fashion.

"As I am his widow, I can sign in your father's place. I'll be able to sell enough of the slaves to satisfy the debt."

Alexandra explodes, "Papa put the villagers on his ledger so he could legally give them their freedom."

"Time to grow up, Alexandra! If I don't sell those slaves, Heaven Hill will be ruined."

"I hate you!" The words fly out of Alexandra's mouth before she can stop them.

"Get out of my house!" Mother's rage triggers so violent a coughing fit, Alexandra's afraid she's going to drown in her own blood.

"I didn't mean it, Mother. I don't hate you. I didn't mean it," Alexandra says.

Mother crumples to the floor. Alexandra kneels beside her. Every time she reaches out to touch Mother, she jerks away.

Finally, the coughing subsides. Mother stands without help and looks Alexandra in the eye. "This is my house. Get out, and don't come back."

Alexandra runs out the front door, her eyes brimming with tears.

CHAPTER THIRTEEN

The sun's directly overhead when Alexandra climbs to the top of the hill that overlooks Papa's village. She's drenched in sweat. Odd. There are no people in sight, no chickens or pigs, not even any goats. Have the villagers gotten word that Mother plans to sell them? Did they run North? Did the sheriff march them off to a slave auction?

Keep them safe, Alexandra prays.

A branch snaps. She crouches behind a bush and scares up a cloud of gnats. Someone's coming up behind her. She barely breathes. The gnats feast. Footsteps move closer. Closer. One of the sheriff's men? A patroller?

Something touches the back of her neck. She screams. A horse neighs. She wheels around and buries her head in Cabai's mane. He nickers as she strokes his neck. Then she heaves herself up onto his back.

Cabai trots into the sacred forest and picks his way through shadow-dappled woods. When they come to the edge of the swamp, Papa's stallion splashes toward them through the marsh waters with Oeyi on its back.

"This way," Oeyi commands. "Hurry."

Cabai follows the stallion, picking his way through a labyrinth of waterways and forest paths. They come to a narrowing passage where the canopy of trees is so thick barely any light reaches the forest floor. Alexandra's afraid the foliage will become so dense they'll have to stop and turn back. Then sunlight breaks through a stand of thinning cypress, and she catches the scent of Mamou's secret tea. They round a corner. Alexandra laughs out loud when she sees her little brother standing on the "veranda" of Mamou's tree-house.

"Jimi!" Alexandra calls.

"Keep your voice soft," Oeyi warns.

Mamou emerges from around the trunk on the first of three levels of the treehouse. She moves to the railing and stands by Jimi's side. She's wearing the indigo skirt and matching head wrap that makes her skin look like black velvet.

Mamou once told Alexandra she had a secret house, but Alexandra never guessed it was built in the branches of a towering oak on an island in the middle of the swamp. Mamou lets down a ladder made of twisted vines. Alexandra slips off Cabai's back and climbs up as Mamou sings the chant she claims makes all beings within the range of its sound safe from enemies.

Jimi allows Alexandra to smother him with kisses. Then Mamou hugs Alexandra. Oeyi slides off Papa's horse and whistles. The horse turns down a path toward a jungle of vines. Cabai follows. The old priest scrambles up the ladder, nimble as a spider.

"Come," says Mamou. She sweeps a reed curtain aside and ushers her guests up a second rope ladder to "the sitting-room" on the upper level. Alexandra admires the wall mats that are decorated with river pearls. A rug made of woven reeds, worn to a bronze patina by years of use, covers planked wood floors.

When they've settled themselves on deer-hide floor cushions, Mamou hands each guest a large clam shell filled with her famous red tea. The warm liquid, sweet, with a bitter after-taste, fulfills its reputation and quenches Alexandra's thirst.

Sorrow glistens in Mamou's eyes. "Just last month, your father was sitting right where you are now," she says. "He told me he'd had a dream that the end of this life was near. He wanted you to have this." Mamou hands Alexandra a large doeskin pouch.

Alexandra unties the laces and takes out a hand-made book filled with parchment-like pages and bound in a birch-bark cover.

Mamou seems to be looking into a hidden world. "Siopama, our ancestor, was just about your age when he first saw this land we now call home. These are his words, written almost three hundred years ago. Normally they would be passed to you when you turn seventeen. But I'm going to give them to you now. Commit them to memory. Remembering where you come from will give you the courage you'll need to survive the coming storm."

Storm? A chill grips Alexandra as Mamou hands her the book.

"You have a good reason to tremble!" the Ahoelra says inside Alexandra's mind.

"Get away from this girl," Mamou tells the Ahoelra. Then she turns to Alexandra. "Don't let that old ghost feed on your fear."

"You can hear it?"

"And see it, too. Whenever it comes around, tell it to go away and imagine your body is surrounded by light. That ghost wants you to think it's more powerful than you, but that's only true if you give into the fears it's trying to stir."

Mamou pats the book. "Read the first part out loud, so Jimi can hear, too."

Alexandra opens the cover.

April 14, 1558

"Dearest Son,

I am writing to you because I sense my transition from this life to the next is at hand. Consider this as you read my letter: We are united by blood and by a common purpose; Africa and the New World are married within our souls. We are

called to be a bridge between peoples, to create a path of
understanding and harmony.

By now, you have heard many stories and experienced much
that tells you of our Diola people's life in the world. I would
like to tell you more about your roots..."

Mamou puts her finger to her lips. Alexandra stops reading.
Mamou raises her hands, closes her eyes and tests the air with
her fingertips. Worry creases her aunt's face. "No time to read
the whole thing now," Mamou says as she presses a polished
tourmaline hummingbird into Jimi's hand. "This was carved by
Old Marcello when hummingbird was named your ewuum."

Jimi holds the hummingbird up to a patch of sunlight.

Mamou continues. "Hummingbird is a symbol of quickness
and intelligence. He's powerful, but not boastful. He's alert and
able to read sounds and sights as well as you read words. And he's
brave, just like you."

Jimi hugs Mamou.

Oeyi whistles a signal. "Stay out of sight," Mamou says as she
stands and walks to her railing.

"Miss Mamou!" Marcello's voice drifts up from below.
Alexandra tenses. *Has Marcello tracked her? Has the sheriff
followed him?*

"Marcello, I haven't seen you in a while."

"Miss Mamou, I've come to carry Miss Alexandra home.
Miss Josephine took a bad fall. She be needin' her little girl."

Mother fell? Was it because of me? Alexandra wonders.

Marcello is a master iron-worker who earned his freedom by
selling his wares after he satisfied the demands of his owner. He's
the only person at Heaven Mother doesn't reprimand for
speaking low-born English. "The way my mama talk be good
'nuf fo' me," he tells anyone who raises an eyebrow when he
speaks his mind.

Mamou taps her foot three times, sending a message to Oeyi that Alexandra can't decode. The priest leans over and whispers, "Jimi, stay down. Alexandra, stand and show yourself."

Alexandra stands. She's about to ask how Marcello found her when she sees Moon Baby, Marcello's hound; that dog has the best tracker nose in the low country.

"I sure is aggrieved about your daddy and your brother, Miss Alexandra. But this ain't no time to dwell on sorrow. Miranda fin' your mama lyin' on a stair fightin' for air. She call for Sampson, and he run for de doctor. Miranda say your mama not long for dis world. But I seen miracles in my time. When she come to herself, Miss Josephine say if de sheriff's men get wind that she be dyin', dey gonna round up all de slaves in de big house an' carry 'em off to de August auction in Georgetown. De villagers is meetin' at a secret spot in de swamp as I speak, figuring how to escape the clutches of de sheriff and his men."

Oeyi stands.

"What you doin' up dere, Oeyi?"

Oeyi scrambles down the ladder. He and Marcello speak too softly for Alexandra to hear what they're saying. Now and then Marcello glances up at Alexandra and nods. She can tell Marcello hasn't guessed that Jimi's kneeling by her side.

Alexandra tenses when Marcello says, "It be my pleasure to take Miss Alexandra home."

Oeyi scampers back up the ladder. He speaks so low and so fast that Alexandra has to listen hard to understand him. "Marcello will take you to your Mother. Soon as the way is clear, I'm going to piggyback Jimi to the entrance of the secret passage that leads to the big house. It wouldn't be right for your mama to be carried into the next world believing her only son is dead."

"Is that safe?" asks Alexandra.

"I brought him here on horseback. As long as his feet don't touch the ground, the sheriff and his hounds can't track him. While you were at your father's funeral, your mother gave the sheriff and his men permission to search your house. They found no trace of Jimi. It's the safest place for him to be."

Oeyi turns to Mamou. "You need to leave this place, Miss Mamou."

"I will, when the time's right," Mamou says.

Alexandra feels a wave of dizziness when Oeyi looks into her eyes. "If your mother passes to the next world, you and Jimi run to Marcello's. He'll help get you to your grandmother's in Charleston. Be strong, Analai."

Alexandra whispers, "Mother doesn't want me in her house."

Oeyi's words reassure her. "Marcello said she asked for you. Some folks have a change of heart before they pass over. Hurry now, give your mother some peace before she leaves this world."

Mamou tucks the pouch with Siopoma's letters into an oiled goat-skin satchel and slips the strap over Alexandra's shoulder. Alexandra feels numb and dizzy.

"Follow your lights," says Mamou, "and one day you may be able to pass along the story of your father's people.

Alexandra hugs Mamou. *Please let me see Mamou again on this side of life*, she prays.

Chapter Fourteen

It's dark when Alexandra and Marcello arrive at the ridge that overlooks Mother's grounds. They watch as the sheriff and five of his torch-bearing cronies gallop down the tree-lined lane toward the big house. A man tied behind the last rider's horse runs as fast as his legs will carry him so he won't fall and be dragged. When the men pull up on their reins in the circle of light cast by lanterns in the circular drive of the big house, the young man collapses on the cobblestones. The sheriff nods to one of his men, who dismounts, races up the stairs and pounds on the front door.

Alexandra steals her way down the hill, careful not to break a twig and give herself away. She hides behind the laurel hedge. Horrified, she watches fourteen-year-old, Zachariah, Miranda's youngest grandson, pick himself up from the carriage drive.

Does Miranda know about Jimi? Will she give him up in exchange for letting her grandson go?

Alexandra abandons caution. She runs toward Zachariah and plants herself between the sheriff and the boy. "Untie that child!"

The sheriff's alcohol-blooded eyes range over Alexandra's body.

"This is between me and the owner of this house, Girl. You sneak out in the middle of the night to meet a fella'?"

"I was bringing herbs to the kitchen house so cook could brew the tea Mother likes," lies Alexandra. She keeps her voice even. "The doctor says her health is improving steadily, but she must have her rest, so she's asked me to handle her household affairs." Alexandra nods toward Zachariah. "This young man is Mother's best stable boy. Sometimes the horses get stirred up by panther or a bear, so Zachariah goes out at night to check on them. You have no right to truss him like an animal."

She tucks her hands under her folded arms so no one can see she's trembling. "Release Zachariah this minute!"

"I don't take orders from children—or darkies."

Zachariah struggles to stay on his feet. "I was searching for that new colt, Miss Alexandra. I don't know what spooked him. He jumped the fence and ran toward the woods."

"I ask you to speak, Boy?" The sheriff whips Zachariah in the back of the legs with his metal-tipped horse quirt and draws blood. Zachariah falters, but he doesn't fall.

"Leave my baby alone!" screams Miranda, running out the door of the big house.

One of the sheriff's men twists Miranda's arm behind her back and forces her to her knees. There's a sound like a branch snapping. Miranda screams. Her arm goes limp.

"You derive pleasure from breaking the arms of defenseless women?" Alexandra asks. "Zachariah is registered on Mother's property ledger. When our family's long-time friend, the George-town Mayor, finds out what you've done, you'll find yourself on the wrong side of jail bars."

From the corner of her eye, Alexandra sees Dr. Higgin's cabriolet driving up the lane toward the house. The sheriff and his men make way as the carriage rolls to a stop at the foot of the stairs. When Dr. Higgins is within hearing distance, Alexandra stands tall and says, "As I told you, Mother's convalescing, and I'm acting in her stead. Release the young man."

"What are you? Thirteen years old?" asks the sheriff.

"Almost seventeen."

"My, my." The sheriff removes a document from his shoulder pouch and hands it to Alexandra. "The assessor was more than generous in extending your mother's tax payment for a year, contingent, of course, on her being alive. But as Mrs. Josephine Degambia has expired . . ."

"Who told you Mother's dead?" Alexandra asks. She sees Mr. Ball give the sheriff a wink and a nod.

"Release the boy!" All eyes lift up to Mother, who stands erect on the upstairs balcony. Alexandra can see that she's gripping the railing to keep her balance.

Color drains from the sheriff's face.

"I thought you were . . ."

"Dying? Dead? How convenient that would be for you. As my daughter said, I am recovering. The boy is my property. Let him go, or, as my daughter explained, I will have a conversation with the Mayor. He has the power to relieve you of your responsibilities since you were appointed, rather than elected. We have a reputable witness who can testify that you are abusing this boy's rights against the will of his owner."

Mother turns to the doctor. "Good evening, Doctor Higgins. Give your wife my regards."

"Evenin', Mrs. Degambia," says the doctor.

Alexandra notices he doesn't meet her eyes.

Mother smiles one of her condescending smiles that makes its recipient feel small and stupid.

"Y'all ever heard of the colored curfew?" asks the sheriff.

"I'm well aware that slaves are not allowed to be wandering at night. I will see that Zachariah carries a pass next time he goes out to check on the horses. And of course, I would be happy to show you his name on my slave ledger. If you value your position as sheriff, you'll let Zachariah go. Now." Mother turns to Mr. Ball.

"I trust my sister is well, Mr. Ball. Do give her my regards."

Mother turns back to the sheriff. "Return in a year with the assessor, as we agreed, and I'll pay my debt in full. In the meantime, you'll receive a doctor's bill for the repair of my servant's arm. Cut the boy loose.

"See to Miranda's arm, Dr. Higgins. When you're done, I'll have Sampson escort you to the main road." Mother turns and disappears into the house.

Mr. Ball lingers, Alexandra follows his gaze up to her room. She gasps. Jimi's face is pressed against a window pane of her French door. Alexandra thinks fast. "Miranda, I told you not to let little Noah wander into my room. I'll give him the switch myself if he ever presses his face against my clean windows again."

Miranda, who's nursing her arm, doesn't seem to hear.

Finally, Jimi disappears from view and someone closes the drape. Had Mr. Ball seen Jimi clearly enough to identify him? After glancing up at the window one more time, Mr. Ball grins and kicks his horse to a gallop.

When all the sheriff's men are out of sight, Alexandra runs inside and races up the stairs to scold Jimi. She finds Mother slumped on the floor in the hallway just outside her room. Alexandra drops to her knees. Mother's breathing is shallow and labored.

"Help!" shouts Alexandra.

Sampson comes running. He scoops Mother into his arms as easily as if she were a child, carries her to her room and lays her in her bed. Alexandra smooths the hair out of Mother's face and kisses her forehead. Mother opens her eyes, sits up, and nods to an entity Alexandra can't see.

"I'm coming," says Mother.

"Not yet!" Alexandra kisses her Mother's hand. "I love you, Mother. You can't die."

But death listens to no one. Alexandra stands transfixed, watching as Mother's eyes light up with wonder. Mother smiles. Then, she exhales one long breath.

Sampson feels for Mother's pulse. "Did you see her eyes glow with happiness, Miss Alexandra?"

"I wonder what she was looking at."

"Your mother was peering into the face of a loving angel who came to carry her home to heaven."

"She seemed so strong when she spoke to the sheriff."

"Some people do it that way—quicken and speak their piece, just before they pass."

Alexandra draws a steadying breath and buries her feelings too deep for other people to see. She is now the mistress of this big house. She must be strong to honor Papa—and Mother. In her last moments on earth, Mother was courageous and compassionate—if only she had told Mother that Jimi is alive and well.

Sampson reaches over to close Mother's eyelids.

"No. Leave them open. She liked to see what was going on," Alexandra says with such authority that Sampson stands up straight and backs away.

"Fetch the priest!" orders Alexandra. "Swear him to secrecy."

"You sure that's a good thing to do?" asks Sampson.

"I'm in charge now," says Alexandra.

As soon as Sampson leaves, Alexandra picks up Mother's hand. It's still warm. She kisses each finger.

"I love you, Mother." Alexandra whispers. *I wish you had loved me.*

Miranda explodes into the room with her bad arm tied up in Dr. Higgin's sling. Sampson follows, fidgeting.

"I told you to go for the priest," Alexandra tells him.

Tears well in Miranda's eyes when she sees Mother. Then she stands erect and faces Alexandra. "Since you're in charge, you need to know that our lives depend on you making wise decisions. Samuel won't be going for the priest."

Alexandra stiffens. "I'm the mistress of this house."

Miranda continues as if Alexandra hadn't spoken, "The

sheriff's spies are camped out all along Heaven's border, their eyes and ears are trained on this house. If Sampson calls for the priest, they'll know your mother has passed. They'll sweep down like locusts and lay claim to this house. They'll scoop up the villagers along with the house help and add them to their own slave ledgers.

"You have to make them believe your mother is still improving."

"She would want a priest to pray over her," says Alexandra, determined to honor Mother's wishes.

"Fetch that priest, and the sheriff will know your mother is dying—or dead. Is that what you want?"

Alexandra thinks fast. "Not if Marcello goes for him." Marcello claims he can steal through the woods without a soul knowing because of the Cofitachiqui blood that runs in his veins. "They have no reason to be watching the blacksmith shop. Sampson, can you slip out the side door and get to Marcello's without being seen?" asks Alexandra.

"Say the word, Miss Alexandra."

"Might work," says Miranda. "Wouldn't want to do anything to ruin Miss Josephine's chance at going to heaven. But you'll have to have a quick tongue if you're going to convince the sheriff that your mama's alive, especially if you want to keep Jimi safe."

Alexandra shivers. "You do know about Jimi." Miranda's eyes search for a place to land. "Were you planning to trade his life for your grandson's?"

Shock registers on Sampson's face when Jimi runs in the room. "Mama, Oeyi brought me here." Jimi wriggles out of Alexandra's grasp and climbs up on Mother's bed. "Mama?" Jimi questions Alexandra with his eyes.

"She's gone to heaven."

Jimi throws himself on the bed and hugs Mother.

Miranda leans down to Jimi and whispers, "Tell her what

you want her to know. She can still hear you for a little while."

Jimi sniffs up his tears. "I love you, Mama. Tell Papa hello when you get to heaven."

"Now you need to go into your sister's room so Alexandra can get your mother ready for her burial," says Miranda.

Jimi clutches the bed. "I want to stay with Mama."

Miranda smooths the hair out of Jimi's eyes. "Alexandra has to dress your mother so she can be laid to rest and her soul can go up to heaven. She wouldn't want you making a commotion. Help us out, now, Jimi. For your mother's sake," Miranda says.

Jimi loosens his grip and kisses Mother's hand. "I'll see you in heaven someday, Mama."

Alexandra holds Jimi close and whispers so only he can hear, "Mother would want you to stay hidden from those bad men." Then she turns to Miranda. "Take him to my room and stay with him until I come in. And make sure he stays away from the window."

"Yes, Miss Alexandra," Miranda says as she takes Jimi's hand and takes him to Alexandra's room.

"I'll find a reliable man to dig the grave after I summon Marcello." Sampson hurries out of the room.

Alexandra's glad to be alone with Mother. Ever so gently, she draws Mother's delicate eyelids down. "Maybe you've seen enough of this world." As she anoints her with lavender oil, Alexandra notices that Mother looks young again, and beautiful, unburdened by life's trials. Alexandra dresses Mother in the red silk gown she loved. She takes a rose from the bud vase and tucks it behind Mother's ear. Then, she winds Mother's pink rosary around her delicate wrist and crosses her emaciated hands over her heart.

Miranda returns to the room. "She looks beautiful. I'll sit here. You go on in with Jimi. He's asleep. Sampson stopped in and said Marcello's going for the priest."

Alexandra stretches out next to her little brother. She

struggles to keep her eyes open, but she falls into the oblivion of sleep. Two hours later, she startles and sits up. She hears Papa as clearly as if he were standing in the room.

"Run. Now."

"Papa, if that's you. Give me a sign."

The flame in her lantern flickers, even though the window's closed, and there's no breeze. Alexandra shakes Jimi. "Wake up!"

Jimi opens his eyes.

"Is it time to lay Mama to rest?" Jimi asks.

"Papa told me we have to leave."

"Papa's dead."

"He spoke to me in his spirit body."

Someone pounds on the door downstairs. Alexandra and Jimi hear shouting, hear Miranda's protest, hear the sheriff's voice. Footsteps stomp up the stairs. Alexandra runs to the wardrobe and opens the trap door. Jimi pulls on his shoes.

Alexandra whispers, "Go to Marcello's shop. Slip in through his back window if he isn't there. Don't let anyone see you."

Jimi nods.

Bedroom doors open and slam shut all along the hall.

Jimi grabs her hand. "Come with me, Ali."

"I have to fix up the wardrobe so no one will know about the passage."

Alexandra hands Jimi the small lantern.

"Don't drop this. Be brave."

Jimi trembles as he climbs down into the secret passage.

Alexandra locks her door and runs to the wardrobe. Her fingers fly as she lays the rug on top of the trap door and rearranges her shoes. Then, she hurries toward the hearth. Before she can open the safe to retrieve the key to Papa's gold, someone hammers on her door.

"Open up, or I'll kick this door in!" yells a man.

She looks around to make certain there's nothing that will give Jimi away.

When she unlocks the door, the tallest man she's ever seen pushes his way inside. His pale skin has a yellow cast. His black beard and mustache make him look like an etching of the devil Alexandra once saw in Mother's illustrated Bible,

"Where's your brother at, Girl?" he asks, grabbing her arm.

"My brother's gone from this world." She tries to squirm out of his grip. "Let go and get out of my room!"

The man twists her arm behind her back and forces her to her knees. "Where's your brother at?"

"He's gone to a better place. Leave me alone."

"Mr. Ball seen him peering down from your bedroom window."

"That was our cook's son."

"Not what our spy from this very house told us."

"What spy?" Alexandra struggles to make an unreadable mask of her face. Sampson? Miranda? No one else from this house knows Jimi's alive.

"Thirty pieces of silver buys a heap of information."

Who had betrayed Jimi, Alexandra wonders? She struggles not to collapse.

The tall man digs his fingernails into her wrist, shoves her across the room, and presses her into a chair. Then he whips off his belt and winds it around her neck.

"Where's your brother at?" He tightens the belt.

"Don't damage her," says the assessor who's stolen into the room, silent as a rat. "If the boy is on the premises, we'll find him."

The assessor scours the room. Alexandra stares at her French door, determined not to reveal the secret passage. She relaxes when the assessor looks inside the wardrobe, then slams the door shut.

Plucking a document out of his satchel, the assessor curls his lips into a thin smile and reads the agreement signed by Mother: "In the event I should die before Heaven Hill's debts are settled in full, all of my property shall be conveyed to government agents of the State of South Carolina."

"The debt will be settled in full in one year, as agreed," Alexandra says. "Mother is recovering."

The assessor adjusts his monocle. "Fortunately, the sheriff had the foresight to detain the doctor on the main road, out of fear your mother might need his services."

The assessor takes a second document out of his case. "Josephine Degambia's death certificate, certified by Doctor Henry Higgins."

Traitor!

Alexandra takes a deep breath to keep from vomiting.

The sheriff limps into the room and tells the tall man, "Take her. Do what we agreed to."

The tall man squeezes Alexandra's elbow as he steers her toward the hall

"Let me put on a dress and some shoes," Alexandra pleads.

The tall man shoves her into the hallway. He stops in front of Mother's doorway, Alexandra gasps. Mother's bed is empty. Miranda is leaning against the wall holding Mother's red funeral dress in her one good hand, her eyes cast to the ground.

"Where have they taken Mother?"

Miranda shakes her head.

"Tell me where they've taken her."

Miranda shuffles toward Alexandra like a sleep-walker; her eyes are dull and unfocused. When she touches Alexandra's cheek, the tall man tightens his grip and manhandles Alexandra toward the stairs.

"Where did they take Mother?" Alexandra screams.

The tall man wads up his dirty handkerchief and jams it into Alexandra's mouth. Her mind races. *Concentrate on helping Jimi,* she tells herself. They haven't caught him, or they wouldn't be asking her where he is.

Think! Don't lose control.

The handkerchief swells. She gags. The tall man presses his mouth close to her ear. "Keep your damn mouth shut, or I'll shut it for good." She nods. He rips the handkerchief out of her mouth and pushes her out the front door onto the porch. Mr. Ball smirks astride one of Papa's Arabians.

"Make you a deal. I'll tell you where your mother's body's at, and you tell me where your brother's hiding," says Mr. Ball.

"My brother's dead, and you know it."

The sheriff comes up behind Alexandra. "Think we're stupid? My deputies are gonna scour these grounds." He fixes the tall man in a threatening stare. "Persuade the girl to tell you where her brother's hiding, and there might be something nice in it for you. But don't damage her permanently. She could bring a good price at the Charleston auction."

A rim of morning sun peeks up over *Rise-and-Shine Hill*, so named because that's where Grand-mère claimed the risen Christ appeared to her on the day Alexandra was born. Where is Grand-mère's Jesus now? And where is Papa's Emitai?

CHAPTER FIFTEEN

The tall man winds a rope around Alexandra's wrists and pulls her down the road. Her eyes bulge when she sees armed deputies on horseback herding Papa's villagers up the path toward the indigo fields. Planted on high ground, Heaven's indigo was never affected by the onrush of salt water that ruined the rice.

Hatred smolders in the eyes of the newly enslaved. Angry men trudge past Alexandra with cadyendos slung over their broad shoulders and gathering bags tied to their backs. Wary women balance reed baskets on their heads. Mothers carry babies in cloth slings dyed to match their head wraps. Children old enough to walk hold tight to their mother's skirts.

Alexandra hoped the villagers had gotten away. She looks around. No sign of Lulu.

A lanky, bleached-out white boy with pale eyes and slicked-back black hair, a younger version of the tall man, runs toward Alexandra and her captor. "Theya comin', Pa."

"You sure?" asks the tall man.

Child-like agitation in the man's voice surprises Alexandra. "Seen 'em close up, Pa."

Alexandra guesses the boy's thirteen or fourteen.

The tall man pulls Alexandra's arms behind her and binds her hands with the rope. He shoves her off the road. "Sit down," he says, pushing her to the ground. She jumps up and tries to run. None of Papa's people look in her direction. The tall man bends her arm up behind her so hard, she thinks it'll pull out of the socket. She sinks down by the side of the gravel road.

"Keep fightin' me, and I kin do some things that won't show if the sheriff does decide to put you up on the auction block."

Alexandra fumes as the man ties her to a pine tree.

"Be a good girl now, or you'll be sorry you was ever a pretender to high-born society."

The washed-out boy dances from foot to foot in the middle of the road, his eyes fixed on the carriage coming toward them. "Theya almost upon us, Pa!"

The tall man licks his fingers and slicks back the boy's hair. "Stand up tall and wave when they pass by, Steven. Or, if they should stop, look them in the eye. If they speak to you, don't fidget."

Steven slouches. "My belly's achin', Pa. You promised me fancy victuals."

"Mind me on this," says the tall man as he draws his hand back to slap the boy.

"Whatever you say, Pa," Steven says, standing at attention.

The tall man clamps his hand on the boy's shoulder, as if posing for a portrait.

A black carriage with gold scrolling approaches. The coachman, a light-skinned mulatto dressed in a maroon velvet cloak that must be suffocating on a day like this, reins four matched Andalusians to a stop. When the boy turns to look at her, Alexandra is struggling to wriggle free.

"Whatcha doin' there?" the boy asks Alexandra.

"Rope's itchy. I'm trying to scratch my wrist," she lies. Alexandra sees a woman inside the coach. She's leaning toward the open window, holding tight to an ostrich-plume hat that looks like it could take flight.

"Stop the carriage!" the woman calls up to the driver in a cultivated canary-voice. The woman's rouged lips break into a smile when she recognizes the tall man. "Is that you, Mr. Hodges?"

"Yes, Ma'am," says Mr. Hodges, tipping his bowler.

"So nice to see you again!" she says, dripping so much honey into her voice it makes Alexandra reassess Mr. Hodges. His chiseled features might appeal to some women.

The woman waves her gloved hand like one of those moths that emerges from its cocoon, grows to maturity, mates, and expires in the course of twenty-four hours.

"Mr. Hodges! Do come tour my little girl and me around the big house that's to be our new home." The woman motions for Mr. Hodges to sit on the carriage seat opposite hers. She addresses the coachman. "Harold, where are your manners? Climb on down and open the door for Mr. Hodges. He's handy with a hammer and saw. I want to tour the house with him so I can surprise my husband with my ideas for fixing up our new home."

The coachman hesitates.

"Do as I say, Harold," she says with more flirt than command in her voice.

This ridiculous woman plans to take Mother's place in the house Papa built?

When Harold opens the carriage door for Mr. Hodges, Alexandra sees a frail little girl dressed in a pink satin dress and a white hat, trimmed with lace and pink rosebuds. The shy child crouches down on the seat, hugging a porcelain doll dressed in an outfit that matches her own.

Mr. Hodges leans toward Steven. "I'm going to tour the house with the missus. Keep your eyes glued on that uppity girl."

"I won't let her out of my sight, Pa."

"Do me proud, Boy!"

Mr. Hodges removes his bowler and climbs into the coach. Then he leans out the window to say something. The clatter of wooden wheels swallows his words.

As soon as they're out of view, Steven sits on his haunches and flicks pebbles at Alexandra's bare feet.

"Stop that!" she says.

A flash of red in the field behind the boy's back catches her attention. She sees Oeyi motion to her from behind a bottleneck bush. She has to find a way to make Steven leave her alone.

"Mmmmm. Smell that?" Alexandra asks.

"What?"

"Cinnamon buns. In summer, Cook bakes peach pie and cinnamon buns on Tuesdays. You hungry? You like cinnamon buns?"

Steven stops throwing pebbles. "They got pancakes up at that kitchen?"

"Cook'll make crêpes, those are French pancakes, even on Cinnamon Roll Day, if that's what a body craves." She has his attention. "The kitchen house is just on the other side of that hedge."

Steven stands on tiptoe to see where the kitchen is.

"If that lady takes your father on a tour of the big house, he'll be gone long enough for you to go to the kitchen and come back without his ever knowing you left my side. You poor thing. If you haven't eaten all morning, you must be starving."

"I could eat a horse."

"Just go around to the back of the kitchen house and knock three times, wait a second, and knock once more. That's my secret code. Old Mary, the cook, will open the door. Tell her Alexandra sent you and said to make you a plate of whatever you hanker for."

The boy glances toward the big house.

"You can't see the kitchen from the big house. Of course, you shouldn't go if you aren't hungry, or if you're afraid."

"Why are you telling me your secret code?"

"My throat's parched. I'd like you to bring me back a lemonade. Never give something for nothing. Know what I mean?"

Steven hesitates. Alexandra adds, "Old Mary might still have some of her custard from dinner last night. If she does, ask her to add it to your breakfast plate. That is, if you like custard with caramel sauce.

"If you don't leave soon, your daddy'll come back and find you out."

Steven's eyes shift toward the kitchen house. "Stand up," he tells her. Steven double-ties the rope to the tree. "Stay put till I get back—or I'll hurt you. If my daddy comes, tell him I had to take a piss. Tell him I'll be back in a wink."

"Don't forget the lemonade," says Alexandra.

The boy races off. As soon as he's out of sight, Oeyi, now dressed like one of the sheriff's guards, steals up behind Alexandra, unties her, and whispers, "Act like you're still tied up. Run and climb in the back window of the blacksmith shop as soon as I distract the sheriff's men," he whispers before slipping out of sight.

How can Oeyi distract all these gun-toting men without getting caught? What if the boy comes back before she has a chance to run? Alexandra's doubts run wild until she hears Oeyi shout, "Fire!"

Deputies spur their horses toward the edge of the tree line, jump off their horses, and use horse blankets to beat out the flames of a brush fire. When no one's looking in her direction, Alexandra hunches down and runs toward the blacksmith shop, grateful the worn trail softens the impact on her bare feet. When she's almost to the back window, she hears a horse galloping toward her. She flattens herself behind a bush, peers through the branches, and sees the sheriff ride to the black-smith's door. He slips off his saddle and leads his horse toward the shop.

"Boy!" he shouts.

Marcello saunters out the door, wiping his bear-paw hands on a leather apron. "Someone shout fire? Or was my mind playin' tricks?"

"My men will take care of the fire and find the scoundrel who set it. My horse needs a shoe. Front right," says the sheriff.

Alexandra panics. Is Jimi in the shop?

Marcello smiles. "Blink of de eye, and your horse, he fly." Marcello takes the reins and leads the horse to a stall. The sheriff follows. Alexandra tenses. The sheriff has probably used this excuse to find Jimi. Who told him to look in Marcello's shop?

She hears the clank, clank, clank of Marcello's hammer. Finally, Marcello leads the horse out of the shop, followed by the sheriff.

Where's Jimi?

"Board up that back window and lock up your place. Then get yourself over to the corral down by that African village. Don't come back till all the horses down there is fed and combed. Got that, Boy?" asks the sheriff.

"Yes, Sir."

"And if you see that little guy who used to live in the big house, let me or my men know."

"I gots to cool down the forge before I can go."

"Get to it, then."

The sheriff canters up the road without a good-bye or a thank you.

Marcello opens the back window. "Lucky the sheriff didn't see you."

Alexandra climbs into the shop.

"Get on over to de far corner, Miss Alexandra." Marcello points with his chin. "Draw de blanket over your head and lie still as a dead cat."

"Where's Jimi?"

"I passed him on to Mamou. Oeyi's goin' to collect him. Your daddy tol' me you have a key to his stash. Let's get your gold so you and Jimi can get away from dis place."

Alexandra looks into Marcello's eyes and finds no deception. "The key's in the safe in my room."

Marcello pounds a few boards over the window, making it

impossible for anyone to climb in—or out. He leaves enough space between the slats to see out—or in.

"Don't worry your sweet head, we find a way to get you and Jimi to Charleston wid or widout dat gold. Go on over to de blanket and lay still while I think on what to do," he says. "Pull de extra blanket over your head if you hear someone comin'."

The bellows heave a sigh as the forge fire dies. Alexandra curls up on a scratchy blanket that smells like smoke and sweat.

She hears Marcello say to himself, "Why her mama have to be call away so soon?"

It's quiet for a while, then Marcello starts muttering again. It takes her a minute to realize he's speaking to her.

"We tryin' to keep y'all safe, but, if dey finds you and sells you and Jimi for slaves, you gots to be specks on de wall. Stay still 'nuf, and dey come to decide dey ain't seein' nothin'. When dat happen, turn on your ears and fire up your thinking cap.

"Flies on de wall don' never flap dey mouths. So, don' y'all be buzzin' round till you find a friend you know you can trust wid your life. And don' you never let dem know you can read and write." Marcello shuts the window and pulls down the shade. "I gots to go see to de horses. I gonna lock you in. I be bringing you vittles soon as it be safe."

Marcello locks the door from the outside. Suspicion unnerves Alexandra when she hears muffled voices. Marcello is talking to someone, but she can't make out who the other person is, or what they're saying. Then she's alone, enveloped in silence.

"Papa," she whispers, "Jimi's safe, and I'll do all in my power to make sure he stays that way."

She tries to hold her feelings in, but she's so tired, she cries herself to sleep. When she wakes up, it's dark and there's a chill in the air. Her throat's dry, and she's hungry. She sits up and tips over a tin cup. Whatever was in it is a patch of mud now. Her hand brushes something lying on a cloth. She picks it up and smells it. A biscuit. She crunches something gritty and gags. Her mouth's too dried out to swallow anyway. She spits out the bite of biscuit and flings the rest across the room. Why did Marcello come and go without even speaking to her?

The next day passes with no word from Marcello. Alexandra's throat is parched. Her stomach aches with hunger. She relieves herself over in the corner.

When night falls, something taps on the window. She scoots close to the wall and pulls the blanket over her head. Is Jimi trying to get in? She waits until her eyes have adjusted enough to make out the shapes of things. Tap. Tap, tap, tap. She crawls over, raises up on her knees and peers through an opening in the boards.

She sees a firefly flinging itself against the thick glass. Its translucent wings shimmer in the light of the newly risen moon. Didima's ewuum was a firefly. Is her grandmother bringing her a warning? The hairs on Alexandra's arms stand on end.

She knows without knowing how that she has to get out of the shop now and get the key, so she and Jimi will have enough money to make their escape. When she crawls back toward the wall to make an escape plan, she overshoots the blanket and ends up near the coal pile. Then it occurs to her, she's barely fatter than the raccoons she and Papa saw one night when they were walking by Marcello's. They heard a noise and thought a thief was in his shop. Papa told her to hide; he took a revolver from his vest pocket. Then two raccoons waddled out of the coal chute, their faces smeared with soot. She and Papa laughed so hard their sides ached.

Maybe she can get out through the chute. She knows where the outside entrance to the secret passage is. If she can get out of this shop, she can get into her room.

Scrambling to the top of the coal heap, she digs herself into the narrow channel that connects the shop to freedom. The passageway is only as long as an average man is tall. As she pushes her way through the pile of coal, she struggles for air. She stops when she hears whispering, only to realize she's listening to the sound of her own ragged breaths.

She inches forward. Her eyes are squinted shut; coal dust burns her throat, sharp chunks of coal stab her hands and knees. What if the coal's packed so tight at the end that she can't push her way through the five-ply oilcloth door that Marcello hinged to the top of the chute the day he found the timber rattler coiled in the ashes of his forge?

She braces her toes against the ground and pushes past the "snake stopper." Exhausted, she emerges into the warm, humid embrace of the Carolina night. She lies on her stomach to catch her breath. When she lifts her head, she can see light winking through the trees from the direction of the big house.

Hunching down, she runs to the hedge that borders the manicured grounds, trying not to cry out when pine needles and stones stab her feet. When she comes to the rose garden, she drops to her knees and crawls. Keeping herself low to the ground, she makes it to the well. She pulls the bucket up and drinks her fill. She hears someone laugh. She peeks through the hedge that shields the well and gasps.

More than a dozen surreys are parked in Heaven's circle drive. Torches set in sconces blaze with light. A man throws open the French doors that lead from the parlor to the west veranda. The sound of someone banging on Mother's piano spills out.

All the ballroom doors on the top floor of the house have been thrown open. Candelabras inside the ballroom are turned up bright enough to illuminate a soirée in full swing. Alexandra nearly cries out when the woman Alexandra saw earlier in the carriage strolls onto the veranda on the assessor's arm, wearing Mother's red funeral dress.

Light flickers in her bedroom window. Is someone in her room? She looks more closely, hopeful that what she'd seen is the reflection of the lighted lawn torches that line the drive.

The upstairs chambers are removed from the parlor and the ballroom. With luck, she can slip through the secret passage into her room without attracting attention. Keeping to the shadows, she inches her way to the white oleander that conceals the passage and pushes her way through the branches, relieved when she finds the rope handle. She pulls up on the rope, and the trap door lifts soundlessly. She can only see as far as the first three stairs, hewn from earth and covered with woven flax to absorb excessive rain.

She feels her way down the stairs to the tunnel and pulls on the chain that lowers the trap door. Fetid darkness wraps around her like a funeral shroud.

Lose your way, and no one will find you, chortles the Ahoelra.

Cool, wet ground soothes her bare feet as she extends her hands and feels her way along the damp tunnel wall. When she comes to the first fork, she hesitates. Papa had said left led to the house and right led to the river. Hadn't he? The scent of earth and musk soothes her nerves as she turns left down a narrowing passage. When she's all but given up hope, she comes to the rope ladder that leads up to the trap door in her bedroom.

The party must be over. There's no music or laughter to mask whatever noise she might make. She tucks her skirt into her pantalets and climbs to the second-floor landing. Then she drops to her knees and inches through a passageway until she comes to a dead-end. Running her hands along the low ceiling, she feels for the edges of the trap door that opens up into the wardrobe.

When she pulls the brass ring, the door springs open. She hears her shoes slide and hoists herself up, surprised by the stream of soft light that curls in through the bottom of the closed door.

Maybe it wasn't a reflection she'd seen in the window. And what's that smell? Peppermint? Is someone in her room?

"Mama!" calls a little girl between fits of coughing. Sweat coats Alexandra's body. She hears her bedroom door open, followed by padding feet. A woman says, "Swallow down this tonic, Baby. I have a mind to tie you in. Don't want you sleep-walking these unfamiliar grounds."

"Don't tie me, Mama," pleads the little girl. "I won't wander."

Alexandra hears the child choke down the medicine.

"You look like a queen in that lovely gown," says the woman.

"It's silky, but it's too big. Mama, you sure my cousin wanted me to have her clothes?"

"Why else would she have left them in your new room?"

"Mama, before you go out, could you light another lantern please? To keep the haints away."

"Aren't any haints in this room, Baby."

"I saw a little brass lantern on the desk," the little girl says hopefully. "Wouldn't hurt to light it."

"Tell you what, I'll send in the girl who's cleaning up downstairs. She can sit with you till you fall asleep.

"Is she nice?"

"I expect she is, otherwise her former owners wouldn't have had her working in the big house."

There's a lull in the conversation, then the woman says, "Baby, you're shivering. Let me fetch something from the wardrobe to take off the chill."

Alexandra scoots behind her cloaks and prays the woman won't notice the shoes are in a jumble. When the wardrobe door opens, a slice of lantern light illuminates a diamond and ruby ring on a dainty white hand. Alexandra holds her breath while the woman sorts through her clothes and pulls out the blue satin bed-coat Grand-mère gave her for Christmas. She doesn't exhale until the door closes.

"Isn't this a lovely little thing?" she hears the woman say.

"Mama, I don't recall meeting any cousins who are older than me. And why does she want me to have her clothes? Won't she need them?"

"Not where she's goin'."

"Where is she goin'?"

"Far away."

"Why?"

"It's not my place to ask, Baby."

"What if she comes back and gets mad at me for wearin' her lovely things?"

"She isn't coming back."

"Not even to visit?"

"Enough, Sally Ann. Sit up now, Baby, so I can slip this bedcoat around your shoulders."

"It does fend off the chill. Thank you, Mama."

"Go to sleep now, so the Sandman can come and give you lovely dreams."

"But, Mama . . ."

"I'll send the girl right in."

As soon as the mother leaves, Sally Ann starts to cry, which leads her into a coughing fit. Alexandra's mind drifts to Mother's illness. Then she hears the bedroom door open again. The little girl stops coughing.

"I'm here till you fade off to sleep."

Lulu's voice!

"Want me to cool you with this peacock feather fan?"

"That'd be nice," says Sally Ann.

Alexandra hears the rocking chair squeak as Lulu sits down, followed by the swish-swash rhythm of rocking. When all is still, Alexandra opens the door just enough to see that Lulu is turned toward Sally Ann, trying not to nod off. Sally Ann's breathing smooths into a sleeping rhythm.

Alexandra drops to her knees and crawls toward the fireplace. Then she hears someone coming down the hallway. She slides under the bed just before the door opens.

"You're not allowed to sleep while you're tending my daughter!" scolds the girl's mother.

"Just resting my eyes," Lulu says; she jumps up and stands at attention.

"I will not have you nodding off while you're supposed to be watching my baby. I'm worried about Sally Ann's cough."

"She's sound asleep, Ma'am."

"Go on down to the kitchen and make her a lemon water with a little honey."

Lulu hesitates.

"Right now, if you don't mind."

"Yes, Miss Masters."

"Call me Miss Gweneth."

"Yes, Miss Gweneth."

Alexandra hears the door open and close, then Lulu's footsteps pad down the hall.

"Fly away to dreamland, dear . . ." sings Missus Masters, oblivious she can't carry a tune.

Finally, Lulu returns. "I warmed up some lemon water and put in two spoons of honey, Ma'am."

"Test the temperature on your wrist before you give it to Sally Ann. Come wake me if she has a bad coughing fit. I'm down the hall, two doors to the right."

This woman has moved into Mother's room? Already? Tears stream down Alexandra's cheeks. How could so much have happened in so short a time?

"Might be best to fold that bedspread down, so she won't take a fever."

"Yes, Ma'am," says Lulu. When she bends down to tuck the blanket around the little girl's feet, her eyes meet Alexandra's and she emits a little scream.

"What is it? A mouse? I knew I shouldn't have agreed to live here."

"I just hit my knee on the bed frame, Ma'am."

After Missus Masters has left the room, Alexandra slides out from under the bed.

"How long have you been there?" Lulu whispers.

Before Alexandra can answer, Sally Ann stirs, and Alexandra slips back under the bed.

When Sally Ann settles, Alexandra re-emerges. A torrent of words spills from Lulu. "That assessor moved his family in so it would appear they were well-established in case the State inspector came by. They've retained me to dust the silver and to be the little girl's personal attendant—until they can find someone 'more suitable.'

"I heard the assessor say that occupying the big house so soon after your mother died will help them gain title to the property. The sheriff said they have to get rid of you and Jimi like they did your father before some judge in Charleston gets wind of what happened and comes to investigate. You have to get away from here."

"I need something from my fireplace safe."

"Just leave!"

Alexandra ignores Lulu. She's nearly to the fireplace when Sally Ann sits up and screams. "Who are you?"

Alexandra races to the wardrobe.

"What are you doin' in my room?" asks the little girl.

Alexandra grabs a dress and a pair of shoes. She lets the shoes fall to ground, drapes the dress around her shoulders and pulls the trap door shut. As she scurries down the ladder, she hears the little girl call out, "Mama!" over and over again.

It seems to Alexandra like she'll never come to the other side of the passage. Has she made a wrong turn? she wonders. Then, she sees moonlight streaming in from the edges of the trap door at the end of the tunnel. She pushes hard. The trap door opens. She heaves herself out of the tunnel, puts the dress on over her night clothes, wipes her feet on the grass and slips on the shoes.

She's about to step onto the path that leads to the village when she hears footfalls coming toward her. She crouches in the center of the cascading bridal veil bush that has been her hiding place since she was a little girl. Alexandra peeks through the leaves. A pair of brass-buckled boots stops inches from her face, joined by a second pair of boots. Tongues of torchlight lick the sheriff's ghoulish face. Mr. Hodges stands next to him.

The sheriff picks up a twig, touches it to Mr. Hodge's torch and lights his cigar. He drops the twig.

"Well?" asks the sheriff.

"Well, what?"

"You do her? Cotton in your ears, Hodges?"

The sheriff pauses. "Don't need to know how. Just want to know if you dropped her body down that dry well shaft on the north side of the pasture, like we planned if things got moving too fast?"

Mr. Hodges twists the toe of his boot, smothering the fire that has sprung up on the unburnt end of twig.

"Speak up!"

Mr. Hodges clicks into high gear. "Missus Masters asked me up to the house to offer some suggestions on decoration. Wouldn't have been good manners to refuse. Left my boy by the road to guard the girl. After I got Missus Masters and her sweet little gal situated, I went on back to where I'd left Steven with that uppity girl. But they wasn't there. You do recall, Sheriff, how I attracted your attention, several times throughout the day. But ever' time I caught your eye, Sir, you nodded and smiled and waved me off.

"Naturally I took that as a signal that you'd switched to that other plan we had to lure the girl to the blacksmith shop, do her and wait till night to dump her body in the swamp. When I didn't find Steven or the girl, I believed with all my heart that I was right about my notion you'd sent my son on an errand.

"I went over to the blacksmith shop to confirm my suspicion. I looked in the window and saw two little feet was stickin' out the bottom of a blanket: brown on top, pink on the bottom. Belonged to the girl, I figured. She wasn't moving none. It come to me that she must have become a nuisance you couldn't abide."

The sheriff flicks ash from his cigar. "Figuring can get a fellow in a mess of trouble." The sheriff drops his half-smoked cigar and crushes out the smoldering butt with the brass toe of his boot.

"Mr. Master's family come sooner than we expected, otherwise, I wouldn't have left her in Stevie's charge," offers Mr. Hodges.

The sheriff takes a fresh cigar from his pocket, bites off the end, and spits it out. The slimy brown tip bounces off Mr. Hodge's boot and comes to rest inches from where Alexandra crouches.

Mr. Hodges continues, "Surely you are aware that my time and attention was consumed by Missus Master's early arrival. You remarked several times on how it was to our advantage to make a good friend of the assessor's wife. I thought if I helped her out when her husband was over to the lawyers getting those legal papers in order . . ."

The front door of the big house slams shut, interrupting Mr. Hodges's flood of excuses.

"Mr. Hodges?" Missus Masters calls.

"Over heah!" shouts Hodges.

"Why'd you tell her where we are?" growls the sheriff.

"Say again," calls Missus Masters.

"They're over by the well," Alexandra hears Sampson say.

Judas!

Sampson comes up the path, carrying a torch. Missus Masters follows, holding the wheezing Sally Ann in her arms.

"There was an intruder in Sally Ann's room, Sheriff!"

"'Twas a haint," whimpers Sally Ann.

"Let mama do the talkin', Sweet Pea. Well, Sheriff, Sally Ann was screaming so loud, she was like to wake the dead. I ran to her room. And there she was, standin' on her bed yellin', 'I saw a haint! I saw a haint!' 'Where's the girl I sent to your room?' I asked her. 'There,' says Sally Ann, pointin' to the door. Sure enough, that lazy girl was just standing by the bed staring at the wardrobe door. I asked the girl why she wasn't helpin' my baby, and she said, 'I tried to calm her. I took the lantern to the wardrobe to show Sally Ann there was nothing there.'"

"That haint disappeared soon as she shut the wardrobe door," Sally Ann said. "Don't open it, Mama. It's full of ghosts."

"Something sneaky about that girl. I'm gonna sell her down South soon as the speculator comes by. Anyway, I says to the girl, 'Bring in a bigger lantern.' I was thinking to myself that Sally Ann must've had one of her nightmares. But then I took that bright lantern over to the wardrobe, and I saw muddy footprints on the floor. That mud was fresh! And, the shoes were in a jumble. I ordered the girl to show her feet. There wasn't one speck of mud on 'em. I know she can't've washed off her feet that fast. But haints don't make muddy prints, Sheriff."

The sheriff turns on his heel and double-times it toward the house.

"Sheriff! I'm talkin' to you!" calls Missus Masters, but the sheriff keeps running.

Alexandra stays crouched inside the hollow of the bush.

Mr. Hodges slides his hand under Missus Masters' elbow. "Allow me to escort you and the little miss back to the house, Ma'am."

"Call for our buggy, Mama. Let's go home to Williamsburg," pleads Sally Ann.

"This is your home now, Darlin'," says her mother.

"I'm never goin' in that house again!" screams Sally Ann.

"Weren't no haint you saw," says Mr. Hodges. "It was that girl."

"What girl?" asks Missus Masters.

"My cousin who used to live here?" asks Sally Ann.

"Wasn't no cousin of yours," says the sheriff.

"Whose clothes am I wearing?"

Mr. Hodges tells Missus Masters, "Plantation houses sometimes have secret passageways."

Their voices fade as they hurry toward the big house.

Alexandra hears the sheriff bellow from the front portico, "Mr. Hodges, find the blacksmith! Now!"

"I won't go in!" Sally Ann screams.

CHAPTER SIXTEEN

Two of the sheriff's men are stationed in front of the blacksmith shop. Alexandra has to find Marcello and tell him she's not in the shop. She's sneaking around to the back of the shop to find the path to Papa's corral when she sees the sheriff and his deputies riding toward her, carrying pine torches. She flattens herself in thigh-high grass.

"I got the boy!" shouts a man from down the road.

Men waving torches gallop toward the shop. Alexandra's heart lurches when she sees a man riding toward Marcello's with Jimi trussed and slung across the neck of his horse. Another rider follows, dragging Oeyi's unconscious body at the end of a rope. The deputy lets out a whoop as he hands Jimi down to Mr. Hodges.

The sheriff glares at one of his men. "Saw the boy's body float down the river, or did you just see his hat?" The sheriff strides over to the man. "Lock the boy in the shop, and see if his sister's inside."

The sheriff nods to a man the size of an ox. He takes a branding iron from a loop in his belt and breaks the padlock off the shop door with a single blow.

Alexandra slithers backward through the grass, and inches her way to the cherry tree. Frantic to think of a way to save Jimi, she climbs to the highest branch so she can get a better view. Four men hold their torches high, lighting up the road in front of Marcello's.

She's sees Jimi trying to kick free of a huge, bearded man. "Let me go!" screams Jimi.

"Put 'im in there," says the sheriff. "When y'all have confirmed the girl's in there, bar the door and pour creosote around the perimeter," orders the sheriff.

Mr. Hodges runs up and grabs Jimi. He pushes him inside the shop.

Alexandra's about to yell at them to let Jimi go when Marcello bursts out of the bushes, races toward the sheriff, and falls to his knees.

"Please, Sir. De girl's in de shop. No need to hurt her and her brother. Let 'em go."

A skinny man comes from around the side of the shop, carrying a can of creosote. The sheriff bars the door.

"Let de babies go, and I'll work for you for free. You could sell 'em for a good price at de Savannah Market, and make a bundle of money with my wares. Nobody over to Georgia know who dey be. I can work iron into gates and window boxes. I can make you a mountain of money."

The sheriff slides off his horse and barks instructions. "Bind that aider-and-abettor to a tree so he can see the tragedy his collusion has wrought."

It takes four men to tie Marcello. The sheriff takes his flintlock out of the scabbard attached to his saddle.

"Jimi! Alexandra! I'm sorry!" wails Marcello.

Someone shouts, "Two fer one. Hallelujah!"

The sheriff primes the pan of his flintlock, slides the lock back and aims at Marcello's head. Alexandra sees Jimi's face pressed against the window. She starts down the tree. The flash of powder and the boom of the gun startles her. She falls and hits her head. Her world goes black.

When Alexandra comes to, she's lying on her back, hidden by the branches of her bridal veil bush. She looks up through a cascade of white flowers at a slice of pearl-grey sky. Birds haven't started up their morning songs yet. When she's certain no one's around, she crawls out from under the bush and stands up. Smoke, hanging in the air, stings her eyes. She struggles to catch a breath. Then she realizes this isn't where she fell. Someone hid her in her secret hiding place. Her head throbs. She can't make the puzzle fit together.

The smell of burnt creosote conjures Jimi's face pressed up against the glass. She sneaks through the tall grass toward the blacksmith shop. Cold sweat washes over her when she sees the chimney of the forge rising from a heap of steaming ash. She inches closer, her eyes drawn to something shining in the debris. Jimi's hummingbird! She picks it up, wipes the tiny bird clean on her skirt, and presses it to her heart. Her memory flashes to life: A gun pointed at Marcello's head, a man ready to torch the shop, a gun shot.

"Jimi!" Her cry shatters the silence.

As the rising sun spills color across the world, she hears something thudding. Alexandra tucks the hummingbird into her pocket and follows the sound to a moss-bearded oak. She raises her eyes to where Oeyi dangles from a rope. His withered body sways in the breeze, striking the tree trunk. Marcello sits at the bottom of the tree, holding his severed head on his lap.

She vomits, then collapses. A whisper of wings draws her to look up where a white owl is circling. It peers at her with golden eyes that seem human. She remembers the Cofitachiqui story Old Marcello told her when she was little. "An owl that flies in the day is a guide that's come to take the newly departed from this world to the next."

When her legs will hold her, Alexandra dances as much as she can remember of the Nyakul funeral dance. Then she speaks to the yahls of Oeyi and Marcello, her resolve growing. "I'll tell my children and my children's children your story."

She's too grief-stricken to take note of the footfalls of the man sneaking up behind her. He grabs her and shoves a gag of cotton into her mouth.

"I'm not going to hurt you. Don't fight me now, or you'll be dead," the man whispers in her ear. Before she can turn to look at his face, he pulls a bag over her head, ties it so it won't fall off, drapes her over his shoulder, and runs.

The sound of barking hounds waxes and wanes as the man splashes through marsh water. When the braying of the dogs fades, the man turns and walks a ways without making a sound, then he lays her down in sweet-smelling grass that has wilted in the heat of early-morning sun.

"You won't scream if I take out the mouth rag, will you, Miss Alexandra? Your life, and mine, depend on it," he whispers.

She shakes her head.

He removes the gag, but not the itchy head-sack.

"That better, Miss Alexandra?"

"Jeremiah? Is that you?"

"Yes, Ma'am, Miss Alexandra. I come to carry you away from danger."

Marcello's cousin, Jeremiah, lives on a little farm up the road from Heaven.

All that grief Alexandra has pushed down erupts in wracking sobs.

"I seen what happened, Miss Alexandra, but giving yourself to remorse pains the spirits of those who's passed over. Pull yourself together, now. You wouldn't be here if the Creator didn't have a purpose for your life."

"Can you take this thing off my head?" she asks.

"The head-cover be there for your own good. Keep still as a possum now, Miss Alexandra. We have to step out for a bit more."

Jeremiah picks her up piggy-back style. She wraps her arms around his neck and holds tight as his feet pad steadily. From the musky smell and the flitting shadows, she guesses they're on the Indian trail that leads to the north end of the swamp.

After a long time, she hears trickling water followed by the sound of Jeremiah's feet squishing through stinking mud that sucks at his feet. He slogs into bright sunlight. The air thickens with heat and humidity. Finally, he sets her down, but not on the bare ground. Her hands brush over a woven mat.

"We gonna lay up here till they give the signal."

"Who?"

"The ones who are gonna help you."

She starts to pull the bag off her head, but he catches her hand. "Like I say, it be for your good and mine."

A whistle splits the air; Jeremiah jumps to his feet.

"A little more travelin' and we'll be there," he says, hoisting her into his arms. "Hold tight."

The cool water he's wading through must be up to his chest. It feels good on her bare feet and legs. Another shrill whistle rents the air. As they wind down a trail, she catches the scent of jasmine. Jeremiah ducks. Alexandra feels vines brush over her feet. Coolness tinges the air.

"Whatcha got under de blanket, Mr. Jeremiah?" asks a child.

"That's for me to know."

"Praise the Creator," says a woman with a beautiful lilt in her voice.

"Bet he got one o' those totem carvings," says a little girl.

"I'll thank y'all to pull aside the curtain," says Jeremiah. "You children run along now." Jeremiah steps into a dark space; the warm air is perfumed with the scent of cedar. He sets Alexandra down on smooth, firm ground, but he leaves the hood in place.

"Wash her in the smoke," says a woman with a voice almost as deep as a man's.

Jeremiah whispers, "Be at peace, child. You be with people who cares."

"Take that thing off the poor girl's head," says the woman.

"This here's a Maroon Village," Jeremiah says as he lifts the bag off Alexandra's head. "Been here for a hundred years, helping runaways on their way to freedom."

Alexandra looks around. Firelight from four small fires stripes the cave walls. Four ancient women, one with African features and three with the high cheekbones of native people, sit cross-legged, gazing into the flames of the large fire in the center.

Using deer antlers, a lithe young man, whose dark skin and straight hair suggest mixed heritage, adjusts the logs.

"The fires take care o' their own self now, Woodpecker. You git up that tree," orders Jeremiah. "And don' be tellin' what you saw."

"Already made my promise, Mr. Jeremiah." Woodpecker walks clockwise around the outer edge of the cave and bows respectfully to each of the fires. Then he ducks out the opening.

"Do all the grandmothers tell you, Miss Alexandra. It be for your good."

Jeremiah leaves before Alexandra has time to thank him.

The grandmothers move with the easy grace of girls. They seem much younger than their wizened faces and white hair suggest. They stand in a row, facing Alexandra. The tallest woman motions for Alexandra to approach. When Alexandra is close enough, she sees that the toothless grandmother has skin as veined and wrinkled as a decaying leaf, but her youthful, black eyes dance. The toothless woman kneels and scoops a burning ember into a large clam shell.

Alexandra recalls one of Marcello's stories. *Dawn Singer say de smoke be de purifying breath of de Great Spirit. Dat why we wash ourself in de fire's gift. Dat smoke clean away de obscuration of de mind and open de heart to hear de voice of de Creator.*

The grandmother cradles the shell in her hand and draws a stream of smoke over her own head and down her body. Then she extends the shell and nods to Alexandra, encouraging her to wash away her impurities.

After Alexandra washes herself in the smoke, three of the

grandmothers nod to the woman who wears two owl feathers in her hair. The woman with feathers carries a bucket of water. She gestures for Alexandra to kneel, then she dips a soft cloth in the warm water and washes the grime from Alexandra's face and arms and legs.

A woman wearing a cowrie necklace approaches. Her clam shell is filled with ground corn. She leads Alexandra next to the main fire in the center and walks around her, stopping at each of the Four Directions to sprinkle cornmeal into the smaller fires. The woman hands Alexandra the shell, gesturing for her to offer the rest of the silky meal to the large fire in the center of the room. As Alexandra scoops up the cornmeal, she senses that whatever she prays for will come to pass.

Help me do something good to honor Jimi's memory, Alexandra says inside her mind.

As soon as she has formed her wish and sprinkled the cornmeal on the fire, the grandmother with blue eyes beats a pattern on her drum. All four grandmothers nod and smile at Alexandra. Then the tallest woman picks up a fringed shawl made of bleached white deerskin and decorated with pearls and shells. She places it around Alexandra's shoulders, takes a pine torch from its holder on the cave wall, and motions for Alexandra to follow.

But Alexandra can't move. Chills wrack her body. She falls to the ground, the world spins. Swamp miasma? Maybe death will come and take her to the Diola Housandioume where contrite souls go to learn from their past life before they are permitted to enter a new body. Alexandra knows she hasn't been good enough to become a benevolent helper like Didima. She broke her promise to Papa. She didn't save Jimi.

Or, maybe she'll be forced to live a tormented life in Mother's Catholic hell. Her thoughts scramble as her world goes dark.

When Alexandra wakes up, she's lying on a wooden pallet in a log house with a thatched roof. The deerskin shawl is wrapped around her. Light, filtered by tree branches, trickles through an open window. The birds are in full song. It must be morning.

She tries to sit up, but she's too weak. She turns her head and sees steam rising from the pot hung in an earthen fireplace. A little girl comes in. Smiles. And disappears. Alexandra hears the little girl shout, "She woke up."

Footsteps draw her attention to the doorway. She thinks she must be dreaming when she sees who's standing there.

"Lulu?" Alexandra stretches out her arms. But Lulu comes in and sits apart from her on a three-legged stool.

"Where am I?" asks Alexandra.

"Like Jeremiah told you, this is Maroon Village. It's hidden away in the swamp that borders the north end of Heaven. Indians and Africans have been living here together for more than a hundred years. They helped the Swamp Fox during the Revolution. Some of them knew your father. They harbor slaves and help them escape. I stay here and at the big house taking care of Sally Ann. I come here to help out when I can. Miranda comes and goes, too. We're working with Mamou to help Heaven's slaves find their way to freedom."

"But Jeremiah ran for miles."

"He was making a confusion path that hounds can't track."

"Where is Mamou?"

"Nobody knows for sure. She sends Jeremiah here with messages that tell the people who're running, when to go and where to meet their helpers."

Lulu takes a silver-handled mirror that belonged to Alexandra's mother out of her shoulder pouch.

"It was all I could carry off without them noticing," Lulu says.

Alexandra snatches it.

Anger flares in Lulu's eyes. "I was going to hand it to you. I'd have been whipped to the bone, if they'd found me taking it out of the big house."

Alexandra swallows her pride. "I'm sorry for grabbing it. Thank you, Lulu."

Alexandra's shocked a second time when Miranda steps through the door. "Moses will be here in five days!"

"Miranda!" Alexandra never thought she'd be so happy to see Mother's head of house.

Miranda feels Alexandra's forehead.

"Your fever's broken. Now we have to make you strong. You have a big trip ahead of you."

Five days later, after resting and choking down bitter herb tonics, Alexandra's strength has returned. Miranda comes in the cabin door at the break of dawn, followed by Lulu.

"She's well enough. Lulu, take her to the pond and get her ready," instructs Miranda. "If Woodpecker gives the signal, take cover, like I taught you."

"I remember what to do," snaps Lulu.

Miranda hands Alexandra a small leather bag tied together with a loop of sinew long enough to slip over her neck. "Oeyi said to give this to you and to tell you that your daddy's people carried it here in the long ago. It's river sand from the banks of the Gambia. Maybe it'll bring you some luck. Lord knows you'll need it."

"Oeyi is..."

"His body may be gone to dust, but his soul's flyin' high and free."

Miranda hands a flax shift to Lulu. "Take Alexandra down to the pond and help her on with this."

The shift looks like the clothes field slaves wear on plantations where cruel masters work them hard.

"I won't wear that."

Miranda grabs Alexandra's wrist and peers into her eyes. "That sheriff's men are looking for you. Some of them aren't convinced you burned to death in that fire. If you want to stay alive, you'll do exactly what I tell you. There's a big reward for your capture. You won't wear this? You eager to share Oeyi's fate?"

Alexandra brushes the tears out of her eyes.

"You are dead to Heaven Hill, dead to the world you've known. You have to get away from here. Do you understand?" Miranda squeezes Alexandra's chin and forces her to look her in the eye. "Old Marcello gave his life to save you. His life! He saw you start to climb down from that tree. He knew Jimi was doomed, but he also knew he could save you by making them think you were in that shop. He never gave you up, even when they..."

Alexandra presses her hands over her ears. Miranda pries them away.

"Even when they put a gun to his head and..."

"Stop!" Alexandra begs.

Miranda pries Alexandra's hands away from her ears.

"... and shot him."

"I know!" Alexandra screams. Her pent sorrow escapes in an anguished wail.

Miranda makes no effort to comfort her.

"Jeremiah was hiding in the forest too. He saw Mr. Masters hand the sheriff a bundle of money. He heard that pretender-to-the-law say there wouldn't be any problem with Mr. Master's deed to Heaven Hill, seeing as you and Jimi died in the fire. Most of them think you're dead, but they didn't find a trace of your body, so they're still lookin'. You're not safe here."

Miranda crosses her arms over her chest. "Your daddy made an arrangement for you and Jimi to run to your grandmother in Charleston."

Alexandra nods. She starts to tell Miranda about Papa's gold, then she thinks better of it.

Miranda continues, "Let me finish. When your father died, your mother changed the plan. She set you up to be an indenture."

"An indenture?" Alexandra can barely breathe. "I knew Mother hated me."

"She was trying to keep you safe. Your grandmother is

staying with Callie's family until things settle down. You can't wander into Charleston and survive without her help.

"Your mother wanted to get you out of sight and out of mind of anyone who might be looking for you. The Marchands live up on the Pee Dee River. No one's likely to look there. Your Mother arranged for you to be Marchand's granddaughter's personal servant. They promised your mother you would live in their big house and have a room of your own. After seven years, you'll be free."

"I'll be twenty-three years old by then."

"Would you rather be dead?

Alexandra reels.

"As soon as you're ready, Lulu will take you to the meeting place where a wagon driver will pick you up and carry you to the Marchand Plantation. The driver's name is Moses. You'll know him by the yellow feather he wears in his hat. Do exactly what he tells you.

"I asked Missus Masters for permission to gather some herbs, so I could help her little girl breathe better. I have to get back in time to give Sally Ann her morning bath, as I'm taking over Lulu's responsibilities until Lulu returns."

"Why don't you just live here?" asks Alexandra.

"Soon as I help all our folks who want to slip away from Heaven, I'll say good-bye to that rotting plantation."

Miranda turns to Lulu. "When she's dressed, take her to the meeting place. As soon as she's safe with Moses, come straight back to the big house. Take the main road. Skulking through the woods will only stir suspicion. And carry yourself with confidence."

Lulu pulls herself up to her full height. "I know what to do and how to do it."

Miranda hands Lulu a clay jar filled with honey comb. "If patrollers stop you, show them your pass and this honey. Tell them you had to stay at your auntie's longer than you expected because your cousin's sick, and her people wanted to make sure you didn't carry the yellow sickness back to Heaven Hill. Tell them you sneaked out when your auntie wasn't looking because you knew Sally Ann needed the honey to make her medicine. Then cough a little. That'll make them step out of your path quick enough."

"I told you, I understand, Miranda." The steely edge of Lulu's voice surprises Alexandra.

"Moses might be delayed," Miranda cautions. "But wait for him."

Miranda presses Mother's rosary into Alexandra's palm, turns, and walks into the shadows.

How dare Mother hire her out as an indenture. Alexandra plans to throw the rosary in the river and let the tide carry it away. Then she thinks that Mother really might have been trying to save her life, and she puts it around her neck.

"Come on," says Lulu. "Follow close."

The trees thin. They come to a pond fed by water trickling through a wood-lined trench. Lulu keeps one eye on the murky water as she soaks a towel and wrings it nearly dry.

Lulu hands the towel to Alexandra. "Time you learn to wash yourself."

Alexandra looks at the scum floating on the surface.

"Last chance to get clean." Lulu says.

"Clean?"

"Hurry up!"

Alexandra slips out of her dress and grimaces as she sponges off.

"Dry off with this," says Lulu, handing Alexandra her dress.

"Use my dress to dry off?"

"We'll have to burn it to ash tonight, if it's safe to light a fire."

"Do you know how much that dress cost?"

"I can imagine." Lulu sighs. "We can't leave any trace you're alive," Lulu says in a flat voice. "You'll have to leave your pantalets behind too."

Alexandra scowls.

Slaves don't wear undergarments.

Alexandra takes off the pantalets. Lulu hands her the shift. She pulls it on and poses, "The gentlemen at my coming-out ball will be stunned into silence when they see my attire." Her bitter-sweet laugh turns into sobs.

Lulu softens. "Miranda told me that your mother set you up with the best family she could find. She said the Marchands are prosperous and well-mannered. They've been told you were educated by nuns when you were an orphan in Martinique. They want you to teach their granddaughter French. It's not all that terrible, you'll be an indenture, not a slave, you may even be allowed to read."

Someone whistles a poor imitation of a mockingbird.

"That's Woodpecker telling us we have to go so we can be in time to meet Moses. I have something to show you on the way." Lulu continues to chatter as they follow a narrow Indian trail through the swamp. "Moses, from the Bliss place, plans to sell three hogs to the Taylors who live near Georgetown. Everyone around here knows Moses, and he always gets a good price for their livestock. No one will harbor a suspicion that you're hiding in his wagon seat compartment.

"He'll pick you up and deliver you to the Marchand's carriage driver, who will meet the wagon at the crossroads west of Georgetown.

"Your mother made the Marchands promise to feed you nourishing food and to go for a doctor if you get sick."

"How generous."

"Don't be so sarcastic. At least you'll be alive."

Alexandra wonders if she deserves to be alive.

Lulu turns left on a deer trail that leads through a grove of birch trees. "Miranda said I could take you to say a final good-bye to your mother."

They come to a bluff that overlooks the river. Alexandra is astonished to see hundreds of grave mounds decorated with flowers, bits of bright cloth, broken pottery, pieces of glass, shells and hand-carved wooden statues.

"It's the slave cemetery. See how the heads of all the graves are pointed toward the river? Some folks believe the water carries the souls of the departed all the way home to Africa." Lulu points to a new grave surrounded by pink flowers. "Your mother's over there."

Alexandra tenses. "Mother would have wanted to be with her family in the Catholic cemetery."

"Jeremiah overheard the assessor say he's thinking of turning your family's cemetery plot into a cotton field."

"And defile the dead?" Alexandra pauses. "He'll go broke planting cotton on this land. That'll serve him right."

Lulu leads Alexandra to the grave. A silver cross is imbedded into newly turned soil.

"Mother's cross!" Alexandra kneels. Begonia cuttings have already been planted all around the perimeter. "This is beautiful."

"Me and Miranda sneaked out after midnight and fixed it up."

Tears flood Alexandra's cheeks.

"We better go. Best leave that mirror and the rosary with your mother," says Lulu softly. "Mamou told me when you lay a mirror so it's shiny side is pointed up to the sky, it'll signal to good spirits to come and carry a soul to the place where folks can decide if they want to tuck themselves into a new body right away or become a guide for a living relative."

Alexandra winds the rosary around the cross and places the mirror, face-up, in the middle of the grave. Then she says the *Hail Mary* Mother loved.

"We have to hurry," says Lulu.

When the sun is directly overhead, they come to a wagon road. They walk in the tracks, through a meadow of grass and wild flowers, until they come to a fallen oak stretched out like a slumbering giant by the side of the road.

"This is the place," Lulu says. Alexandra follows her around to the back of the huge tree. Wooden slats, that can't be seen from the road, have been nailed to the back. Lulu climbs up. "Come on," Lulu say.

When Alexandra joins Lulu, she sees the rope ladder that extends down into the hollowed-out trunk.

"Miranda told me this has been a hiding place for runaways since the time she was a little girl. Hardly any people even know about this road anymore."

Alexandra stiffens when she sees a fly struggling in the spider web stretched across the opening. She hopes Moses will come soon.

"We don't have to go down unless we see a stranger coming. Turn around, I'll fix your hair." Lulu takes a tortoise shell comb out of her apron pocket and works Alexandra's hair into a top-knot.

"Rubies, or the emeralds, Miss Alexandra?"

They burst out laughing as Lulu secures Alexandra's hair with the comb. "Your hairdo will show the Marchands you want to keep up your appearance."

"Thank you," Alexandra says, her voice stripped of pretension.

Stretching out on their backs, they find shapes in the clouds to pass the time. When an angel floats by, Alexandra's consumed by a feeling of emptiness. She will never see Papa or Jimi or Mother again in this life. Are their souls really alive and well in some other world? She hopes so, but part of her fears that life beyond the grave is a story people tell themselves to keep from going crazy. As she is about to give into despair, a hummingbird zips into view, hovers, circles above her head, and flies out of sight. She smiles. "Jimi, is that you?" she whispers.

"What?" asks Lulu.

"Nothing," says Alexandra.

"Why are you smiling?" Lulu asks. Before Alexandra can answer, they see a carriage coming around the bend.

"It's not Moses," Lulu whispers.

They scramble down the ladder, careful not to touch the spider web. Huddling on the rough-hewn floor, they listen to the muffled sound of carriage wheels passing by. When they're sure it's gone, they climb up out of the trunk. The sun's now two fingers above the western horizon.

Alexandra asks the question that's on both of their minds. "What are we supposed to do if Moses doesn't come before dark?" See sees fear flit across Lulu's face. "That note Miranda gave you is only good in the daytime. You'll be in trouble if patrollers catch you outside at night." Lulu trembles. "You have to go," says Alexandra.

"I'm not leaving you here alone."

"Maybe Moses had to fix the wagon wheel. Maybe the business with the hogs took longer than he expected. Whatever happened, you have to get back to the big house before they send someone out to look for you."

"Miranda said to wait."

Alexandra hadn't saved Jimi, but maybe she can help Lulu.

"You have to go now."

"I promised Miranda . . ."

"I don't want you here. I order you to go!" Alexandra says.

Tears fill Lulu's eyes as she slides off the log without another word and shuffles up the road toward the big house.

Alexandra aches to call her back, but she holds her tongue.

Lulu passes out of sight.

Frightened to be all alone? asks the Ahoelra. *Night's coming.*

PART TWO

CHAPTER SEVENTEEN

The sun is a sliver on the rim of the horizon when Alexandra hears hounds braying in the distance. Did Lulu tell the sheriff where to find her? No time to brood. The dogs are closing in.

Think!

Hounds can't track in water.

She climbs down the trunk and races toward ribbons of black water that spread through the mangrove and cypress swamp. The sound of hounds howling wanes, then bursts into a cacophony of triumphant barks. In the distance, she hears a man shout, "She was hiding in this tree trunk!"

Pushing her fear of snakes and alligators out of her mind, Alexandra wades into waist-high water near a stand of reeds. She ducks under the surface and pushes herself along the bottom until she comes to a tree root protruding into the water. She breaks off a reed to use as a straw to draw air, and takes hold of the root to pull herself farther below the surface.

She feels the vibration of running feet. Hears the muffled shouts of men. Pulls herself closer to the muddy bottom. A school of tiny silver fish brushes her cheek. The distorted braying of hounds reverberates through the water. Even though it's murky, she can make out a dark shape swimming toward her. Something thrashes; she hears a yelp; tendrils of blood spiral toward her. Had an alligator just attacked a dog?

She hears the muffled sound of men whistling their dogs out of the water. She waits. Listens. Thinks she's alone. She swims toward the bank of the river. She's about to break the surface when something clamps on to her leg. She opens her mouth to scream. Foul water fills her lungs. Gasping for breath, she's yanked to the surface by an unkempt monster. The huge, bearded man holds her upside down by her ankles. When she stops vomiting, he lays her out on the ground and clamps his hand over her mouth.

He has pale skin, greasy brown hair, and eyes the color of wet ash. One of his front teeth is chipped, and the other is missing. His body reeks of fish and tobacco. He digs his filthy fingernails into her shoulder and pulls her toward him.

"You're hurting me!" she says.

"Shet yer mouth!" He pulls a hunting knife from his belt and presses the razor-edge to her throat. "Or I'll shet it fer good."

She clamps her teeth so tight, her jaw aches. He heaves her over his shoulder and runs along the edge of the swamp, keeping a steady pace as he traces his way through the web of swampy channels. Trees thin. He splashes across a marsh without breaking stride, leaps onto the shore of an outcropping of land, and continues to run until he reaches a clearing where three crude cabins squat in a meadow of matted-down grass. He dumps Alexandra on the ground near the largest cabin in front of two men armed with guns and knives. Their features appear similar to her captor's, except for the red hair of the youngest; she guesses they're family.

All three wear tattered moccasins laced up to their knees and rain-stained, broad-brimmed, leather hats. They're sinewy and disheveled. Her wet dress clings to her. The unsated hunger in their eyes fills her with dread.

"You check this black bitch for a brand?" asks the one with grey streaks in his beard.

"Weren't time, Pa," says her abductor. "Sheriff's dogs was

after her. Like I said, weren't no time to make a careful check."

"Sheriff's dogs? I told you to skedaddle if the law got close!"

"They never seen me, Pa. I was hid up in a tree when I saw a big ol' gator take one o' their dogs. Soon as they changed directions and ran up stream, I dropped down, quiet as a weasel, and grabbed the girl."

"Sheriff ain't got no jurisdiction this side of the river, Pa," chimes in the younger brother.

"I ask your opinion, Red?"

"No, Pa," Red says, as chastened as a small child.

Pa turns back to Alexandra's kidnapper. "Now might be the time for you to find out if she's marked, Clem," Pa says, his toe tapping with impatience.

Before Alexandra realizes what he's doing, Clem yanks her shift off. She sinks to the ground, covering her private parts with her hands.

Clem grabs her by the hair and yanks her to her feet. "Arms to your sides. Turn when I say turn!"

When she refuses to move, Clem leans into her from behind, wraps one boney arm around her waist, and flicks his knife back and forth inches from her face with his free hand.

"Put that away. Spoil her looks, and her price'll drop," says Pa.

When Pa strides toward her, she sees he's missing three of his front teeth. His breath, a mixture of rotten eggs and something dead, nearly makes her gag. "Stand up straight and let us have a look." He points the barrel of a flintlock pistol at Alexandra's head.

She drops her hands to her sides and makes a mask of her face, determined not to give any of these men the satisfaction of seeing her fear.

"Turn," says the one they call Pa.

She senses Pa's eyes slide over her body.

"Ain't branded," says Clem.

"Not even marked by a whip," adds Red. Then he grabs her hands and inspects her palms. "Hands is soft as cotton balls."

"Dusky for a house darkie," says Clem. "Nothing wrong with her shape, though." He moves behind her, cups her breasts and squeezes. She clamps her teeth together as he rubs his stubbled face across the back of her neck.

"Want me to see if she's pure?" asks Clem.

"As you will. But spoil her, and I'll spoil you," says Pa.

Clem scoops Alexandra into his arms and carries her to an old quilt laid out on the grass like it was waiting for a picnic. He lays her out on her back and straddles her chest, with his head facing her feet.

"Could use a hand. Git that, Red? 'Twere one o' them puns."

Clem forces her legs open; Red spreads her legs and leans the full weight of his knees across her feet.

"No! Please!" Alexandra shouts, angry at herself for losing control.

Red slides his little finger inside Alexandra's female part, smiling as she writhes in pain.

"I'll be damned," says Red, clicking his tongue. "Tight as a clam."

"Make sure she stays that way," warns Pa.

Clem jumps to his feet and tosses Alexandra her clothes. Trembling, she pulls the wet shift over her head. Red opens the door to the largest shack and shoves Alexandra inside. The stench of sweat and human waste blasts her. Red slams the door and bars it from the outside.

Streaks of light filter through misfit boards. Alexandra's eyes adjust. The room is long and narrow and reeks of fear. She hears breathing. A child coughs. Her eyes adjust, and she makes out the shapes of people. She jumps when someone touches her on the shoulder.

"It's me."

"Lulu?" Alexandra hugs Lulu and starts to whimper.

Lulu disengages. "Nasty ol' boys did de same to me. Put it from your mind."

Put a thing like that from her mind? Alexandra's thoughts shift. "I just told you to leave that log because I wanted you to be safe. "

"I figured."

"How did you wind up here?"

Lulu takes hold of Alexandra's hand and leads her to the back corner. They turn their backs away from the others and squat down.

"When I was almost to the house, that boy with the red devil-hair jumped down from a tree and grabbed me. 'I gots a pass,' I told him. He crumpled my papers and slipped a rope around my neck, like I was a dog, then he headed toward the swamp. I had to run to keep the rope from choking me. When he tripped over a rock, I looked back toward Heaven. People were shouting and running every which way. The kitchen was on fire."

"What happened to the big house?"

"I don't know.

"Alexandra, we have to do whatever we can to survive." Lulu whispers. "I have a plan. Some of the sheriff's men are looking for you. They know Alexandra Degambia hasn't got a sister. So, if these fools ask who you are, tell them I'm your sister. We can say we were born in the same slave cabin to the same mother."

"You? My sister?" Alexandra laughs without meaning to.

"So that's how it is."

"Lulu, I'm sorry, I'd be proud to say you're my sister."

"Like Miranda told me, the truth comes out when your feet are to the fire. Stay away from me." Lulu makes her away to the other side of the room.

Before Alexandra can figure out how to make things right, Clem flings the door open. "Come outta here, y'all. Move!"

Pa fires his pistol in the air, and the slaves scramble out into the blinding light.

Alexandra sees Red herding four strong, young men bound together by a chain looped through thick metal neck bands. The metal bar strung through their hand and leg irons causes them to move like they're old. Scars crisscross their sweaty backs.

Clem shoves three young women about the same age as Alexandra and Lulu into a line. They hold their heads high with the kind of pride that says, do what you want to my body, but you can't touch my spirit.

Two little girls, one about seven- or eight-years-old, and the other no older than three, cling to the youngest woman. Their wide eyes are fixed on the rawhide whip looped around Red's shoulder.

Two old women stand apart from the others, their eyes watchful in their haggard faces. One of them has a severe limp, the other, a shriveled eye socket. Their metal neck bands must be burning hot on a day like this.

Pa picks up a pointed stick and draws a line in a patch of dirt on the far end of the meadow where no grass grows. "Little ones ova heah! Toes on the line. Step it up, now!"

The little girls don't move.

Kneeling, the young mother gathers the little girls close. "Go on, babies, like we practiced. Don' give nobody a cause to hurt y'all."

"Come with me, Mama," begs the smallest girl.

Red cracks his whip and stirs up a clod of dirt.

The young woman smiles and nods, encouraging the little girls. They inch forward until their toes are on the line. The big girl holds the little girl's hand tight to stop her from running back to her mother.

Red shoves Alexandra and Lulu into line next to the girls. Then he snaps his fingers and motions for the other young women to line up on the other side of Alexandra.

Clem picks up a pair of neck bands and a link of chain and starts toward Lulu and Alexandra.

"Wait till they're shined," says Pa. He pulls the chain that connects the men's neck irons tighter, loops the end around a tree, and secures it with a twisted wire.

The woman with the missing eye moves behind the little girls and leans down to speak to them.

Pa grabs her by the arm. "I tell you to move?"

"Beg your pardon, Masta," she says in a sweet-pea voice that doesn't match her aging body.

"Don' hurt my mother!" shouts one of the young men.

"Hold your tongue, Emory," cautions the old woman.

Pa pushes the old woman into the line beside the littlest girl. Then he nods at Red, who saunters over to Emory, draws out his whip, and lays a lash across his chest. Emory barely grimaces as blood trickles from his wound.

"Don' hit my Daddy!" screams the smallest girl.

"Don' worry, Angela," says Emory. "It was jes' a tickle."

Clem kneels next to Angela, winds his hand through her hair and pulls it taut. He laughs when she kicks at him.

"Angela! You be a good girl and tell the man you're sorry for speakin' outta turn," says Emory.

"Angela, do like your daddy told you," says the young mother.

Angela presses her lips tight.

Red swishes his whip back and forth in front of Angela's face. Before Red can lay down a lash, Pa grabs the whip out of his hand.

"Want the speculator to think we got uppity slaves?" demands Pa.

"She was lookin' at me funny," whines Red.

"That's 'cause you're funny to look at," says Clem.

"Shet up!" Red shouts.

"Gonna make me?"

"I'll make you," says Pa.

Pa grabs them both by their ears and twists hard enough to bring tears to their eyes.

Alexandra now sees that those grown men are more than six feet tall, but Pa's half a head taller. The sons are lean muscle and sinew. Pa's thick as an ox.

"Sorry, Pa," his sons say in unison.

He lets them go and turns toward the slaves. "Oil yerselves up," commands Pa.

Clem pops the cork top off a clay pot filled with fat and sets it on the ground in front of the slaves. Pa keeps his flintlock cocked and ready as Red releases the men from the tree. Lulu copies the women and children and slips out of her clothes.

Alexandra stands perfectly still, arms akimbo.

Clem moves toward her, ready to crack his whip. "Do a good job, or I'll do it for you," he says, fondling her behind.

She wills herself to look indifferent. He loses interest.

The oldest of the woman steps forward, dips her hand in the grease, and smears it on her arms. "Dis de same stuff they use to polish horses 'afore a sale," she says. "Won' hurt you none." The woman gestures to Lulu and Alexandra. Both stare at the jar.

"Trust me. You don't want those boys to do it for you," says the woman.

Alexandra takes off her clothes. The women dip their hands into the jar and smear their bodies with slime that makes the day's rising heat even more oppressive.

When they're greased, Clem hands out fresh rosemary branches. Alexandra longs to apologize to Lulu. She tries to catch her friend's eye as they crush rosemary needles in their palms and rub their bodies with the fragrant herb.

"Toes on the line," Pa says.

The women and children scramble to obey. Pa motions for the tallest of the young women to step forward. She folds her arms over her ample breasts and shuffles toward him.

"You the one whose mama popped out seventeen live 'uns?" Pa asks.

The sound of approaching horses draws their attention to the road.

"Put on these clothes!" commands Pa, gathering the filthy shifts and distributing clean hand-me-downs.

Just as Alexandra's slipping a worn calico over her head, a cream-colored carriage pulled by four black horses rounds the bend. The mulatto driver's eyes are the same faded blue as those of the elderly man who peers out from the silk curtain hung in the carriage window.

The slaves step back to let the carriage pass, but the driver reins the horses to a stop. Clem leans toward Pa, whose face is screwed into a frown. "Funny conveyance for a speculator."

"That's not the speculator," Pa whispers.

"Shit!" says Clem, straightening up to his full height.

The coachman climbs down and summons Pa with a nod of his head. When Pa's face-to-face, the coachman announces his master, "Monsieur Noel Marchand." He offers his hand and helps the elderly man step from the carriage.

"How do you do, Sir?" says Pa, extending his hand.

Monsieur Marchand ignores Pa's gesture.

"To what do we owe the pleasure of y'all's esteemed company?" asks Pa.

"Je crois que vous tenez ici une chère femme pour qui j'ai donné beaucoup d'argent," says Monsieur Marchand in a silken voice.

Miranda said Mother had given Monsieur Marchand money. But it was the other way around.

Pa stares.

"You are unacquainted with the French language? Allow me to translate," says the coachman. "You have, in your company, a young woman for whose indenture Monsieur has paid a handsome sum. Monsieur has no interest in detaining you, or in revealing your location to the authorities, as long as you release the servant for whom he has given fair price. His widowed daughter is to marry, and he wishes to present her with a servant who speaks French, so her little girl may learn to converse with people of culture."

Pa puffs out his chest. "You're mistaken. Ain't no slaves who speak no French in this group."

"Not what our man told Monsieur," says the coachman.

"What man?" asks Clem.

"Shut it, Clem," Pa barks.

"There will be dire repercussions for your enterprise should we inform the authorities about the business you're conducting in stolen slaves," says Monsieur Marchand, using perfect English.

Pa plants his feet.

"Y'all cain't roll in heah and steal our property." sputters Red.

Pa kicks Red in the shin. Then he turns to Monsieur Marchand. "Which one is she?" Pa asks.

"Qui parle Français?" asks Monsieur Marchand.

While Alexandra decides whether or not to respond, Lulu says, "Je parle Français, Monsieur."

"Mademoiselle Degambia?" asks the driver, breaking into a smile as he steps forward.

"Mais, oui," Lulu says. "Please call me Alexandra."

"She's lying," blurts Alexandra.

The driver raises an eyebrow, indicating his disapproval of Alexandra's outburst, and gestures to Lulu to follow him.

Alexandra steps forward. "But . . ."

Lulu scowls at Alexandra. "Ingrate! After all I've done for you, despite the deep hue of your color." She turns to Monsieur Marchand and says, "I look forward to meeting the little girl." Then she curtseys and drops her eyes.

The driver drapes a cloak over Lulu's shoulders and helps her into the carriage. The old man opens a purse. Pa looks inside.

"My lips is sealed," says Pa.

"Thank you for your cooperation." The old man places the purse into Pa's palm.

"Anytime at all," says Pa, counting the money.

Lulu opens the carriage drape and speaks loud enough for Alexandra to hear her say, "How did you know how to find me?"

"En Français, s'il vous plaît," says the old man.

"Bien sur."

They drive off before Alexandra has a chance to hear Monsieur Marchand's response. She swallows her tears, takes a deep breath, and wills herself to be strong.

A peculiar look lights up Pa's face as he fondles his payment. "Red, ride on over and see if you can find out how much it would be worth to tell authorities that I know where the Degambia girl is. By my lights, there's a price on her head."

"I'll go, Pa," volunteers Clem.

"Your name Red?" Pa turns to the son with the flaming hair. Ride the horse."

"Yes, Sir!" Red jumps on the back of a skinny grey horse and trots out of sight.

Pa hands Clem the rifle. "Take the men around back to do their business."

As the men shuffle around to the back of the shed, the littlest girl starts to cry. "Where you takin' my daddy?"

Pa slaps her to the ground. "Shet your ugly mouth!"

The little girl hugs her knees to her chest and hides her face.

Her mother kneels by her side. "Stop cryin', Angela."

Pa draws back his foot to kick the wailing child.

Angela screams, "Papa, help me!"

Pa withdraws his foot and laughs.

The slaves turn toward Pa, rattling their arm chains and chanting in a language Alexandra's never heard. They run toward Pa, their speed barely impeded by the chain that connects their leg irons.

Clem takes aim.

"Don't shoot! They's numba'-one boys," shouts Pa.

Clem swings the barrel of the rifle around and aims at the little girl. The slaves lower their arms and cast their eyes to the ground. Pa yanks her to her feet.

"Mama!" cries the little girl.

Pa jabs the butt of his flintlock into Angela's back. Angela lays on the ground, limp as a rag.

The youngest woman rushes toward Clem, her eyes blazing. She scoops up Angela and runs toward the trees.

A shot rings out.

"Millie!" shouts the woman's husband.

"Emory . . ." calls the young woman, her voice faint. A circle of red blooms on her back as she crumples to the ground. She reaches for Angela, who is regaining consciousness. The woman's body goes limp. The little girl hugs her mother.

The older girl runs over to help the little girl up. "Your mama would want you to be brave." Angela won't let go of her mother. "Come on, Angela, put your toes on the line like your mother would want you to," the oldest girl urges.

"White Devil!" screams Emory.

Emory lunges at Clem, but he pulls back when Clem grabs Angela and presses a knife to her throat.

Pa circles Clem, who's grinning like he's won a prize. Pa takes his axe out of the loop on his belt. He screams, "Idiot! That girl was one of the breeders!" He smashes Clem in the temple with the blunt end of his axe. Clem stumbles and falls. When he's down, Pa kicks him in the groin. Clem screams, then passes out.

Alexandra hears something that sounds like thunder, but there's not a cloud in the sky. She follows Pa's gaze down the road.

"Goddam it!" Pa shouts, pointing his pistol at Angela as he unfastens the chain that binds the male slaves together. He turns to the men. "Put my boy and the dead girl in the barn. Bar it shut from the outside. Hurry up!" Pa presses the butt of his flintlock into Angela's temple for emphasis.

The biggest of the slaves heaves Clem over his shoulder. Emory lifts Millie, kisses her forehead and heads toward the shelter. Pa keeps the barrel of his flintlock butted up against Angela's head.

"Pickaninny dies if any one of y'all makes the wrong move."

Pa keeps his gun trained on Angela and kicks dirt over the pools of blood.

Pa's distracted. Alexandra looks around for an escape route. If she can make it to the trees, she might have a chance. She steps out to run; the oldest woman leans close and whispers, "You wanna git dat baby kilt?" Alexandra moves back in line.

"I want Mama!" wails Angela.

Alexandra searches for words. "Your Mama lives in your heart now. She'd be proud to see you're a brave girl."

Angela straightens up.

Alexandra watches the dust cloud rolling toward them, which seems strange since the air is as still as death. Then she hears people break into song, singing praises to the Lord.

The two slaves return.

"Toes on the line. I'll be watchin' y'all." Pa releases Angela and fondles the deer-antler handle of his hunting knife.

Alexandra's stomach knots when the slave coffle comes into view. She's seen long lines of slaves pass down the road that leads past Heaven Hill. Until now, she never paid much attention. As they come closer, she sees that a slave boy dressed in a blue suit beats a drum as he leads a line of about fifty men and women linked together four abreast by a chain strung through the metal eyes of their neck collars.

Pa's eyes alight on the blood splattered on Emory's pants. "When they ask about them stains, tell 'em you just butchered a hog."

The speculator, a tall, thin man dressed in a beaver stove pipe and black tailcoat, rides toward Pa on a high-stepping bronze-and-tan horse. When he raises his brass-tipped staff, the slave coffle stops and the singing ceases. Even the birds fall silent.

Alexandra and the others stand in a single row, spit-polished like old shoes that can barely hold a shine.

The speculator dismounts, his tongue flicks in and out of his mouth like a lizard's. He removes the kid glove on his right hand and walks down the row of slaves, stopping at the prettiest of the young women. He slides his manicured hand underneath her shift to feel her breast. She stands statue-still, her eyes fixed on the middle distance.

Without warning, the speculator yanks her shift off over her head. It sickens Alexandra to see his eyes roam over the young woman's body. He turns her around and cups his hand over her buttocks as if he's checking the muscles on a horse. She keeps her hands to her sides as he pries her mouth open and inspects her teeth.

"Number two," he says.

"She's a numba' one, and you know it," says Pa.

As soon as the speculator moves down the line, the young woman pulls her shift back on over her head.

"She's a numba' one," repeats Pa.

The speculator steps toward Emory. "That boy give you trouble, Sir?" the speculator asks as he runs his riding crop along a line of dried blood.

"No, Sir," replies Pa.

The speculator rolls his eyes and waits for an explanation.

"He was butchering a hog, Sir. Woulda changed his clothes, but you came earlier than we expected."

"That true, Boy?" asks the speculator.

"Yes, Sir," mutters Emory.

Suddenly the speculator grabs Alexandra's arm and pulls her out of the line. He runs his fingers over the palm of her hand. "Speak up and tell me about yourself, Girl." He inspects her skin. "You got mighty soft hands for a field worker."

"I've been in the big house all my life." She'll be dead if they find out who she is and give her over to the sheriff for a reward.

"In a big house? With that dark skin?" inquires the speculator.

"Hasn't been touched by a man," Pa says.

"You pure?" asks the speculator, raising one eyebrow.

Alexandra's mind races, searching out the right thing to say.

"Speak up, now," the speculator says in a dangerously soft voice.

"I've never known a man," Alexandra says.

"You have a high tone for a dark nigger. Which place you come from?" the speculator demands.

"Virginie," says Pa, quick to cut her off.

"That why you speak so fine?" asks the speculator. "You've been in one of those fancy Virginia houses that coddles its slaves? Don' know who'd want a girl like you in their house. Hands are too soft to work the fields. Numba three," says the speculator.

"She's a virgin. She's a two," Pa says, holding the man's eyes in a steady glare.

Alexandra's mind spins as she tries to think of a way to work herself into a position in a house. She can't let them know she can read and write and play the violin, and speak French and Greek. An idea flies into her mind. "I can sew, and I can make lace, which is why I was in the big house."

"She can make lace," says Pa, "and she's pure. She's a numba two at the least. And that high yellow breeder over there, she's a numba one."

Clem, who must have roused himself, pounds on the inside of the barn wall.

"Damn horse," says Pa, "like to kick the door down one of these times."

Pa motions for the speculator to come close. Alexandra overhears the speculator tell Pa he's going to march the coffle down the main street of Georgetown to the harbor where they'll be boarded onto schooners headed for Charleston. Charleston! Her chance to escape and make her way to Grand-mère's house.

She'll have to keep her head down when they go through Georgetown in case the sheriff's men are looking for her. If she can just get to Charleston, she'll try to escape. She'll tell Judge Calvin about the gold and ask for his help.

The speculator presses some money into Pa's outstretched hand, then he turns to his men. "Chain 'em. Leave the little ones free."

His beefy assistants slide off their horses, collars and chains slung over their shoulders. They walk toward the line of slaves.

CHAPTER EIGHTEEN

$\mathcal{A}$lexandra is surprised by how heavy the neck collar is, and how hot to the touch. From sitting out in the sun, she supposes. A big man with vulture eyes and a black handle-bar mustache chains her to the end of a line in a row of four, next to one of the young women from the shack. The neck of the white-haired woman chained in front of her is rubbed raw in places and scabbed over in others. Alexandra runs her fingers under the steel band, grateful she has one free hand.

When the slaves are hooked together, the skinny mulatto on the horse at the head of the line shouts in a shrill voice, "No talkin'. No laggin'. Sing when I say. We'll stop along the road ever so often for y'all to do your business. Follow the rules, or suffer the whip."

"Forward!" commands the speculator.

Untethered young children try their best to keep up as the coffle moves down the road. Alexandra sees Angela up ahead, sitting on the ground, sucking her thumb. A man on horseback scoops her up and starts over to the wagon where babies too young to walk have been set on the laps of slightly older children.

"No room. Gotta pick up that hog. Don't want it walking and burning off fat," says the speculator. The man drops Angela to the ground like she's a bag of rice. The speculator leans down from his horse and tells the little girl, "Keep up, or the buzzards'll eat you."

Angela doesn't even blink when he cracks his horse quirt in front of her face.

Chains clink to the rhythm of all those feet marching in unison. In a few seconds Alexandra will pass close enough to grab Angela's hand and pull her along. She's about to reach down when a guard rides up fingering his rawhide whip.

Angela looks into Alexandra's eyes, pleading for help. But Alexandra turns away. As soon as she's passed by, an image of Jimi's face pressed up against the window flashes in her mind. Shame washes over her. She didn't save her brother; she didn't save Angela. But she spared her own life and saved herself from being whipped.

Alexandra is shocked out of her dark mood when a white boy with hazel eyes weaves through the coffle line, holding Angela's hand. He looks to be nine or ten years old. At first Alexandra thinks he must be the son of one of the guards, and it strikes her as odd that he would be helping a slave. Then she sees his calloused feet are bare and his britches are tattered, and she realizes he must be an indenture on his way to being contracted out when the slaves are sold. The two children walk along, close enough for Alexandra to hear what they're saying.

The little boy says, "My name's John Fowler. What's yours?" Angela doesn't answer, but she lets him pull her along.

Then John Fowler says, "I heard what happened. Your mama's watchin' over you from heaven. Could be she knows my daddy."

The man in the blue coat at the front of the line shouts, "Sing it out, now! So, the Lord on high can hear y'all."

The slaves sing:

When I get to heben, I gonna sing and shout,
Tryin' to make heben my home.
Ain't nobody there gonna put me out,
Tryin' to make heben my home.

When John Fowler starts to sing, Alexandra joins in, surprised to find the song makes her feel better.

After a few hours, Alexandra tries to divert her attention from her hunger pangs by finding shapes in the clouds billowing up from the west. Rain would make their plight more miserable in some ways, but it would slake her thirst.

A new song starts up:

When Israel was in Egypt's land,
Let my people go!
Oppressed so hard they could not stand,
Let my people go!
Go down, Moses,
Way down in Egypt's land.
Tell old Pharaoh
To let my people go!
Let my people go . . .

Who will let them go? Who will let her go?

Thunder rumbles. The first round of the storm passes over without shedding a drop. Lightning sparks in the next crowd of clouds. The air becomes thick and hot. Alexandra's collar burns her throat. *Please, let it rain*, she prays.

By the time they turn off the road onto a wagon path, fireflies blink on and off. They pass through a cow pasture and come to a haystack packed as tall as the two-story barn it leans against.

The speculator steps up on a tree stump. "Heed my words!" he says. "We're gonna unhook you. Try to run, and y'all's heels will be cut. That's all that'll happen—if you're lucky."

The slaves huddle, casting their eyes to the ground, waiting to be unlocked. The guards sit straight as tin soldiers and trot their horses to form a perimeter around the barn grounds. One of them raises his pistol in the air, fires and calls out, "You'll get my bullet between your eyes if you try to run."

When the sun sinks below the horizon, it starts to rain. Frogs start up a serenade. A man who reminds Alexandra of Papa unlocks the chain on her neck collar.

"Thank you," she says.

"Better get some food before it's gone," he says. Then he shuffles toward an open fire where soup bubbles in a suspended iron kettle covered with an oiled cloth to keep out the rain.

"One chicken for a hundred people in that pot," whispers the high-yellow woman Pa claimed was a number one.

Alexandra hears Angela's hacking cough and watches the little girl creep over to the woman. Alexandra edges close enough to hear their conversation. "I feel poorly, Auntie," says the tiny girl as she reaches for her aunt's hand.

The aunt pulls away. "Fin' yo'self a dry place to lay your head. You be better in the morning."

Angela shuffles away.

"Aren't you her aunt?" asks Alexandra.

"Don' be judgin' me, Miss High-and-Mighty. Ain' no time to be catching someone's sickness. We gonna be up on de block. De rich Marses don' want nothin' to do wid no sick slave."

The woman snatches a wooden bowl and a mussel shell to use as a spoon, then strolls over to get her portion of stew.

Alexandra fumes. How can this woman ignore her niece? Then it comes to her that she has no right to judge.

The white boy comes up and interrupts her thoughts. "Howdy, Ma'am. My name's John Fowler."

Alexandra doesn't dare use her real name. "My name's— Louise."

"You know that little girl who's coughin' up a storm?" asks John. "Angela's her name." John Fowler holds two bowls of stew in his hands. Alexandra's stomach turns when she sees a chicken feather floating on the surface. "You see which way she went?" he asks.

"I saw her go over by the barn. I'll help you find her," says Alexandra.

Lightning cracks the sky open, and it starts to pour.

They weave their way around a small garden plot that's gone to seed and find Angela huddled close to the barn, shivering. Her bare arms are wrapped around her knees. Alexandra feels her forehead.

"She's burning up," says Alexandra. "We need to get her out of the rain."

"Maybe we could take her inside the barn," says John Fowler.

Alexandra picks Angela up. They steal around to the back of the barn where a young man, atop a grey roan, holds his lantern high so he can see any runaways who might cross his path. Alexandra grabs John Fowler's sleeve and pulls him back around the corner of the barn, out of the sight of the guard.

"I saw a chain stretched across the entrance, but it's loose and the door's not shut tight. Think you can slip inside and push it open wide enough for us to squeeze through?

John Fowler takes a look. "I'll try to do that, Ma'am."

When the guard in front of the barn shifts his attention to the fence-line, Alexandra holds Angela close and follows John Fowler around the corner. He pulls the door open as far as it will go, and they slip into the barn which is lit by a lantern hung on the wall. The roof's leaking, but there are some dry spaces. Alexandra carries Angela to a place where the floor's covered with hay. She sits and pulls Angela onto her lap. John Fowler holds a mussel shell filled with soup to Angela's lips. Angela shakes her head.

"My tummy hurts," says the little girl, grimacing.

Alexandra and John Fowler huddle close, with Angela between them. Alexandra vows to stay awake and guard John and Angela, but after a few hours, she can't keep her eyes open. Toward morning, Alexandra wakes up and sees John kneeling next to Angela. The rain has stopped and the moonlight that streams through a broken place in the roof pools around the little girl. She looks peaceful curled up on the dry pile of hay.

Alexandra feels her forehead. Cool to the touch. Her hope soars, then she sees the sadness on John Fowler's face, and she feels for Angela's pulse.

"No!" Alexandra cries out. She leans close to the sweet little face. "I'm sorry. I'm sorry," she whispers. She's about to surrender to her grief when she sees the stricken look on John Fowler's face. She has to be strong for this dear little boy. She smooths the hair out of John Fowler's eyes and hugs him.

He whispers, "They might throw her body down a dry well if they find her. I saw them do that to a baby."

Alexandra says, "Let's slip outside and find a nice place to lay her to rest. I'll carry her. See if you can find a long stick for digging. Be careful not to let the guards see you."

The guard in front of the barn is turned the other way. Alexandra holds Angela close and follows John Fowler out the door. They flatten themselves against the barn wall and inch their way around the corner. The speculator's men have maintained their positions around the perimeter, but they're half asleep, and no one pays them any mind as they sneak to the garden plot on the south side of the barn, aided by the light of a bright moon.

They stop at the east end of the garden where bean vines grow up the trunk of an oak tree.

"This is a good place," says Alexandra.

John uses a branch to dig a shallow grave.

"Put some of that long grass on the bottom to soak up the rain and make it softer," says Alexandra.

John pulls up fistfuls of knee-high grass and smooths it into a bed on the bottom of the grave, then Alexandra sets Angela down, tears off a swath from the bottom of her dress and covers Angela. She shovels dirt over the perfect little body with her bare hands and breaks off a twig of flowering Oleander to set on the grave.

John binds strands of a vine around pine twigs to make a

cross. He lays it at the top of the little grave. "Daddy, Angela's a good girl. Help her find her mama, please, Sir."

Slowly, careful not to attract attention, Alexandra dances as much of the *Nyakul* funeral dance as she can remember. Very softly, she sings the Diola song Mamou used to sing to her when she was a little girl.

"Was that an African dance?" John Fowler asks.

Alexandra nods.

"Is that where you're from?"

"My people came from there. It's getting light. We better go," says Alexandra.

Alexandra's surprised when John reaches out and takes her hand. "My daddy told me if Jesus were alive, he would be an abolitionist."

When they're close to where people are sleeping, Alexandra pulls her hand away. "Better not hold my hand, and don't let these people know about your daddy being an abolitionist."

"I understand, Ma'am."

The rooster crows in the dawn, and the camp begins to stir.

"Rise and shine," calls out the speculator. "We have a boat to catch at the end of this march."

Four days later, they arrive in Georgetown. Alexandra soon learns she needn't have worried about being recognized. As the slaves are paraded down the main street, townspeople look away. She'd done the same when coffles passed by Heaven. It seemed as though if she didn't look at the slaves, they didn't exist. The coffles passed by like a dream, out of sight, out of mind.

She turns her thoughts to her escape. If she can sneak away when they reach Charleston, she will try to get to her grandmother's and retrieve the papers that prove she's free.

CHAPTER NINETEEN

As the schooner nears Charleston, the slaves are permitted to stand at the rail to quiet their stomachs by breathing in sea air—or by retching over the side. Alexandra's certain she's being turned inside-out and that she'll die before they reach the port. But when they're herded onto dry land, her stomach settles.

She guesses the guards will unchain them when they get close to the auction block. She figures there will be distractions, and if she's alert enough, she'll be able to fade into the shadows and find Grand-mère.

Doubt assails her as they're herded down King Street. Alexandra's eyes stray to the sidewalk where a little black boy dressed like a carriage driver stands and rings a silver bell. As she passes by him, she reads the note attached to his top hat, "Boy for sale."

Up the street, a woman dressed in a calico dress and a matching head wrap stands beside three little girls who sit on overturned boxes, their hands folded on their laps. The sign next to them reads, "Mother with three well-mannered children. Together, or separately."

Alexandra gags. The metal band cuts into her throat.

"Stand up straight," says the woman next to her. "You're choking me."

Alexandra shuffles forward. It seems like kindness has been drained from the world. The coffle turns and marches past the south edge of town. They come to three large, white-washed barns.

Burly guards separate men from women and herd them into two identical buildings.

Once they're all inside, the massive doors are barred. Alexandra discovers the windows are up at least twenty feet, near the ceiling. There will be no escape from this place.

An old man with kind, sad eyes unlocks the women's neck band chains.

"Thank you," says Alexandra, rolling her head to loosen up her muscles. When she reaches back to soothe her neck, her hand comes away streaked with blood.

"Strip down and wash all your parts," says an enormous woman with grey-tan skin and muddy brown eyes.

Last month Alexandra would have preferred an easy death to revealing her naked body to people she'd never met. Now, she doesn't hesitate to slip out of her dress.

A big iron tub squats in the middle of the building. It's lit up by torches set into the sconces in the plastered walls. The women are given rags as they step up to the tub, six at a time, and sponge off. Now Alexandra knows what Mamou meant when she said life is like a hurricane that can change directions before you have a chance to blink. At Heaven Hill, Lulu had bathed Alexandra in a porcelain tub refilled with fresh, warm water by a trio of house slaves.

"Let me get your back, Baby," says an old woman with a patched eye. The woman has a soft touch. Alexandra closes her eyes and imagines she's back home. But she pulls away when she feels the woman's hands creep toward her private parts.

The old woman rattles on as if Alexandra never pulled away. "Seen how you and de little boy cared for dat poor baby girl. It's plain as day you ain't used to slave ways." The woman pauses. "Dey catch you and carry you down from up North, Baby?"

Alexandra tenses as the woman continues. "Dos devils be sorry 'nough when dey stands 'afore de Maker at de Judgment. One piece of advice: don' be speaking' no high-born talk wid dese folks. Dat get you into a mess of trouble."

A hefty butter-cream woman wearing a faded blue dress and a starched white apron with a matching headdress struts through the door. Eyes drop. Silence falls. "Time to put on your new clothes," she announces.

The old woman leans toward Alexandra. "Dey gonna dress us for de parade."

Alexandra falls into the back of the line so she can watch and see what she's expected to do. More than a hundred slaves, ranging in hue from cream to night-sky, line up behind a matronly mulatto woman wearing the cast-offs of some wealthy patroness with a preference for pastels. Three long tables, marked 'one,' 'two' and 'three,' are piled up with clothing in the north end of the room.

Alexandra's would-be mentor leans close and whispers, "Make dat inspector feel important when you stand afore her."

Alexandra gets close to the front of the line and notices that the inspector's face is pinched into a mask of exaggerated self-importance. Penciled-on eyebrows arch up at the ends making her look more like a clown than the elegant lady she's trying to emulate. As each slave steps forward, the inspector woman traces the line of breast and buttock with the long, pointed fingernail of her index finger. Young, light-skinned women are directed to "Table Number One" where they're given pressed calico dresses with headdresses to match and white linen collars, some with lace, designed to set off the features of their high-yellow faces. It's obvious Number Ones will work in fancy houses.

The majority of the women are delivered to "Table Number Two", where "gently-worn" dresses are handed out.

The women and girls directed to "Table Number Three" are old or lame or dark-hued. Number Threes are given flaxen shifts, similar to the one Lulu gave Alexandra to wear, except they're clean and the holes have been mended.

Alexandra's so determined to figure out how to get to Table Number One, she doesn't realize she's arrived at the front of the line. She stands naked, inches from this woman who will decide her future. She covers her private parts with her hands.

"Arms to your side," says the inspector.

When Alexandra refuses to remove her hands, the woman nods to "the enforcer," a muscular black man with a scar that runs from his nose to his neck. The enforcer cracks the air with his bullwhip as he walks toward Alexandra. She drops her hands and stares into the mid-distance while the inspector squeezes her breasts so hard, they ache. The woman slams her hands onto Alexandra's shoulders and turns her in a slow circle, her eyes running over every inch of Alexandra's body.

"Why you standin' here with your nose in the air. You have no call to be uppity, far as I can see." The inspector grabs Alexandra's hands and turns them over and over again, as if turning them will change them into something else.

"How come your hands so silky-soft?"

"I've been in the big house all my life."

"Doin' what?"

"Embroidering and making lace."

"They had no sewing house where you were at?"

Before Alexandra can answer, the inspector asks, "How many been wid you?"

"What?" asks Alexandra.

"How many men had their way wid you?"

"None!" blurts Alexandra.

"Don't use that sour tone with me. Something wrong wid you?"

Alexandra stares at the ground.

"Bring de sheet ovah heah," the lady tells a little girl who's a shade lighter than Alexandra. The little girl returns with a stained sheet which she smooths out on the ground.

The woman turns to Alexandra. "Lie down and spread 'em wide."

Mortified, Alexandra doesn't move.

The woman motions to the enforcer.

Alexandra lies down with her legs squeezed together.

"I said, spread 'em,'" the inspector woman says as she kneels by Alexandra's feet.

When the inspector's satisfied Alexandra's a virgin, she asks, "You had an impaired master?"

Alexandra doesn't understand, so she says nothing.

"Didn't hear your answer, Miss Silver-Spoon."

Alexandra searches the woman's face for clarification.

"She a three."

The inspector shoves Alexandra toward Table Three.

Alexandra's 'mentor,' who has also been sent over to Table Three, whispers, "We be taken to de private viewin' pen for afore we go up on de block. If a master you take a fancy to come by, stand tall and convince him he should pick you. If a master you don' favor come close, put on de dog face. You know de dog face?" Alexandra watches the old woman drop her jaw and squish her eyes until they're nearly shut.

Alexandra surprises herself by laughing out loud.

"This yellow'd look nice on you," says the old woman, handing Alexandra a worn, yellow shift.

Alexandra has already chosen a light purple with more than a few patches.

"Quiet ovah theah!" shouts the inspector.

When all the slaves are decked out in their 'new clothes' and lined up single-file, the barn doors are opened and the parade begins. Buyers lined up on the walk that leads into the sales building, a third barn, crane their necks and write notes to themselves in leather-bound tablets.

The "Ones are led by a tall, muscular, mulatto teenager, who wears a top hat and swings a brass staff back and forth as if conducting a band. They strut their stuff into the third barn, into spacious pens with smooth oak benches that wrap around the perimeter of plastered enclosures.

A robust coffee-colored man heads up the "Number Twos." There are families in this group; slender girls who haven't seen their first time; untested boys who have yet to do a man's work; women who've passed their child-bearing years. Many are fine looking human beings, siphoned from the "Number Ones" because of the hue of their skin; the young children they hold in their arms; their lack of experience, or some minor blemish.

"Number Threes" are too old or too young or too dark or too thin or too fat or too scarred—an indication they may be unruly. They're herded past indifferent buyers into a run-down pen with a floor of matted hay.

Alexandra is surprised to find John Fowler sitting on a pile of straw at the back of the "Threes" pen. A cloth band tied around his head reads, "Seven-year indenture."

When she sees he's fighting back tears, she knows he's no more used to being treated worse than a pig brought to auction than she is. It's rumored that some white indentures are worked harder than slaves, so their owners can exact full value before their allotted term is up.

Sometimes, they're worked to death.

Bargain hunters viewing the "Number Threes" pen remind her of a gaggle of turkeys as their voices rise to high-pitched judgment then fall to whispered speculation: ladies looking for someone to wash the floors; men seeking fence menders—or bed warmers; children who've come to pick out a birthday present.

She's heading over to console John when she hears Mr. Ball's voice. She holds her breath and edges to the front of the pen where she cranes her neck to confirm her suspicion.

Callie and Mr. Ball are headed straight toward her. Callie sees her. Her cousin's eyes dart from Mr. Ball to Alexandra. If Mr. Ball notices Alexandra, she's doomed. Alexandra sidles into the back corner of the pen and turns her back, but she knows this won't protect her for long.

She squats down. "Please. Stand in front of me," she whispers to John Fowler. He complies without questioning her.

Alexandra crouches and peeks around John, watching Callie dally before the slaves in the "Number Twos" pen.

"You sick, Miss Louise?" John asks.

Alexandra shakes her head.

John Fowler reminds Alexandra of Jimi, the way he's always looking out for other people.

Alexandra and John Fowler huddle in the back of the stall until a wiry little man, with a pointed beard, and a finely waxed mustache that makes him look like a goat, glances in their direction. He plants his feet, and does a double-take. A female slave, whose face has been ruined by a terrible burn, moves up to the rail.

"Lookin' for a cook, Mister? You fancy lemon chiffon cake that's light as a feather?"

But the goat-man is staring at John Fowler. "Monsieur Beaufort, come on ovah heah and take a look," he says in a deep, melodic voice.

Alexandra watches a tall, white-haired man with sideburns weave his way through the crowd.

"Ovah heah, Monsieur Beaufort," repeats the goat-man.

When Monsieur Beaufort sees John Fowler, so much blood drains out of his face that he looks like a ghost. His mouth forms an "O" of surprise. Alexandra wonders if he might be having a seizure.

Finally, Monsieur Beaufort shakes himself out of his spell. "Come here, Son," he says in a voice choked with tears.

"Me, Sir?" asks John.

Monsieur Beaufort nods and motions for John to approach.

John Fowler walks right up to the white-haired man and extends his hand to shake, just like Jimi would have done.

Alexandra moves forward and looks for Mr. Ball. She can't see him or Callie. She can't hear them either. Hopefully, they've made their purchase and left. Alexandra refocuses when she sees Monsieur Beaufort take John's hand and press it to his heart, tears glisten in his eyes. What kind of man is he, to cry like that in front of a child? Alexandra can tell John's uncomfortable, but he's too polite to draw away, so he stands still, waiting for the man to release his hand.

Finally, the man speaks, his voice tender. "What's your name, Son?"

"John Fowler, Sir."

"What brings you into these circumstances, John Fowler?"

A flood of words pours out. "My daddy went home to Jesus just after we'd come down to Kingston from Greensborough. My mama and daddy, my three sisters, my two brothers—and me. We thought we were lucky to be followin' the tar trade south. When we had enough money, Daddy planned to take us on back to North Carolina and buy a farm of our own. Imagine that!

"We'd only been in South Carolina for two days when the tallest pine tree I ever saw fell on Daddy. I ran over to him. He was lying on the ground. 'Be strong,' he told me. 'Follow Jesus and help your mother,' He didn't have a peaceful passing, like some folks. He seemed to see someone—or something—from the other side coming for him. He strained to sit up. "No!" he called out, then he fell back and his spirit went up to Jesus."

John takes a heavy breath, "I might've saved him if I'd run fast enough for help. The day after Daddy passed, a government man tried to talk Mama into parceling out all of us children so that we could be indentured and learn a trade. Mama told him his suggestion might be all right for us three boys: William, Elvis and me. But she insisted on taking the three girls and going back up to North Carolina, where we have family and friends. The man convinced her he could set up a good indenture for each of us boys. When she agreed, he gave her enough money to take my sisters back up North.

"Mama fretted, afraid she'd done the wrong thing. I told her we boys would be all right, and that we would come and find her when our indenture was up. William and Elvis went off to different plantations, close to where I was supposed to be, but two days after Mama left, the man who owned my indenture caught swamp fever and died. The wife told me she was sorry for selling my indenture to a speculator she barely knew, but he had offered her enough money for her to carry her children back to Virginia, where her sister lived. That speculator brought me here so a new placement could be found for me."

"Can you read?"

"Yes, Sir, and I can do figures."

Despite Monsieur Beaufort's well-tailored clothes, he has an unkempt look about him, as though he lacked the time, or perhaps the inclination, to involve himself with his appearance. He wears an expertly cut, dark green tail coat. His light green cravat, interwoven with gold thread, compliments the color of his eyes. But he hasn't bothered to shine his boots or comb his hair. Even though sadness plays around his eyes and mouth, he exudes kindness.

"You say your name is John?" the man asks, barely above a whisper.

"Yes, Sir. John Fowler."

"How old are you, Son?"

"Almost ten, Sir."

The big man stands up and paces.

"Do you speak French?"

"No, sir." John wilts when he sees that this disappoints the big man.

"No matter," says the big man. Color comes up in the man's cheeks, and a light shines in his eyes. He waves his hand. "Speculator!"

"Monsieur Beaufort, how may I assist you?" asks the speculator, cocking his lizard-like head.

"I'd like to spare this boy from the humiliation of further interviews," says Monsieur Beaufort, resting his hand lightly on John's shoulder.

"Certainly, Monsieur. Come, we'll draw up the papers."

Monsieur Beaufort turns to John. "I'll be back."

Alexandra's so consumed with scheming a way to persuade Monsieur Beaufort to take her too, she's forgotten about Mr. Ball—until she hears him say, "Callie, I know you were disappointed when your new girl drowned. But the one you chose to replace her is too expensive. You must make a reasonable choice."

Sadness sweeps over Alexandra to think of that nice little girl, who tried so hard to please Callie, lying in a shallow grave in Pinnacle's slave cemetery.

"Let's take a look over there," says Mr. Ball.

"You expect me to choose from the "Number Threes?'" Callie asks, loud enough for God and his angels to hear—and loud enough to warn Alexandra.

"You never know when you might find a diamond in the rough," Mr. Ball replies, matching Callie's volume. After a pause, Mr. Ball says, "That can't be. I think I saw your cousin in that pen."

"Alexandra's with the angels," says Callie, taking Mr. Ball's hand and leading him back toward the entrance. "I've had enough shopping for the day, Daddy."

Alexandra senses Mr. Ball looking for her. She waits for her world to crash. Then, Callie screams and Alexandra hears her cousin's body thud to the ground. She wants to look, but that could prove fatal.

"Sir! Your daughter's twitching," says a woman. "Call for a doctor!"

"Get up, Callie! Now!" Alexandra hears Mr. Ball say.

"Sir, is she your daughter?" the woman asks, her voice full of scorn.

"She has these spells from time to time. She'll be all right," says Mr. Ball. "Stand up!" he tells Callie.

"A brown spider bit me!" says Callie, her voice trailing to a whisper.

Alexandra nearly laughs out loud. She and Callie have enacted the spider-bite ruse since they were five years old.

"One of those poisonous brown spiders bit that poor little girl," says the woman.

"Get up!" Mr. Ball says, obviously aware that Callie's playacting.

"A person can die from that kind of spider's bite! Doctor! We need a doctor," calls the woman.

Doctors are always present at slave auctions. Some are privately retained so that they can inspect the "merchandise" before a purchase is made. Others stroll about, hoping to be hired by a wealthy planter.

"Over heah, Doctor," says the woman.

"Carry that child out into the sunlight where I can get a better look," says the doctor.

Alexandra guesses Mr. Ball's hanging back, trying to get a better look at her because she hears the doctor ask, "Are you coming, Sir?"

"Hurry, Sir," chides the woman.

Alexandra hears Mr. Ball say, "I'm coming, but I have every confidence my daughter will recover in time for Spencer's Ball."

"But that's tonight," says the woman.

"Indeed. I saw a girl I might want to buy," Mr. Ball says.

"Sir, where are you going? I need you to stay by your daughter's side," says the doctor.

Alexandra has to get away. She sees Monsieur Beaufort coming back with legal papers in his hand. "Pardonnez moi, Monsieur Beaufort," Alexandra says in flawless French. She switches to English, "My people are from Martinique. I could teach the young man you've indentured to speak French."

Monsieur Beaufort questions her in French and finds her pronunciation is perfect.

"Are you familiar with the duties in a plantation house?" he asks.

"Mais oui, Monsieur. I have lived in a big house all my life."

"No, no, that would never do," cautions the goat-man, rushing to Monsieur Beaufort's side. "Miss Cynthia chooses the house-help."

John Fowler takes a step forward. "Sir, may I speak?"

"Go on."

"This is Louise. She sews and embroiders and makes lace."

"Who taught you to make lace?"

Alexandra's grateful she and John Fowler had traded life stories, although she had borrowed from Grand-mère's childhood. "The nuns taught me when my parents were killed in an uprising in Saint Pierre."

"Where did you say?"

"Saint Pierre, in Martinique. The invaders stormed into the front door of the big house. I sneaked out the back and climbed a tree. When it was night, and I was safe, I climbed down and ran to the convent. The kind Mother Superior gave me sanctuary. The nuns taught me how to make lace. Then, a woman I'd never seen convinced the nuns I was her property. She took me with her to her plantation in Virginia, where I lived until my master died, and I was sold to the speculator who brought me here."

"How much for this girl?" Monsieur Beaufort asks.

CHAPTER TWENTY

$\mathcal{A}$ lexandra steps aboard Monsieur Beaufort's schooner and considers the cruel irony of traveling all the way to Charleston without making contact with Grand-mère, only to be returned to the Georgetown area. Monsieur Beaufort's plantation, *Rose of Sharon*, is up on the Black River. At least it's in a different region than Heaven Hill, so it's unlikely she'll run into her enemies.

She's glad the goat-man, who was touring with Monsieur Beaufort, stayed behind in Charleston. Something about him made her think he would sell his soul to the devil if it would put a penny in his pocket.

It's dusk when Monsieur Beaufort's schooner arrives at the Georgetown port. Most people are inside their homes enjoying supper, so, even if someone who knows Alexandra strolls by, the shadows will most likely conceal her. Monsieur Beaufort leads her and John Fowler to an elegant barouche that stands in a pool of light cast by a street lamp.

Alexandra has never seen such a fine carriage. The dark blue chassis is scrolled with silver designs; it's similar to Monsieur Marchand's conveyance, but there's more attention to detail. The coachman, a smartly dressed mulatto with finely chiseled features and wavy black hair, wears a well-cut scarlet waistcoat and a bowler encircled with a satin band that matches the coat. He springs down and helps Monsieur Beaufort step up into the carriage.

"Come sit by me, John Fowler." Monsieur Beaufort pats the seat opposite him.

The coachman raises an eyebrow as John, who now wears a ruffled shirt, a pale blue linen coat, and dark blue velvet pants, climbs aboard.

"Et l'esclave, Monsieur?" the coachman asks, indicating Alexandra, who stands on the boardwalk with her head down.

"Oh, yes," says Monsieur Beaufort. "Have Hephaestus make room for the girl in the jump-along."

"Go over there," barks the coachman, switching to English as he points to a one-horse buggy.

Alexandra doesn't realize the coachman's speaking to her until he flicks his whip and draws blood from her ankle. She looks up, her eyes filled with shock and rage. *Hold your tongue*, she tells herself, pressing her lips tight to avoid riling the arrogant man. Monsieur Beaufort is so focused on John, he doesn't notice the abuse—or he doesn't care.

"Don't make me tell you again, Girl," says the coachman.

Alexandra shudders. This is the same tone she'd used with Lulu when she was in a bad mood. Why hadn't she told Lulu that she would be proud to call her sister? No wonder Lulu stole her identity in order to take up residence with the Marchands. Alexandra hopes Lulu's safe.

When the coachman lifts his whip to strike again, Alexandra hurries over to the horse-drawn cart.

"Help Hephaestus with the luggage, then climb in the back." The coachman waves Hephaestus over.

"Marse picked this girl up in Charleston along with that boy," says the coachman.

"Without Miss Cynthia's consent?" Hephaestus clicks his tongue. His mouth falls open when he sees John Fowler.

"Could be young Jacob's twin, eh?" asks the coachman, arching his eyebrows.

"Dat de truth, awright," says Hephaestus.

"Have the girl help you, then have her climb on top of the luggage in the back of the runabout." The coachman's voice softens to a whisper, but Alexandra hears what he's saying.

"With any luck, Miss Cynthia will be asleep when we get to Rose. We can stash this girl somewhere until Marse finds the nerve to tell his wife about his new acquisition." The coachman starts back to the carriage, then stops, turns back around, and hands Hephaestus Alexandra's bill of sale. "In case patrollers stop y'all."

Hephaestus does not match his namesake as Aphrodite's disfigured husband. He flashes her a smile that lights up his handsome, young face. Muscles ripple beneath his white linen shirt as he heaves a trunk up into the back of the runabout. Then he hops up on the fender, balancing with a dancer's grace as he ties the trunk down with leather tongs. Alexandra struggles to pick up one of the heavy suitcases.

"I'll take dat," says Hephaestus. "I'd be glad to have you ride in front wid me, but if de coachman tol' Miss Cynthia I deviated from her protocol, I'd spend de night hanging by my wrists from de hook in de wine cellar."

Even though Hephaestus uses sub-standard English, he puts his words together with the precision of a poet. *Interesting,* Alexandra says to herself.

When the coachman brings the carriage abreast of the runabout, he glares at Alexandra, telegraphing she's supposed to help. She tugs at the remaining trunk, but it doesn't budge.

"How 'bout handin' me dat hat box over dere," says Hephaestus.

When all the trunks and boxes are tied down, Hephaestus offers his hand to help Alexandra step up. She smiles when she sees that he's draped a rabbit skin blanket over the carefully arranged suitcases and created a comfortable seat for her. Hephaestus keeps the horses trotting along at a steady pace. She lays her head back and watches horsetail clouds fly across the sky.

Hephaestus breaks the silence. "Miss Cynthia, de mistress of Rose of Sharon where we goin', she have a delicate temperament," he warns. "Best to put her up on de pedestal, if you know what I mean."

"I'll be respectful," Alexandra tells him.

Alexandra is admiring the clarity of Cassiopeia in the clear night sky when Hephaestus turns the runabout onto an oak tree-lined lane. It's too dark to make out all the contours of the house, but from the distance between the torches set into the Doric columns supporting the wrap-around balcony, she can tell Rose of Sharon's big house is even larger than Heaven's.

The coachman is helping Monsieur Beaufort out of the barouche when Hephaestus reins the round-about to a stop.

"I need your help," Monsieur Beaufort says to the coachman. Through a series of gestures, Monsieur Beaufort makes it known that he wants Hephaestus to lift John Fowler out of the carriage without waking him. Hephaestus jumps down from the driver's seat and opens the carriage door.

"Carry him to the top of the stairs. I'll fetch help," says the coachman. "Monsieur Beaufort wants to lay him down in Jacob's room."

The coachman and Hephaestus exchange a look. Alarm? Disapproval? Alexandra can't tell.

Torchlight illuminates the marble steps to the portico. Alexandra watches Hephaestus climb the stairs and transfer the sleeping boy to a waiting butler who must have heard the carriage approach. Monsieur Beaufort kisses the boy on the forehead and follows the butler inside.

Hephaestus trots back down the stairs. "No tellin' what Miss Cynthia gonna say about all dis," he says barely above a whisper.

The coachman glances at Alexandra, grimaces and shakes his head. "Marse said to put the girl where Miss Cynthia won't find her until after he's told her about the purchases he made. Settle the girl where you see fit, then tend to Marse's trunks."

Alexandra follows Hephaestus's eyes to the roof of the big house where a tall, narrow turret is backlit by a bright moon. Hephaestus unhooks the runabout lantern with one hand and extends the other to help Alexandra climb down.

"Dat woman won't never think to look up dere," he says to no one in particular. Then he turns to Alexandra. "Follow me."

She follows Hephaestus around to the back of the big house and up the winding slave stairs. On the narrow landing of each of the three lower floors, there's a door that apparently leads to the main hallway.

When they come to the fourth-floor landing, they enter a narrow passage and climb a steep, circular staircase. Hephaestus unlatches a brass hook and pushes up. He folds the door backward on its hinges, then climbs up and nods, indicating that Alexandra should come up onto the rooftop.

"Tread soft. Miss Cynthia's ear can catch de sound of a moth wing flutterin' on de other side of a room."

Alexandra steps onto the roof and drinks in the clear, starlit night.

"I'll come back with the supplies you'll be needin'. You enjoy dat sky while it still be available." Hephaestus climbs back down. The roof door closes. Alexandra hears the lock on the other side snap shut.

A low moaning drifts up from below. Alexandra tiptoes toward the back edge of the roof, squats down, and peers over the parapet that runs around the roof perimeter. The moon casts bluish light on a cemetery which is filled with raised white tombs, each overseen by a marble angel taller than a grown man.

A woman clad in a gauzy white dress dances around the angels. She stops before each statue, stoops and places a white rose at its feet. In the moonlight, the statues look like they're alive. Some have faces full of compassion, some exude anger, and some appear coldly indifferent to the flower-offering placed at their feet.

Alexandra startles when the lithe woman leans her head back, wails and then throws herself across a grave overseen by an angel carrying a dead warrior, clutching a sword in his right hand. Chills wash over her when she hears the woman sing the same French lullaby Grand-mère lulled her to sleep with when she was a child.

A figure dressed in a hooded cloak emerges from behind an angel.

"Time to go inside now, Miss Cynthia."

Alexandra's breath catches. *This is Miss Cynthia?*

"Please, just a little longer, my poor baby isn't asleep yet."

"Yes, he is, Miss Cynthia. I can see him in my mind. Your Jacob's eyes are closed; his sweet little mouth is curled up in a happy dream."

"Oh!" says Miss Cynthia. Her voice sounds more like it belongs to a child than to the mistress of a grand plantation.

Alexandra's so engrossed in the scene that she doesn't hear Hephaestus padding across the rooftop. She nearly cries out when he taps her on her shoulder.

"Shhh." Hephaestus puts his finger to his lips and guides her to the center of the roof where she can't be seen from below.

Miss Cynthia's voice drifts up. "What was that noise? Did you hear that?" she demands, her voice rising to hysteria. "Someone's on the roof."

Alexandra and Hephaestus freeze.

"Just the wind playin' through the trees, Miss Cynthia."

"I heard a voice. Listen . . ."

"Come on, Miss Cynthia, I'll make you a nice glass of warm milk with a little of that clover honey you're so fond of."

"And a little rum, to help me sleep?"

"And a little rum."

Alexandra and Hephaestus don't move until they hear the back door to the big house close.

"Can't never let her know you're up here," Hephaestus

whispers as he takes Alexandra by the elbow and steers her toward the turret. Hephaestus slips the key in the lock of a wood door carved with fairies and forest animals. When it opens, the scent of old flowers and linseed oil assaults Alexandra. She stands in the doorway while Hephaestus goes inside and lays a clean quilt on the floor.

"Gots a few more things to fetch," he says. "Go on in and stretch yourself out on de blanket, but keep de door open and give de room a chance to breathe."

Alexandra doesn't want to go inside. She leans against the outer wall of the turret and looks up, searching for Cassiopeia. Then, she hears footfalls crunch across the gravel road down below. She crouches and inches her way back to the railing.

"Hide!" someone shouts. "Peter's comin'."

She hears people running. The footfalls fade. She hears a horse clopping up the cobblestones. It comes to a stop in the front drive. She raises her head high enough to see a one-horse Cabriolet with two lanterns fitted on the front. A young man steps down. He wears a waistcoat, knickers and a frock coat with tails that reach the calves of his white-stockinged legs. Dark curls spill out from under his derby.

Alexandra's heart stops when she hears the young man hum a bar from Corelli's Opus 6, the piece she was to play in the Christmas concert. Tears flood her eyes as she remembers Mamou's words, "There are no accidents in this world. You must always be alert to the signs and opportunities life brings your way."

"Quiet now, Master Peter. Your step-mother sleeps light as a feather." That voice sounds like Monsieur Beaufort's carriage driver. He must have come out when he heard the carriage stop in the drive. The young man ignores the cautionary words, bounds up the front stairs, and slams the door.

Alexandra hears another man tell someone, "Too much Blackstrap." To which someone else replies, "Good thing Eusebia slipped a little extra rum in Miss Cynthia's milk. She be sleepin' good till the rooster crows."

Alexandra tilts her head up in time to see a shooting star. A few minutes later she hears the door to the roof unlatch.

"A little help, if you wouldn't mind," whispers Hephaestus. He hands her another gourd with a string tied to the top. Then he climbs up carrying a wooden box and a lantern with its flame turned low.

"Time to step inside your residence."

Hephaestus hangs the gourd on a nail and sets the box against the wall opposite the door and lifts the lid. "I put de chamber pot inside dis box so you can close de lid and hide de smell. Don' know when Marse Beaufort'll call for you to come over to de big house. He have to prepare de missus to meet you." Hephaestus slips a bundle out of the oversized-pocket of his coat. "Biscuits is wrapped in de napkin and dere's clean water in de gourd. I'll come back with more for you to eat as soon as the opportunity present itself. Don't be movin' around in de day when de folks downstairs is up and about." Hephaestus slides the box over to the side of the room, steps up, and opens up one of the small windows spaced at intervals around the lower half of the turret.

"These lower windows was installed to gib a body some air. De ones up top is for viewing. You'll be able to see dem when de sun come up."

"Lay yourself down, Missy," he says, "Let yourself drift into a sweet dream. I do apologize for lockin' you in and takin' away de lantern light. But it be for your own safety."

When he closes the door and turns the lock, terror rises up in Alexandra and makes it hard for her to breathe.

When she was six, Mother made Miranda lock her in the cellar without her supper for pounding on the drum Papa had given her for her birthday and waking everybody up in the middle of the night. Miranda forgot about her till mid-morning. By the time Miranda opened the door, Alexandra was convinced she'd been forgotten and would waste away.

What if Hephaestus leaves, or forgets she's here? She makes her way over to the far part of the wall, sits down on the comforter he brought up for her and draws her knees up to her chest. Closing her eyes, she sorts out odors: rat droppings, mildew; some sweet thing she can't identify; linseed oil; the faint scent of dead flowers.

Memories taunt her. Not very long ago, she was worried she'd make a fool of herself at her coming-out ball; she was preparing for the Christmas concert. Monsieur Martin told her she was a musical genius. She basked in his praise. Now, she's a nobody.

Part of her wishes she could die and disappear, rather than face what this new life might bring. How will she ever tell people that her ancestors brought the knowledge of rice cultivation that made South Carolina prosperous?

Mamou speaks inside her mind, *"When you're at the bottom of the well of despair, call happy memories to mind."*

But happy memories want nothing to do with this place. She sits up and feels for the gourd that Hephaestus hung from a nail in the wall. She's surprised when she takes a sip; honey and lemon have been added to the water. Hephaestus' kind gesture conjures a memory of how Cousin Callie took a risk when she distracted Mr. Ball and saved her life.

A moth darts in and out of the open window. *Lucky moth*, Alexandra thinks just before she lies down on the soft comforter and drifts off to sleep.

A rooster crows. She wakes up with a start and takes in the oddest room she's ever seen. Its diameter is so small that when she lies down and stretches out, her fingers and toes touch the edges of the surface. But the domed ceiling is at least twenty feet from the ground. A ladder leads up to a circular platform above which viewing windows have been placed all around the turret top. It reminds her of a drawing of a lighthouse she once saw. A person must be able to see a great distance from such a height. The rounded ceiling is painted with an intricate pattern of vines and birds and exquisite blue flowers.

Then she notices the walls. A musical score has been painted all around the smooth white surface. She rises to her knees and hums the melody. She's so enthralled that she forgets the injunction to be quiet. At first, she thinks someone's copied a Corelli score. But this music is something she's never heard before. Anguished riffs are threaded through with hope and longing. Even in its darkest place, there's a hint of light, reminiscent of Bach. Her voice rises from despair to a surging crest of joy. The music ends so abruptly, she guesses the piece must not be finished.

She hears the door downstairs close, hears footsteps coming up the ladder. She falls silent, scoots close to the wall and wraps herself in the comforter. Leaving a slit to peek through, she watches the door. Her body tenses. These footfalls sound different from those of Hephaestus. Someone fiddles with keys on the other side of the turret door.

"Mother?" the urgency in a man's voice stuns her.

Alexandra holds her breath. The lock turns. The door opens. The young man she saw come to the big house late last night stands in the doorway. He stares at her. Peter, that's what someone had called him.

"Take that blanket away," he says.

Alexandra lowers the comforter and casts her gaze to the floor.

"Who are you?" he asks, stepping inside. His voice, redolent with kindness despite its alarm, offers an invitation. "How did you get in here?"

Alexandra's emotions stir into such a frenzy, she's afraid to say a single word.

"Speak up, or would you rather have me call the authorities?"

"Hephaestus hid me here—until Monsieur Beaufort has time to tell his wife he bought me."

"Bought you? Without my step-mother's permission?"

"Hephaestus said I had to stay hidden until Monsieur Beaufort gathered the nerve to tell her about me, or she might do something terrible."

"That's the truth. This is my secret place. My step-mother had it locked up the day Hephaestus said he saw Mother's ghost looking out a viewing window. She doesn't know I have a key. Apparently, Hephaestus has one too.

"Mother used to bring me up when I was a child. She'd tell me stories, and I'd play my violin for her. She said I would be a great composer one day.

"She died of a heart attack when I was twelve."

"I'm sorry."

Peter frowns. "When I was down in the yard, I thought I heard Mother's ghost humming my music."

"You wrote this? It's spectacular. At first, I thought it was Corelli's . . ."

"You know Corelli?" He studies her. "How can that be? Dear God. It was you singing."

"I forgot I was supposed to be quiet."

"Look. I know it isn't your fault you're up here, but you can't stay."

A door slams. A scream down in the yard rents the air.

"My step-mother's awake," Peter says. "I hope she didn't hear you singing."

"Adam! Who have you brought into this house?"

"She's found you out," says Peter. "Now she'll find my music and have it painted over."

"I don't think it's me she's talking about," Alexandra says.

Peter rushes out of the turret, hunches down, and creeps over to where the roof looks down onto the front drive. Alexandra follows him. They crouch and peek over the railing. Alexandra gasps. Peter puts his finger to his lips, a warning to be quiet. Miss

Cynthia doesn't look up, she seems so eager to chastise John Fowler, that she isn't paying attention to what's happening on the roof. Miss Cynthia grips John's arm with one hand and slaps his face with the other.

Peter stares. "Who is that?" he mouths.

"The indenture your father acquired when he bought me," Alexandra mouths back.

They continue their silent conversation.

"He could be Jacob's twin."

"Who's Jacob?"

"My half-brother. The day he turned nine, he got thrown by his new horse, hit his head on a rock and died. Miss Cynthia lost her mind."

Alexandra winces when Miss Cynthia slaps John again. That brave little boy doesn't utter one word of complaint.

Peter glowers. "I'm goin' down. Get back in the turret."

Alexandra tiptoes back inside the turret. Peter locks her in. Ever so quietly, Alexandra climbs up the ladder to one of the viewing windows. There is no glass on the windows; a cleverly built overhang protects the turret from rain.

She sees Miss Cynthia standing in the middle of the drive holding tight to John Fowler's wrist while she berates Monsieur Beaufort. Even from this distance, Alexandra can see a bruise coming up all around John Fowler's eye. When Peter approaches them, Miss Cynthia starts speaking French. "You brought him into my house without my permission?"

Monsieur Beaufort stares at the ground, hat in hand. "I thought you'd be pleased."

"Idiot! My Jacob cannot be replaced by this pauper." Miss Cynthia stomps her foot like a child throwing a tantrum and slaps John Fowler on the back of the head.

"Stop that," says Peter.

"Apologize to this boy!" Monsieur Beaufort commands; his voice shakes with rage.

"Why? I have half a mind to lock him in the tower and let him starve."

Alexandra ducks down.

"Act like a lady and lower your voice," commands Monsieur Beaufort.

"Why? Who here can understand me? My good-for-nothing step-son? This little boy? The slaves? None of whom understand French?

"You bought his indenture for me? Don't tell me how to treat him."

After a pause, Monsieur Beaufort switches to English and says, "I have business in Savannah. This boy had better be in one piece when I return."

"Savannah? This time of year? Is she pretty?"

Monsieur Beaufort whistles. Alexandra moves around and looks out another window. Monsieur Beaufort's coachman is bringing the barouche around to the front of the house. A few minutes later, Hephaestus straps suitcases on the back of the carriage.

Monsieur Beaufort climbs inside the carriage and closes the door without uttering another word.

"When are you comin' back?" Miss Cynthia demands from the top of the portico stairs.

Monsieur nods. His coachman urges the horses to a fast trot.

Miss Cynthia turns to John Fowler. "Take off those clothes," she says, her voice full of venom.

The little boy stares at Miss Cynthia.

"Take them off."

Alexandra clamps her teeth tight to keep from yelling for Miss Cynthia to stop humiliating John Fowler.

"Do as I say!" screams Miss Cynthia.

The little boy hesitates, then he slips out of the clothes and stands in his drawers.

"All of them!"

"That's enough, Mother," protests Peter.

"I thought I made it clear. You are never to call me mother."

"That child didn't do anything to hurt you," Peter protests.

"Your father left. Now, I'm in charge. Get out of my sight, or I'll cut off your allowance. Who knows when your father will come back to restore it?"

Miss Cynthia swings back around to face John Fowler. "I told you to take off my son's clothes, all of them."

Peter stalks toward the horse stable while John Fowler drops his undergarment to the ground. He covers his private parts with his hands, gazes toward the horizon and sets his jaw like Jimi used to do when he was being punished.

Alexandra expects to see Peter burst out of the stable on a fine horse, but he's leaning against the doorsill, drinking from a silver flask.

"Eusebia!" screams Miss Cynthia. The nimble mulatto from last night's garden episode glides down the front steps wearing a white, Grecian-style dress. She curtseys before Miss Cynthia, cocks her head, and waits for instructions.

"Take my Jacob's clothes to the laundress. Tell her to wash them twice, then set them out to dry so they'll be purified by the sun."

Eusebia avoids looking at John Fowler as she gathers up the clothes pooled around his feet.

"You're slow as a sow bug! Hurry up!" commands Miss Cynthia.

Eusebia hugs the clothes to her and runs down the path toward the slave quarters, a beleaguered row of cabins on the far side of the north lawn.

"Lower your hands!" says Miss Cynthia.

"Excuse me, Ma'am, but I don't think that would be the proper thing to do."

"Pierre!" Miss Cynthia calls. A pecan-colored man, who seems to be a few years older than Peter, twenty maybe, trots around the corner of the big house dressed in a brown leather jacket, black pants and a broad-brimmed leather hat.

"I told this boy to lower his hands, but he doesn't seem inclined to comply."

Pierre whisks his whip from the sheath attached to his belt and taps the iron-beaded strands of leather on his palm. John Fowler drops his hands to his sides. Eusebia returns, breathless from her run back from the laundry. She curtseys, then stands at attention looking everywhere but at John Fowler. The little boy stands in front of Miss Cynthia shivering, even though it's a warm morning.

"Have this scrawny pauper taken to Musu's cabin. He's to eat and sleep with the slave children, but he must do a man's work in the fields."

"According to your pleasure, Miss Cynthia," says Eusebia with the touch of a British accent that catches Alexandra by surprise.

Miss Cynthia sashays up the marble steps.

"Hephaestus," says Eusebia. "Come see to this poor child's needs."

Hephaestus, who has been watching from the shadows, rushes toward John and gestures to someone outside of Alexandra's sight-line. A young child, whose hair is tied up in a white head scarf, darts out from behind the hedge. Alexandra can't hear what Hephaestus says to her, but the little girl unfastens her scarf and hands it to him. Hephaestus kneels down, and fashions a loincloth out of the little girl's gift.

"Come along," says Hephaestus, when John is slightly more presentable. He leads the little boy toward the quarters.

An old man gripping a metal bar emerges from the direction of the kitchen house, which, in Alexandra's estimation, is too close to the big house to prevent the spread of fire. He strikes the metal triangle hanging from the branch of a magnolia tree. Children clutching mussel shells run out of the slave cabins. Alexandra moves to another window and sees the children fall into line behind a tall, elegant, dark-skinned woman with high cheekbones and straight, black hair. She is so regal, Alexandra thinks her mother may have been an Indian princess who married a man from Africa, like the Queen of Cofitachequi in one of Marcello's stories.

The biggest boys crowd to the front of the line; girls come next, and the smallest children, of both genders, line up in back. After passing the tall woman's clean-hands inspection, each child lines up behind one of two young girls, seven or eight-year-old miniatures of the woman who inspected their hands. The girls stand back to back, holding baskets filled with rice cakes. After stuffing a cake in their pocket, the children run to a pig trough that's filled half-way to the top with a white liquid, which Alexandra supposes is milk. The children scoop the liquid into their mouths with their mussel shells as fast as the windmill motion of their arms permits.

John Fowler follows Hephaestus toward the line of children from the direction of the slave quarters. He's dressed in a long hemp shirt, the usual attire of much younger slaves. Hephaestus leans down and says something to the little boy, then turns and walks out of Alexandra's sightline.

John tries to edge in behind the big boys. They jostle him to the end of the line, behind the smallest child. Many of the children point at him and laugh. John stares straight ahead.

Alexandra wants to slap those rude children and tell them they aren't half as brave as John Fowler.

When John finally arrives at the food baskets, he dips his hand into the basket and tries to pick up the few crumbs of rice cake that are left. The little girls step back, as though they're afraid of him. The woman grabs those girls' baskets and scolds them. Then she pours all of the remaining crumbs into John's outstretched hands, smiles at him and directs him toward the milk trough.

John races over and squeezes in between two small children.

Since he has no mussel shell, he tries to scoop up what remains of the milk with his bare hands.

"He's using his hands!" cries a girl.

Before he can bring the life-saving liquid to his lips, Pierre strides over, grabs John by the arm, and pulls him away from the trough.

"A day in the sun'll teach you not to touch Marse's milk with your bare skin."

John tries to wiggle out of Pierre's grasp. Pierre pulls John's arm behind his back and forces him to his knees. "I'm the driver on this plantation. Do what I tell you, or you'll rue the day you was born."

Alexandra has never understood why white men who manage plantations are called overseers, while their darker-skinned counterparts are called drivers. In Papa's fields, where everyone was free, there were no drivers or overseers. Villagers took turns at the helm, the common practice in Diola communities.

The punishment place consists of two pillories and two leg-stocks placed a few feet apart in a fifteen-foot square of bare dirt. Pierre drags John to the child-size pillory.

"Kneel down." John kneels. Pierre pushes his head down into the neck cutaway of the wooded frame. John tries to get away. Pierre catches him by the scruff of his neck and bends his arm up behind his back. "Don't make me break your arms," Pierre says, loud enough for Alexandra to hear.

John lays his arms in the wrist-holes. Then Pierre closes the top and locks the cross-bar. Alexandra can see that the bottom part of the frame chokes John when he relaxes his neck. He struggles to use his muscles to lift his head.

How long is Pierre going to leave him in that thing? *I'll run away and take you with me,* Alexandra promises.

She hears a fight break out. The children at the trough push and shove as they try to scrape the last of the milk into their shells. When they see Pierre heading toward them, they pour their precious drops of milk on the ground, stand at attention, and hold their empty mussel shells out for inspection.

Pierre puffs his chest out when Peter approaches and says something that Alexandra's unable to discern. Pierre glances over at the pillory where John Fowler is doing his best to keep from crying. Peter opens a pouch, takes out some of gold pieces, and offers them to Pierre. Pierre counts the coins, shakes his head and starts to hand them back. Peter puts more coins in his hand. Pierre motions to Hephaestus, who's walking toward the trough with a bucket of water and a rag. Probably to wash out the trough. Pierre tells Hephaestus something. He sets the bucket down. Pierre gives him a key and nods toward the punishment place.

Pierre walks over to where the children are assembled in two lines. He puts two fingers to his lips and whistles. The children march toward the fields to do their day's work. Peter returns to the barn.

Alexandra smiles when Hephaestus unlocks the pillory and lifts the top bar. John Fowler throws his arms around the big man's neck. Hephaestus gently disengages the little boy's arms, steps back and hands John the gourd that had been tied to his belt with a leather tong. Alexandra suspects John must be aching with thirst, but the little fellow tells Hephaestus thank you before bringing the gourd to his lips.

Jimi would have done it just that way, she thinks.

After John's drunk his fill, Hephaestus motions the boy to follow him toward the path that leads to the field.

Alexandra sees Peter riding toward John on a marsh-tacky, an ancestor of one of those escaped horses brought over in 1526 in the failed attempt to create the first Spanish settlement in South Carolina. The sturdy horses are praised for stamina and steadiness. Peter leans toward John Fowler and shakes the little boy's hand. Then he turns his horse and urges it to a gallop toward a copse of vine-covered trees that separate Rose's manicured lawns from the untamed swamp.

Alexandra climbs down from the viewing platform, takes the gourd Hephaestus hung by a cord on the wall, and sips honey and lemon water warmed by morning sun.

CHAPTER TWENTY-ONE

—✦—

One night, when Hephaestus visits Alexandra, he tells her, "Peter said I have to find another place for you to be at. I'll see to your needs till then."

"No place to put you yet," he says every time he empties the chamber pot and brings food: crab cakes, or shrimp boiled in rice; an occasional piece of ham; biscuits with jam; and sometimes, an apple. Best of all, he gives her a thicker quilt that she doubles up and uses as a mattress. She tries to stay awake so she can thank him, but she always falls asleep before he comes.

A wetter than usual beginning of September follows an unusually dry August. It rains. It rains. And it rains. Good thing the overhang on the turret prevents water from seeping through the top-tier windows, which have no glass.

In the sticky, warm darkness, she lies on her back, sifting through memories. One night her mind drifts to Callie's unnamed slave. She sees that little girl in her mind's eye so clearly it seems like she could reach out and touch that sweet slave's face. No wonder that child had cried at night, torn away from her mother and father and all the people who knew and loved her.

Alexandra feels a constant ache in her heart. Will she ever see Mamou again, or Lulu, or Miranda? Sometimes, when she closes her eyes, she sees Jimi's face pressed against the shop window; she hears him calling out to her. "Help me." Guilt wraps her in a garment of shame. "Let me die," she whispers one night. But when Hephaestus doesn't come for two days, and she thinks she really might be forgotten and starve to death, she wills herself to do all in her power to stay alive.

At the beginning of the eighth week in the turret, she wakes up at dawn and finds Hephaestus, kneeling by her side. He leans close and whispers, "I tacked twelve gourds filled with water to the wall and set a clean chamber pot and a basketful of biscuits against the wall. Miss Cynthia's suspicion has been aroused. She has all eyes trained on me. Miss Louise, I won't be able to come up till dey turn dere minds in a new direction."

Alexandra keeps her mind occupied by memorizing Peter's entire score. She hums his music inside her head, over and over, in order to keep her terror at bay.

When all the water's nearly gone and only two dried out biscuits remain, Alexandra stops marking the days. The chamber pot overflows. Nausea turns into bouts of vomiting. She loses track of time. Nothing more seems to be left in her stomach, diarrhea plagues her. She uses that nice, thick quilt as her toilet; she's surprised no one down below has caught a whiff and sent someone up to see what died.

Maybe odors rise, like heat.

Sometimes her cramping is so severe, she begs to die. When the pain abates, she curls into a ball and yearns for the oblivion of sleep. But chills wrack her body.

Mamou appears. She cups Alexandra's face with her warm hands and kisses her forehead. Tears pour down Alexandra's cheeks in this vision, which seems more real than dream-like.

Mamou's voice is clear and strong. "*One day you will be in a position to share the legacy of your father's people with those who have ears to hear, colored and white alike. Fight. Stay alive.*"

The next morning Alexandra is so limp, she can barely bring the gourd with the last of the water to her lips, but her stomach seems more settled. This time, when she drifts into sleep, Jimi does not appear at the window of the blacksmith shop.

She feels like she's falling into a void, swirling like a feather, angling toward the forest floor from a great height. As she spins, she hears Lulu voice, *"Tell them I'm your sister."*

"Yes," Alexandra says. *"You are my sister."*

Lulu laughs as her face materializes. *"Too late,"* she whispers. Lulu's image fades.

"Forgive me!" Alexandra cries out, but Lulu has disappeared.

Then Jimi comes to her. As Alexandra reaches out to touch him, his face morphs into John Fowler's face. *"Help me,"* John Fowler pleads.

"I will," she replies.

In this fevered dream, she floats on a river of light; the sound of its rushing chimes, like tiny bells. She hears Didima laugh.

Didima, I need your help.

So, you want to live? Good, says Didima.

Alexandra is thrust into the vision of a meadow with silver grass where drops of dew shimmer in the moonlight like diamonds. Her dream-body stops, afraid to move from the shadows of trees into the open. She senses that if she takes one step onto that meadow, she'll die.

"Step into the meadow," commands a deep voice.

Papa?

"Step into the meadow," he says again.

"I don't want to die. John Fowler needs my help."

"Stay alive and thrive. Step into meadow," says Papa a third time.

Alexandra takes three steps into the meadow. A peacock appears, standing less than two feet from her. It spreads its fan into a kaleidoscope of glowing colors. As it peers into her eyes, its feathers turn into glass and tinkle to the ground.

She feels lighter, cooler. The peacock disappears. Alexandra knows, without knowing how, that she will live.

The vision fades. An ephemeral woman with dark curls and

blue eyes the same shade as Peter's stands by her side. The woman smiles.

The ghost of Peter's mother, Alexandra thinks before falling into a restful sleep.

When she awakes, it's dawn. She's weak, but her chills are gone and her appetite is returning. Someone has washed her, dressed her in a new shift and wrapped her in a soft, clean blanket.

The room smells like lavender. Two new gourds have been filled with fresh water. Biscuits and mulberries have been set out on a checkered napkin. There's a sprig of rosemary in a clean chamber pot. Hephaestus must have changed her clothes. Gratitude edges out her humiliation and aching loneliness.

She hums. Peter's melody breathes life into her. Then she comes to the abrupt ending of his composition, and her mind turns to their first meeting. She had felt an instant connection with Peter. He must have felt it, too. Why else would he have told her about his life? Why hasn't he come back up?

Then she remembers how the overseer sneered when Monsieur Martin kissed her hand, and she knows Peter is repulsed by the color of her skin.

CHAPTER TWENTY-TWO

October: her fourth month of captivity. Alexandra climbs to the upper windows expecting to see a repeat of Miss Cynthia's nightly ritual. Ghost-like clouds race across the full moon, creating the illusion that spirits are dancing on the graves below.

Miss Cynthia appears on cue, but tonight, she wears a ball gown and a white satin cape that shimmers in the moonlight. She lays a bouquet of white rosebuds on her son's grave. Then, she stands erect and sings the French lullaby that still sends chills chasing up her spine.

"A bientôt, mon chère," Miss Cynthia says to the little grave.

"You sure you want to travel by night?" Eusebia asks from the shadows.

"The voices told me to. It's dangerous to deny my voices." Miss Cynthia turns toward Eusebia's cloaked figure. "Are my trunks secured to the carriage?"

"Yes, Miss Cynthia."

Alexandra watches Miss Cynthia and Eusebia leave the cemetery and step through the opening in the jasmine hedge to the circular drive of the big house; street lamps cast a pool of light. Pierre steps down from the driver's seat of an elegant carriage and opens the door for Miss Cynthia and her dutiful servant. When the ladies are settled, Pierre urges the horses to a trot. Lanterns attached to the front and back of the barouche swing back and forth, like drunken ghosts, as the carriage rolls down the tree-lined lane and out of sight.

Alexandra is about to climb down from the platform when she hears drums beating out African rhythms and people whispering. She looks through the window closest to her and sees nothing, but when she moves around to the east window, she makes out people moving through the stand of pines Miss Cynthia refers to as her garden of guardian trees.

Alexandra hears someone running up the stairs that lead into the turret. She hurries down from the platform and wraps herself in her blanket just as the lock turns and the door opens. Hephaestus comes up into the room like Hades emerging from the underworld; his lantern spills out sepia light that distorts the features of his face.

Alexandra's alarmed by the urgency in his voice. "Miss Cynthia hab it in her mind for Pierre to drive her to Georgetown so she can visit a necromancer," confides Hephaestus.

"A what?"

"A lady able to go back and forth between de living and de dead. Miss Cynthia convinced herself that if she can contact her little son and hold a conversation that lets her know how to make him happy over dere on death's side, her heart will be soothed and she can move onward with her life. That's dangerous business, I tell you. Mr. Beaufort would have stopped her if he'd been here. Anyway, Miss Cynthia, she assemble de house help and announce dat her grandmother be near to death. She tol' 'em since she didn't know how to get word to Marse, she made up her own mind to travel with Eusebia in order to pay her respect.

"Everybody know Miss Cynthia ain't got no grandmother in Georgetown. Dey also know if Miss Cynthia got a hint dat Eusebia told dem she was travelin' wid Miss Cynthia to de necromancer, dat witch would cut out sweet Eusebia's tongue. So, everybody jes' say, 'We be prayin' for your grandmother. Y'all have a safe trip.'"

Hephaestus smiles. "Her absence afford me de opportunity to get you situated in de quarter—if you do know how to make lace."

"I do," Alexandra says between sips of the lemonade Hephaestus has brought up in the gourd.

"Musu, be de head of de only cabin with a porch, she be tickled to have a lace-maker in her place, as long as you willin' to share your profit."

"Profit?"

"De planters up and down dis river gives dere slaves from Thanksgiving to Christmas Day de opportunity to sell dere products, long as dey keeps up with dere work—and long as dey be willin' to share dere profit with dere betters. You willin' to gib Musu a percentage of your lace profit?"

"If I make a profit."

"If your lace be as good as I expect, I guarantees it. My cousin Betsy gib me de supplies of ol' Eloise, Rose's last lace-maker, who now be makin' lace for de angels."

Hephaestus hands a large cloth bag to Alexandra. She looks inside and finds a lace-making pillow, hardwood bobbins, pins and three cones of tatting silk—everything she needs.

"I already tuck John Fowler into Musu's cabin to keep him outta of Miss Cynthia's sight. Musu got a spot in her heart for de babies. But since he white, she jes' take him on trial."

Hephaestus ducks out the door and comes back in with a new chamber pot and a larger box made of cedar and lined with hardened clay. "Sanded off all de rough places," he says as he sets it against the wall. Then he hands Alexandra a bouquet of rosemary and lavender.

Alexandra tears up. "You made this box? It's beautiful, Hephaestus, thank you."

"Pinch de lavender buds 'tween your fingers and rub it under your nose; it'll carry off any nasty smell. Bite down on de rosemary needles, and your breath be sweet as a new baby's.

"Make a piece of lace for me to gib to Musu, and if be high quality, I swear on my mama's soul dat you gonna be a welcome addition to Musu's cabin family."

"Thank you."

Two days later, Alexandra finishes a square of lace intricate enough to please a queen. She hopes it'll be good enough for Musu.

The next day at dawn, a loud conversation down in the drive awakens her. She climbs up to the viewing windows.

"You sure Mr. Pierre ain't around?"

"Still in Georgetown. The young master's in charge."

That night, she hears someone coming up the stairs, she assumes it's Hephaestus coming to tell her whether or not Musu has agreed to let her stay in her cabin. She smooths her skirt and chews on a rosemary needle to freshen her breath.

Then her nerves spark. She can tell from the pattern of the footsteps it's not Hephaestus. She lies down, pulls the blanket up around her and presses herself against the wall.

The lock turns. The door opens. Alexandra peeks through an opening in that blanket and sees Peter standing in the doorway, holding a violin case in one hand and a lantern in the other. Maybe he thinks she has already left.

His lantern, fitted with colored glass, scatters blue and purple patterns across the circular wall. Peter takes his violin out of its case and lifts it to the chin rest. *Play your own music*, she tells him inside her mind. But he chooses Bach's *Concerto in A Minor*. His brilliant rendition thrills Alexandra into forgetting her misery.

When he finishes, she sighs. He whirls around. "Why are you still here?" he asks, more embarrassment in his voice than anger.

"Hephaestus thinks he found another place for me," she says. "It depends on whether or not Musu likes my lace. If she does, I'll be gone from here."

Peter draws near. The kind look in his eyes causes her words to spill out as if they had a mind of their own. "Bach would have loved the way you played. But I wish you'd played your own music."

"How is it you recognize Bach?"

She doesn't trust him, yet. A lie trips off her tongue. "My master in Virginia taught me all about music."

"That's odd."

"Why didn't you play your own song?"

"Who are you to ask me that?" He pauses, then continues. "I haven't committed it to memory yet, and obviously I can't see it in the dark." He stands up, a confused look on his face. "What did you mean back when you said my piece wasn't finished?"

"You like the way it ends?" she asks.

"You're audacious for a slave." She's pondering whether or not she should tell him that she composed an ending, when he says, "How would you finish it, if you're such an expert?"

"It'd be hard to tell you, but I could show you."

"Play," he says, in a voice mixed with skepticism and curiosity. Peace washes through Alexandra as she closes her eyes and touches the bow to the strings. She picks up Peter's composition somewhere in the middle, then she plays all the way through to the ending she'd composed in her head.

She offers the violin to Peter and drops her eyes.

"My God!" he says, cheeks flushed, eyes welling with tears.

"Your mother would be so touched that you wrote this for her."

"How did you know it was for my mother?"

"The title: 'Tribute to My Dearest Mother.'"

"You read French?"

"My mother was from Martinique."

The conversation is cut short by a tattoo of gunfire followed by the sound of galloping horses and the shouts of excited men.

Peter takes the violin out of Alexandra's hands and lays it in the case. "With any luck, they didn't hear you playing. And even if they did, they'd think it was me." Peter tenses. "If they find out about my coming up here. They'll erase my music."

"I stopped playing as soon as we heard their horses. They were pretty far away."

"I have to find out what's going on. Latch the door from your side. Don't make a sound." He holds her in his eyes. His hand brushes her cheek. Then he steps back, flushed with embarrassment, picks up his lantern and leaves the room.

Alexandra's so stirred up, she finds it difficult to get back to sleep. Finally, she drifts off, only to be awakened too early by men shouting down in the yard. She hurries up to the platform, careful not to make a sound, and looks out the first window she comes to. Peter steps out from the shadows as Pierre slips off his horse.

"I thought you were staying in Georgetown awhile," Peter says.

"Got word of a runaway. Came to get my dogs. I knew I shouldn't have left you in charge."

"Someone's running from here? Who?"

"Ares," Pierre snaps.

"Hephaestus's daddy?"

"You acquainted with another Ares?"

"Wait on me. I'm coming with you," says Peter.

A few minutes later, Peter and Pierre gallop down the side road that leads toward the woods, trailed by baying hounds. After a time, someone whoops. It sounds like Peter's voice.

"Make that fool runaway pay."

She brings the palm of her hand to her cheek where Peter had touched her. Alexandra's heart thuds in her chest. Tears chase down her cheeks. She'd thought Peter was different from the others. Her mind twists with longing and fear. She stands there, paralyzed for a long time, by a kind of grief she didn't know existed. She returns to her blanket.

A few hours later, the ruckus of dogs barking and horses clomping over the cobblestones snaps her from her depression. She climbs to the viewing platform and looks down on the circle drive. Pierre pulls his horse to a stop and slides off the stallion's back. His friends tie up their horses and gather around like bored ladies eager for gossip.

She can't make out what he told them, but they slap each other on the back and shake hands. Some of them throw up their hats in celebration. Some of them even hug and pat each other on the back. Then they part and make way for a burly man shoving a defiant slave who has some kind of wire cage on his head.

"That'll teach you not to run," Pierre tells the slave whose eyes smolder with hatred. "You don't look like a god of war now."

Ares!, Alexandra thinks.

The proud slave holds his head still. If he moves a fraction of an inch, the iron spikes pointing toward his head from the edges of the head contraption will pierce his nose or put out his eyes.

Pierre laughs. "Hephaestus, you think I'm a fool? Come on out from behind that bush and prove your loyalty to Miss Cynthia by giving your daddy a tap with my flogger. Or, if you'd rather, we can put a cage on your head, and you can join old Ares at the whipping post."

Alexandra sees Hephaestus crouching behind a bush. She can tell Pierre's only guessing he's there by the way his eyes dart around.

Without warning, Pierre strikes Ares' bare chest with a spiked whip that looks like it came from a pirate's cache. A web of blood crawls down Ares' torso. His muscles quiver, but he stands still and keeps his gaze steady. When Pierre draws his hand back to strike again, Hephaestus starts to come out from his hiding place. Before he has time to reveal himself, Peter rides up and brings his horse to a stop between Ares and Pierre. "Stop that!" he shouts.

Hephaestus sinks back down.

"I told you you'd miss the fun if you went searching down by the river." Pierre glares at Peter, his hooded eyes dark with challenge.

Peter dismounts. "Take that cage off. Where'd you get a thing like that?" demands Peter.

Their voices are identical!

"Never seen a Gorée special?"

"Take it off."

"Just followin' your step-mother's orders, Master Peter," says Pierre, his voice smooth as an eel's. "Your daddy went off on one of his larks and left Miss Cynthia in charge. When I took her to see that necromancer, she told me when I came back, I would be in charge. She said if I caught any runaways in her absence, I was to make an example that would wag the tongue of every slave up and down the Black River. If I were you, I'd pray your daddy returns before your step-mother comes back and gets a whiff of your yellowbelly ways."

Peter composes himself. "Tell you what, you leave that cage on and do what you want to Ares. When Miss Cynthia does get back, I'll tell her your punishment was so harsh, Ares wasn't able to make the roof repairs she ordered."

Pierre paces.

Peter glares. "Remember the time Miss Cynthia had a fit, after you whipped Hermes so bad he couldn't harvest rice?"

Pierre unlocks the cage. When he pulls it off, threads of blood streak Ares's cheeks. Pierre moves close to his quarry. Alexandra strains to hear.

"Put Ares in the hole with enough bread and water to keep him strong enough to do his work." Pierre leans close to Ares. "Try leavin' again, and this cage goes on your son's head."

Alexandra gasps when she sees Peter and Pierre standing side by side. Except for the color of their skin and eyes and the texture of their hair, they look like twins.

They have the same father! Alexandra's sure of it. She watches as Pierre leads his horse into the stable; watches as his men go their way. When they're out of sight, Peter gestures for Hephaestus to come out from behind the bush. He whispers something in the slave's ear. Alexandra's too far away to make out the words. But he must have said something kind. A smile lights up Hephaestus's face.

Alexandra promises herself that she'll help Ares and Hephaestus escape, along with John Fowler, or she'll die trying. If she lives, she'll tell the story of her people.

The scent of gardenias suffuses the air.

CHAPTER TWENTY-THREE

When Hephaestus comes up that night, shame weighs down his shoulders. He hands Alexandra a basket without looking at her. His voice has lost its lilt. "Brought you crawdads wrapped in banana leaves. Cooked 'em my own self. Minerva, one of de cooks, say she only have one biscuit to spare. It's sort o' burnt up on de underside. I seen a whole stack settin' right there on de kitchen table. When Minerva seed my eye alightin' on dos fine vittles, she put on a scowl and turn her face away.

"Yesterday morning, she favor me wid a smile, and a pat on de arm and de fluttering eyes dat say, 'You can ask, and I won' object.' He sighs. "But all dat change when dey catch my daddy while I hid behind a bush jes' watchin'.

Hephaestus heaves a sigh. "Soon as you finish dat piece o' lace, I gonna take it on down to Musu's cabin. Her full name be Musukebba de Mandinka, meaning de senior wife. We call her Musu, but you should call her Miss Musu. And don't be using none of your fancy talk."

Alexandra muses. Mandinka helped the Portuguese enslave her ancestors. Now she'll be living side by side with them, if she's lucky.

"Hephaestus, what's your real name?"

"My mama gib me de name, Jato."

"You know what tribe your people came from, back in Africa?"

"On my mama's side, we was Mandinka, like Musu. Don't know who my daddy was."

Maybe people will become one tribe here in America, muses Alexandra. "What does Jato mean in Mandinka?" she asks.

"It mean de lion," Hephaestus says, a spark of pride lighting up his eyes.

"May I call you Jato when no one else is around?"

"I'll think on it, Miss Louise. Where y'all's folk from?"

"Most people call us Diola, meaning someone who pays back for what was done to them. Among ourselves, we are Ajamatau. Our people have lived along the Gambia River for hundreds of years."

"You been to dat river?"

"I've read about it."

"Read about it?" Hephaestus shrinks into himself.

She realizes her mistake. Just associating with slaves who know how to read and write can earn a slave a night in the stocks.

He lowers his eyes. "Call me Hephaestus. I ain' nothin' like no lion. Lions stand up for dere own blood."

"Maybe the lion inside of you is just waking up, Jato. You've been very brave to help me."

"You a fortune reader, Miss Louise?"

"Sometimes I see things that come to pass. But one thing's for certain, we all make mistakes. Deciding not to repeat them and holding to it is what makes us strong." She studies Hephaestus. "I can see the lion inside of you."

He gazes at the floor. "It'll go poorly for you if you tell folks you can read."

"Will you keep my secret?"

Hephaestus nods. She hopes he has the strength to keep his word. "How has John Fowler settled in?" she asks.

"I was mistaken when I thought Musu could warm to dat little fella. Her ol' mind can't pass over de color line. She no better den de white folk in dat regard. John Fowler don' have a place to turn in dis cruel world." He sighs.

"If she takes me in, maybe I can help," she says. She fishes a piece of lace out from under blanket. "I finished it." He holds it to the lantern's light.

"Praise de Creator! Musu gonna beg you to stay in her cabin." He takes a burlap bag out of his pocket and lays the lace inside. "I be back to get you after I showed her."

It's past noon when Hephaestus awakens Alexandra from an afternoon nap.

"Musu took one look at de lace and say, 'Bring dat chil' to my cabin.' Musu a sly lady. Last year, she bartered a piece of Penelope's woven cloth for a ham. A swatch of your lace might bring a whole pig shank to her cabin. Musu say to gib you a token o' her admiration."

Hephaestus hands Alexandra a handful of shelled pecans.

"Thank you, Hephaestus."

"I got to sneak you into her place under de cover of night. Miss Cynthia's day-time spies who live in de Quarters got potato eyes; dey everywhere." Hephaestus looks around, seeing no one, he continues, "Miss Musu axe me if you also do embroidery."

Alexandra nods.

Hephaestus winks. "Be ready. I be back tonight."

She puts the pecans on her blanket and looks at them, allowing her desire to ripen. She imagines what it will be like in Musu's cabin. Then she hears horses clopping up the road, their feet striking the cobblestones in unison. She climbs up and looks out a window. A fancy carriage she doesn't recognize is coming toward the drive.

Maybe Monsieur Beaufort bought himself a new conveyance. If he's come back, maybe he'll find a place for her in the big house, and she won't have to move in to the slave cabin.

When the carriage stops, a white-haired man carrying a doctor's bag emerges, followed by Monsieur's regular coachman and two men dressed in white.

Doctor's attendants?

"We need a table to balance the stretcher on," says the shorter man.

The coachman runs up the front steps. Alexandra hears him knock on the door.

A house-servant Alexandra doesn't recognize comes down the stairs. The young woman stops in her tracks when the taller man opens the carriage door and she looks inside.

"What happened to Marse?" she asks.

The coachman and another man carry a table down the stairs and set it by the door of the carriage. The attendants lay the stretcher on top. They struggle to lift Monsieur out of the carriage.

"What happened?" the servant asks again.

"He was struck by apoplexy. He nearly died," says the coachman.

"Where's the lady of the house?" asks the doctor.

"She's out of town seein' to family business," says the servant.

The doctor presses his finger to Monsieur's wrist and feels for his pulse. "We have to make your master comfortable. Show me to his rooms."

"Jesus help us. Follow me, Sir." The servant leads the doctor into the big house. The attendants start to follow with the stretcher.

"Stop!" shouts Pierre as he rides up to the carriage and dismounts.

Pierre's dressed in a bowler and cloak identical to Peter's formal attire.

Odd, Alexandra thinks.

"A friend of the doctor's brought me word that Father's had a stroke. Is that true?" asks Pierre.

Did he say father? Chills creep up Alexandra's spine. What's Pierre up to?

Pierre pulls a portable writing desk out of the pouch attached to his saddle. He slips the strap that secures it over his head and opens it up; it forms a smooth surface. He speaks as he removes a bottle of ink and a quill from an inset drawer. "I was grieved to learn of your illness, Daddy," he says, as he takes a paper from his satchel and lays it out.

Pierre had referred to Monsieur Beaufort as his father—twice.

Pierre offers the pen to the old man. "Miss Cynthia sent word that as she's a woman and has no standing in court, you should designate me as your conservator until you recover your health."

"We have to get your father into bed," says one of the attendants."

"This has to be done now," replies Pierre. "Lift his head so he can write."

"If this is to be legal, he must be in his right mind and sign of his own accord," says the first attendant.

"Are you of right mind, Daddy?" asks Pierre. "He nodded yes," says Pierre. Alexandra didn't see the old man's head move. The attendants don't dispute Pierre's declaration. The coach-man, who has returned from the house, starts to protest. Alexandra sees Pierre put his finger to his lips and press a money pouch into the coachman's hand.

"The affliction affected his right side," says the other attendant. Pierre folds Monsieur Beaufort's left hand around the pen.

Alexandra panics. She wants to call out. The attendants don't realize Pierre isn't Monsieur Beaufort's son. Pierre guides Monsieur's hand to the signature line. Then Monsieur looks more closely at Pierre. Only the left side of his mouth works when he ekes out his words. "Wear a hat when you go out in the sun, Peter."

Monsieur Beaufort spasms. The attendants lay him back down.

"Doctor!" calls the attendant.

The doctor runs down the stairs. Monsieur struggles to breathe. The doctor places a pillow under Monsieur's head. "Follow me."

The attendants carry the stretcher into the big house.

Just as Pierre is putting the signed document inside his satchel, Peter races down the stairs, tucking his shirt into his trousers.

"Why didn't anyone wake me earlier? Athena said Daddy is ill, and I am supposed to sign a paper."

"Everything's been taken care of," Pierre says as he secures the writing box with a saddle strap.

Peter stares at Pierre. "Where did you get those clothes?"

"From my tailor, I believe he's yours as well. Now, if you'll excuse me, I have business to attend to in Georgetown," Pierre mounts his horse and rides out of sight.

Miss Cynthia's carriage pulls into the drive. She nods to Peter as she steps down. "I thought it'd be better to put the driver in charge of your father's affairs, being as you're only seventeen years old. That way, you'll be able to attend to your music."

The young servant calls from the top of the stairs, "Master Peter, your father is calling for you."

Peter runs up the steps two at a time. Miss Cynthia follows, close behind.

Monsieur's coachman looks up at the turret. Alexandra ducks down, A wave of nausea passes over her. Had he seen her?

She stays awake all night, fretting.

Hephaestus comes into her room just before dawn.

"Change into dis," he says, thrusting a worn calico dress with a matching headdress into her hands. "Musu say you can come to her place, but she'd throw you out on your ear if she seed you in dat smelly rag."

Hephaestus hands Alexandra a patched calico dress with a headdress to match.

"You got to hurry. Manny, Monsieur Beaufort's coachman, saw you peekin' out de window. Manny convinced himself Pierre'll give him some money if he tells him someone's up here.

Manny gonna tell Pierre soon as he gets back from seein' de lawyer in Georgetown."

"Turn away while I change," Alexandra says.

Hephaestus sweeps biscuit crumbs into his hand and gathers the blanket, the chamber pot, and the gourds. "Can't leave one speck of evidence you was up here."

When she's dressed, she follows Hephaestus down the dimly lighted slave stairs. As soon as she emerges into the fresh September dawn, she stretches her arms wide, twirls around, and throws her head back.

Hephaestus grabs her arm. "Stop dat. We gots to hurry."

They steal from shadow to shadow, ducking under glassless windows of slave cabins. Hephaestus leads her to the only one with a front porch. He leans close and whispers, "I tol' Musu you was deaf and dumb."

"What?"

"Dey hears one word outta your mouth, and dey know you ain't seed one day as a slave. Don' be tellin' me no more stories about workin' for a master in Virginie."

Alexandra starts to protest, then thinks better of it.

"De way you talk and de tone of your voice turn dem against you sure as rain is wet. Even if she like your fancy lace, Musu ain't gave me her final word about lettin' you take up permanent residence."

Hephaestus hands Alexandra the bag of lace-making supplies.

"Guard dis with your life," he warns.

Boards creak when they step onto Musu's porch. They stop and wait, listening. Not a single sound comes from the cabin. Alexandra's mind turns to food as she breathes in the lingering aroma of last night's pig cracklings.

Hephaestus spits on the hinges to keep them from squeaking. He opens the door just wide enough for Alexandra to slip inside. Snoring and erratic breathing of so many people sleeping in the same room fill Alexandra with dread. Hephaestus takes her hand, guides her across the room and motions for her to climb onto an empty wooden pallet built into the wall. When she hesitates, he leans close and whispers, "Your life depend on makin' dis plan work. Remember, you is deaf an' dumb."

She puts the bundle of lace close to the wall and lies down, careful not to bump her head on the platform above. When she turns to thank Hephaestus, he's already tiptoeing out the door.

A little boy on the platform above hers cries out in his sleep.

"Shet your baby mouth!" yells a woman with a voice almost as deep as a man's.

"Sorry, Miss Musu, I was dreamin' on home."

John Fowler's on the platform directly above her!

Alexandra listens to make sure everyone has settled back to sleep, then she stands on the edge of her platform and hoists herself up until she comes eye to eye with the little boy. In the quietest voice she can manage, she says, "They think I'm deaf and dumb."

John pats her hand and whispers back, "That's a good idea. Nice to see you, Miss Louise."

He hands her a threadbare blanket.

"I don't need two blankets, Ma'am."

"Thank you."

Alexandra presses herself close to the wall, and pulls the blanket up so it covers her whole body.

All too soon, a rooster crows in the dawn. Shadowy shapes begin to stir. Alexandra makes a peep hole in her blanket. She's surprised when she sees the woman she thinks must be Musu, lighting a pine torch from the dying flames in the fireplace. From her voice and the way Hephaestus talked, she'd imagined Musu had barrel-shaped arms and tree-trunk legs. Moving through the cabin like a queen in her castle, the real Musu is tall and slender. Her face is unlined by age, but her black hair is salted with grey. Her dark eyes are huge and fawn-like, her lips full, her neck as graceful as a doe's.

Musu knows magic, Alexandra thinks. Why else would a woman with grey in her hair appear to be so much younger than her years?

Musu plucks a metal rod from its nail on the wall and strikes the steaming iron pot that hangs in the fireplace. The bell-like peal reverberates in Alexandra's head. She wraps the blanket tighter, flattens herself against the wall and stays still as a dead cat. John Fowler slides down from his bed and lands with both feet on the floor, taking care not to step on her.

Musu strikes the pot a second time. The cabin's lazier occupants jump to attention next to their platforms. Musu marches around the room, wielding a pine torch as she scrutinizes the cabin's occupants.

"Where be Penelope?" Musu asks, searching people's faces for signs of deception.

Alexandra sees a young girl's eyes fly to the door then turn back to meet Musu's gaze.

Musu glides toward the little girl whose corn-rows are pulled so tight it makes her eyes slant.

"Spider-girl, you have somethin' to tell Musu?"

Before the frightened child has a chance to answer, an ample-breasted, long-legged, almond-colored, young woman about Alexandra's age waltzes through the door, balancing a basket on her swaying hips.

"Forgive me, Miss Musu," she says in a feathery voice, "I was up at the big house helpin' Pierre move into his fancy new room."

"Helpin' who?" asks Musu.

"Pardon me. I thought y'all knew the driver's name. In exchange for my attentive services, Pierre put in a good word with the cook, and she gave me this basket filled with biscuits. There's enough for everyone to have one of his own. And there's peach jam, too."

Musu snatches the basket and distributes the biscuits to the slaves, still standing at attention by their platforms.

"Why you usin' silver-spoon English?" mutters Musu.

"Penelope rememberin' de big house up to Fairchild Plantation where she be de personal slave of de mistress," offers Spider-girl.

A boy retorts, "Everybody in de world know dat."

Musu stops distributing biscuits when she comes to John Fowler.

"Dey's a crumb or two left," says Musu, her voice tinged with prejudice.

"Thank you, Miss Musu," says John Fowler as Musu pours biscuit fragments into his outstretched hands.

Alexandra sees John Fowler reach into the pouch tied around his neck and take out a mussel shell. He folds his hand around it. He'll need it when the children line up to dip into the milk trough.

Musu turns her attention to a tiny, sweet-faced girl.

"Aesco, it be your turn to help Penelope weave de cloth," says Musu.

"Yes, Ma'am, Miss Musu," says the grinning little girl.

"Hector caught himself a possum last night," announces Musu, indicating the pot. "I throwed in some carrots and a onion and some broke rice. De stew be ready tonight. Whatcha y'all have to tell Hector?"

"Thank you for providin', Hector," the slaves say in unison.

Hector, who Alexandra guesses to be fifteen or sixteen, flashes a smile. "My pleasure,"

Musu raises her arms straight up in the air and arches her neck. The slaves and John Fowler kneel on the bare floor, fold their hands in prayer, and close their eyes.

"Let us go forth for de glory of de Lord," says Musu.

"Amen," say the slaves.

Outside, the breakfast triangle proclaims milk is being served in the children's trough. The little ones grab their straw hats off hooks nailed to the door jam and race into the drizzle of the autumn morning.

Alexandra wonders why little John Fowler has no hat.

Later, the adults traipse out the door. Alexandra sighs, grateful to have escaped Musu's notice.

She figures if she were really deaf and dumb, she wouldn't be expected to hear Musu's wake up call. That will be her excuse if Musu asks why she didn't properly present herself. But how will she convey her message?

She wants to lay still and try to figure out how a person who's deaf and dumb should communicate, but she'll burst if she doesn't relieve herself soon. She peruses the room. No sign of a chamber pot. She'll have to find an outhouse as quick as she can. Pulling off the blanket and making certain she's alone in the room,
she inches toward the edge of her platform,

The dirt floor feels cool and damp to her bare feet. She makes her way to the door. Her heart drops when she looks through the tiny glassless window and sees Penelope sitting on a bench on the covered porch. Aesco kneels by her side, passing up strands of the flax thread wound around her hands.

Alexandra looks around the cabin. Her eyes light up when she sees a back door. She tiptoes toward that exit, thankful the floor is made of pressed earth instead of squeaking boards.

She spits on the hinge, like she watched Hephaestus do, and pushes open the door. She slips out onto the narrow ledge that separates the cabin from a wide trench where water carries off debris in a steady stream.

She's about to wade through the water to the other side when a bloated rat floats by, its claw-like forepaws raised in supplication to the grey sky. As she stands there in the drizzle, debating whether or not to wade to the other side, she sees what she thinks is a log moving along with the current. If she can angle herself into the correct position, she can pull it up, float it across the water and jam it into the other side of the ditch. When she digs her toes into the mud and leans down to catch it, the log's jaw opens to reveal razor-sharp teeth. The young alligator twists toward her. She backs into the cabin and shuts the door, shaken.

The pain in her bladder bears down. She has no choice. She walks out the front door, pretending more confidence than she feels. She uses a series of gestures to ask where the outhouse is.

Penelope leaps to her feet. "What are you doing in our cabin?" she demands.

Alexandra lays her head on her pressed-together-hands and closes her eyes, trying to convey that she was sleeping. Inventing her sign language as she goes, she ends by gesturing she has to relieve herself and wonders where the toilet facilities are.

"Want me to take you to do your business?" asks Aesco.

"Sit right where you are," Penelope tells Aesco. She lays the cloth she's weaving over the top of the loom and picks up a pine-handle broom; she lifts it above her head and stalks toward Alexandra.

Alexandra jumps off the porch. She hears the broom handle, meant to crack her skull, break when it hits the porch rail.

Alexandra splashes through the channel of filthy water and runs toward the swamp at the back of the cabins.

In the distance she hears Penelope yell, "Aesco, get me a straight branch to fix this broom."

By the time Alexandra reaches the swamp, thunder is roaring in the distance. Lightning bolts flash down from boiling clouds.

Alexandra steps up onto solid ground, wondering if the storm will wash snakes out of their dens. She goes around to the other side of a tree, pulls up her dress and squats, smiling as the pressure is relieved. As soon as she's done her business, it starts to pour. The stream she just crossed rises. What if a freshet comes roaring down from the Piedmont?

She comes to a sturdy pine. Hand over hand, she climbs to a fork of broad branches and winds her arms around the trunk.

The wind blows. The tree sways. An hour or more passes before the rain softens to a patter and sunlight streams through a hole in the clouds, revealing a blue sky. The eye of the storm that Mamou cautioned her about? Is the worst yet to come?

A curtain of dark clouds rolls across the sun. Alexandra maneuvers so she's facing the rice fields and holds tight to the stout trunk. Wind screams through the branches like a maenad gone mad.

She closes her eyes and braces her head against the trunk, startled to hear the voice of the Ahoelra shouting inside her mind. "*Why not give up? Let go. Fall. What is there for you in this world?*"

She hears a horse whinny. Her eyes spring open. No horse is visible. Is Cabai speaking to her from his spirit body?

"I won't give up," she tells the Ahoelra without much conviction.

"*Fool,*" whispers the Ahoelra, its teeth clattering.

Memories of the smoke-filled blacksmith shop and Jimi's face in the window assault her. She loosens her grip and imagines herself falling to the ground, the constant, stabbing pain of her guilt dissolving in her throes of death, her terror about what her life might become ebbing into the damp earth. The storm taunts her. She calls on her ancestors to give her courage. But she knows if she takes her own life, she'll carry her burdens into the next world.

"*Let go,*" says the Ahoelra.

She's tempted.

But if she gives in, she'll never fulfill her promise to help John Fowler and tell her people's story.

Movement draws her attention to the crook of an oak where a black panther, like the one at Papa's funeral, stares at her. Power flows from its yellow-green eyes, filling her with new resolve.

"I won't give up," she shouts.

The Ahoelra vanishes.

Finally, the last of the clouds rolls away and sunlight streams down as if there had never been a storm. New-washed leaves sparkle like jewels. Alexandra looks for the panther. All she sees is a burl in the tree's trunk.

A song she's never heard plays in her head. African drums interweave with Mozart. A gift from Emitai?

It occurs to her that she could slip away from this plantation prison, and no one would come looking. Mr. Beaufort isn't in his right mind. Maybe he never had time to register her name on his property ledger. Less than a handful of people at *Rose* knows she exists: John Fowler, who's proven he can keep a secret; Hephaestus, who would incriminate himself if he acknowledged he's been helping her; Peter, who fears someone will find his secret sanctuary. Monsieur's coachman is happy to accept money from Peter in exchange for his silence.

Musu, who now has Alexandra's patch of lace, could present a problem. But odds seem to be in Alexandra's favor.

She'll find a way to sneak back to Heaven Hill and retrieve Papa's gold without anyone seeing her. She could buy passage on a schooner to Charleston and find Grand-mère. The sheriff must believe she's dead by now, and if she never makes a claim on Heaven, he and his men won't come looking for her.

Just as her despair is turning to hope, a scream rents the air.

"Help!" calls John Fowler.

Is someone hurting little John?

"Help! Hurry!"

Alexandra scrambles down from the tree and runs toward the curve of swamp that opens onto the rice fields. As soon as she's clear of the trees, she sees John Fowler's head bob up from a row of rice.

"Over here!" he calls, frantically waving his hands.

She sloshes through ankle-deep mud and finds John trying to keep Hector's head above the water of a flooded irrigation ditch. Hector's eyelids flutter as he struggles to remain conscious. Alexandra jumps in the water.

"We were working in the rice; then it started storming. The driver galloped around on his horse and ordered everyone to go home soon as lightning started raining fire," says John Fowler as he strokes Hector's cheek. "I was at the back of the line, behind Hector. He started swaying, then he fell face down. He would've drowned if I hadn't turned him over and put his head up on my lap."

Alexandra checks Hector's face and arms.

"It doesn't seem like lightning struck him." She looks closer and sees Hector's engorged wrist. In the center of the swelling, there are two points of blood: fang marks.

"A moccasin bit him." She rips a strip of cloth from the bottom of her dress and wraps it tight a few inches above the bite.

"You have anything sharp?" she asks.

"No, Ma'am."

Hector's eyes flutter and open.

Alexandra tells John, "Hold his shoulders as tight as you can. Tell him a snake bit him, and I'm gonna try to suck out the venom. Tell him I've got to open up the wound, or he'll die. Tell him it'll hurt more if he moves."

Poisonous snakes were a problem at Heaven, too. Mamou taught her how to suck venom, but she never thought she'd have to do it. Lacking a sharp tool, she sinks her teeth into Hector's skin and rips open the wound.

Hector jerks.

"Hold him still."

When Hector starts to thrash again, John lays his mouth next to Hector's ear and hums a tune. Hector quiets down.

Alexandra sucks salty blood mixed with bitter venom and spits it out. When there's no more vile taste, she wipes her mouth and presses her thumb over Hector's wound. She rips a strip of cloth from the bottom of her shift and winds it tight a few inches above the wound. Then, she nods to John and gestures that they need to get him to Musu's cabin. It takes all their strength to lift Hector to a standing position, but it's impossible to help him walk, and he's too heavy for the two of them to carry. They inch Hector out of the irrigation channel onto the land.

Alexandra looks into John Fowler's worried eyes. "Get help! And remember, I'm deaf and dumb. Hector's too far out of his mind to remember me talking."

John sprints toward Musu's cabin.

Hector shivers. His eyelids twitch. Alexandra holds his head on her lap and hums Peter's music.

Finally, John comes racing back with Chiron, a big man with a child's mind. He has a slow, loving nature. Chiron scoops Hector into his arms and cradles him as if her were a baby. "You my strong boy, Hector. You hang on!" Chiron says as he kisses Hector's forehead and heads to Musu's cabin.

When no one but John can hear, she says, "You go on. I have some personal business to attend to. Thank you for keeping my secrets. I'll be back."

Alexandra wants to take the little boy in her arms and hug him and tell him that she's making her escape, that as soon as she straightens out her own affairs, she will buy his indenture. But it wouldn't be wise to tell him her plan.

When John runs to catch up with Chiron, Alexandra turns back toward the swamp, determined to escape. She hears the horse coming toward her before she sees it. Pierre trots his stallion in front of her and blocks her path. His sneer turns her blood to frost.

"Penelope told me there was an interloper in Musu's cabin. That's when I understood why this bill of sale was in Monsieur Beaufort's satchel." He waves a paper in front of Alexandra's eyes. "Your name Louise? Where you been hidin' yourself?"

Alexandra's about to speak when she remembers she's "deaf and dumb." She shakes her head and gesticulates, indicating that she can't understand one word he's saying.

"You slow?"

Alexandra shrugs and lowers her eyes, searching her mind for what to do next.

"Look at me when I'm talking to you. Where do you belong?"

She doesn't look up. Pierre slides off his saddle and loops a long leather strap around her hands. He remounts and ties the other end to his saddle horn.

How can a man with such lovely eyes be so cruel?

"Keep up," he warns as he kicks his horse to a fast cantor. Alexandra jogs, careful to keep some slack in the tether.

When they arrive at the crossroads, Musu comes running over to the driver's horse, waving her arms and shooting fire from her eyes.

"Where you goin' with my girl?"

"Your girl?"

"Didn't Master Beaufort tell you? She lives in my cabin. She cain't hear and she cain't talk, but she do make lace fit for a queen. Surely you remember how disappointed Miss Cynthia was when her last lace-maker died," says Musu.

Pierre scrutinizes Musu. "I caught her heading toward the swamp. Looked to me like she was fixin' to run."

"Sent her to get some herbs for Hector—who you left in the ditch to die of snake bite. Dis girl stay with my boy while de little white fella run to fetch Chiron. No tellin' what Miss Cynthia'll do if she find out you abused the one person on this plantation who can make lace."

"Why wasn't I told about this girl?"

"Miss Cynthia don't know about her yet. Marse Beaufort was fixin' to make this girl a Christmas present after he surprise Miss Cynthia with lace for her Christmas Eve ball gown."

"You have a piece of this lace to show me?" Pierre asks.

"Follow me."

When they get to the cabin, Musu brings out Alexandra's square of lace all laid out on a clean, black cloth. "This here's for you to look at—not to touch."

Pierre's eyebrows shoot up when he sees the intricate lacework. He squints at Alexandra like she's a puzzle to be solved. Then, thunder rattles the sky, announcing the arrival of another band of storms.

"I'll be watching y'all," he warns. "Untie her and take her in your cabin." Musu complies. Pierre puts on his oilcloth slicker and gallops toward the big house.

When they're inside the cabin, Alexandra sees Aesco cooling Hector's fevered brow with damp cloths. "Dat baby have de healer's touch," says Musu.

Alexandra sits on her platform and wraps her arms around herself to ward off a chill.

Penelope points at Alexandra. "She's the one I tol' you about, Miss Musu. Why are you bringin' her in here?"

Musu scowls. "She save my Hector's life. Dis child likely to catch pneumonia in dis wet rag. Give her one of your dresses."

"Nothing I have will fit her."

Musu throws a hard-eye at Penelope. "She kept Hector from driftin' to de next world. You find somethin' dry for her to wear."

Alexandra sees John sitting in a dark corner, his knees drawn up to his chest, his teeth chattering. She takes his hand and leads him over to a stool in front of the fire. No one objects.

Musu motions for Alexandra to stand up.

"You cain't hear or speak, is dat de way it is?" Musu asks.

Alexandra nods.

"But you can comprehend?"

Alexandra points from her eyes to her lips.

"You can follow de words de lips make, is dat what you's sayin'?"

Alexandra nods.

"How you learn dat, child?"

Alexandra shrugs.

"All right, you have it your way. Now, you got to win de favor of Miss Cynthia. She de mistress of de big house. Understand?"

Alexandra nods.

"Can you make a collar for her Christmas dress?"

Using her hands, Alexandra asks how large the collar is to be.

"I got de measurement. Can you do it?"

Alexandra smiles and retrieves her bag of lace making supplies.

"Dat be your ticket to stayin' alive."

Alexandra works through the day and into the night. Her fingers keep a steady rhythm with her thoughts—loop and tack, loop and tack—as she creates a lace collar that she hopes will save her from toiling her life away between rows of rice.

It's still dark when Hector opens his eyes. "Where is my Mama?"

Musu has nodded off to asleep, sitting by his side, on a homemade stool. Alexandra touches Musu's hand and indicates Hector with a nod in his direction.

"Praise God!" Tears run down Musu's cheeks as she kisses Hector all over his face then hugs him so tight he has a hard time catching his breath.

"When all de folks run for shelter from de rain, de little white fella' stayed with me. He held my head in his lap and hollered for help. Den dat girl, she stepped out from de trees and ran to my side and sucked out de snake poison. De two together saved my life."

Alexandra watches Musu's eyes travel over to John, who is curled up as close to the fireplace as he can get without setting fire to himself.

"Hades!"

A little boy jumps up out of his sleep and stands at attention by the side of his platform. "Give John Fowler some dry clothes."

Hades eyes spark with the rebellion.

"He saved your brother," says Musu. "Git him de dry clothes afore I get de switch."

Hades looks to Hector for confirmation.

"He saved me, all right. You got cotton in your ears?" asks Hector.

Hades goes over to Hector's platform and fishes dry clothes out from under the bed.

As Alexandra thinks on these things, a little girl hand-springs in through the front door.

"You gots somethin' to tell us, Arachne?" asks Musu.

"Miss Cynthia comin' down de lane. We gonna have a fine Christmas."

"How do you know?" Penelope yawns and stretches her way from sleep to wakefulness.

"Dey never been no Christmas festivity at Rose," says Hector. "Miss Cynthia jes' tryin' to make us work faster."

"Maybe this is one of the deals she made with that necromancer to make sure her boy's soul gets a place in heaven," says Penelope.

"Where you git an idea like dat?" Musu asks.

Arachne ignores them all, cartwheels off the porch and steals around the side of the cabin to spy on John Fowler, who's gone outside behind a bush to change into dry clothes.

"Ladies, pick up your winnowing baskets. Men grab your hoes. Christmas is almost three months off, and a lot can happen between now and then. If y'all want Christmas ham, stand up and make ready to go on out and work."

CHAPTER TWENTY-FOUR

By the time December arrives, Alexandra and John Fowler are accepted members of Musu's cabin-family. The best harvest in five years puts Miss Cynthia in such a good mood, she gathers the slaves in the kitchen house and announces that, in addition to the privilege of selling their wares during Advent, they'll each receive a surprise on Christmas Day. Alexandra keeps up with the lace requested by Miss Cynthia's dressmaker. She also makes five collars, four armrest covers, and two cuffs she intends to sell at the holiday sale, with the hope of purchasing a violin.

"My promise is only good if y'all keep up with your regular work," Miss Cynthia tells the field slaves.

That night Alexandra lies on her platform, reviewing the twists and turns in her life. She'll turn seventeen the day after Christmas. Six months ago, she was worrying about tripping over some boy's feet while she attempted the minuet, and she was looking forward to setting Lulu free. What's happening to Lulu now?, she wonders as she drifts off to sleep.

In the middle of the night, Alexandra is awakened by her own chattering teeth. She tries to think herself warm like Mamou taught her, but her toes are almost numb and her nose feels like it might snap off. She's about to close her eyes and try for more sleep when she sees a shadowy form stealing toward her in the dim light. She relaxes when she sees it's Musu coming close, carrying something in her arms.

Alexandra closes her eyes and pretends to sleep as Musu covers her with one of the duck-down quilts meant for the Christmas sale. Alexandra smiles as she warms up and drifts into a happy dream where Cabai is beckoning to her, his eyes full of mischief. She grabs his mane and swings up onto to his back. They race across a summer meadow.

Alexandra wakes at dawn when she hears Musu ask someone, "Where you been all night?"

There's no apology in Penelope's voice. "Sittin' by Marse Beaufort's side at Pierre's request, offerin' the old man sips of water every time he tapped his thumb on his mattress. I was listenin' too. Arachne was right. That necromancer told Miss Cynthia her little Jacob would go into the light if she'd make a fine Christmas for *Rose of Sharon* slaves and have a tar-and-feather ceremony on New Year's Day."

"A tar-and-feather? Rose has never had one of those nasty devil-parties."

"How is Master Beaufort?" John Fowler asks.

"Right side of his body's limp as a rag, but the left side works fine. He can't spit out all the words he wants to say; he doesn't say much. His eyes lit up when Master Peter came in the room and played a tune on his violin; he even smiled with half his face. Then Miss Cynthia marched in. 'Put that noise-maker away, she said. 'Marse needs his rest.'

"Marse gestured with his good hand, sayin' he wanted Peter to continue, so he just kept playing.

"She said, 'I am in charge, here. Leave this room now if you expect me to give you your allowance.' Peter packed up his violin and left in a huff."

Musu stirs a handful of squirming crawdads into the water boiling in the iron pot hung over the fireplace. "Peter will be in a heap of danger if Marse don't come back to his old self."

"Dat's de truth," Hector says from across the room, where he's making a toy birchbark canoe for Hades' birthday.

Penelope continues, "Soon as Marse opened his mouth to speak again, Miss Cynthia patted him on the head like he was a good old dog and made him swallow her sleepin' tea. Marse nodded off before he could find his words.

"Miss Cynthia smiled and rattled on 'bout all the folks around here are gonna proclaim she has the best Christmas heart in the whole world—the whole world, that's what she said. After that, she got quiet, and I heard her whisper, 'After the tar-and-feather, my Jacob will be taken up to heaven.'"

"Who she plannin' to tar-and-feather and send to an early grave?" asks Musu.

"How would I know?" Penelope unclips a silver hair bobble with a red jewel and rubs it with the sleeve of her dress to make it shine.

"De driver give you dat shiny thing?" asks Musu.

Penelope smiles and nods.

"Don' you be letting' dat Pierre raise your hope too high, even if he do let you call him by his Christian name," says Musu.

Penelope rolls her eyes.

Three days before Christmas, Alexandra's life takes an unexpected turn. Field slaves are out cleaning up the rice beds, except for Musu and Penelope, who are helping to sew the new clothes Miss Cynthia ordered for her winter parties, and Alexandra, who's embroidering roses on the collar of Miss Cynthia's New Year's Eve dress.

Alexandra has just knotted the thread on the last leaf when a young cock of a man with pecan-colored skin and brown eyes flecked with gold struts up the path to the porch.

"Be careful of that boy," Penelope says as he brushes off his new yellow vest like he's a fancy bird preening to lure a mate.

He tilts his bowler hat and slides his eyes up and down Penelope's body, lingering too long on certain features. "Mornin', Miss Penelope," he says in a voice smooth and thick as molasses.

Penelope replies with a snort, and keeps her eyes fixed on her sewing.

"Mornin', Miss Musu," he continues, undeterred.

"Lyle, you been a stranger ever since dey takes you up to de big house," says Musu.

Ignoring Musu's comment, Lyle stations himself squarely in front of Alexandra and speaks loud and slow, making certain she can read his lips.

"Miss Cynthia's callin' for you to bring yourself, your clothes, and your lace-makin's up to the big house." He gesticulates as he speaks, as if flying his hands around will help her to understand what he's saying. "I'll wait here on the porch for you to ready yourself." He gives Alexandra a cotton bag. "To collect your things," he tells her. Then he tips his hat and leans on the railing as close to Penelope as he can get. Musu follows Alexandra into the cabin.

Will she still be able to sell her lace at the Christmas market? Maybe she can slip a couple of her extra pieces to Musu and offer to give her part of the profit.

Musu reads her mind and takes Alexandra out of the range of the boy's hearing. "Miss Cynthia will sniff around. If you don't take every piece of your lace wid you to de big house, Miss Cynthia'll see to it that you pay de piper."

"But . . ."

"I cain't sell one inch of your lace widout dat witch-woman learnin' about it, Louise."

A pall of sadness washes over Alexandra. She's going to miss Musu and Arachne. And she's come to love John Fowler like he was her own brother. How will the little boy get along without her? And how will she get along with him?

Alexandra goes over to her sleeping platform and gathers her lace-making supplies. Musu hadn't told her to take the quilt, so she guesses it was meant to be a loaner and not a gift. She lifts up her straw mattress and takes out the arm coverings and collars she'd stayed up nights making for the Christmas sale.

She's almost certain Musu has guessed she isn't deaf. The other day, when Musu and Alexandra were the only ones in the cabin, Musu had whispered, "Louise," from across the room. Alexandra had spun around to face her. Will Musu keep her secret?

As soon as Alexandra comes out of the door carrying her meager earthly possessions, Lyle snaps to attention.

"Hold a piece o' your lace to the light," he commands.

Alexandra picks up a piece of lace and holds it up. He squints as he inspects it. Then he frowns. "I was told Louise is deaf," says the boy.

"She's readin' your lips. She's real good at it," says Penelope, dropping nettles into her voice.

Lyle turns the lace over and scrutinizes it.

"Ain't no bugs in my house, and you knows it." Musu exclaims.

"I'll take your lace," Lyle says.

He puts Alexandra's Christmas sale lace in the blue-velvet bag that he's brought for that purpose. "You can keep the cotton bag for your supplies," he says, as though he's bestowing a fine gift.

Musu hugs Alexandra. Then she puts her hands on Alexandra's shoulders and looks her in the eye. "Dat quilt be waitin' on you when you come back. Wouldn't do to take it into dat big house where someone else would make a claim on it." Musu kisses Alexandra on the forehead, like Mamou used to do.

It's all Alexandra can do to hold on to her tears. She's surprised when Penelope stands up and pecks her on each cheek, then she recalls someone saying Penelope used to serve a French mistress. When Alexandra turns to wave good-bye, she sees a tear rolling down Musu's cheek. Penelope's eyes are dry.

Alexandra follows Lyle, glad the sun has come out and there's no frost on the ground to freeze her bare toes. As they pass by the kitchen house, aromas of cinnamon and apples spark memories of the festive parties Mother put on during the holidays.

They round the corner. Alexandra looks back. It's the first time she's seen the big house from this angle. It's Greek Revivalist, like Heaven, but it looks like a poor relation. There are no flower pots hanging from the veranda rafters and no glass tea table on the alcove outside the sitting room. The turret on top looks gaudy and out of place. Gargoyles peer down from roof eaves with clownish smiles that make the house look like a pretender.

Lyle leads Alexandra around back. She supposes he means to take her up the slave stairs, but he keeps on going toward a circle of trees. The hairs on the back of her neck stand at attention. She opens her mouth to ask where he's leading her. She catches herself, just in time—she's sick and tired of being deaf and dumb.

Lyle takes her down a sparsely beaten path to a patch of grass surrounded by a wall of pine trees. What's he planning? Should she take her chance and run?

Then she sees a big pot hung in a tree with a pipe protruding from it. She relaxes. It's an improvised shower, like the one slaves at Pinnacle use. She realizes he's bringing her here to wash. At least that's what she hopes.

He stands in front of her, opens his mouth wide, and shouts, "Take off your clothes!"

Alexandra presses her lips into a grim line, folds her arms across her chest, and shakes her head in an emphatic, "No!"

"I could call on reinforcements, but I don't think you'd like that."

If he has to call for help, it'll make him appear weak, she reasons. She wraps her arms tighter.

He points up to the water tank and speaks so slowly, she can barely follow his train of thought. "Once a field slave brought body lice into the big house. Now Miss Cynthia don't allow outside help to set a toe in the door unless they's scrubbed clean as a sea stone."

She frowns, as though she can't follow such a long string of words. He points up at the tank. "Make you clean. Pull string and wash. I bring new clothes."

Through a series of gestures, Alexandra makes it known that she will do as he says. But he must bring the new clothes before she removes the old ones, and he must turn his back until she is dressed.

Lyle returns with a blue house-help outfit without a single patch. Then he turns around. Seeing no spies, she pulls her sweat-stained dress off over her head. She has to restrain herself from crying out when she pulls the string connected to the iron tank. A white liquid that smells like rat poison pours over her. Even though she washes her body and her hair and dries off with the towel he gave her, her skin feels sticky. Then she notices the bucket of clear water over to the side of the shower apparatus, and she washes off the residue.

When she's dressed and has smoothed down her hair as best she can, she taps Lyle on the shoulder to let him know she's ready. He's been so true to his word; she wonders if he finds her attractive enough to spy on.

He leads her in through the back entrance of the big house and indicates she's to put on the shoes set out for her. Those red russets squeeze her toes and rub on her feet in all the wrong places. A tall beanpole of a woman with honey-colored skin and dark brown hair done up in a tight bun comes in and looks Alexandra up and down like she's judging the quality of a milk cow. The woman raises one eyebrow, clicks her tongue and turns to Lyle.

"Well. Show me the lace." She snatches the pouch from his proffered hand. Her eyebrows shoot up when she pulls out a collar and sees the beautiful pattern Alexandra invented.

"Take her in," the woman says with a trace of a British accent, like Eusebia's.

Alexandra follows Lyle through a maze of hallways to a

windowless interior room lit by the flames of hundreds of candles set in a candelabra that hangs from an ornately carved ceiling. Lyle gestures for Alexandra to sit in a straight-backed chair that faces a Queen Anne's chair with gorgeous brocade cushions.

"Good luck. You'll need it," Lyle says. When he leaves, he quietly closes the door. So as not to rile Miss Cynthia, Alexandra guesses. She sits erect in the chair, waiting. Her eyes fasten on the painting of a pale elderly man, who looks like an older version of Peter. The gentleman's eyes dance with life.

She assumes he's Peter's grandfather. The man in the painting wears a light blue brocade waistcoat over an embroidered shirt and knee breeches, identical to clothes she's seen Peter wear sometimes, except for the man's tricorne. Peter usually wears a bowler, or no hat at all.

Alexandra's heart races when the painted man's lips appear to curl into a smile. She closes her eyes to shut his image out of her mind. When she summons the courage to look at the painting again, the man's face has returned to its original, grim expression. Either this is no ordinary painting, or her nerves are playing tricks on her mind.

When she hears footsteps coming down the hall, she crosses her ankles and stares at the floor. The scent of roses mixed with lilac announces Miss Cynthia's arrival. The woman sashays into the room, her pink satin gown rustling. Alexandra stands, curtseys and holds her pose.

"You didn't learn how to bow to a lady like that from living in slave quarters. I suppose they didn't want you sewing in a house where your silk could pick up the scent of those dismal environs."

Alexandra frowns, as if she doesn't understand.

"I forgot!" says Miss Cynthia. She steps right in front of Alexandra and exaggerates as she tilts Alexandra's chin up until they're looking at each other eye to eye. "Always stand up straight and look at me when I speak."

Alexandra's startled by the pain she sees in Miss Cynthia's eyes. The young woman turns away and gazes at the man in the painting. When she turns her attention back to Alexandra, she's masked all trace of vulnerability.

There's a tap on the door.

"Come," says Miss Cynthia.

The servant who met Alexandra at the door enters carrying a pillow on which the lace collar has been laid. As Miss Cynthia studies the intricate patterns, her eyes dart from the lace to Alexandra.

"Who taught you how to make lace this fine?" Miss Cynthia asks.

Alexandra crosses herself and bows her head in prayer.

"I've been given to understand nuns on the island of Martinique taught her," says the tall woman.

Had John repeated Alexandra's made-up story?

The servant sidles to the far corner of the room. *Be a fly on the wall*, Alexandra tells herself, as she focuses on the mid-distance and endures careful scrutiny. Miss Cynthia, who has not yet gained the ability to mask her feelings consistently, like a proper lady, smiles too brightly when she turns to the servant, "Antonia, take this girl to the patio room."

Antonia's mouth drops open in surprise.

Miss Cynthia speaks slowly. "Do you have time to create a narrow edge of lace for the sleeves of my dress before Christmas Eve in two days?"

Alexandra nods.

"Take her to her new room and give her those spools of silk thread that arrived yesterday. I'm goin' to lie down and take my beauty nap. Don't disturb me until supper's called."

"Yes, Ma'am," Antonia says.

Antonia should work on her curtsey, Alexandra thinks.

When they're in the hallway, Antonia's nose flies into the air. "Follow me," she says as she leads Alexandra down a hallway wide enough to accommodate the statues of Christian saints who stand in alcoves built into the wall.

Antonia stops before an elaborately carved door, unlocks the latch, and turns the knob.

"Your room," Antonia announces, "for now."

Alexandra tries not to gawk at the elegant furnishings.

"I'll be back," says Antonia. She locks the door from the outside.

Alexandra folds down a green velvet bedspread and stretches out on the silk sheets of the four-poster bed. An intricately carved rocking chair sits beneath a large window framed by cream-colored chiffon curtains. A marble-topped table, similar to the one in Grand-mère's bedroom, sits beside the rocker. But what impresses her most is the stone fireplace topped with a deep brown mahogany mantle.

Alexandra closes her eyes and imagines she's back at Heaven. She's drifting off to sleep when Antonia flounces back into the room and sets two spools of silk thread on the table by the chair. Through a combination of gestures and simple phrases, Antonia tells Alexandra to complete the lace edging as quickly as possible.

When Alexandra lays out her lace-making supplies, she discovers that some of the bobbins are missing. They must still be in Musu's cabin. She's relieved to find her door's no longer locked from the outside. It's the lazy time of day. Maybe no one will notice if she leaves the big house through the slave entrance.

Once outside, workers pay no mind to her. She's almost to Musu's cabin when the sob of a grown man rents the air. Has a runaway been captured? She hears it again, muffled this time, but filled with such anguish she feels compelled to investigate. She pulls her skirt up above her ankles, turns off the path and wades through tall grass, following the sound.

She freezes when she sees Peter pummeling the trunk of an oak tree with his bare fists. "I'll kill him!" he shouts. Then he sinks to the ground, nursing his bloody knuckles. He senses her presence and turns around.

Alexandra stands paralyzed as she looks at him.

"Get away," he whispers.

"Is it your father?" she asks.

The stone mask of his face drops away as he shakes his head and weeps.

Alexandra kneels by his side.

He stands and throws his hands into the air. "It's lost!" he screams.

When he's calmer, she asks, "What's lost?"

"My music! I went up to the turret this morning. My music is gone." Tears spill from his eyes. "My step-mother ordered Pierre to paint over my score. I've been working on that piece for seven years." He stops crying and frowns. "Why am I telling this to you?"

"Because I know the world needs to hear your music."

Peter looks stunned. "That's what Mother said, exactly those words. I was going to transcribe the music to paper as soon as I wrote the end. I didn't commit it to memory."

"I did," Alexandra says, simply.

"What?"

"I committed it to memory."

Alexandra can't read the odd look on Peter's face.

"You remember the whole composition? I don't understand."

"It's what my grandmother called one of my gifts."

"Your gifts?"

"I can recall whatever I see, if I put my mind to it. I was up in that room for a long time with nothing else to do."

Alexandra hums the first few bars of his score. Her voice trails off.

"Go on," he says. And she does. When she's finished, he gazes into her eyes for a long while, then he asks, "Who are you?"

Afraid to tell the truth, and afraid to get caught in a lie, Alexandra simply smiles. "I'll transcribe your score. Sneak a pen and some paper to the patio room where I'm staying. I'll work on it and have it finished before Christmas Day. I'll start as soon as I finish Miss Cynthia's lace. That should be tonight." She pauses briefly. "Everyone but you and John and Hephaestus and Monsieur Beaufort's coachman think I'm deaf and dumb. It has to stay that way."

"Of course."

Their eyes lock. Peter moves toward her. She doesn't move, or breathe. When he reaches for her hand, she steps back and breaks the spell, afraid that giving into her feelings will only bring heartache—and danger.

Peter stiffens. "I'll bring you some paper and a pen and ink. They let me stay with my father alone a few hours a day. I'll tell him you're coming in his room to transcribe my music."

"All right," Alexandra says, "And bring a ruler," she adds.

"Thank you for doing this." He smiles, then he turns and double-steps toward the big house.

On her way to Musu's, Alexandra's feet skim the ground. She hums a love tune. *Stop it*, she orders herself. The song keeps going in her head until Musu's cabin comes into sight and she spots Hector up on the roof.

A look-out? Alexandra tenses.

Aesco and a smaller girl Alexandra doesn't recognize sit on the porch spinning her lace bobbins like they were toy tops. Alexandra starts to scold them, then remembers she's supposed to be deaf and dumb. She claps her hands together and gestures for the children to bring those bobbins to her. They don't even look up from their game. She's about to give up her charade of being unable to speak when Musu leans her head out of the front door and says, "Christmas cakes with honey's waiting for hungry children in the side yard."

The children leap off the porch. Alexandra scoops up the bobbins. They're a little scratched, but they'll serve their purpose. The problem is they're not all here.

A whistling duck's *wa-hoo*, Hector's best call, brings Aesco and the other little girl running around from the side of the cabin. Musu opens the door. They rush inside. Hector jumps off the roof and follows them. Musu grabs Alexandra's arm, pulls her into the cabin and quietly shuts the door. Alexandra hears horses galloping toward the quarters. Blood drains from Musu's face. When the horses pass by, Musu relaxes.

As Alexandra's eyes adjust to the dimness of the cabin, she sees the little girl from the porch huddled between a man and woman she doesn't recognize. Ares and Hephaestus are hunched over in the corner, hope sparking in their eyes. Alexandra senses what this is about. They're getting ready to run to freedom.

Let John Fowler and me come with you, Alexandra begs inside her mind, hoping Musu will catch her thought, like it happens sometimes.

"When we goin', Musu?" asks Hephaestus, fiddling with his hat.

"Christmas Eve. Just after midnight."

The woman casts a fearful glance in Alexandra's direction.

"Don't worry. She can't tell anyone. She's deaf and dumb," the observant Aesco tells her.

"We goin' before we git our Christmas ham," says Musu. "Miss Cynthia won't expect no one to leave before dey gets de ham and de secret prize."

Musu's appraisal makes sense.

"Y'all who live at *Rose* got to do your work with a cheerful face, and don' tell no one, not even your own blood, what we be plannin'."

They nod in unison, as if connected by an invisible force.

"Uncle Renault and Auntie and little Jane, y'all'll have to stay down under de floor till de time come to run."

Hector pulls a deerskin rug off a trap door and tugs on an imbedded iron ring. Oak planks, covered with dirt to make them look like part of the bare floor, open to a staircase that leads into a fortified underground room. A pine torch set into one of the clay walls provides illumination.

Musu nods at Aesco, who steps forward and cheers up the room with her smile.

"Aesco will bring y'all your food. May not be tasty, but' it'll keep y'all alive. We'll empty your pots two times a day. Go on down, now."

Uncle Renault picks up little Jane. "You gonna be my brave girl?"

Jane nods. Her father carries her down into the secret chamber. Her mother follows.

When Musu gives the nod, Hector closes up the door and smooths loose dirt over the seams.

"De rest o' y'all, go about your work. All 'cept Aesco." Musu kneels down by Aesco.

"Remember what I tol' you 'bout keepin' a secret?" asks Musu.

"I won't tell no one we goin', not even Penelope," promises the little girl.

"Especially not Penelope. Tote dat bouquet of wild flowers up to Miss Cynthia, just like we plan," says Musu.

"And tell whoever answers the door, we's grateful for the promise of a ham," says Aesco.

When everyone else has left the room, Musu beckons to Alexandra.

"We alone, now. You and I both know you can hear a pin drop from across de room."

Alexandra hesitates, then she says, "I'm missing some lace bobbins."

"You heard all what was said here. I trust you not to breathe a word. You and little John is welcome to come with us."

Alexandra throws her arms around Musu. "Thank you!"

"We ain't free yet."

"Best not keep Miss Cynthia's Christmas dress waitin'. We don't want to stir no suspicion."

They scoop up the missing bobbins from under Penelope's sleeping platform.

Musu clicks her tongue and says, "Penelope been livin' most nights in de big house. 'Spose de little ones thought her pallet was a safe place to store their treasure. Pray to God dat girl stay in dat fancy house till dis deed come to completion."

Alexandra looks around. "Where's John Fowler?"

"De driver workin' him to his death. He out there now, wadin' round in de rice water der usin' to leach out de salt—wid no hat to protect him from de sun. We'll gather him in our fold when it come time to go."

"John Fowler knows I can hear. He can keep a secret. Please, take him aside and tell him we're going to escape with you."

"I'll think on it."

Alexandra hugs Musu again.

"Hurry on, now," says Musu. "We gonna meet by de three oaks. You know dat place?"

Alexandra nods.

"Midnight on Christmas Eve. If you ain't there, we cain't wait."

"I understand," says Alexandra.

CHAPTER TWENTY-FIVE

Alexandra finishes the lace edging for Miss Cynthia's dress just as the sun is setting. She's ready to pull the last knot when a knock on the door startles her into pricking her finger. She sighs with relief when the drop of blood lands on her apron, instead of on the lace. Another knock, more insistent.

Is it Peter bringing the pen and paper? Why isn't he being more cautious? When she opens it, Peter stands in the doorway holding a wooden box. The pull of desire and the push of fear play across the features of his face.

"Drafting supplies are inside," he tells her. She thinks he's going to come in. But, he says, "Meet me in the library tomorrow night when the clock strikes nine. All the guests should be at the party in the ballroom by that time, enjoyin' Miss Cynthia's Christmas Eve festivities. Will that give you enough time to finish the score?"

Alexandra nods.

He hands her a lap-blanket. "Cover the box with this when you come out of your room. If anyone asks what you're carrying, tell them it's a chamber pot filled to the top, and they won't bother to look."

Peter leaves without saying good-bye.

Alexandra closes the door and slides the box under the bed, then she settles into the straight-back chair. As she cuts the last thread on the lace, someone knocks. Has Peter come back? Or, is it Antonia? Not likely. Antonia's knock is sharp and quick. Alexandra sets the lace on the bed and goes over to open the door. As soon as she unlatches it, Penelope pushes her way inside the room.

"Lock the door," Penelope demands, drawing the curtain closed. Her eyes are wide with fear.

"Why're you pretending to be deaf all this time?" she demands.

Alexandra gestures in protest, indicating that she is deaf. *Has someone betrayed me? she wonders.*

"Don't put a lie on it."

Alexandra gesticulates, indicating that she can read lips if the speaker is looking at her straight-on.

"Then how could you hear me knock?"

Alexandra indicates she felt the vibration from the floor.

Penelope gives her a hard looking-over. "All right, I believe you, I guess."

As soon as Alexandra picks up the lace, Penelope plops down on the bed. Alexandra's about to gesture for Penelope to get out, when the uppity girl starts to cry, and Alexandra notices blood at the corner of her mouth and a black eye starting to bloom. She wants to ask questions. But Musu made it clear. Penelope can't be trusted. So, she throws her hands into the air, frowns and gestures, begging for Penelope to tell her story.

Penelope plants herself so she's face to face with Alexandra. "They gonna sell me down South."

No wonder she's crying. Alexandra's hands ask, "When?"

"On New Year's Day, at the usual sell off. Speculators come through here from as far away as Savannah and buy up slaves the masters are done usin'. Folks at *Rose* never sold their slaves before, but Miss Cynthia says she needs some extra money—and she has the last word since Marse Beaufort can't talk."

Now Alexandra understands why people at Musu's are running for freedom. Rumor has it cotton planters, who work slaves to death in Georgia, are paying top price for experienced field hands.

"I need you to hide me and get word to Musu. Tell her I'm sorry for how I acted, and I want to come back. I want to beg her to help me run to freedom."

Alexandra gestures, "What happened?"

Tears swell in Penelope's eyes. "Me and Pierre was in the library, kissin'. We couldn't come in here like we used to, because of you. Miss Cynthia walked in and saw us. As soon as she came through that door, Pierre slapped my face and said, 'Stop comin' at me.' I frowned up at him. He glued his eyes to the floor with shame written all over his devil-face."

Penelope starts breathing so fast, Alexandra fears she'll pass out.

"Then Pierre said, 'This girl was in here when I stepped in to fetch a book for Marse. As you know, Marse's left hand works good enough to turn pages, and he can read a little with his one good eye. He asked me to come in here and retrieve *Lady Macbeth*. Well, this girl, who you so kindly brought into the big house, threw her arms around me and started kissing me all over. Can you do somethin' 'bout her?' The lie rolled off his tongue like honey on a hot day."

Tears clog Penelope's throat. "Miss Cynthia started hitting me and scratching me and pulling my hair. I knew I'd make it worse if I protested. I didn't want to be swinging from no rope like the last girl who sparked Miss Cynthia's jealous streak.

"That witch threw me down on the ground. She's little, but she's strong. She kicked me in the stomach. I begged Pierre to help me, but he just stood there and looked out the window with his arms wrapped around himself. Finally, Miss Cynthia tired herself out. She got this crazy look in her eye and handed a fire poker to Pierre. 'Prove you care for me,' she said to him. I nearly passed out right then and there. He looked scared. 'What are you asking me to do?' he says to her. I knew what she was asking.

"'Bash her head,' orders Miss Cynthia. I looked into Pierre's eyes, and I saw he was conflicted. I observed a thought bloom in his mind. He turned to Miss Cynthia and smiled. 'I know somethin' worse than killin,' he says. 'What?' asks Miss Cynthia.

What?, Alexandra wonders.

"'Make her the tar-and-feather?' Miss Cynthia asks, 'That lazy white boy's gonna be the tar-and-feather, you know that.' Pierre tells her to sell me to that speculator who is goin' down to the cotton fields in Georgia. That would be worse, he tells her. I play Br'er Rabbit and cry, 'Kill me!' Then Miss Cynthia laugh, like she is crazy. I don't want to go South, but I'd rather work in the cotton fields than be the tar-and-feather. Miss Cynthia smiles a wicked smile and says, 'You're gonna go South to work the cotton come New Year's Day. If you try to run away, I'll have your nose cut off. You'll be ugly as a manatee. Now get out of my sight.' So, I ran up here to hide."

Penelope glares. "Just last week, Pierre told me he was gonna' ask Miss Cynthia to get me a position in the big house and make this room mine, so we could be together whenever no one was watching. Why did Pierre do me like that? What am I gonna' do? I've never worked in the fields a day in my life." Penelope devolves into a puddle of tears. When she stops crying, she sits up. "The Good Book says, if you're whinin' 'bout havin' no shoes, just look at the man who has no feet—at least I'm not gonna be the tar-and-feather."

Alexandra gestures for Penelope to explain.

"You wanna know 'bout the tar-and-feather?"

Alexandra nods.

"That necromancer told Miss Cynthia it was up to her driver, that's Pierre, to choose a slave who hasn't done his share, to be the tar-and-feather and represent all the lazy slaves who work at Rose Plantation. Pierre told me the person who's gonna be the tar-and-feather is kept a secret until New Year Day to keep all the slaves on their toes. But that necromancer told Miss

Cynthia that, if she wants to be sure her little boy's soul will fly up to heaven, the tar-and-feather ceremony ought to be done at noon on Christmas Day.

"The unlucky slave is made to parade down the road while the others line up on both sides and whisper their sins in his ear, then they hit him hard as they can. When he gets to the end of the line, the folks down there pour hot tar over him and apply the feathers. It's a ways from the end of the line to the curve in the road. If he's still alive when he gets to the finish line, he can try to clean himself with oil.

"If he survives, it's said that the transgressions of all the slaves have been washed clean, and it will be a fine New Year. If he dies, his body will be thrown on a pyre, and it'll be said that all the year's sins are burned up, and it'll be a fine New Year. So, it comes to a good result for everybody—except the tar-and-feather.

"There's never been a tar-and-feather at Rose before now."

Alexandra sucks in a slow breath to keep from throwing up.

"The necromancer convinced Miss Cynthia that the little white boy stole her Jacob's wanderin' soul, and if John Fowler dies on Christmas day, as a blood sacrifice, her Jacob will fly up to heaven where he belongs. Miss Cynthia's gonna make sure that tar's boilin' so hot, not even a grown man could survive. Truth to tell, I feel sorry for that little fella, but I'm glad I'm not goin' to be the sacrifice."

Alexandra must get down to Musu's and ask how to help John Fowler escape before he's tarred and feathered. She also needs to finish Peter's music. Before she can do either one, Penelope must leave her alone.

An idea comes to her. Using her pantomime skills, she convinces Penelope to take a beauty nap. Then she promises to ask Musu to take Penelope back into the cabin.

Jealousy stings Alexandra when Penelope stretches out on

the bed. She shakes off her exhaustion and lays a cloth over Penelope's eyes to block the last rays of daylight. Alexandra slips the box out from under her bed and places the lace on top. She covers it with the chamber pot cloth Peter gave her. When she starts toward the door, Penelope whips the towel off her eyes and sits up.

"You takin' the lace to Queen Antonia for inspection?"

Alexandra nods.

"Good luck with that mean ol' witch."

Alexandra pantomimes that Penelope should lock the door from the inside.

Time is slipping by too fast.

Chapter Twenty-six

Christmas Eve day. Alexandra puts a scrap of lace on top of the writing box and makes her way to the quarters without being questioned. She's about to knock on the cabin door when Musu grabs her by the wrist and pulls her around the side of the cabin to the greens garden, where no one can hear them. Musu's face loses its color when Alexandra tells her what Miss Cynthia has planned for John Fowler.

"Who tol' you dey choose John Fowler for de tar-and-feather?" asks Musu.

"Penelope. She came to my room. She's gonna be sold down South on New Year's Day. She has no place to stay till then."

"Ain't no way Penelope can come in my cabin. Dat girl like a two-face snake. She say one thing to dis person and de other thing to dat person, depending on what she have to gain."

"What about John Fowler?"

"I'll snatch him soon as he comes in from de field. What is de driver thinkin', making de little boy work so hard on Christmas Eve day?

Alexandra, I gots to let you in on de rest o' de secret. All de folks in my cabin is runnin'. No tellin' what might happen if Marse die and Miss Cynthia and de driver take his place. We got boats ready to carry some of us through de swamp to de sea. My tracker friend is gonna guide my brother's family by land along de old trails. Dat be de best way for you and John Fowler.

"You make sure you come to three oaks before midnight, and you keep Penelope from comin' wid you."

"I'll tell her to make herself at home in the patio room. People are so busy; I don't think anyone will bother coming there, as long as Miss Cynthia has her lace."

"Won't work. Miss Cynthia gonna be lookin' for you in dat room if she need somethin' done to her dress before dat big party. Tell Penelope to go over to Cousin Ellie Lyn's place. She got a spare bed and a need for a flax spinner. You be at three oaks by midnight, and we'll carry you and little John to freedom."

"May I leave this with you for a little while?" Alexandra asks. She opens the writing box.

Musu jumps back from that box like it's a snake ready to strike. "You wanna lose your fingers like Virginie? Miss Cynthia had all de appendages on dat poor woman's hands cut off when she caught her writing out a pass."

Alexandra shudders.

Musu steps inside the cabin and closes the door. Thunder roars through the sky. An army of clouds marches up from the horizon. Alexandra has to get back to the big house before rain comes and ruins the paper inside the box.

Alexandra strides down the main hall of the big house like someone on important business. No one questions her. It's supper time; she assumes Cynthia and Pierre are in the dining room. She stops at Monsieur Beaufort's door, gathers her courage, and knocks softly. When no one responds, she opens the door and slips inside. A little boy is curled up on a rug. There's an empty tea cup next to him. He's sound asleep. Had Monsieur Beaufort given him sleeping tea? Monsieur Beaufort watches Alexandra with his good eye.

The clock downstairs strikes two. Ten hours till midnight. She tiptoes over to the old man's bed, slides the drawer of the bedside table open, and hides the contents of the box— paper, ink and quills, under a stack of handkerchiefs.

Monsieur Beaufort grabs her wrist and pulls her toward him. His infected breath makes her stomach roil, but she doesn't try to pull out of his grasp.

"Please, Sir," she whispers, "keep these things safe for me. I'll come back in a little while and write down the music that your son Peter wrote to honor his mother, your first wife. Will you keep my secret, Sir?"

The left side of his face lifts into a smile. "Thank you," he whispers. He releases her and draws his shaking finger across the tight line of his lips to indicate he won't tell a soul.

Alexandra makes her way back to the patio room, expecting to find Penelope sound asleep. Cold sweat drenches her when she finds the door unlocked. She goes inside. Penelope's nowhere to be seen.

Just as Alexandra's sliding the wooden box under the bed, Miss Cynthia charges into the room, followed by Antonia and Penelope.

"I told you!" says Penelope, pointing at Alexandra.

"Give me that!" Miss Cynthia snatches the box. "Where did you get this writing box?"

Penelope must have seen Alexandra take the box from under her bed. She must have run to Miss Cynthia, hoping to use her revelation as barter. Alexandra pantomimes that she found the empty box under the bed and thought it might be a good way to carry the lace, so it wouldn't get soiled.

Penelope's face falls when Miss Cynthia opens the empty box.

"You said she was carryin' writin' materials in that box."

"I thought—" says Penelope.

"Did you see a quill?"

Penelope shakes her head.

"Did you see a bottle of ink?"

Again, Penelope shakes her head.

"Did you see paper?"

Penelope stares hard at the inside of that box, as if trying to conjure a quill, ink and paper.

"Speak up," snaps Miss Cynthia.

"I didn't see inside the box."

"You hoped to divert my wrath to the best lace maker in the low-country?"

Penelope wilts beneath Miss Cynthia's hateful gaze.

"I have already made arrangements for your future."

Miss Cynthia turns toward the ever-obedient Antonia. "Lock Penelope in the potato cellar. Give her water and let her use a pot. Wash and oil her every night. On New Year's morning, make sure her clothes are in good repair. The speculator will arrive at noon."

Penelope collapses.

"Stand up!" shouts Miss Cynthia.

Antonia grabs Penelope's arm and steers her out of the room.

Miss Cynthia plants herself right in front of Alexandra to make sure she can read her lips. "I'll be sendin' you that white silk thread I told you about as soon as it arrives. I have two velvet pillow coverings that have been dyed in our finest indigo. They'll look lovely with your white lace trim. Don't you agree?"

Alexandra nods.

"Time for my beauty nap. But, before I lay my head on the pillow, I'm going to let Cook know you have permission to come down to the kitchen for a meal of your choice. If the lace supplies arrive this afternoon, I'll have them delivered to your door."

Alexandra manages a curtsey.

The second Miss Cynthia leaves, Alexandra collapses on the bed. She speaks to Didima inside her mind. *Please don't let that thread arrive today. And don't let anyone lock this room from the outside. I have to transcribe Peter's music before I go to three oaks. But I guess you know all that—if you're still watching over me.*

Alexandra relaxes a little as the clock downstairs chimes three, and no supplies have been delivered. She slips down the hall into Monsieur Beaufort's room, glad to find the old man is alone. With halting speech, he manages to say he sent the little boy away to spend Christmas Eve in the quarters, with his mother.

"Lock the door," he manages to tell her.

She slides the bolt into place, sits by the bedside table and turns the lantern to full wick. Her fingers fly as she scores the pages and records Peter's music. Five hours later, when she's finished, she throws caution aside and adds the ending she composed during her confinement in the turret. The clock downstairs strikes the half hour: eight-thirty: Peter's music is saved. Alexandra smiles. She starts to put the music back into the bedside table.

"No!" With a shaking finger, Monsieur Beaufort points to the bureau. "Bottom drawer," he manages to say.

She slides Peter's score under Monsieur Beaufort's summer neck scarves and hurries into the hall. She hears Christmas Eve party-goers socializing in the ballroom upstairs. As she makes her way to the library, she doesn't encounter a single person. She'll meet Peter and tell him where to find the music, then she'll sneak out of this house, race to three oaks, and escape to freedom with John Fowler.

She opens the library door and slips inside. An over-sized lantern spills a circle of light on the oak table in the middle of the enormous room. Alexandra's eyes feast on thousands of books that line the walls and fill rows of free-standing bookcases. The scent of oiled wood and stale cigar smoke hangs in the air. She smiles. Peter must have come in early to light that lantern. But where is he?

She freezes when she hears a woman laugh in the hallway; then she hears a man's voice. It sounds like Peter. Has he set a trap? She hears footfalls. Just as the doorknob turns, someone claps a hand over her mouth and pulls her into the shadows of an alcove. She's about to jab her assailant with her elbow, when

Peter leans close. "It's me." His hand slips around her waist; he pulls her back toward the wall. "Duck down," he whispers. They crouch and listen as the door opens and a woman's giggles drift into the room.

"After you." It's Miss Cynthia's voice. "So thoughtful of you to set up the lantern in advance of my entrance, Pierre."

"My pleasure." Pierre sounds exactly like Peter. Why is Miss Cynthia coming to the library with Rose's driver with her party going on?

"Found the brightest lantern in the house, Ma'am," says Pierre.

"Don't you dare call me ma'am when we're alone like this. It must have been dreadful when that slut threw herself at you."

A second or so of silence is followed by another round of giggles. "Not here, you naughty boy."

Alexandra reels. *A lover's rendezvous.* She hears the sound of papers being shuffled.

"Here it is." Miss Cynthia pauses. "The Will and Testament of Adam Pierre Beaufort. You're named after your father, Pierre. I told you I'd found proof. You're his oldest son."

Peter gasps.

Alexandra stiffens. Had they heard him?

"Shall I read it?" Miss Cynthia continues before Pierre has a chance to respond. "'Upon my death, it is my wish that my property be divided between my two sons, Pierre and Peter.' Notice, he put your name first?"

Peter's breath comes shallow and quick.

"'The care of the plantation is to be given over to Pierre, who is to be freed upon my death. Within a week of my demise, Pierre is to be taken to court and declared to be a white man, a precedent that has been established in the case of a wealthy free-colored man in the Charleston courts.'"

Alexandra feels Peter trembling. She covers his hand with hers.

"'My wife Cynthia is to remain in the big house for as long as she chooses. She will retain possession of all the house-help, and she will be given a stipend based on the percentage of yearly profits gained from the enterprises enumerated in the addendum to this document.'"

Peter rests his head against Alexandra's shoulder.

"'The majority of Peter's portion is to be kept in trust until he is twenty-one years of age.'"

Peter nearly squeezes the breath out of Alexandra.

"'However, Peter will be given a monthly allowance, to be administered by my wife, Cynthia, in an amount she sees fit, providing it covers, in full, the cost of his education at the Music Conservatory in Paris. I trust he will fulfill his destiny and become a composer of note. Upon reaching his twenty-first birthday, Peter will be given the balance of the estate owed to him.'"

"Monsieur Beaufort signed this?" Pierre asks.

"You mean your father? Of course, he did."

"He really is my father?"

"Did you never guess why you were raised in the big house and given the position of driver?"

Pierre makes an odd sound, something between a groan and a laugh.

"This is an unpredictable world, Pierre. What if Peter doesn't live until his 21st birthday? An education in France would be expensive. He might meet with an unfortunate accident, in which case you and I would be forced to divide his portion."

"Master Beaufort—"

"Your father?"

"My father is recovering."

"The quickening before the end, most likely."

"Peter *is* accident prone," says Pierre.

Alexandra hears the rustle of Miss Cynthia's skirt.

"Mmmm. I want to, but now isn't the right time," Miss

Cynthia says. "Wait in here for a few minutes after I leave the library. We can't afford to set tongues wagging."

When Miss Cynthia has left. Alexandra hears Pierre say, "When Peter comes to an unfortunate end, you gonna dance to my tune, Miss Cynthia."

Alexandra hears Pierre pick up the lantern and make his way to the door. When he leaves, the library is cast into total darkness.

She and Peter remain still for a long while. When Peter stops trembling, they stand. He shifts around in front of Alexandra, grips her hand and leads her to the door. She knows his world has been shattered, and she wants to help him. But if she's late to the three oaks, she'll never be able to help John Fowler escape certain death as the tar-and-feather.

When they reach the door, she whispers, "Peter, I'm so sorry. Get away to France as soon as you can."

"You didn't transcribe my music, did you?"

"Your composition is under the summer scarves in your father's bottom drawer. When the people at the Conservatory see your score, they'll beg you to be their student."

"You really finished it?"

"It wasn't safe to carry it through the hall and bring it here."

"Thank you," he says, his voice choked with emotion.

"I have to go now and find John Fowler. I have a Christmas present for him."

Alexandra slips out of the library. As she's about to open the door and escape down the slave stairs, Hephaestus comes up behind her and grabs her arm.

"You gotta get back in your room, Antonia's on her way. She got wind that something's going on, and it might involve you. Convince her you been in your room all evening and you intend to stay there till morning. Soon as she satisfied, come down through de stairs at the back of the balcony and run to de three oaks fast as your legs will carry you."

When they arrive at the patio room, Hephaestus unlocks the

door. "Antonia came by and locked your door after you left. Good thing she thought you was still inside. Good thing Marse entrusted me with de keys to all the rooms in de house."

They hear footfalls coming up the marble staircase.

"Hurry," whispers Hephaestus.

Alexandra slips into the room. He locks her in. She crawls under the covers and pulls the comforter up to her chin so Antonia can't see that she's dressed and ready to run. The outside clicks. The door opens.

She hears Antonia rummage through her wardrobe. The mattress jiggles when Antonia looks under the bed.

Alexandra keeps her breathing slow and regular. But she can't stop trembling. Good thing she hid Peter's score in Monsieur Beaufort's room. Antonia sighs. Then, she leaves.

Alexandra sits up and listens. Antonia hadn't locked the door from the outside. As soon as all is quiet, Alexandra starts toward the door. When she touches the doorknob, chills spiraling up her spine warn her. She hurries to the bed and slips back under the covers.

Seconds later, Antonia flings the door open and repeats her original search. This time when Antonia leaves, she does lock the door.

Alexandra turns the wick on her bedside lantern low. *Move! Move!* she tells herself as she fills a pillowcase with the bobbins and silk thread that may become her livelihood if she's unable to retrieve the hidden gold at Heaven Hill. She ties the bundle to her back, the way Diola do with their babies. Holding tight to the lantern, she opens the window and climbs down the trellis. She waits to make sure no one has heard her. Then, she sprints toward the path that leads to the swamp.

Help me be on time! Alexandra begs whatever helpful spirit has an ear to hear.

CHAPTER TWENTY-SEVEN

⁂

Alexandra holds her lantern high as she splashes through bone-cold swamp water. When she steps onto dry land, she can't find the path. Wind rattles dry leaves. She has to help John Fowler escape.

Help me! I promised John Fowler I would help him. Please, help me.

She turns in a circle, looking for clues. She thinks she sees a person slip behind a tree. Has someone followed her? She turns her lantern wick all the way down. Darkness closes around her. She sinks to the ground. A twig snaps. She sees the glow of a lantern. Someone is coming toward her.

"Alexandra?" whispers Musu.

"Musu!" She jumps up and runs to Musu.

"Shhh," Musu says, taking hold of Alexandra's hand. Musu leads her across a rivulet of knee-deep water, onto an island where three oak trees are backlit by a waxing crescent moon. Musu covers her lantern with an oilcloth, cups one hand around her mouth and hoots like an owl.

Someone answers her call.

Minutes later, Alexandra sees two flat-bottom boats fitted with lanterns gliding toward them.

"Where be Ares?" Musu whispers to Hector, who stands on the prow of the first boat, maneuvering close to shore with a pole.

"Filling a trail with lies in case the hounds come sniffin'. Don' fret. He be back in time."

Hector croaks like a bull frog. People come out from behind the trees and gather around Musu.

"Listen good. De ones goin' by land, git in de first boat. It'll carry y'all to de far side of de swamp. A guide'll meet you and take you up the Indian trails dat lead to de Ohio River where you can cross to freedom.

"De ones goin' by sea, put yourselfs with me in de other boat. It goin' by sea up to Delaware."

Hector hops onto the land, grabs a rope and pulls his boat onto a sand ledge. The lantern hung on the prow casts enough light for Alexandra to see that John Fowler is missing.

"Where's John?" Alexandra whispers. "I thought he was going by land."

"Git in de boat," says Musu.

"Is John Fowler here?" Alexandra asks, her fear spiking.

"Keep your voice soft," says Musu.

Before Alexandra asks the third time, Musu whispers, "Dey already put him in de pillory. Nothin' we can do 'bout it. Save yourself and git in de boat."

"Musu, they're going to kill him."

"We got lots o' folks to consider. We got to leave."

"I'm going back for John."

Someone says, "I thought she be deaf and dumb. She'll give us away if she goes back."

Musu stares into that speaker's eyes. "She not gonna gib us away." Then Musu leans close to Alexandra, "When we gone, we gone. You gonna be on your own."

Alexandra nods.

"Give her de bag, Hector," Musu says.

Hector hands Alexandra a large bag with a shoulder strap.

"Hector made all de squirrel skin shoes in dis bag so little John could walk back up North and find his people. De guide was gonna deliver him to my cousin Minnie, who live in de quarters at Fennigan Plantation." Tears shine on Musu's cheeks as she takes hold of Alexandra's hands. "Baby, we didn't know dey was gonna grab de boy so soon. If de Lord see fit for you get him free, go to Fennigan's. Look for a cabin with a porch like we has at Rose. Cousin Minnie help a lot of folks. She always lay de broom against de left side of de cabin door if it be safe to come in her back window. Stay away if de broom be on de right." Wind ripples the water. Musu looks around. "We gots to go." Musu hugs Alexandra and gives her the lantern. "You take dis. Keep de oilcloth handy and cover it up if someone come your way. Dat way you'll have light to see by. When you get close to de punishment place, turn de wick all de way down and hide de lantern in a bush. De driver got dat place lit up."

Musu traces a map of the way back on Alexandra's palm. "Follow all de paths dat lead to de left." Musu hugs Alexandra and whispers in her ear, "Sooner or later, I be seein' you in de bye-and-bye."

"See you in the bye-and-bye," says Alexandra. Alexandra starts off on the path and doesn't look back.

CHAPTER TWENTY-EIGHT

Music and laughter from the Christmas Eve party waxes and wanes as Alexandra steals toward Rose's punishment place. When she gets to the clearing that marks the edge of the Quarters, she puts out the flame and hides the lantern under a bush. She moves toward light streaming from five lanterns hung on the top of pine poles that are at least twelve feet tall.

Careful not to step on sticks that will snap and give her away, she inches forward until she can see John's feet sticking out of the stocks. They must have moved him from the pillory for fear he would choke to death and their ceremony would be ruined. She scans the area. She doesn't see anyone, but lantern light is tricky. She moves close enough to hear John praying in between spells of whimpering.

"Give us this day, our daily bread."

Alexandra feels a sneeze coming on. She tries to smother it in her sleeve.

"Forgive us our trespasses. As we forgive those who trespass against us."

Her sneeze lets loose.

John Fowler stops speaking.

"It's me," she says, coming out of the shadows.

"Miss Louise? Get away. They'll tar you, too, if they catch you."

She studies the lock on the stocks that trap John's feet. She rummages around in the ground that surround this evil place, and picks up a sturdy branch. She wedges it into the loop at the top of the lock and uses it as lever. When she presses down, the branch snaps in two.

"You best go, Ma'am. My Daddy's waiting to usher me into heaven. Please, just pray I'll go quick."

Alexandra searches for a rock. Maybe she can smash the lock. No luck.

Torchlight bobs from down the road. Someone's coming toward them.

"You have to go, Ma'am."

Alexandra stays by John's side. Before she has time to hide, Peter comes into view.

"Miss Louise, you are a hard woman to track," Peter says.

"You were following me?"

"I asked around and found out why you wanted to find John Fowler tonight."

"You takin' me to be tarred, Sir?" asks John.

Alexandra steps between Peter and John. "He's just a little boy. He hasn't done anything to hurt you."

"I'm here to help." Peter takes out a key and opens the lock on the stocks. "Miss Cynthia'll have me tarred-and-feathered if she finds out about this," Peter says as he slips a gentle hand under John's elbow and helps him to stand. "Take off your shirt, Son."

"You gonna flog me?"

"I'm going to set the hounds running the wrong way when they find you're gone."

"You know where Fennigan's Plantation is?" Alexandra asks.

"I've been there. It's up north of Kingstree."

"People there can help John get back to his family. Tell me how to get there."

"You won't find it at night. And it's too dangerous to go in the day."

John lowers himself to a tree stump and rubs his ankles.

"Draw me a map in the dirt, I'll find it," says Alexandra.

"Won't work. You know where the side road forks toward the indigo fields?" Peter asks.

Alexandra shakes her head.

"I been there," says John.

"Wait for me there."

"You gonna trust this white man?" asks the Ahoelra inside Alexandra's mind.

She ignores that devil voice and helps John to stand. "We'll see you at the fork," she says.

"Thank you, Sir," says John, offering his hand to Peter.

John's legs give way.

"How long did they keep you in that thing?"

John shrugs.

"You had any water?"

John shakes his head.

Peter takes a flask and hands it to John. "Sip some and get going."

John gulps down the water then takes Alexandra's outstretched hand, but he collapses when he tries to walk. She squats. Climb on." She carries John Fowler piggy-back, the way she'd carried Jimi after that unbroken colt threw him.

Feathery clouds are flying across the crescent moon when Alexandra and John reach the fork that leads to the indigo. It's a good place to meet Peter because it's bordered by a pine forest just across the road from Rose's property line.

Alexandra eases John off her back and helps him sit on a fallen tree trunk.

"Why are we goin' to Fennigan's?" John asks.

"Musu's cousin lives there. She's lined up some people who can help you get back to your family."

"You're an angel of God, Miss Louise."

Alexandra wonders if angels have to "do their duty." Her bladder's about ready to burst.

John's eyes fix on a tree. "Pecans! There's still some on the tree."

"I've got to step away for a minute. Nature's calling," Alexandra says.

"Don't worry, Ma'am. Go on and find a place in the woods. I'll pick some nuts."

Alexandra crouches behind a bush to do her business. Just as she's about to stand, she hears someone crashing through the trees.

Let it be Peter.

She peeks through the branches and spots a bearded white man on a horse trotting toward John, his lantern lifted high.

"I see you, Boy. Come ovah heah." The man aims his pistol at John.

John stands straight, pecans clutched in his hands. A lie glides off his tongue. "I was pickin' pecans for my mama, to make pies for Daddy and my six brothers and me. We live in a cabin over yonder. My big brother's out lookin' for squirrels to put in the stew. Is that what you're huntin'? Squirrels?"

"Ain't huntin' no squirrels."

"Well, Sir, my brother'll be along any minute. I gotta get more pecans. You want some? I can pick more."

The man shoves his pistol into the home-sewn holster attached to his belt. "Seen any deaf colored girls wanderin' around with a white boy about your size?"

"No, Sir. I ain't seen a deaf girl."

Alexandra's breath catches when she sees Peter driving toward them in a one-horse runabout with lanterns attached to the front and back. His own horse follows along at the end of a tether.

Peter doesn't know about this man. What if he doesn't see him and says something that gives them all away? Alexandra crouches down further behind a bush.

John speaks loud enough for Peter to hear. "That's my big

brother bringing home the buggy my daddy lent to Uncle Charlie. He'll be glad to know I picked enough pecans for Mama's pie."

"Mama's waiting on you," Peter says, picking up on John's cue.

"Glad to see Uncle Charlie's done with the buggy. Get any squirrels?"

Peter sets the brake and slides down from the driver seat.

"This here's my new friend." John turns to the man. "I didn't catch your name, Sir."

"Didn't give it."

"He's looking for a deaf colored girl and a white boy about my size."

"I saw a colored girl and a white boy running south on the wagon road that goes toward Georgetown. Don't know if she was deaf," says Peter.

The man turns his horse. "That reward's mine. You won't be following me, if you know what's good for you." He gallops out of sight.

When Alexandra steps out from the shadows, she hears Peter ask John, "Where'd you learn to tell stories like that?"

"We sometimes hid slaves. Daddy said it was better to spin a lie than let a child of God die. So, we made up a bunch of stories to have ready just in case. First time I ever used one."

Peter motions for Alexandra and John to come close. "Pierre's crew set out on the trail where I laid John's scent. Should buy us time. Don't know who that man was, or where he heard about the reward, but folks from around here will be on the look-out. Put these on and we'll get going."

Peter hands John a girl's funeral dress and a matching bonnet.

"You funnin' me?" asks John.

"They're not looking for a white girl."

Peter puts on his own dress, along with a long black cloak

and a hat with a thick black veil that hides the stubble on his face.

"You ride the horse," he tells Alexandra, handing her a stable boy's white shirt, britches, and a wide-brimmed hat. "Don't lift your head so people can see your green eyes."

She pulls on the pants, stuffs her hair inside the hat, and swings up on the horse. John hops up on the driver's bench by Peter. Peter flicks the reins. The horse steps out.

"If we get stopped," says Peter, "we're goin' to our Aunt Sue's bedside. She's passing fast, so we couldn't wait till morning to start off."

"Poor Aunt Sue," says John.

Chapter Twenty-nine

By the time they come to the pine windbreak that marks Fennigan's property line, the sky's eastern rim is a riot of yellows and oranges. Christmas Day has arrived in a blaze of morning's glory. They follow a two-track road that winds along the east edge of the trees. When they see the plantation house in the distance, a red-brick three-story with white pillars, they veer into a stand of tall pines and hide the horses and buggy close to the river.

They make their way on foot, staying in the cover of the trees. When they can see the house, Peter signals them to duck. He climbs a tree and surveys the premises. When he jumps down and gestures that it's safe, they gather around him.

"Quarters are down the road on the other side of the big house," whispers Peter. "I'll go on ahead. When I motion to y'all, stay in the shadows and come meet me."

Peter zigs and zags his way to a towering magnolia on the southside of the plantation lawns. He waves Alexandra and John forward, then he motions for them to crouch behind a jasmine hedge.

Alexandra's heart drops when she sees two patrollers galloping up the road toward Fennigan's. They duck. The eager men ride past without noticing the trio, stop in front of the house and tie their horses to the hitching post. They run up the stairs and knock.

The door of the big house opens. A slave wearing a pink dress and a starched apron, nicer than the ones the help at Rose wear, opens the front door and steps out onto the porch. An elderly woman, still in her dressing gown, pushes her way in front of the slave. Alexandra's able to hear when the old woman raises her voice.

"It's Christmas morning, we were sleeping in."

The patrollers gesture as they speak, insistent in their demands. The old woman says something to her slave, who motions for the slave catchers to follow her. "I can't understand why you need a tour of my slave cabins on Christmas morning," the mistress of the house calls before she slams the door.

As soon as the patrollers ride away empty-handed, field hands gather in the circular drive of Fennigan's big house.

Alexandra wraps her arms around John to ward off the chill in the air.

"At least it isn't raining," he whispers.

Finally, the old mistress comes out the front door wearing a red, fur-lined cloak. A little girl dressed in an identical outfit joins her. The woman's granddaughter, Alexandra supposes. The little girl rings a brass bell.

Heads turn as a wagon drawn by a matched pair of high-stepping hackneys comes around the corner from behind the house and stops in the front drive. The mistress claps her hands. The male slaves take off their field hats as a show of respect. The children edge in front of the adults, pressing their hands to their sides, no doubt hoping a show of obedience might earn them an extra treat.

Squeals of happiness erupt as the coachman and his assistant hand out Christmas gifts from a big burlap bag: a ham to some of the people, a head-wrap for each woman, a shirt for each man, a small bag for each child, and a new pair of red russet shoes for all of them. A few brave children wrangle taffy out of their bags and pop it in their mouths before the adults have a chance to tell them to be polite and wait.

When all the slaves have their Christmas presents, they stand at attention while the coachman and his assistant lift a huge box down from the wagon bed. Careful to keep it upright, the men place the box in front of the little girl. Her grandmother helps her to lift off the top and peel down the sides. The little girl jumps up and down with delight. Then she takes the hand of her gift, a young, teak-colored slave with a red bow in her hair. The little slave looks like she's ready to cry as the young mistress parades her past the waiting slaves.

Alexandra takes hold of John Fowler's hand.

The slaves line up. Each one bows and thanks the mistress, as if she were a Queen. It's close to noon, judging from the sun. The slaves saunter up the road to their quarters, while the mistress leads her granddaughter and her 'present' into the big house.

Finally, Peter motions for Alexandra and John to fall in behind him. Hunching down, they follow Peter until a row of well-built, wood-plank slave cabins comes into view.

Alexandra sees a broom leaning on the left of the door jamb of the only cabin with a porch. Before Peter can stop her, she runs around behind the cabin. A few minutes later, Alexandra emerges and gestures for Peter and John to follow her. When they all reach the back of the cabin, a woman who could be Musu's twin motions for them to hurry. She leads them around a winter vegetable garden toward a tangle of trees that runs along the edge of a marsh. The woman puts her finger to her lips, indicating they are not to speak, then she gestures for them to follow her toward the woods at the back of the cabins. When they've reached the cover of pines, they follow a narrow trail to a grove of well-spaced beech trees. The woman looks up at a boy sitting on a high branch.

"You know what to do if you see someone coming," says the woman.

The boy waves and nods.

They come to a wood shelter with a flat roof that has plants growing on top. The woman pulls aside the reed mat that serves as a door. When they're inside, Alexandra's surprised to see how orderly and spacious it is. Woven baskets filled with dried fish hang from nails driven into the trunk of the tree that forms one of the shelter's supports. Bundles of herbs and indigo hang from hemp strings attached to the walls. The woman slips a square of oiled homespun off of hooks attached to the ceiling. Light spills in through a square opening.

"I'm Minnie," the woman says, shaking hands with the three of them.

"You look just like Musu," says John.

"We're cousins. People often mistake us for twins." Minnie kneels on the pressed dirt floor next to John. "Musu gave me to think you were a boy," says Minnie.

John grins and takes off his bonnet.

Minnie laughs. "You're pretty enough to be a girl." Color jumps into John's cheeks. "But I can see the handsome side of you, too."

Alexandra notes the slaves at Fennigan's have been schooled in proper English, and it occurs to her that each plantation is like a small country with customs and a culture all its own.

Minnie looks into little John's eyes. "I want you to understand some things before I set you on your way. It's more than a hundred miles to where your folks stay in Greensborough. We have a wagon to take you some of the way, but there will be a lot of night-walking. You're going to have to travel on foot, all alone, for long spells of time. There will be dangers all along the way."

John takes hold of Alexandra's hand. His fingers are as cold as ice.

"You have those squirrel shoes Musu tol' me about to comfort your feet?" asks Minnie.

John shakes his head.

Alexandra slides the shoulder strap off and hands the bag to John. "Hector made these for you."

He takes out a pair of moccasins. "Wish I could thank him."

"What do you say, John Fowler? You want to go on this adventure?" asks Minnie.

He's already putting on his first pair of moccasins when he says, "Yes, Ma'am. I'm obliged to you for helping me, Miss Minnie."

Minnie turns to Alexandra and Peter. "Well, Sir. I believe this young man's ready."

Alexandra starts to take off her hat. Peter catches her eye and signals her not to reveal she's a girl.

"Thank you for giving me this blessed opportunity, Master Louis and Miss Petunia," says John.

"You're very welcome," says Peter, using a falsetto.

"Are you with the abolitionist league from Georgetown, Dear? I don't believe I've met you."

"Petunia Purell. I've come up from Savannah," says Peter.

Alexandra and John struggle to keep from smiling.

"Nice to meet you, Miss Purell."

"Likewise, I'm sure," says Peter.

"I'd like to offer y'all a plate of rice and crab cakes and a place to lay your heads, but it's not safe. Say your good-byes quick, and we'll send John on his way home."

John hugs Peter. "Thank you for saving my life, Petunia."

"Take good care," Peter answers.

Minnie doesn't say a word when Peter's voice cracks into a low register.

John throws his arms around Alexandra's neck. "I love you."

"I love you, too, John Fowler." Alexandra manages to hold back her tears.

"I'll always think of you as my big—brother."

Minnie clears her throat. "Hurry up, now. The wagon will be coming along to take you a ways toward the North."

Alexandra and Peter watch from the doorway as Minnie takes John's hand and leads him into the dappled light of a warm

Christmas afternoon. John looks back one last time, tears stream down his cheeks despite the hope shining in his eyes. Alexandra manages a smile. When little John turns his back and follows Minnie around the turn in the path and disappears from sight, she collapses. She trembles, shaken by the memory of all those lost from her life in the last few months. Papa, Mother, Jimi, Oeyi and Marcello seem to be viewing her from afar. *Be strong* their voices say inside her mind. *You have been saved for a reason. Tell our story.*

Calmness settles over Alexandra. Her tears stop. *Is this grace?,* she wonders.

When she opens her eyes, Peter is kneeling by her side, his Petunia bonnet in his hand, concern written in the lines of his face.

Alexandra senses the war inside him as he reaches out to touch her, then draws back, exhibiting the forward-pull of love and the backward push of all those folks in his head telling him what's expected of a wealthy, white Southern boy.

She doesn't judge him like she might have six months ago. She's come to understand that forces beyond one's control sometimes cause well-meaning people to choose living comfortably over following their conscience. Herself, for example.

He speaks softly. "When you're feeling up to it, we best get back to the horses. We have to get as far away from here as we can before Pierre's people come looking for us."

Peter extends his hand and helps Alexandra to stand. He kisses her. "You'll have time to change your mind on the way to Charleston."

CHAPTER THIRTY

After unharnessing the horse and removing extra clothes, a blanket and an oilcloth from the carry-all, Alexandra and Peter shove the buggy over the bank and watch the river carry it toward the sea.

The satisfaction she expected she'd feel when she helped John on his way is muted by her concern for him. Like Minnie said, he must travel one hundred miles, and his journey will be dangerous. But something inside of her has shifted. It's as though the edges of what she considered herself to be have expanded. She's also noticing things around her in a new way, like sun sprites dancing on the surface of the river.

Her old life seems like a fading dream. The world has changed, and she has changed with it. She is both thrilled and terrified to consider what her future may hold.

Show me what to do now, Didima, she silently begs. She throws a twig in the river, watches it circle around in an eddy, then spin off and float away.

Peter breaks the silence. She'd nearly forgotten he was there. "What now?" he asks.

Alexandra keeps her eyes focused on the flowing water and listens as he shares his thoughts.

"Part of me wants to head back to Rose. I know my Daddy's gonna pass soon, and I want to be by his side. But it won't take long for Pierre to figure out I set John free, and I'm not much good with the pain he and Miss Cynthia intend to inflict. My being there might even make things worse for Daddy."

Peter sighs, "Ever since I was four years old, I've wanted to study at the Paris Conservatory and become a famous composer. Now I barely have enough money to get to Boston or New York, where I might be lucky enough to get a job teaching music to children. The folks at Rose have a long reach and a lot of money. If they find out where I am, they'll make sure I never turn twenty-one, so I can make a legal claim on my inheritance."

They sit side by side in a comfortable silence. Alexandra watches a dragonfly skim across a pool of water. She wishes she were as wise as that little dragonfly, who seems to know where it's going, and why.

Without invitation, a vision flashes in her mind. She can see it with her eyes open or closed, like it's a painting she can touch. Peter stands center stage, conducting an orchestra. She hears his "Mother's Song" playing inside her head. Suddenly the vision shifts, and she sees herself teaching those children in Charleston that Grand-mère told her about.

But how could that come to be?

An image of Papa's hidden bags of gold pops into her mind.

She reaches out and touches Peter's hand; he doesn't draw away. "I know what you should do," she says, grinning at him. Her excitement grows as she speaks. "Go to that music school in France. When they hear your composition, they'll beg you to study with them."

"Even if I could get there, the score that would get me in the conservatory is still in the sock drawer."

"I can transcribe it again."

Peter gives her all of his attention as she continues.

"My path has music in it, too, but it's a little different from what I'd planned. Helping John Fowler showed me part of what my purpose is. I want to teach children, who don't have access to education, everything I've learned: languages and literature—

and all about music. I'm going to tell them how Africans brought their knowledge of rice to this country and provided the prosperity required to create America."

"I hate to intrude on your dream, but we live in a real world, Louise. I barely have enough money to hide out in Boston for a month. How are you even going to survive once you reach Charleston?"

"All the resources we need are waiting for us." She gives him a minute to digest her words. "There's gold hidden at the plantation where I used to live, and only I know where it is."

Peter's voice is a mix of anger and skepticism. "Virginia's a long way off."

"I apologize, but I've been shading the truth."

Don't trust a white man, whispers the Ahoelra.

Peter gave up any chance of a future at Rose and risked his life to help save John Fowler, she argues. She grows strong as she unwinds her web of deception. "My name is not Louise, and I was never the servant of some great lady in Virginia. I'm Alexandra Degambia, heiress of Heaven Hill Plantation. You ever heard of it?"

"The plantation of that famous African who plants all those different strains of rice?"

"Planted. He was my father." Alexandra tells her story to the end. "If the people who took over Heaven Hill find out I'm alive, they'll try to make sure I have an accident, like Papa and Jimi."

"My God. We have a lot in common." Peter puts his arm around her. The color of their skin is of no more consequence than the color of their clothes.

Alexandra rests her head on his shoulder.

"I should have figured it out. You play the violin. You read French."

"And Greek."

Alexandra draws back so she can look into his eyes.

"Peter, no one but me knows where Papa's stash of gold is

hidden. If we can get to it, I can give you the money to go to France and have enough left over to make a good life for myself. There are several free women of color in Charleston who own property and conduct prosperous businesses. And Thomas Bonneau, a free man, is a renowned teacher. I feel Charleston calling to me. I may lose my life going after that gold, but I'm going to try. You want to come along?"

Peter stands and looks out over the river. "It'll have to be a loan. I'll pay you back," he says.

"We can see about that when the time comes."

"Let's get goin'," says Peter.

They create a new 'story'. Peter changes from his mourning widow's disguise into a dapper planter, and Alexandra, still in boy's togs, becomes his servant. When they put their few belongings in the saddle bags, they're careful to safeguard Alexandra's lace-making supplies, in case they can't get to the gold.

"Pierre will have an eye out for these horses." Peter says as he tightens the saddle cinches.

They mount and ride. Late afternoon sunlight sifts through pines as the horses pick their way up an old Indian trail. Luck is with them. When they cross the river that marks the district boundary, they come upon a new plantation, more of a farm, really. The owner doesn't recognize Peter. It takes little convincing to trade champion Arabians for a pair of Appaloosas.

They camp off the road. Three days and nights pass. Peter has enough money to buy blankets and food from local planters. They're less than a half day to Heaven when darkness forces them to stop for one more night. The falling temperature encourages them to put on all the clothes Peter had stuffed in his satchel. Since they only have one oilcloth to use as ground cover, they lie together, with their backs touching for extra warmth.

The cadence of Peter's breathing makes Alexandra feel safe. Sadness she's hidden deep inside rises to the surface.

"You cryin'?" asks Peter.

"I miss John Fowler. He reminded me of my little brother."

Peter turns, pulls her close and strokes her hair. "It's the oddest thing, do you know what I see when I look at you?"

"What do you see?" Alexandra asks, even though she's afraid of what he might say.

"A song."

"A song?"

"A song about a beautiful woman." He holds her hands and hums an original melody. As she listens, she remembers how he stood up to his stepmother in order to help John Fowler; how he made Pierre take the head-cage off of Ares; how he risked his life leaving bits of John's shirt on bushes along the path to draw the hounds away from their prey.

When he comes to the end, he says, "I think I'll call it *Alexandra's Song*. If we get to the gold, come with me to France. We could live together in Paris. Folks have a different way of thinking there." He traces her cheek with his fingertips and then curves his hand down over her shoulder.

"I'm grateful for the offer. I'll have to think about it," she says. "Now we need to sleep."

He withdraws his hand. They lie down, back to back, but it takes a long while for them to drift off to sleep.

They awaken the next morning to a chorus of crows squawking at them from a tree branch.

It's past noon when they come to the fence that marks the boundary of Callie's plantation. Alexandra longs to see her cousin. It's true, Callie hadn't helped her out on the back porch, but she'd saved her life at the Charleston auction. She considers telling Peter she wants to stop and visit, but she's too afraid of what Mr. Ball might do if he finds out about her—and Peter. So, they continue on to Heaven Hill.

Alexandra's spirit lifts when they arrive at the meadow that marks the property line of Heaven Hill. The December air is cool and clear, and she can see Papa's corral in the distance.

"Race you," she says, spurring her horse to a gallop. Peter follows in her wake.

Alexandra slows to a walk when she comes to the corral gate. Most of the railing has been burned to ash. All the horses are gone. She takes in a slow, deep breath to quell her nausea.

"Where are you, Cabai?" she whispers.

She grips the reins as they ride to the top of the hill and look down on Papa's village. Thatch has been burned off all the rooftops, and the mud and waddle walls are crumbling. The smell of burnt straw hangs in the air. They dismount, tie their horses to a tree and walk side by side through the ruins, lost in their thoughts.

Alexandra kneels down in Papa's ruined house and rubs her hand over the clay floor. "Papa lived here," she says.

Peter puts his arms around her and draws her close. Over her shoulder, he sees four men riding toward them. They move apart. "Tuck all your hair into your hat and walk along behind me. Look at the ground so they won't see your eyes" Peter whispers.

The leader, a tawny-haired man Alexandra doesn't recognize, rides up on one of Papa's horses and blocks their way. The other three men box them in.

"Mind tellin' me what you're doin' here?" asks the leader.

"Just bought this boy. Takin' him back to my place in Georgia. Must have taken a wrong turn." Peter looks around. "What happened here?"

"Fire."

"Terrible—to lose so much property." says Peter. "We're lost, and we're thirsty. We came into your place looking for a well. I don't trust the water in these streams. Can you help us out?"

Alexandra tenses when the tawny-haired man dismounts. She relaxes when he shakes Peter's hand.

"Must have lost your way back where the road forks. Been known to happen." The man takes a stick, draws a map in the dirt, and marks an 'X' to show Peter their location. He sketches in a few landmarks, then he draws a line. "This road'll take you to Charleston. It's three or four days from there to Savannah."

"Could you spare some water?"

"Follow that trail," the man says, pointing to a path. "Drinkable well's up by where the big house used to be. Most of the rest are polluted with—dead things."

Where the big house used to be? Alexandra feels sick.

"Help yourself to as much water as you need. Something wrong with your boy?"

"Nothing a little flogging won't cure."

The man mounts and kicks his horse to a fast canter, his cohorts follow him, like fragments of his shadow.

"A little flogging?"

Peter grins at her. "I convinced him."

"Those were Papa's horses," she says, gritting her teeth.

"Your father knew a thing or two about horses." He puts his hand on her shoulder. "I can see how hard this is."

Alexandra takes a deep breath. "Maybe luck is with us. That well is close to where the key to the safe should be."

"He said the house burned down."

"But not the chimney where my safe is hidden."

Alexandra's insides tie in knots when she sees the ruin where Mother's house had stood. She was wrong about the chimney. It has collapsed into a pile of rubble. Someone must have found the safe that held the key to the gold—and the family treasure Mamou had given her. She'd forgotten about Siopoma's letters.

As they're sifting through the wreckage, two slaves Alexandra doesn't recognize come around the corner pushing wheelbarrows. They pay no attention to Alexandra and Peter as they pile in a load of tumbled bricks, then head in the direction of the family cemetery.

Alexandra and Peter sift through bricks. She cries out when she sees the corner of the leather pouch Mamou gave her sticking out from under a burnt beam of wood. Maybe Siopoma's letter is still inside, and maybe the key's nearby.

Alexandra trembles as she opens the oiled leather pouch. Empty. She rakes through debris. Finding the key will be impossible. If they can get to Papa's safe, they'll need another way to open it.

Alexandra's breath catches when she sees Miranda ambling toward a pile of bricks balancing an empty bucket on her head. Mother's head of house looks so old. The feeble woman stumbles. Alexandra's first instinct to run and help her, but she stops herself. Last time she saw Miranda, she was going back and forth between the Maroons and the big house, allegedly helping. She'd told Alexandra where to hide. Not long after, the sheriff's men were on her trail. "Don't let that old woman see my face," Alexandra tells Peter, pulling the hat down farther. As it turns out, there's no call for Peter to block Alexandra from Miranda's view. The old woman fills her bucket, then turns down the path toward the cemetery, never once looking in Alexandra's direction.

Alexandra gasps when she sees the assessor driving toward them in a one-horse carriage. "Don't let him see who I am," she says as she falls a few feet behind Peter and bows her head.

The assessor pulls his horse to a stop and steps down.

"My employees told me you're taking that boy to your place in Georgia," says the assessor, extending his hand.

Peter shakes his hand. "Yes, sir, I am," says Peter. "He's strong and obedient, with a lot of years left on him."

"I been looking for a boy that size to clean out my chimneys. I wonder if I might persuade you to part with him. For a fair price, of course. Walk with me."

Without missing a beat, the assessor turns toward Alexandra. "Boy, take my horse over to that patch of grass, hold him there till I get back."

"Let me help you with that, Sir." Peter unharnesses the horse and hands the reins to Alexandra.

"Stay put, or I'll have a piece of your hide," Peter commands. A chill runs up Alexandra's spine when she hears the ease with which Peter's voice deepens and takes on an imperious tone.

She hears the assessor ask, "Where are your horses?"

"Left them tied up near a pasture so they could graze. Your man said it would be all right to fill our gourds with well-water."

"Help yourself to all the water you want," says the assessor. "I'd like to show you something." The assessor leads Peter around a bend in the road, out of sight and out of earshot. What could they be talking about? Papa's gold isn't a sure thing. Turning her over to the sheriff would more than pay for Peter's trip to Paris.

"Get to the horses and get out of here," says the Ahoelra.

Alexandra's stomach churns. *Peter won't hurt me. He's good.*

"Is he? Ride away from here, fast as you can go."

Peter's different from most men. Isn't he? Being a musician is his goal, not reaping a fortune at the expense of others. That's right. Isn't it? In the back of her mind, she knows gold is an alchemist that transforms men's intentions.

Still, if she can't trust Peter, she can't trust anyone in this world. Except Mamou. *Where is Mamou. Is she alive?* Alexandra's flood of thoughts is interrupted when the assessor's horse nickers and another horse answers its call.

Alexandra turns around. "Cabai!"

Her horse stands less than twenty feet from her, partially concealed by the copse of pines that borders the south edge of the village. She senses Cabai's power as he looks into her eyes. He seems to say, *Stay the course. Be strong.*

Then she hears Peter and the assessor talking, walking her way, laughing. Cabai turns, flicks his tail and gallops out of sight.

Alexandra lifts her head just enough to see Peter and the assessor talking in low tones like they're old friends—and they're smoking cigars.

Papa used to smoke a cigar when he had made a deal with someone.

Alexandra's heart pounds. She wants to take a closer look and see if she can read their faces, but she doesn't dare.

"Boy, hook that horse up and bring it over here," says the assessor.

"Let me do that," says Peter, taking the reins from Alexandra.

"Thank you for your advice, Mr. Reynolds," the assessor says, as Peter hooks up the horse.

"Call me Jake," says Peter.

"Sure you won't part with that boy of yours?" asks the assessor.

"I'll get back to you, if I change my mind."

Peter and the assessor shake hands and pat each other on the back like old friends.

"Boy, hold my horse while I climb aboard," says the assessor.

"I'll hold him for you," Peter steadies the horse as the assessor climbs up in the driver's seat. Finally, the assessor rides out of sight.

"Let's get away from here," says Peter, dropping the cigar on the ground and grinding out its smoldering tip with the toe of his boot.

"What did he want?"

"Advice. Showed me a parcel of land. Good thing I'd read up on Eli Whitney's invention and studied up on crops. I advised him against cotton on land like this. Then he offered me a pittance to part with you. He said you were the perfect size to sweep his chimneys. That man has a slow fuse that burns hot when he doesn't get what he wants. I assuaged his disappointment by inviting him over to Sunrise, my cotton plantation in Georgia, for a quail hunt. And I held out the hope that I might be willing to sell you to him at that time."

"You have a plantation in Georgia?"

"I've never set foot in Georgia, and I don't intend to. Let's find that gold and get out of here."

Alexandra locates the trail that leads to the mound. When they get there, she's relieved to see that the ivy curtain that covers the fissure appears to be intact. But dread takes hold of her when they step inside. A fire blazes in the stone ring. Someone's in the man-made cave.

"Let's leave," Alexandra whispers.

They're halfway out of the opening when Mamou steps into the light, wearing a grin that covers her entire face. Alexandra flies into her aunt's arms and holds onto her so tight, she can feel her aunt's heart beating.

"I've been waitin' for you," says Mamou, holding Alexandra at arm's length and looking her over. "I prayed my visions weren't deceiving me. Look at you. All your chaff's been burnt to ash. You're a young woman now." She turns to Peter. "And this is the young man who wants to go to Paris. Peter, is that your name?"

Peter gives Alexandra "a look," inquiring how her aunt could know all of this.

Alexandra shrugs, but Mamou answers him, "The fire's been talkative these last three days."

Peter frowns.

"She's a seer," Alexandra explains.

Mamou turns to her. "Good thing your father showed me this place and gave me a duplicate key. He had eyes to see the future too, you know."

Alexandra considers some of the things Papa told her; maybe he could see the future.

"Let's get what you came for and get you out of here," says Mamou.

Alexandra's bursting with questions as they follow Mamou down the narrow passage toward the hidden gold.

"I saw Miranda. Where are the others?"

Mamou turns and faces Alexandra, her face a mask of calm. "There are no others here. Some ran. Some were sold. Some are living with the Maroons and me—and more than a few died. My sister-in-law Sadie went crazy. The day after her husband disappeared, Mr. Masters told her to gather her children. He intended to sell them. She fed those babies rice cakes soaked in an Oleander concoction. They died quick. She lowered their little bodies into the well down by your Papa's corral. Then she ate her own poisoned cake and jumped in after them. There's something more you need to know. Lulu died."

"No!" Alexandra's anguished cry echoes off the cave walls. Her knees give way. Mamou kneels by her and holds her as she tells her what happened.

"Mr. Masters got wind of the man who indentured Miss Alexandra Degambia. Lulu was found floating face down in the river. Good thing the man he hired didn't know what you looked like. Mr. Masters is convinced you're really dead, so you should be safe in Charleston."

Tears stream down Alexandra's cheeks.

"Say a prayer for Lulu, and put the past behind you, Analai. You must look to your own future now."

Peter helps Alexandra to her feet.

Mamou leads them deeper into the cave and shines torch-light on the opened safe. "Your daddy told me the pattern to tap a week before he died."

Alexandra and Peter stare at six bags of gold stacked on the ground beneath the open safe. Alexandra would give it all up if she could bring Lulu back to life—and Papa—and Jimi—and Mother.

"I know you'll make good use of it." Mamou kisses Alexandra on the forehead.

"Take half," Alexandra says. "Share it with the Maroons."

"Thank you, but one bag is all I need."

"Take two," Alexandra insists.

"One's more than enough. Before you go, I have a few things for you."

Mamou reaches back into the safe and takes out a leather

pouch. Alexandra smiles when she looks inside. "Siopoma's letters!"

"I fished 'em out of the debris where the main house used to be."

"Thank you, Mamou." It's a sign. Now, Alexandra knows for certain she shouldn't go to France with Peter. She has her own work to attend to.

Next, Mamou hands Alexandra her mother's rosary and her own cowry shell amulet.

"I retrieved these under a full moon the night before the assessor's people leveled the whole slave cemetery and started building an outdoor pavilion right on top of those graves."

Alexandra sighs, puts the rosary and the amulet around her neck, and tucks them under the neck of her boy's shirt.

"One more thing you might like to know. I came across your grandmother on her way back to Charleston. Seems she made a fuss when Mr. Ball arranged for Callie to marry an elderly Georgia planter against that poor child's will. Mr. Ball kicked your grandmother off his property and told her not to come back. He made it clear he doesn't need that parcel your grandmother was dangling in front of him. I'm sure he believes he'll inherit it when your grandmother dies. Won't happen though. She wrote him out of her will. Won't matter much. He has a fortune guaranteed to come his way when Callie's husband, who's way too old to bless Callie with a child, passes into the next world."

"Poor Callie!"

"Your cousin's a shadow of what she used to be. There's always a bruise on her arm. Your aunt never raised her voice against that heartless man's decision. Out of fear for her own life, I guess."

Alexandra plants her feet so she won't collapse from the weight of grief.

"Sorry to load you up with so much bad news, but wondering can eat away at a person. The good thing is your grandmother is thriving in Charleston."

Mamou places her hand on Alexandra's head, conferring a blessing. Her eyes shine with love. "I have to get back to the Maroons, before it's too dark to see my way. We had to change our location. We're deeper in the swamp. You need to leave this place before it's too dark to see your way."

Mamou hugs Alexandra, then she ties the bag of gold into a sling she's fashioned from her head wrap. "I'll carry you in my heart," Mamou says as she takes a bucket of water and douses the fire. Then, Alexandra watches her beloved aunt walk out of her life.

Peter pulls her to him. "Come to France with me," he says.

She melts into his kiss, then she draws back and looks into his eyes. "I do have feelings for you, Peter. But I have work to do in Charleston, and you have to go to Paris for your music."

He brushes her lips with a kiss and releases her, still gazing into her eyes. "These bags are too heavy for us to carry. I'll get the horses. You have time to change your mind on our way to Charleston."

She doesn't have a change of mind. Grand-mère sets her up in that house on Chalmers Street.

"I love you," Peter tells her before he boards the ship to Bordeaux. "I promise, I'll be back."

"I love you, too," she whispers.

After all that's happened, Alexandra doesn't dare cling to the hope that Peter will return to her.

CHAPTER THIRTY-ONE

Four Years Later

L ate May light floods the classroom in the back of the Old
Bethel Methodist Church. Alexandra, a teacher for four
years now, stands at the chalkboard recording her student's
responses.

"Who were the first colonists to live in South Carolina?"
Alexandra asks.

Hands shoot up.

"Yes, Charles?"

Eight-year-old Charles, whose loquacious proclivity makes up
for his short stature, jumps up by the side of his desk. "Africans!"

"Complete sentences, please."

"In 1526, African slaves from along the Gambia River were
brought to work in South Carolina."

"Excellent, Charles."

Charles basks in his teacher's praise.

"What happened next?" Alexandra asks.

Maria, a demure twelve-year-old, raises her hand. Alexandra
gestures for her to speak.

Maria rises by the side of her desk. "When Spanish captors
mistreated the slaves, they stole into the forest and joined with
the Cofitachequi natives. The terrified Spaniards sailed back to
Hispaniola. The slaves stayed and made South Carolina their
home."

Alexandra smiles. "Thank you, Maria."

"You're welcome." Maria takes her seat.

A little boy, who has lost his front baby teeth, raises his hand as high as it will reach.

"Yes, Terrence?"

Terrence stands tall. "Africans taught the people of South Carolina how to plant rice and helped to make America strong and rich."

"Good job, Terrence," whispers Charles.

Someone down the hall starts to play "Mother's Song" on a violin.

"Do you hear that, Miss Alexandra? That's the song you taught us to play," says Charles.

Heads turn toward the doorway where Peter stands beaming.

"You came back!" Alexandra exclaims. She runs toward Peter, then stops, aware that her students are watching. She wipes tears from her face, takes a deep breath and turns toward the class.

"Forgive me students, I was so excited, I lost my composure. This is my friend, Peter Beaufort. I haven't seen him for four years."

"Peter Beaufort, the great composer who wrote "Mother's Song?" Charles asks.

Alexandra nods. The children jump to their feet and applaud. Peter flushes.

"How do we welcome visitors, class?"

Still standing, the children chime, "Good afternoon, Mr. Beaufort."

Charles marches right up to Peter. "May I shake your hand, Sir?"

"What's your name, young man?" asks Peter.

"Charles M. Tate."

Peter offers his hand. "It's a pleasure to meet you, Charles M. Tate."

As Charles returns to his seat, he announces, "I have just been touched by greatness."

Alexandra longs to tell the students they will be dismissed

two hours early, but she says, "Take out your readers and excuse me for a moment, class."

Trembling from the shock of seeing Peter, Alexandra has a hard time catching her breath. *Composure*, she reminds herself as she leads him around the corner, out of sight and hearing of her students.

"Are you staying in Charleston for a while?" she asks.

That was a stupid way to greet the man I love, she tells herself. But she can't take it back.

"I'll be here a while," Peter replies, matching her formal tone.

Her dashed hope revives when he winks at her. *Maybe he just had something in his eye*, she warns herself.

Protect yourself. Is this her thought? Or is the Ahoelra lurking? She hasn't sensed that obnoxious spirit's presence for years.

"Sorry for interrupting your class," Peter says, bringing her back to the moment. "May I meet you later? I have something to give you."

Something to give me? Alexandra's curiosity is piqued.

"You remember the house I showed you on Chalmers Street when we first came to Charleston?"

Peter nods.

"I live there now."

Peter smiles. "I think I can find my way."

"I'll see you when I finish working."

A war rages in Alexandra's mind when the dismissal bell finally rings, and she starts to walk home.

Peter's letters stopped coming six months ago. Grand-mère insinuated he might have found a bride in France. Grand-mère told her not to fret because she had a full life, teaching children and playing her violin for small, appreciative audiences. But the longing Alexandra feels for Peter is a constant ache for which teaching could never compensate.

She doesn't need a man to complete her. Alexandra wants to

be with Peter because he lifts her spirit and fills her life with a sense of beauty.

At least that's what she's been telling herself.

Why does she feel so confused now that he's actually returned?

Maybe he hasn't come back because he loves her. He said he would be here a while. Unless the wink meant he had come to stay. She probably imagined his wink.

And what is it he wishes to give to her? The money she lent him for his studies? She told him he could keep it. His pride. That's probably why he's come back.

Still, is it possible to feel this over-powering desire to be with Peter, if he doesn't feel it too?

Her mind leaps to his last letter. He made a point of telling her that mixed-race marriages aren't illegal in South Carolina, like in most southern states. She knows of a few mixed couples in Charleston who have managed their lives quite well.

Why would he have mentioned marriage if he wasn't thinking about the two of them?

The truth slaps her in the face. It's often the case that a white man has a secret side lover and secret side children of dark complexion, and sometimes they refer to their union as moral marriages. But there's no ring and no church service.

"I won't be any man's side lover," Alexandra says, speaking aloud without meaning to. She looks around to see if anyone overheard, glad that her only audience is a tabby cat sitting on a fence rail, eyeing her with suspicion.

Words fly out of her head when she turns the corner and sees Peter waving to her from her front porch. It's the first time she's understood that weak knees, sometimes mentioned in romantic novels, are rooted in actual feelings.

Determined not to make a fool of herself, she takes three deep breaths, straightens her spine, and walks up the front steps. Her hands shake so badly, she can't get the key in the lock.

Peter pulls open the door.

Unlocked? Alexandra remembers locking up the house before she left to teach. She steps inside and gasps. The room is filled with gardenias.

"You brought these?"

"The back window was open," says Peter, his eyes dancing with delight.

This is just the way a man might court a side-lover, she cautions herself.

"Why did you stop writing?" she asks.

"I didn't."

"I haven't gotten a letter for more than six months."

"I'm sure you're aware there's a war on the horizon. The British have been intercepting French and American ships. I was lucky to get here."

Alexandra is taken back by the brittleness in his voice. She did know the British had captured enemy ships. It should have occurred to her that mail, along with many more important things, had been lost.

She wants to confess she prayed he would come back to her every night for four years. Instead, she says, "Thank you for the flowers. They're exquisite."

So many people she has loved have disappeared from her life. Now, she's terrified to open her heart only to have it broken again.

"I'm glad to see you looking so well," he says.

"You also look well." *That sounded stupid.* "You said you have something for me?"

"If you want it."

Before she can say one more word, Peter drops to his knee and displays a ring in the palm of his hand. "I love you. Will you marry me?"

Alexandra is so stunned she can barely breathe. Then, she looks into his eyes. She inhales the fragrance of gardenias and hears Didima whisper as clearly as if she were standing next to her in the flesh. "Trust and dare, Ali. Live. Now or never."

An unexpected calm washes over Alexandra as her pent-up fear and grief and guilt, as well as the need to contain her feelings, gives way to the love she feels for Peter.

She sinks down to kneel beside him. "Of course, I will marry you, Peter."

They slowly stand, barely breathing as they look into one another's eyes. He slips the gold band, set with diamonds and rubies, onto her finger.

"It was my mother's. It fits you perfectly."

He starts to kiss her. She steps back.

"I want to keep teaching," she says. "And I play my violin at small gatherings."

Peter smiles. "And I want to compose and conduct. The St. Cecilia Society has offered me a permanent position."

Concerts organized by the St. Cecilia Society have made Charleston a prime destination for music lovers. Peter will be able to share his gift. Alexandra laughs out loud.

Then they both become still.

"I realize ours won't be an easy path," Peter says. "But wherever life takes us, I want us to be together . . . forever."

"I love you," Alexandra whispers as he draws her into his arms.

They kiss and surrender to this precious moment when all is still right with their world.

A Note from the Author

I was inspired to write this novel when I read W.T. Dugan's account of *John Fowler, The Story of a White Slave,* published in 1901 in the *Emporia Gazette,* Emporia, Kansas.

When his father died, John Fowler, a young indentured servant, was placed in the slave quarters of a plantation in South Carolina. The slaves, with whom John worked side by side, became his friends, and they risked their lives to help the young boy escape and travel one hundred miles back to his family in Greensborough, North Carolina.

The Underground Railroad had not yet been established, but many slaves and abolitionists helped John along the way.

When he was older, John Fowler married Millie Glass. They had nineteen children and 199 grandchildren.

I am one of John Fowler's descendants.

ᴀCKNOWLEDGMENTS

Deep gratitude to those who helped make this book a reality: Dr. Robert Baum, Dr. Lee C. Brockington, and Dr. Avery Campbell who gave time and provided expertise;

Raymond Bear, my second cousin, who told me John Fowler's story;

Authors and editors: Justin Cronin, Andre Dubus III, John Dufresne, and Kathleen Anderson, in whose workshops *Once in a Blood Moon* was tweaked and revised;

Katrina Diaz Arnold, my content editor;

Scott Evans, editor of *Blue Moon Literary and Art Review*, who empowers writers with his generosity of spirit and wisdom,

Blue Moon Writers, especially: Anne Da Vigo who cheered me on; Dorothy Place who had confidence in this project; Fallon O'Neil who pushed me to go deeper; and David Sutton for his editorial genius;

The gifted writers of the Wednesday afternoon writing group: Beulah Amsterdam, Charlene Logan Burnett, Ann Wyant Halsted, Carole Stedronsky, Erie Vitiello, Carlena Wike, and Ann Wright for intelligent, heartfelt feedback;

My grandmother, author Opal Skov, whose spirit guided this project;

My mother, for fostering my creativity;

My sons and step-sons, Gregory, Chad, Jason and David Fisk and Chuck, Justin and Matt Bonneau for teaching me too many things about life to enumerate;

Laura Taylor, a prolific writer and talented editor, who contributed her patience and skill to help me polish this novel;

Jessica Therrien and Holly Kammier, of Acorn Publishing, thank you for believing in *Once in a Blood Moon*;

Abundant love and appreciation to my husband and best friend, Charles, who provided constant support on many levels.

SOURCE MATERIAL

Diction used in *Once in a Blood Moon* by African Americans and Caucasians, is derived from original sources including journals and the *Slave Narratives*.

Bagdon, Robert Joseph. "Musical Life in Charleston, South Carolina from 1732 to 1776 as Recorded in Colonial Sources.: Ph.D. diss., University of Miami, 1978.

Banat, Gabriel. *The Chevalier de Saint Georges.* (New York: Pendragon Press (2006).

Baum, Robert M. *Shrines of the Slave Trade: Diola Religion and Society in Precolonial Senegambia,* (Oxford: Oxford University Press, 1999).

Berlin, Ira, *Slaves Without Masters: The Free Negro in the Antebellum South* (New York: Vintage Books, 1974).

Bland Jr., Sterling Lacater. *African American Slave Narratives.* Westport,Connecticut; London: South Carolina Press, 2001.

Blassingame, John W. *Slave Testimony.* Baton Rouge: Louisiana State University Press, 2003.

Brockington, Lee G. *Plantation Between the Waters.* Charleston S.C.: The History Press, 2006.

Dugan, W.T. *The Story of a White Slave.* Emporia, Kansas: The Emporia Gazette, 1901.

Green, Harlan & Harry Hutchins Jr. (2004) *Slave Badges and the Slave-Hire System in Charleston, S.C. 1783-1865.* Jefferson, North Carolina: McFarland & Company Inc, 2004.

Horton, James Oliver & Lois E. Horton. *Slavery and the Making of America.* Oxford: Oxford University Press, 2005.

Katz, William Loren. *Black Indians.* New York, NY: Aladdin Paperbacks, January 3, 2012.

Koger, Larry. *Black Slaveowners: Free Black Slave Masters in South Carolina.* University of South Carolina: South Carolina Press, 1995.

Lause, Mark A. "Borderland Visions: Maroons and Outliers in Early American History": *Monthly Review, Vol. 54. No. 4., 2002.*

Linford, Scott V. "Stories of Differentiation and Association: Narrative Identity and the Jola Ekonting." *Yearbook for Traditonal Music, January 1, 2016.*

Littlefield, Daniel C. *Rice and Slaves.* Urbana and Chicago, Illinois: University of Illinois Press, 1981.

Lockley, Timothy James. *Maroon Communities in South Carolina.* Columbia, South Carolina: The University of South Carolina Press, 2011.

Maillard, Kevin Noble. "Slaves in the Family: Testamentary Freedom and Interracial Deviance" College of Law Faculty—Scholarship. 76. http://surface.syr.edu/lawpub/76., 2012.

Milanich, Jerald. *First Encounters Spanish Exploration in the Caribbean and the United States: 1492-1570, 1989.*

Myers, Amrita Chakrabarti. *Forging Freedom: Black Women and the Pursuit of Liberty in Antebellum Charleston.* Chapel Hill, N.C.: The University of North Carolina Press, August 1, 2014.

Reynolds, Rita. *Wealthy Free Women of Color in Charleston, South Carolina during Slavery*, A dissertation: Graduate School of the University of Massachusetts, Amherst, 2007.

Stoudemire, Sterling. *Dictionary of North Carolina Biography*, The University of North Carolina Press, 1979.

INTERVIEWS

Dr. Robert Baum (an interview, May, 2016, Dartmouth College) Associate Professor of Religion and African Studies: Dartmouth College.

Dr. Lee C. Brockington (an interview, July 2004 in Georgetown, S.C.), researcher and writer for the Belle W. Baruch Foundation at the Hobcaw Barony of Georgetown County, South Carolina. Ms. Brockington is a graduate of Columbia College, Instructor at the Coastal Carolina University. Her research regularly appears in newspapers and magazines and on educational television.

Dr. Emory S. Campbell (an interview, July 2004, Sullivan's Island, S.C.), a native of Hilton Head Island, S.C., Dr. Campbell has been immersed in Gullah traditions and customs all of his life. He is considered to be one of the nation's foremost experts on Gullah culture and the history of rice cultivation in the United States.

Made in the USA
San Bernardino, CA
08 June 2020

72829366R00205